IN TH

∽

*Love is friendship set on fire...*but what do you call it when you fall for your enemy?

*Meredith*

Most people have never met the real me. No one needs to when I'm their favorite party girl. The one person everyone wants, but the one heart that can't be tempted.

I've worked so hard to establish my footloose facade that even I'm starting to believe it.

So why can't I stop thinking about Nick Rhodes?

*Nick*

The smart me would turn and run the moment he laid eyes on Meredith Pryce.

The strong me would walk away from her as easily as I do every other woman.

But the first kiss makes me dumb. The second kiss makes me weak. The third kiss makes me certain…

Being with Meredith for one night won't do it. Maybe not even two.

But every night after the first is a chance to break each other's hearts. The only question is which one of us will do it first.

# IN THE BEAT OF THE MOMENT

## HEART BEATS BOOK 2

BREANNA LYNN

*Ally,*
*Love like it's never*
*going to hurt*
*xoxo,*
*Breanna Lynn*

BREANNA LYNN PRODUCTIONS

ISBN: 978-1-955359-02-3 (ebook)

ISBN: 978-1-955359-03-0 (paperback)

Cover Design by: Y'all That Graphic

Edited by: Jessica Snyder Edits and VB Proofreads

Printed in United States of America

https://breannalynnauthor.com

❀ Created with Vellum

*For my kiddos...*

*Twinx, I couldn't have done this without you.*

*Love,*
*Mom*

＊

*"The risk of love is loss, and the price of loss is grief—*
*But the pain of grief is only a shadow when compared*
*with the pain of never risking love."*

-Hilary Stanton Zunin

＊

# CHAPTER 1

*MEREDITH*

*W*ith a sigh, I flip off the TV. The cameras had captured Jax and Charlie's fiery hot lip lock as the awards show ended and the credits rolled. Add in Jax's speech and Charlie's face as he spoke to her—there's a reason why they're currently what one magazine called *America's Favorite Love Story*. I can't help the way my stomach drops.

I *want* that. I want someone to feel the way about me that Jax feels about Charlie. But how? It's not for lack of trying, that's for sure. I've gone on a few dates in the last year and nothing. Zip. Zilch. I have zero prospects lined up. In fact, is it possible to claim less than zero? Can I claim negative prospects?

The warm weight in my arms shifts and draws my attention away from the path of depression that currently wanders through my lack of love life.

"That's okay, Mac. You're my favorite date anyway." Leaning down, I kiss her downy, dark hair and breathe in the sweet baby scent of lotion and powder. This smell is more addicting than the most potent drug. Little rosebud lips part, even breaths washing across my t-shirt where McKenna has been snoozing since right before her daddy won the award of the night. "Not everyone is as lucky as they are, baby."

"Did I miss it?"

The deep voice sets my teeth on edge.

Why, oh why, did Jax and Charlie issue an open invitation to Nick the Dick? On second thought, who uses that open invitation when their friends *aren't home?*

He lives to irritate me, and no level of man candy sexiness is worth the headache he creates whenever I have to deal with him.

His question is so stupid I don't bother to stop the visceral eye roll accompanying my response. "Well, maybe if you weren't so concerned with stuffing your face full of free food, you wouldn't have missed it."

He smirks, ladling more ice cream straight from the carton and into his face. The moan that rumbles from his chest is both exaggerated and obnoxious, and my teeth clench.

"What were you, raised in a barn?"

He shrugs, but amusement lights his eyes as he smiles around the spoon. "Close enough."

I stand and shift McKenna to my shoulder. She starts to stir, and I rock gently and rub my hand along her back.

"So? Did he? Win?"

I'm not his lackey. With perverse pleasure, I head toward McKenna's room, holding my breath as I pass him.

Dick he may be, but whatever cologne he wears magically makes me want to climb him like a damn tree. It's maddening. Why does such an asshole of a person need to smell so damn good? Too bad my traitorous body refuses to clue in to what my head keeps laying out. Even without a conscious inhale, hints of bergamot and sandalwood follow me up the stairs. Those subtle teases of scent create a skin-tingling, core-clenching, *unwelcome* response.

*Get it together, girl. He's an enemy in Armani, a douche in Dior. He is not attractive in the slightest.*

I concentrate on the baby snuggled in my arms and relax in a room that explodes in shades of pink. It's an oasis to escape the tantalizing cologne that still tickles my nose. The small lamp casts a warm glow on the frilly pink bumper and sheet against the stark white crib, both of which scream princess in training. I'd blame Charlie for all the pink, but since I watched Jax consider a pint-sized pink guitar right after McKenna was born, I know it's not just her. Only by persuading Jax to let McKenna pick her own guitar when she was old enough did I drag him out of the music store without spending a small fortune.

I lay her down, and cool air rushes in where her warm body was snuggled into mine. Her lips pucker and relax almost immediately. *Sweet baby.* I grab the monitor and take several steps toward the guest room, ready to leave Nick to his own devices.

But actually—no. I'm the one with a reason to be here. He doesn't get to make me feel uncomfortable. Descending the steps, I formulate my attack. First, I'll kick him out, then I'll curl up to watch a movie.

That plan goes out the window and I bite back the primal growl that threatens to escape when I get back to the living room to find him now kicked back on the couch watching a football game, shoes off like he's going to stay awhile. Is it too much to ask that he go bother someone else?

*Remember your manners.* I swear the voice of my conscience is actually Mom. And it's that voice that prevents me from telling him to go fuck himself.

"Don't you have a TV at home?" We aren't friends. Charlie and Jax are at the hotel, or at least on their way there. He doesn't need to be here.

"Not like this," he replies.

He might have a point. Jax has fitted out their family room with a massive TV—it's one of those projection ones that makes it perfect for movie night. Not some damn replay of the game from last season.

"They lose." Tossing the spoiler over my shoulder, I head for the kitchen.

"Who?"

"Whoever you want to win," I grumble. His laugh is raspy, like he hasn't used it in a while.

It's not sexy. Nope. Not at all.

"LA?"

"Yep."

"Well, good thing I want Kansas City to win." His laughter rings out again, and I count to ten with the hope of reining in my rapidly fraying temper.

Ice cream drips from the open container on the counter, with the spoon rising like a silver popsicle stick from the middle. Growling, I pick up the partially eaten container. The spoon hits the sink with a loud clatter, and I jerk on the faucet, rinsing ice cream down the drain.

*I will not go dump this over Nick's head. I will not go dump—*

"Everything okay in here?"

Surprised by his voice so close, I whirl and hold up the offending ice cream container. "Are you for real?"

"You dumped it?" He looks crestfallen, and I can't help the evil smirk that spreads across my face. "I wasn't done with it."

"Then why'd you leave it on the counter?"

"I was flipping on the game and coming back. By the way, I googled and saw Jax won," he gloats.

If he thinks I'm going to feel bad for not telling him, he needs to buy a damn clue. "Good for you. You can use Google."

The side of his mouth quirks up, drawing my attention to his lips. Are they as soft as they look?

*Oh my god, Meredith, stop it.*

Forcing my anger back to the forefront, the emotion that constantly simmers under the surface whenever he's around, I push out the unwelcome questions about how soft his lips are and if he's a good kisser.

"I wouldn't have had to if you'd just told me," he says.

"It's not my job to tell you shit." Crossing my arms, I level a glare his way. Instead of saying anything, he leans against the doorjamb and studies me like I'm an intriguing puzzle. "What?"

His undivided attention makes me self-conscious. Do I have spit-up on my shirt? Food in my hair? I run a hand through my curls but don't feel anything. Shrugging the shoulder of my shirt back up where it's fallen down, I toss the now empty container into the trash can and remind myself to tell Charlie she's out of ice cream *and* that it's not my fault.

"What what?" he asks.

He drives me insane. I turn back to the sink and load the spoon into the dishwasher.

"You don't like me, do you?"

The question catches me off guard. I've never made it a secret that I think he's a douche canoe, but I've never openly admitted it to anyone—especially Charlie or Jax. Taking my time with the dishwasher, I keep my face averted and secretly hope he'll go back to what he was doing. Or, even better, he'll finally go home. As much as I want to tell him *exactly* what I think of him, something tells me he'd take some sort of pleasure out of riling a response from me and making things more awkward than they are right now.

"Ignoring this question too?" His voice holds the hint of a challenge. One I'm trying really hard to ignore.

Standing back up, I stare at him. Curiosity is evident in the furrow of his brow, but he doesn't look away. Once again, the need to squirm under his intense gaze intensifies while heat licks along my skin.

"I'm not ignoring it." With a shrug, I head back to the family room and grab the remote before flopping on the other couch.

"You're not answering it either." His long legs eat up the

distance between us. With ease, he snags the remote, plopping down where he was when I first came downstairs.

"Hey!"

"Hey, nothing. I was watching the game."

"Ugh. Then go home. Charlie and Jax didn't ask you to babysit —thank fucking god—they asked me." Anger tightens my stomach and the rage that simmers there begs to be released. Why does he constantly push me like this? Why can't he just be a normal person and go away when it's clear he's not welcome?

"Hey, I'm a good babysitter."

My sarcastic laugh nearly chokes me. "Yeah, okay sure."

"I've watched McKenna before," he counters.

"When? When Jax was in the studio and Charlie had to pee. So what? A whole five minutes?"

"Yeah. It was fine."

I whistle and clap slowly. "Good for you. You watched a sleeping baby for five minutes for Charlie to go to the bathroom. You couldn't last an hour by yourself with her awake. Which is why they asked me." I lean forward and attempt to keep my temper in check when all I want to do is unleash it. "God, please go home so I can watch my movie in peace."

"What movie?" The half-smile that plays on his lips is another match to the fire. And yet it's like I can't help *but* react to him.

"Anything that will make you go home." He's trying to bait me. I need to ignore him, not react. It worked on kids in elementary school who used to tease me about my wild curls, so surely it will work on him. Right?

"Jax said I was welcome here anytime."

"He didn't mean that fucking literally." Flinging myself off the couch, I pace. "And he's not even here."

"I want us to be cool."

The change in his tone from defensive to persuasive freezes me mid-step, and I blink at him as I process what he's just said.

Did I hear him correctly?

6

"What?"

"Jax asked me to clear the air with you. He's tired of us bickering at each other like kids. He said it bugs Charlie." He runs a hand through his caramel brown hair before he stands and walks away from me. He's pacing too, striding toward the kitchen then spinning to face me again. "Clearing the air" with me wasn't his idea, so what's with that?

The idea was Jax's. Like Nick couldn't be bothered to be a decent human being. *He's a dick, remember?* If left up to him, he would continue to be his obnoxious self. Something snaps with that realization, and I'm done with holding back.

Done.

"Fuck you." My words start off quiet, some small part of me conscious of McKenna sleeping upstairs. "Fuck you and fuck your act. You may have Jax and Charlie snowed, but you don't fool me for a second. Get the fuck out!"

He blinks and confusion registers on his face. "My act? What act am I supposedly putting on?"

Like he doesn't know. I may not be as tall as he is, but squaring my shoulders and confronting him with facts makes me feel like a giant. "You're not a nice guy, you're not their friend. You're a fucking snake and I can see right through you."

Anger replaces his confusion. "What the fuck? A snake? Is that what you think?"

"It's what I know," I fire back.

"How the fuck would you know anything about me? It's not like you say more than two words to me. This is the most you've ever spoken to me in the years I've known you."

"I fucking heard you!" Frustration bubbles inside me, the truth punching out like a heavyweight champion. Red shrouds my vision.

He frowns, playing confused. "What the fuck are you talking about?"

"You said you didn't think McKenna was Jax's. You were on

7

your phone in the hallway." I point in the general direction like it matters.

The evil words I'd heard that day still slice me with pain. I'd been so happy that Jax and Charlie had made up, so happy that my two best friends had found love with each other, that I was going to be an auntie.

Until I'd listened to Nick the Dick talk shit about my best friend in her own fucking house.

I snatch his shoes from the floor and launch one and then the other. They hit barely to his right, thudding against the wall. He flinches but doesn't move. "I don't want you here. Jax and Charlie aren't here, and I don't want you around. I can't stand you. But you won't *leave*."

"You have no idea what you're talking about, little girl," he snaps back.

My vision tunnels and my ears buzz as fury boils to the surface.

Advancing on him, I shove at his chest, but he doesn't budge. "Little girl? Really, asshole?"

He looks contrite, but I don't believe it for a second. Then he steps deeper into my space, sucking away all the air in the room. My hands burn against the heat of his body, and I jerk them back. "I'm sorry, I didn't—"

"You're a horrible actor."

"I'm not acting." His voice is calm as he takes another step, and I back up in response. Bump into the wall.

It's suddenly very clear that I've bitten off more than I can chew. Warning bells clamor, adding to the cacophony of disbelief and anger, but I won't concede this. I *know* what I heard.

I give an unladylike snort. "Do you think I'm stupid? That you can say whatever you want—"

His lips against mine stop my tirade. I tense at that first touch, ready to push him away. Until. Until…my body turns traitor and melts into him. His lips *are* soft, pillowed expertly against mine as his fingers wrap around my upper arms to haul me closer to him. The smell of his cologne up close overwhelms all rational thought. His tongue runs the seam of my lips, pushing insistently until I open for him.

Fuck me. Nick the Dick can kiss.

He slants his mouth, and his scruff scrapes against my chin while his tongue drags against mine.

He tastes like chocolate and mint—*the ice cream*. His fingers grip my hips and align our lower bodies in a way that drags me deeper into the kiss's spell. White hot need claws through me at the feel of his thick erection pressed between us. My fingers slide up his chest, bumping along ridges of thick muscle I ache to feel against my skin.

I wrap my arms around his neck and grip his cool, silky hair. Then he shifts us, pressing me to the wall and grinding his pelvis against mine. Fireworks explode. There's no other way to describe the sensations that swamp me with his kiss. The moan that hums from me doesn't make it beyond his lips as his hand flexes against my leg. He lifts it and bends me to the angle where the heat of him transfers through the thin layer of my shorts.

"Oh god." Ripping my lips from his, I lean my head back against the wall, the need to breathe finally greater than the need to keep kissing him. Warm breath hits my neck, spreading delicious goose bumps, and I brace myself for another onslaught from his mouth and—nothing—what the hell? I lift my head.

He freezes, and his eyes open to reveal swirls of emotion that morph from lust to surprise as they widen. His hand drops from the leg I have wrapped around his and my foot crashes down without the warm pressure. As he steps back several feet, the distance he puts between us blows the cool air conditioning across my overheated skin.

I trace my swollen lips with one hand, the heat and wetness a reminder that I've just been thoroughly kissed by the man standing in front of me.

"Shit." His Adam's apple bobs with a swallow, and his hands weave through his short hair where my fingers clung just seconds ago. "I'm gonna go."

Turning, he trips over his shoes before grabbing them. He doesn't stop to put them on, doesn't turn around, and between one blink and the next, the door opens, and the dark night swallows him.

I blow out a breath, using the wall as a support for my shaky legs. What the hell was that? Why did he kiss me? Holy shit, he should have a job as a professional kisser. Is there such a thing? Shaking my head, I follow his path to the front door, twisting the deadbolt even as I steal a peek to see if he's still there.

Why am I disappointed he's not?

# CHAPTER 2

*NICK*

$\mathcal{J}$t's well past sunset and the dark night holds a balmy wind that carries the smells and sounds of the ocean. It drives away the apple scent of the spell Meredith put me under. That's the only excuse I have for it. What had started off as a way to get her to stop talking so I could think past her barb-shaped words had shifted.

Finally learning what those glossy, pink lips tasted like—the ones I'd been thinking about since I met her—was a bad idea. Because instead of wondering, now I know. Kissing Meredith was like biting into a fresh Honeycrisp apple, the flavor tart and sweet. She tasted somewhat like I expected, considering the trail of sun-kissed orchard scent that follows her wherever she goes. It reaches out and wraps temptation around me whenever we're both in the same room.

So how did I go from wanting to get her to stop talking to every impulse other than to keep kissing her taking a hiatus? What happened when our lips collided? That's a fucking mystery to me. The little sounds she'd made, the heat of her through her thin shorts, had short-circuited my brain until it mutely flashed *what the fuck* at me over and over.

I'd only meant to quiet her. But that mouth made me ready to fuck Jax's childhood friend—someone he's described as his best friend—against his living room wall.

The irony of my retreat is not lost on me. She'd tried all night to get me to leave. Instead, I'd stuck around, deliberately doing shit to piss her off—like a twelve-year-old with his first crush—because I was curious what her reaction would be when she finally unleashed that brewing temper.

Joke was on me though. Once her snow queen demeanor melted, I found myself face to face with a layer of heat so intense I'm surprised I'm not sporting second-degree burns to go along with my hard-on. Thank god my instincts had finally demanded I retreat before I either a—dove back into her like an Olympic Gold Medalist diver—or b—stuck around to let her flay me alive with her tongue. And not in the good way.

My dick—traitor that he is—is all about the first option. Fortunately, he's not in control. Even if the image of her leaning against the wall, watching me, is still burned into my brain.

Reaching my car, I sit in the driver's seat to slip my shoes on.

No more kissing Meredith. Losing my recently formed friendship with Jax isn't worth it. Not when there are plenty of other women in LA ready for what I have to give.

One night only. No encores. No exceptions.

Decision made, I put the car in gear. The Tesla Roadster is used but new to me and the fact that there's no key, no ignition button, and no rumble of the engine to signal my departure from Jax and Charlie's still trips me out.

The short ride to my condo is silent despite the near-constant vibrations of my cell phone in the cupholder. I'll check it when I get home.

My condo is the same one Jax stayed at when he and Charlie

were broken up and he was cutting his last album. He couldn't believe I wanted it, and Reverb Records gave me an amazing deal. He didn't understand since I'd already had an apartment downtown. I'd shared that my lease was up, traffic would be a bitch regardless, and now I could have a beach in my backyard. And the fact that Reverb wanted to sell? It was an opportunity I couldn't turn down.

It's dark when I let myself in. There are no lights on to welcome me back. Toeing off my shoes, I grab a beer from the kitchen before flopping on the couch and scrolling through messages on my phone congratulating me on Jax's two awards for the night. The news outlets are already running.

*Bryant Wins Big*

*Jax and Charlie—could they be any cuter?*

I settle back and relax with a sigh. All the articles sing Jax's praises, in large part thanks to Charlie's sweet presence. She's the best thing to ever happen to him, and I'm glad he finally pulled his head out of his ass and fought for her.

My phone vibrates in my lap, dragging me back from the edge of sleep. I debate letting the call ring to voicemail, but the caller won't leave a message anyway.

"Rhodes."

"Nick." Randa Miller, President of Reverb Records, is all business. "Nice work tonight."

I'm Jax's label rep, but I also co-wrote several of the songs on his latest album. I don't fit the true definition of any one job at Reverb.

I shrug and play poker the only way I know how—never let on what you're holding. "Jax is a talented kid."

He hates when I call him that too. Even though at thirty, I'm only three years older than him, it often feels like a span of decades. So *kid* he shall be. I wince at the reminder of calling Meredith *little girl* tonight. Nothing about her is little, despite her diminutive size.

Randa chuckles, but not in a way that inspires warm and fuzzy thoughts. "He is and, thanks to you, he's doing very well."

Playing humble has never worked in our industry. Lesson number one. "Thanks. We worked hard on his album."

"Album of the year." She purrs, sounding like some movie villain, and I almost picture her twirling a mustache. "You helped write his songs."

It's a statement, not a question. Where is she going with this? "Some," I respond warily.

"I'd forgotten you did that." Twelve years ago, I'd shown up in LA with notebooks full of songs. I hadn't written anything new until recently.

Unease and memories sour the beer in my stomach. The only time I usually hear from Randa is when Jax is in trouble. Since he's not, why else is she calling? "Was there something you needed, Randa?"

"Another album for Jax. Followed by a ten-month tour." Ten months? His last tour was six, and it practically killed him. That plus another album? "I want you to write more songs with him, Nick. See what else the two of you can come up with."

"Okay, I'll touch base on Monday—"

"I want an answer tomorrow, Nick. I'll be waiting."

With a click, she's gone. I already know Jax's reaction to another edict issued by the label. Firing off a few texts, I congratulate him and ask him to call me. When they go unread after a few minutes, I head to bed. Tomorrow better be less complicated than today. Guilt gnaws at my stomach, the feeling of disloyalty washing through me.

Jax is my friend. Friends don't kiss other friends' sisters. Pseudo or not. They also don't get hard thinking about her, but that doesn't stop my cock from thickening. Memories of the weight of her body melting into mine, the little sounds she'd made as I'd pressed her against the wall, have me at full mast in the blink of an eye. As if her eyes and lips weren't enough temptation, miles of toned, silky skin make me want to beg to touch her. But I won't. Tonight was a one-off, and I'm just going to ignore that I can smell her fruit-infused scent as I drift off to sleep.

***

"You didn't answer my texts last night." With a tone full of irritation, I sound the same as I did before I'd gotten to know Jax and we'd become friends.

He chuckles. "We were a little busy last night. Been awhile since we had a kid-free evening."

I'm not touching that comment. "Randa called."

"What now?" The happiness in his voice is gone, like I expected, the words bitten off. Jax and Reverb haven't seen eye to eye for a long time—if ever—and I mediate more between them with every directive they toss at him.

"They want another album. More songs from the two of us."

"That's it?" He sounds wary, not that I blame him.

"After the album is cut, they want another tour—a ten-month tour."

Jax is silent for a moment. "Are you serious right now? Ten months? That's insane." He's not wrong, but I don't know what else to tell him.

"We can talk about it next week. You should enjoy your weekend. Relax, you earned it."

He snorts. "Yeah. Relax."

"Look, I didn't mean to bring down your weekend. I just wanted you to hear about it from me."

"I get it. And I appreciate it." He exhales. "We were going to head back to the house today anyway. Charlotte misses Ken."

I bark out a laugh. "Yeah, sure, *Charlie* misses McKenna." That baby has him wrapped around her little pinky, a combination of her mama's eyes and her daddy's dimples makes it impossible for anyone to say no to her. My wallet's already lighter from all the toys I've picked up since she was born.

He laughs, his happiness restored for the time being. "You caught me. I do too."

"How about I pick the two of you up? We can talk about this latest turn of events," I offer.

"That'd be great. Four?" Though muffled, his next words still come through. "No, gorgeous, let's stay this morning and we'll head back."

I'm happy for him, even though I feel more alone than I have in a long fucking time. Might be time to break my dry spell and get laid. It's been…I give up counting. A while.

"All right, I'll see you then," I say. "Let me know if that changes."

"Thanks, man."

He hangs up, and I'm alone with my thoughts again. Jax has never mentioned anything to me about a phone call Meredith overheard. I don't have anything bad to say about Charlie—then or now. If she's so sure about what she heard, why hasn't she told them?

# CHAPTER 3

*MEREDITH*

"Okay, Mac, what am I missing? Anything?" The baby looks at me from the plaything she loves. She's already smacked the little flower rattle and is currently drooling on the pink plastic bumper that surrounds her. "Is it weird I'm talking to a baby who can't answer?"

Probably. But her gummy smile is enough to tell me I'm not crazy. It's not any different than talking to myself, and I'm definitely guilty of that. Maybe if I knew who to talk to besides myself or a six-month-old, that would be great. But I don't know who to talk to—Jax and Charlie are in their private bubble of happiness with McKenna, and Derek is busy with a movie he got hired on to right after Jax's tour wrapped.

"What am I gonna do with my life?" McKenna babbles at me, smacking the flower decoration next to her again. I've done a few tours—both without Jax and with. "Touring with your friends is definitely better. Except when you quit."

I grimace. During Jax's last tour, I had quit after the surprise I helped Charlie with—showing up to an awards show—had turned into a nightmare when Jax had shown up with a date. It all ended up okay. More than okay. *America's Favorite Love Story*.

Letting out a deep breath, I keep talking. Maybe hearing it out loud will help me decide what's next?

"Don't get me wrong. I love dancing. And I've had a few jobs since I quit the tour, but they're temporary. A day here or there, maybe." I shrug. "And don't even get me started on dating. It was impossible on tour. And since I've been home, I want someone interested in me. Not—"

I break off before I utter the word. Yes, she's a baby, but the word "sex" sticks awkwardly in my throat in front of her.

She blows a raspberry at me, and I grin at her. "Cutie pie."

Her dark hair is a fuzzy halo around her head and clean again after I had to wash rice cereal out of it earlier. She's not a fan and I don't blame her. I wouldn't want to eat it either. That stuff had the consistency of watered-down oatmeal. With her bathed and in a cute romper dotted with baby elephants, I'd changed out of my rice cereal smeared t-shirt and into one I borrowed from Charlie.

She'd texted me shortly after McKenna had woken me up to tell me that she and Jax were heading home early. My packed bag sits haphazardly next to the front door, and I'm using the semi-quiet opportunity to talk through the biggest questions that have been eating at me. Mom and Dad don't care if I live with them forever—we have our own personal spaces since I moved into the pool house. But I'd actually like to find a job that doesn't involve traveling all over the country since my friends are all based in LA. And it has to be easier to meet someone—my someone—if I'm not constantly changing locations every other day.

"We're home." Charlie's words end in a high-pitched squeal as she races into the room. She lifts McKenna out of her contraption and dots kisses all over the laughing baby. Jax follows behind, tossing a suitcase and garment bag near the stairs.

"Gorgeous, we were only gone for a day and a half." His smile is indulgent, but he still joins in lavishing attention on the baby.

Knowing when I'm not needed, I wave to them both and tell Charlie I'll call her later. I grab my bag and jump when I open the door and see the silver car parked in front of their house. Nick taps something on his phone, then glances up. Even through his sunglasses, the heat of his gaze burns my skin. Ignoring him is best, but it's difficult when his lips narrow to a flat line after the locks chirp on my red Audi convertible.

"Bite me, douche dick." I crank the ignition and listen to the quiet vibrations. Mom gave me the hand-me-down car when I moved back from New York, and I love it despite not being home enough to drive it until recently.

I avoid peeling out—barely—and smirk as I put Nick the Dick in my rearview. So why do I feel weird when I let myself into my house a few minutes later? Am I missing something? A quick mental inventory tells me, no, I have everything I took with me to watch McKenna. My calendar is depressingly blank—no appointments, no nights out with Derek, no jobs, and no dates. Sighing, I toss my bag toward my room, then drop onto the couch and hug a pillow.

Jealousy. That's what this feeling is. My friends are all busy with their lives, and I'm stuck in some weird sort of waiting room. I didn't feel this way after graduation—I'd already been signed to start my first tour. Now I'm five years past graduation, so why do I feel like I'm starting over? Like I never even started?

Images flash of Jax and Charlie on TV last night, of them wrapped around McKenna a little while ago, and the ache in my chest pangs. When does that happen for *me*?

Another memory surfaces. Nick kissing the living shit out of me last night while I drowned in the heat and scent of him. It's been on repeat in my head all day. Can I have a different movie please? Anything. I'll even pick my breakup with Daniel, which, up until now, had been my least favorite memory. But the universe is cruel and keeps playing Nick's smooth lips claiming mine and the heat of his fingers wrapped around my thigh.

*Calm down, idiot, he's the enemy.*

An enemy who had picked up Jax and Charlie at the hotel but hadn't come inside when he'd dropped them off. No, instead he waited in their driveway long enough to judge me again. *Little girl.*

"Asshole." Tossing the pillow in my lap to the far side of the couch, I hop up to go unpack. He probably acted like he hadn't been a mooch while they were gone. Whatever.

But I won't complain about him. I'm too afraid. Nick is Jax's friend, Charlie's too. Even though I've been their friend longer—hell, since I was in diapers—it didn't stop me from siding with Charlie when Jax fucked up. Who's to say they would pick my side over his? Where would that leave me?

"Mer?" Mom's voice calls from my front door.

"In here."

She steps inside, looking casual in a pair of cut-off shorts and a faded concert t-shirt with her lighter brown curls tucked into a messy bun on top of her head. "Hey, honey, you're home early."

"Yeah, Charlie and Jax came back early."

"This was their first time away from McKenna. Well, overnight," she amends. "I'm surprised Charlie lasted as long as they did."

We both laugh. She and Dad have practically adopted Charlie and McKenna as a surrogate daughter and granddaughter. Jax was already the son Dad never had, so we see them all pretty often.

"Yeah, they both accused the other one of ending the trip early." I don't doubt it was a joint decision, despite what Jax says.

"I was hoping to get some baby snuggles in."

I shrug. "It's not like they don't live ten minutes away."

"Smart-ass." She points her finger at me. Dad says I got my sassy attitude from her since neither of us knows how to filter what we say. "But we should invite them to dinner soon. See what night they're available. And have Jax check with Nick too."

Her request has me choking on oxygen. "Honey, are you okay?"

Coughing, I wave her away and try to get my breathing to cooperate again. "Why?"

"Why not? He's such a nice boy."

Great. Another member of the Nick fan club. Though I can't blame her for being confused. I usually ignore Nick when he tags along for dinner. "I'm sure he doesn't want to come."

Mom and Dad are amazing people. If they'd have had their way, I'd be the oldest of a big family. Instead, it's just me and they adopt *any* stray that crosses their path.

"Well, we won't know unless we ask." Reaching over, she gives me a quick hug. "Your dad and I are going out to dinner tonight. Did you want to come?"

Usually, I'd take her up on her offer in a heartbeat, but my lack of a dating life is too raw. I'd rather not be a third wheel tonight. I spend all my time with Mom and Dad, Jax and Charlie, or Derek. I'm too young to feel this alone. "That's okay."

Mom nods and wiggles her fingers at me in a wave. "See you later. Behave."

She no sooner leaves and my phone chimes with a text.

**D-MAN: What are you doing? Babysitting?**
**MEREDITH: Nah. Unpacking. Why?**
**D-MAN: I haven't seen you in years.**
**MEREDITH: *laughing emoji***
**MEREDITH: You saw me last weekend.**
**D-MAN: It feels like years.**
**D-MAN: I want to go out this week. You game?**

Maybe I'll have better luck meeting someone for more than one date this time.

**MEREDITH: When and where?**
**D-MAN: Eek! Friday.**
**MEREDITH: Derek!**
**D-MAN: What?**
**MEREDITH: It's Monday.**
**D-MAN: If I didn't have to be at the studio at ass crack o'clock, I'd pick a night this week. Friday.**
**MEREDITH: Fine.**
**D-MAN: I'll pick you up. 8 PM.**

★★★

Friday has taken a million years to get here. I texted a bit with Charlie, but it's otherwise been another quiet week of applying for a few jobs and not seeing anyone except my parents. But finally, Derek texts me that he's out front.

His perfectly arched eyebrow rises above his mirrored sunglasses when I walk around the corner of the garage from my house. I'm relieved that Mom and Dad are engrossed in a movie and I don't share a door with them. Dad wouldn't have let me leave the house in what I'm wearing, twenty-three years old or not.

Wolf-whistling, Derek lifts the sunglasses and motions for me to spin. I comply carefully on the four-inch, red-soled shoes. My toes are already pinched, and by the end of the night, my feet will hate me, but I couldn't resist the black and red ombre peep toes since they complemented my red dress.

"Damn, baby girl." He drags out the *girl* until it's three seconds long, and I laugh.

It's exactly the reaction I wanted. The dress hits a little short of my knees, but where it seems demure in length, it has a deep v and shows off way more cleavage than I normally do. But the dress helps me feel sexy, confident, and ready to tackle the world.

It's exactly the boost I need. Maybe I'll meet someone interested in more than just a good time for the night?

I climb in the car and Derek follows—his charcoal slacks and plum colored button-down look tailored. Knowing him, they probably are.

"Look at you, fashion guru," I tease. "Where are we headed?"

"Eclipse?" he asks, and I nod. Eclipse is our favorite club. "What's all this?"

He lifts a hand, indicating my conditioned and styled curls that fall softly against my back, the fire engine red dress, and my peep toes. I don't tell him I'm also waxed, shaved, and moisturized to within an inch of my life. To him, yes, I like to go out and have fun. But it's more tonight. I'm on a mission.

Operation Forget Nick's Kiss. Since the memory hasn't faded over the last week while I've been alone, it's time to try forgetting it with someone else.

"It's Friday night," I tell him with a wink.

The bouncers at Eclipse know us and motion us ahead of the long-ass line winding down the sidewalk. Music thrums through the building as we enter, and I let Derek take the lead through the packed crowd. I duck behind him and snag his shirt so we don't get separated. The energy coming off the people and thumping through the speakers seeps into my feet, but I want a shot or two of liquid courage before I go on the hunt.

"I want two shots of Spirytus," I say when we reach the metallic bar. The vodka's extra oomph will be hidden in the smooth taste.

Derek raises both his eyebrows at me, and I do the same. He'll either order the shots or I will. After a moment, he spins toward the bar, but winning that little staring contest feels hollow. I down my shots in an effort to fill that hollowness, and Derek barely has the chance to throw back his rum before I drag him to the dance floor. I'm ready to lose myself in the music for a while.

We dance for hours until my feet are screaming inside my gorgeous shoes.

"Baby girl, I'm sorry," Derek yells in my ear as we stand at the bar again. "I've got to be at the lot way too early to stay any later."

Perspiration clings to the back of my dress, but I'm not leaving yet, despite his whiny ass. "Derek, it was your idea to come tonight." I want to stomp my foot, but refrain. It would hurt too much.

"I didn't know they wanted us to work tomorrow. I just got the text." He shows me his phone where there is indeed a text that tells him to report tomorrow at five. In the morning? Ugh. "C'mon, let's get you home."

He starts to steer me toward the door, and I set my feet. "I can't leave yet."

He looks at me in confusion. "What do you mean you *can't* leave yet?"

I'm not ready to admit to my secret mission. I've been too caught up dancing with him to even attempt to talk to other guys. Too bad he bats for the same team I do, otherwise, I'd try my luck with him. "I don't want to go."

"Mer." His concern is obvious in the tone of his voice, in the way he gently attempts to guide me toward the front of the club.

"No. I'm going to stay. Just a bit longer. Then I'll Uber home." The look I give him is all confidence as I firmly ignore the nerves that jangle in my stomach. Or maybe that's the shots I've done? Regardless, I have a goal in mind and the fact that I can even now pull up that kiss with crystal-clear clarity, despite the drinks, tells me I'm failing.

"Mer—"

"It's fine, Derek. I'll be okay. I'll head home soon. Love you." Kissing his cheek, I push him toward the door. Mission in mind, I turn and weave my way back through the crowd to an open barstool. Heaving myself up is a nearly impossible feat with my tight dress and sky-high shoes.

"What'll it be?" The bartender glances at me expectantly, his attention already on another customer.

"I'll take a shot of Spirytus and a water please."

The bartender comes back with my shot and a tall glass of ice water. Before I grab my card out of my little bag looped around my shoulder, cash flashes in my peripheral vision.

"I've got it." The voice that vibrates in a low tenor belongs to a tall man with a fresh shave. He winks at me with one brown eye while his dark hair slides over his other eye.

"Thanks." He's cute, put-together. Definitely an option.

We clink glasses and drink. The warmth flows down my chest to pool in my stomach. He moves our empty glasses and leans a bit closer.

"Is it hot in here or is it just you?" A blinding white smile accompanies a line so bad I almost fall off my chair when I giggle at him. "Now that I've got your attention, I'm David. What's your name?"

Taking his outstretched hand, my lips curve. "Meredith."

"Pretty name for a pretty girl." His gaze dips to my chest and travels back up. "You wanna dance?"

I nod and set my full water glass on the bar. Standing, I wobble briefly and save myself from falling on my face with a hand on his chest. Disappointment floods me when it's not followed by any electric shock, but I blame the lack of feeling on the amount of alcohol I've consumed. He wants to dance and I'm not admitting defeat.

He leads me back to the dance floor and pulls me close, his hands warm on my waist. My gaze moves to his lips. Staring at them doesn't make me wonder if he's a good kisser or how soft they are.

But can they help me forget?

# CHAPTER 4

*NICK*

     *T*his place is fucking wall-to-wall people tonight. I know better than to hit up Eclipse on a weekend, but tonight's the night. It's time to break my dry spell, come hell or high water. I'd wanted to come earlier in the week, but meetings had locked me in the office each night until all I wanted to do was go home and relax. Too bad that relaxation also meant reliving last weekend. After the kiss that never should have happened, tonight's activities aren't optional.

They're a requirement.

Good music, top shelf alcohol, and gorgeous women always up for a few hours of fun. That's what I need. Swirling the Johnnie Walker in my glass, I take a sip and survey the bar. The blonde directly across from me makes eye contact, the knowing look and come-hither smile inspiring me to polish off my drink and order another and a refill for Blondie. I stand, ready to make my way around and introduce myself.

Until my gaze snags on the dance floor several steps above the bar and locks on a candy apple red dress wrapped around smooth skin that's occupied more than one fantasy this week. What the fuck? Her head is leaned back, eyes closed, while some slick Wall Street wannabe stares at her chest. When the loser licks his lips like some B-movie bad guy, I clench my empty hand in a fist.

Blondie nearly forgotten, I keep my attention on Mer and the douchebag. He leans down close to her ear and says something before he pulls her off the dance floor with an arm wrapped around her waist. She teeters down the few stairs on shoes that seem like they'll snap with the next tilt of her ankle.

The sharp edges I normally associate with Meredith are blurry, smoothed out by whatever or however much she's had to drink. I look around, expecting Derek or maybe even Jax or Charlie to come to her rescue. Anyone can tell that the guy wrapped around her like an octopus is a twat waffle. I grip my drink tighter when no one steps forward. Shit. Is she here alone? Dressed like *that*?

I step back out of their line of sight with the assumption that they're heading for the bar. I'm only going to keep an eye on her. It's what I'd want done in my place. The hairs on the back of my neck raise when they continue past the bar and step into the corridor that leads to the bathrooms and a door that exits into the alley.

*Don't do it. She won't welcome your interference.*

Hesitation delays my first step. She's probably here to do what I came here to do—get laid. I'm an equal opportunity kind of guy. What's the harm in her hooking up? She's young, single, and smoking hot, even if I shouldn't notice that last fact.

*Asshole, she's fucking drunk.*

The voice of my conscience sounds an awful lot like Cara, but it's rare that my sister drops F-bombs.

*Fine, okay.*

I'll just check. If Meredith is okay with the wolf-pup of Wall Street, I'll leave her to her less than epic night.

My glass hasn't been touched when I set it on a table behind me and follow them into the dimly lit hallway. Something akin to panic spikes when, for a minute, it seems I've missed them, until movement catches my eye. Dumbass has her caged in the corner. Fucker. Crossing my arms, I wait. If anyone sees me, they'll assume I'm some sort of voyeur, but I'm not leaving until I know she's safe.

Meredith says, "I'm going to go home," and my ears perk up.

His voice is too quiet to hear, but his arms move closer, trapping her further. I take a step closer and unbutton my cuffs. She circles her hands around the guy's arm that has her forced into the corner as she tries to move around him.

"I want to go home." Her voice is stronger, the fire I expect infusing her words. *Good girl.* "Excuse you."

I fold my right cuff up once, twice.

Asshole moves even closer to her, pinning her to the wall with his body. His hands grab hers and hold them to her sides. *Fuck that.* I'm advancing when she responds.

"Let go." The waver in her voice stabs me. Stalking right up behind him, I yank at his shoulder.

"What the fu—"

Since I have several inches and a good twenty pounds on him, the fight dies on his lips. That's right, asshole, pick on someone your own size. I smirk when his eyes dart down the hallway and back toward the club. *Coward.*

"My friend doesn't want your attention," I explain quietly. Unequivocally. Meredith doesn't argue the *friend* statement. Instead, she yanks her hands free and slides farther away from him. Closer to me. I watch him, ready to deck him if he decides he wants to play with the adults.

"We were just getting to know each other." He leans toward

me like I'm some sort of co-conspirator. "She's fucking hot as fuck, dude. I've been waiting all night to get her alone."

He's been watching her? Waiting for her? Red haze fogs my brain and a knuckle pops as I tighten my fists.

"She's not alone." I grab her hand to pull her away. "For all intents and purposes, she'll never be alone for you, pup."

His jaw clenches at the nickname but, gutless wonder that he is, he won't tangle with me, well aware that he'll lose. Instead, he'll creep on girls too drunk to put up a fight or without friends to keep assholes like him from pouncing. I step forward to make a very clear and physical point, but stop when Meredith's fingers clutch mine.

"Don't leave." The tremble in her whispered words has me shifting closer to her. A slight tremor in her hand transfers to mine, and I suck in a quiet breath when she crowds next to me. The heat of her arm through the back of my shirt has lust warring with the anger.

"She's not worth it anyway." Wall Street's parting shot is tossed over his shoulder while he heads back to the main area of the club. I track him as he walks away and don't shift my attention until he disappears in the crowd.

When I turn around, Meredith seems softer than normal, likely thanks to whatever she drank, and I want to throttle her. It's her eyes that stop me from losing my shit, the words dying on the tip of my tongue. Normally, they remind me of devil's food cake and inspire me to imagine all sorts of dark, sweet sin. Right now, they're filled with a mix of relief and residual fear.

"Are you okay?" I question softly.

She nods but flinches when I use my finger and thumb to tilt her chin up. Even as she holds my gaze, the bricks shift and she rebuilds those walls. With the last stone in place, she yanks her chin out of my grasp.

"I'm fine." She steps back and nearly turns her ankle in her ridiculous shoes.

Clearly not fine. My molars grind together. Maybe I should say fuck it and toss her over my shoulder and take her home. The idea only gets half a second of consideration though. I don't trust myself to have her delicious ass in my line of sight like that.

"Yeah, 'fine.' Just like you were fine with Junior Wall Street." My temper snaps as images of what I witnessed, of what could have happened, hammer at me. I can't be attracted to her, which leaves anger as my only other option right now. "What would you have done if I hadn't seen you? Seemed to me like the twat waffle didn't want to take the hint. Are you here alone? Dressed like that? Grow up, Meredith."

The *oh, shit* realization hits me a second too late as my words tumble out unfiltered. I shouldn't have said that last part.

Her head snaps up and fire burns in her gaze. "Where I am, who I'm with, and what I'm wearing are no fucking business of yours."

"It's my business when I have to rescue you from your own bad decisions." I drag a hand through my hair, even as frustration mixes with relief. I don't want to think about what would have happened if I hadn't been here. If I hadn't seen her. "It's dangerous for you to be out by yourself. What would Jax say? Or Charlie?"

Doesn't she realize bad guys exist? In her opinion, I am one, I'm sure. But I listen when a woman says no. My gut tells me that other asshole wouldn't have.

Maybe it's the mention of Jax and Charlie that kills her fire, and the fight leaves her in a rush. Her body curls in on itself. "I know."

When a shudder racks her, I pull her close and wrap my arms around her. She hesitates for a breath then burrows closer, her face warm against my neck. Touching her, holding her, is as much for her comfort as it is to calm my own anger. She's safe. Music filters into my awareness and I jolt. I'd forgotten where we were. How does she make me forget? To tune out the music and crowd fifty feet away?

"Ready to go home?" My throat feels filled with gravel as I whisper against her sweet-smelling hair. She nods, and I force myself to ignore the way her arms tighten around me for just a second before she drops them. When she faces the dance floor, I nod my head behind us. "Let's go this way."

She doesn't ask me how I know where I'm going, and I don't volunteer that I've used this alley plenty of times for less noble activities. Outside, my ears ring in the silence from the absence of music. The air is thick with the smell of trash that overflows from the dumpsters and litters the ground.

I find the small of Meredith's back with my hand and guide her toward the sidewalk.

"Want to share a ride?" I pull out my phone and shake it with my question.

She stops to look at me. "Thank you." Those doe-eyes are wide open, her message clear. I know why she's thanking me.

"It's just a ride." I tease, needing to lighten the serious mood that surrounds us. It's the same need to see her smile that simmers in my blood.

"No." She places her palm on my forearm, her heat branding me through my shirt. "You know what I mean."

I nod. "Consider us even."

"Even?"

"I want to apologize," I tell her.

"Why are you apologizing?"

Running a hand through my hair, I look up. The one thing LA doesn't have is stars. No matter where I am in this city, they're never visible. I take a deep breath and let it out as I lower my face again. "You were right. You did hear me on the phone. But it wasn't me who was questioning McKenna's paternity. A gossip mag had published the story, and I was doing damage control." I realized a few days ago what conversation she must have overheard.

"What?" Her mouth drops open while her fingers tighten on my arm. "I've hated you for months."

I laugh, directing her back toward the sidewalk. "Message received. Loud and clear."

The sounds of LA traffic and weekend club hoppers grow stronger. Fuck, I feel old. I'd rather be at home, staring at the ocean from my deck. I'm tired of the club scene.

"So, you're apologizing for that?" The confusion is clear in her voice.

"It just...felt right. To say sorry about that." Shrugging, I keep my gaze averted as I ask, "Do I need to apologize for the other night?"

She stops again, and I look at her. Tilting her head, she considers me in silence for a minute before she shakes her head. "No."

"No?" That's surprising.

"It was only a kiss." The pulse fluttering at the base of her throat and the way her tongue drags across her lips expose the lie. But I don't call her on it. I can't. Regardless of the way my attention rivets to her mouth, she's complicated. On so many different levels. And I don't do complicated.

"Yeah. Sure." My phone chimes, announcing the ride I ordered. "Car's here."

A Nissan Altima idles at the curb.

"Nick?" The driver asks.

I nod and turn back to Meredith, comfortable with my decision to choose a woman driver.

"Why don't you take this one?" I offer.

"I thought we were sharing?" Confusion furrows her brow.

"I'll grab the next one." Time slows to a crawl as the moment stretches between us. The driver clearing her throat breaks the spell, and Meredith turns to fold herself into the back seat. "Meredith?"

"Yeah?" From this angle, the amount of cleavage on display threatens to kill me.

"Take care of yourself."

∗∗∗

"Emily?" We're in my truck, Em curled against my side.

"That's what my mom calls me." She giggles and smacks my chest. This isn't right.

*Shut the fuck up. She's here.*

"What are you doing here?"

The look on her face tells me she questions my sanity. "What do you mean, goofball? Jeez, LA must have knocked a few screws loose."

"LA?" She ignores me like I haven't spoken.

"I can't believe you're going to record your songs." She squeals as she loops her arms around me and squeezes.

"My songs?"

She reaches up an index finger, rubbing at the lines between my eyebrows. "You're turning into an old man, Nick." She laughs again and leans her head against my shoulder. When I inhale, the smell of the dirt in my truck mixes with the scent of her sweet pea body lotion. I know the exact one since Em makes me buy her a bottle for Christmas every year.

"You're really here?" I reach out, resting my hand on her smooth, warm skin.

"Where else would I be? Poor baby, you're exhausted. Are you sure we should leave tomorrow?"

I can't respond. My throat is paralyzed with emotion.

She's here. I can touch her, smell her, hear her.

"Nick? Nick? NICK."

My name is a scream accompanied by shattering glass.

"FUCK. Emily." I launch upright with her name whispering from my lips

My heart races while sweat grows cold on my skin. The sheet is tangled around my legs.

"Fuck. Fuck. Fuck." Resting my head in my hands, I take several deep breaths to help my consciousness reject the nightmare.

That's what it is. A nightmare from start to finish, and it's the same dream every time—driving around with Emily like we used to. Goofing off. Her calling me an old man. I've heard it all before. She said it so many times when she was alive.

Alive. My brain stutters on that word, not willing to fully accept that she's not. It's been twelve years since the car accident. That's the part in my dream I don't know for sure, but my subconscious is more than happy to fill in the blanks since I wasn't with her when she died.

Tossing aside the twisted sheets, I grab my shorts off the floor and pull them on. No more sleep tonight, not after those dreams. I haven't had one in a while, but sleep never returns easily after. Grabbing my phone, I stagger down the hall and turn on the TV for noise to cut the static in my head. My coffee machine beckons, and I wait for the cup to brew as I lean against the counter. Fuck, I'm exhausted.

As the night lightens to morning, I head out the back door and off the deck, my bare feet sinking into the cool sand. Another half a dozen steps and I sit down, staring at the water while the sky changes from silver blue to peach. The water shines like gold in the rising sun. The brine of the water and the rich brew of my coffee give me something to focus on as I time my breath with the surf.

The shakiness is leaving my fingers, so I take a sip of coffee, relishing the warmth in the morning air. It's not cold, but a hoodie wouldn't have been a bad idea.

A few joggers make their way down the beach and surfers dot

the waves farther south, but my section of the beach is quiet. Like the universe knows I need the peace. This feeling is one of the main reasons I bought the condo when I could have easily kept my apartment. But on nights when the nightmare decides to pay me a visit, I can come out here and lose myself in the ocean for as long as I need.

What brought it on this time? Usually, it has something to do with home. A phone call, an anniversary, a birthday, a song. They came back with a vengeance when I started writing again but have fallen away over the past few months. Why now?

My joints are stiff when I finally stand up and dust the sand from the back of my shorts. *Old man.* Fuck that noise. I'm thirty, even if this morning, my soul feels eighty.

More human after a hot shower, I crack my laptop and access my emails. It may be the weekend, but Reverb Records is a 24/7 operation for people like me, tasked with keeping talent from screwing up too badly, damage control, and recording schedules. You name it and I've done it.

My phone rings and rescues me out of the legalese hell of an email from our lawyers. How many *whereto*s and *whereas*es are needed in one message?

"You're up early." I don't bother with hello, too happy to stop the bleeding in my brain as I attempt to decipher what is on my screen.

"When you have a six-month-old, you're up when they're up." Jax's voice is raspy with sleep, but still happy. McKenna babbles near the phone, which must mean he's holding her. The sounds make my lips twitch with a smile.

"Aren't you the sweet family man?" I joke, busting his balls.

"Fuc—funlover," he corrects quickly, and I laugh.

"Cleaning up your language for the baby who isn't even old enough to talk yet?"

"She said daddy the other day," he counters.

"Uh-huh. Sure, she did." I've heard Charlie tell him that babies

McKenna's age only make repetitive sounds that don't necessarily mean anything. "Who else heard it?"

"It was just me and Ken." He sighs. "And yes, Charlie asked me to stop cussing so much because she didn't want to pass on bad language."

"Good thing she didn't hear you."

"Oh, I slip when she's awake too. Don't I, Ken?" He blows a raspberry and McKenna giggles. "I'm on daddy-daughter duty since Ken here decided that her mama didn't need sleep last night, didn't you?"

"You calling me so I can share that on your social media?" Photos of Jax with the baby always spike engagement numbers. But I also know that Jax and Charlie value their privacy, so I hesitate to do shit like that without running it by them first.

"No. I wanted to talk to you about what Randa said. I've been thinking."

"Okay?"

"Another album sounds good. Especially if you tell me you're going to help me with songwriting again."

My fingers twitch with the urge to write. "Absolutely." I'd been rusty at first, the words hard to find after twelve years of silence. But once they came back to the light, they were impossible to stop.

"Hell yes. Er, I mean. Shit. Wait."

I chuckle at his struggle to censor himself. It's a really good thing Charlie isn't awake. She'd have his ass. Which would also be good entertainment. She's sweet until she's not, a fact Jax experienced firsthand.

"So now that that's settled, was there something else?" I rescue him before he can utter another foul word.

"Mama's gonna beat my behind, isn't she, Ken?" He clears his throat. "Do you think Randa's flexible at all on the ten-month tour thing? Nick, I don't want to be on the road for ten months."

With a sigh, I pinch the bridge of my nose. "I don't think so, man. I can check, but don't count on it."

"Fu—fudge."

"Nice save." He groans and I huff out a laugh. "Let me run something by you."

"Shoot."

"Why are you still at Reverb?" I ask hesitantly.

"What do you mean?" He's wary and I understand why. He and Reverb—hell, up until recently, he and I—haven't had the best relationship.

"What if there was another option?" I've been thinking a lot about Reverb lately.

"Another option?"

"Reverb is a machine. Long hours, politics, no creativity. But it also gave me a lot of experience after all these years. I've been wondering what it would be like to maybe start up my own label, try for something different."

Something less soulless than the machine I work for now. Something I feel good about.

"Seriously?"

"Yeah. I remember what it felt like as an artist. The demands, the pressure. I don't like some of the directives coming down lately."

"That would be fucking awesome."

"*Jackson Matthew.*" Charlie's voice is clear through his end of the line.

"Busted." I don't hide the glee in my voice.

"Good morning, gorgeous. Sleep well?" He's probably flashing her apologetic dimples right now.

"Have you been cussing like a sailor around our daughter all morning?"

"*Yes,*" I holler through the phone, throwing him under the bus for my own entertainment.

"Dude," he whispers into the phone. "I already owe like $100 to the swear jar. Shut up."

"The swear jar?" My stomach hurts from laughing so hard. "Good luck."

"Wait," he says as my finger hovers on the disconnect button. "Let's talk more about your idea. You want to come over tonight? Dinner? Maybe grill some burgers?"

My stomach rumbles. "Sounds good. Want me to bring anything?"

He relays my question to Charlie. "Charlotte said no. We got it covered. Six o'clock."

I hang up, and the first hit of excitement sings through my blood. Am I actually ready to do this?

## CHAPTER 5

*MEREDITH*

"'*L*o?"

"Finally. Jesus, baby girl, I thought I was going to have to send a search party." Derek's voice is full of concern. "You never texted me when you got home. I've been worried sick."

I yawn while twinges of a hangover shimmer around the edges of my brain.

*Take care of yourself.*

I push away the flash of sapphire blue eyes that accompanies that memory and sit up. "Sorry."

"Why didn't you text me?" Usually if we're out and get separated, that's what I do. But last night had been different.

"I got home and crashed." Not exactly, but Derek doesn't need to know that.

Just like he doesn't need to know about the guy Nick dubbed Junior Wall Street. I can smile about the nickname now, but the fear had been real when I was backed into a corner by a guy who didn't want to take no for an answer.

"I'm not doing that shit again, Meredith. I shouldn't have left last night," Derek says.

If he knew any of what happened after he left, he'd never leave my side again. I'll be taking that story to the grave. Having my gay best friend accompany me everywhere is not on my to-do list.

"It was fine, D. Seriously. Aren't you at work?" I do not need one more pushy male trying to dictate my life. I have a dad, thank you very much. He and Jax both like to think I am required to listen to everything they say. And Nick is bossy as fuck too.

My head is starting to pound as I wake up. Aspirin would be good.

"Hello?" Derek's voice is sharp through the phone. Like he's tried to get my attention more than once.

"Sorry, what?" Focus, girl.

"Jesus, how much did you have to drink?" The assumption stings even if it is based on past behavior.

"I had one more drink after you left." I bite the words out, defensiveness creeping into my tone.

"Well, pay attention to what I'm telling you."

"I'm tired," I whine. Sleep would be even better than aspirin.

"Time to get up, baby girl. I may have a job for you—a long-term job."

His words have me wide awake. I sit up. "Really?"

He chuckles. "Yep. One of the actors here on the set was talking about another job they auditioned for. They're looking for an assistant choreographer."

"Here in LA?"

"Duh. And guess what?"

I'm bouncing on my bed like a toddler hyped up on Halloween candy. "What?"

"We know them. Or, rather, Charlie does. It's Meric and Garrett."

"Shut up."

"Right?" There's a muffled noise on his end, then he says, "Sorry, baby girl, I gotta go. Back to the grindstone."

He says it like it's a bad thing, but I know how much he loves what he's doing right now.

As soon as I hang up with Derek, I call Charlie.

"'Lo?"

Oh, shit. I forgot to check the time first.

"Charlie?"

"Mer? Everything okay?" Her voice is raspy but awake.

"Shit. Sorry. I didn't look at the time."

"It's okay. I need to get up anyway." She yawns and I might hear her jaw pop.

"McKenna let you sleep in?" Do six-month-olds do that? She had me up at the ass crack of dawn the two mornings I watched her.

"Jackson." She sighs. "She didn't sleep much last night, so that meant I didn't either. He said he'd grab her this morning when she woke up."

"Awww. Well, call me later. Get more sleep," I offer.

"It's okay. Like I said, I'm up. And I can only imagine what Jackson is teaching our daughter. What's going on? You're up early."

"Derek just called me." I don't tell her the reason for him calling me so early. That I'd forgotten to text him when I got home. I also won't be telling her about the necessary rescue last night. "He told me about a job here in LA. Assistant choreographer."

"Mer, that's great."

"It's with Meric and Garrett. Think you could put in a good word for me?" Since she works for them, maybe this is the chance I had hoped to find.

41

"Absolutely. I'll text Garrett in a little bit," she promises me.

"Thank you." If she was here right now, I'd tackle her in a hug. Instead, I settle for wrapping my free arm around my body.

"No thanks needed. Hey, you wanna come over tonight for dinner? Hang out? I feel like I haven't seen you in forever."

"I saw you last weekend, remember? When I was watching Mac," I tease.

"That doesn't count." Her eye roll is evident.

I laugh. "I know. Just giving you shit. What time?"

"Um, six?"

"'kay. Want me to bring anything?"

"We can handle it. Just bring yourself."

"That I can do."

✳✳✳

"Hey, sorry I'm late."

I shiver at the smoky voice I hadn't expected to hear. McKenna wriggles in my arms and draws my attention back to her, even though I've never been more aware of another person.

After fist bumping Jax, Nick hands Charlie a bottle of wine and untucks a six pack from under his arm.

"I told you that you didn't have to bring anything." Jax shakes his head at Nick, who shrugs.

"It's rude to come empty-handed."

Like I had. My stomach sinks at the unintended barb.

Charlie walks into the house with the bottle of wine while Nick pops off the tops of two of the bottles and passes one to Jax.

"Cheers." They clink and drink.

"Oh, in case I forget." Nick pulls out a $50 bill. "Pre-payment for the swear jar."

Jax rolls his eyes and nods in Charlie's direction. "Go give it to the warden."

"Swear jar?" I've clearly missed out on a joke everyone else already knows. Loneliness swamps me.

A little hand grabs a fistful of my curls and distracts me.

"Jax cusses like a sailor," Charlie replies, sitting down next to me. Nick hands her the money while barely acknowledging my existence. What the hell?

"Okay?" I ignore the sting of rejection from his dismissive nod hello and glance between Charlie and Jax.

"I don't want McKenna repeating it." She shrugs. "So I made Jax start adding to a swear jar."

I crack up and the baby giggles with me.

"Your daddy's going to go broke, Mac." I tell her.

"Hey! I'm not that bad." Both Charlie and I give him a look. "What about you?"

His question is directed to me. I definitely have the same problem he does. Huffing out a breath, I respond. "I'll deposit my money later."

Better to pay up front.

A heated gaze singes me, and I glance up to catch Nick's eyes traveling my body. This hyper-awareness of him is unexpected. When his gaze meets mine, he stares intently for a moment, like he wants to say something, then shakes his head and turns to face Jax.

My temper fires, frustrated by his hot and cold reactions. It's quickly followed by embarrassment over last night. I breathe a sigh of relief when he and Jax head into the house.

"What's all that about?" I make faces at the baby and glance at Charlie out of the corner of my eye. Her teeth dig into her lower lip while her attention stays trained on the door.

"The label wants another album and a ten-month tour from Jackson."

"Ten months? That's insane."

She nods unhappily. "He mentioned earlier that he talked to

Nick. He's hoping they'll shorten the time frame. Or that Nick has a different option for him. What's going on with you?"

Avoiding eye contact, I squirm at her sudden change of topic while I keep my gaze fastened on Mac. "What do you mean?"

"Usually you have some snarky comment about Nick," she explains. I shrug. "So, you guys cleared the air then?"

The way he'd looked at me when he explained the misunderstood phone call surfaces, as does the sincerity of his apology.

"I guess so? I mean, we'll never be BFFs..."

McKenna's face scrunches up, distracting Charlie, who reaches for the baby before the face can turn into a cry. "Are you hungry, Ken?"

Her use of Jax's nickname for McKenna is bittersweet. Part of me is ecstatic that they have such an adorable family, but a small piece of me is so jealous I nearly choke on it. She gets the baby set up in the highchair and snaps a bib around her neck. I cringe and wait for the huge mess of rice cereal that I'd dealt with over the weekend, but she expertly avoids that disaster. Jax and Nick are nowhere to be seen—probably in Jax's home studio—and I sit at the table while Charlie feeds the baby bird strapped in the chair in front of her.

"You guys *do* make cute babies." When she and Jax first started dating, I'd told her they'd make cute babies.

She laughs. "We're pretty partial to her."

"You guys gonna have any more?" I ask.

The look on her face is a mix of exhaustion and excitement. "We've talked about it, but we're not in any rush."

Lucky them. They've found each other so they don't have to be in a rush. Dating is hard. And disappointing. My thoughts drift while Charlie alternates talking to me and the baby. I must answer her questions, but I can't say what she talks to me about.

Once McKenna has her dinner, Charlie takes her upstairs to put her to bed. When we head back outside, we find Jax and Nick arguing over the grill and the placement of burgers.

"You two are ridiculous." Charlie says as she wraps her arms around Jax from behind. "You fight more than a married couple."

"We don't fight. Do we, gorgeous?" Jax turns and snags her lips with his without waiting for a response.

Nick's laughter spreads an annoying warmth in me that's better than the late evening sun.

"Dude, she double named you this morning," he says.

I can easily picture Charlie doing that and chuckle while Jax flips Nick the bird.

"That wasn't a fight," he grumbles.

Charlie sighs. "You two. Maybe we don't fight since we didn't have much of a wedding?"

She sits next to me, but mentally she's miles away.

"Gorgeous." Jax abandons the grill and sinks in front of her until they're eye level. "I've told you before. I'll marry you again in a heartbeat."

He kisses the tip of her nose and her face lights up with love for him.

"I know. It's just a lot of planning. With McKenna not sleeping great lately and you're going to be busy recording and touring—" Her breath hitches. "It's…it's not the right time. Once I have more time to plan, maybe."

"I'll do it," I volunteer. Charlie and Jax deserve the wedding they should have had all along. And if I plan it, maybe that means no more inside jokes with Nick.

Charlie and Jax both glance at me, surprised by my offer. Why is this a surprise? I have the time to do it. I've known both of them for years. I can do this and I can do it really well.

"You'll do what?" she asks.

"I'll plan your wedding." Ideas are already spinning, and I can't wait to dive into Pinterest.

"You'll…you'll plan our wedding? For us?" She motions between her and Jax.

I nod. "Absolutely."

"Mer, it's going to be a lot of work," she warns.

"Char, I got this."

Jax groans. "Why do I suddenly feel like this wedding is going to have sparkles and be over the top?"

I stick my tongue out at him. He should know me better than that. "You can request an ambassador too."

"Ambassador?" Jax asks.

"Someone to give the guy's perspective, I explain." I point at Nick, since Jax seems to have a bromance going with him. "If you're so worried about just me planning it, he can help."

Nick's skin turns a shade lighter than normal, but I don't get to ask why since Jax interrupts. "No, that's okay, Nick doesn't have to—"

"I'll help." His voice is more uncertain than I've ever heard it. Why does the thought of planning a wedding kneecap the guy who is always in control? Or is it the thought of spending time with me?

"Great," I say too cheerfully. "Then I just need dates."

Now all I have to do is plan the dream wedding for my two best friends—without killing or kissing my co-planner.

# CHAPTER 6

*NICK*

What the fuck did I agree to earlier? One minute I'd been trying not to stare at Meredith's plump lips as she spoke, and the next, I had agreed to help plan a wedding. Something I have no idea how to do. Emily and I hadn't gotten that far. Hell, the only ring she had when I left for California was the cheapest one I had found at a department store in Grand Island.

"You sure you're going to be okay?" Jax studies me warily as he walks me to the front door. Charlie is upstairs checking on McKenna, and Meredith left a few minutes ago.

"With filing the paperwork for the new label?" I have no idea how I've managed to maintain coherent conversations tonight. My brain froze the moment I got conscripted into wedding planning service.

He grimaces. "Not what I meant."

I shrug, not used to sharing with anyone. "It's fine. I'll try to keep her in line for you."

With a laugh, he slaps me on the back. "Yeah, good luck with that."

Something tells me I'll need all the luck I can find.

∗∗∗

I expect Meredith to call or text me the next day, but it's radio silence for most of Sunday. This is her show, but my patience is thin. If she doesn't want me to help her plan this, fine. I don't have to.

I text Jax for her number, then call her.

"Hello?"

"Do you still want my help or not?" Jax had once told me that my phone etiquette could use a refresher course. But I avoid bullshit when I can—I'd rather use my time on valuable activities. Waiting for Meredith to call me is not one of those activities.

"How'd you get this number?"

I take several deep breaths until my fingers relax on the phone. "I had to get it from Jax since you hadn't called me yet."

"Oh." There's a long beat of silence. "I didn't have your number."

How can someone go from sounding apologetic to back to sassy in the span of a sentence? If I wasn't so turned on by the sass, I'd probably be pissed off. "Yeah, kind of like I didn't have yours and had to get it from Jax."

She huffs at me. "Don't get your panties twisted. I figured I put you on the spot, voluntelling you like that." Her voice is a strange mix of attitude and sheepish quiet. Not what I normally associate with her. "So this is a get out of jail free card. You don't need to feel obligated to help."

A bark of laughter escapes with her words. "Yeah, you did put me on the spot."

"I'm just trying..." Her words fade.

Is that a tiny crack in the front she usually hides behind?

"What?" I ask.

"I want to help Jax and Charlie," she says.

I'd bet that shiny new label I'm working to get off the ground that wasn't what she meant to say, but I don't press her.

"I know. You're a good friend, aren't you?"

As brash and ballsy as she comes off, anyone can see how much she cares for those two. Three if I count McKenna. At Jax and Charlie's last weekend, I'd been hypnotized by the way she stared at the sleepy baby. The way she soothed her the rest of the way to sleep while she kept an eye on the awards show. I'd used nabbing the ice cream as an excuse to avoid saying or doing something I shouldn't. It still hadn't stopped me in the long run.

"I'd like to think so." The bravado is there, but the tremble in her voice hints at something deeper.

"I'd like to be your friend." *Whoa.* Not what I had planned on saying, but the words are true, nonetheless.

"You do?" She's as surprised as I am by my admission.

"So, what do we need to do to plan this wedding?" I tuck the phone between my neck and shoulder to start dinner. Meredith's mom makes the best enchiladas, and I finally begged the recipe off her the last time we had them.

"You're sure?"

I grunt my agreement, concentrating on not burning the meat or dropping my phone.

"What the hell are you doing?" she asks.

"Making enchiladas." My mouth waters at the thought of the cheesy, melty goodness.

"You cook?" Again, she sounds surprised.

"Uh, yeah. Otherwise, I'd starve." I roll my eyes even though she can't see me. "Don't you cook?"

"Nope." She pops the *p*. "I've been banned from attempting to cook in my kitchen and Mom and Dad's. Mom said she didn't have the insurance to cover whatever science experiments I create."

"It can't be that bad," I goad.

"Trust me. It's worse than you could imagine." There's a lightness to her voice, a teasing, and I find the corners of my lips curving in response. Is this what it's like to be friends with her? This easy conversation?

"I could always make you dinner," I offer.

She snorts a laugh. "Save your Casanova schemes for someone who'll fall for them."

"Hey. I *can* cook." I just don't usually cook for anyone but me. The women I sleep with are a distant memory by the next morning, let alone dinner the next night.

"Sure," she accuses.

"Pfft. Whatever. You only wish you got to eat this enchilada awesomeness."

"Wait. Are you making my mom's enchiladas?"

I hum and stir the browning beef a little more. "Yeah. She gave me her recipe. Why? Want some?"

"Umm..." There's a pause before she continues, her voice stilted. "No more enchiladas for a while."

"What, why?"

"That's all she would make you. Every time she knew you were coming over. Any time she asked Jax to invite you. Always enchiladas. I need an enchilada break."

"She really made me enchiladas because I asked?" Warmth blooms in my chest. Meredith's mom *had* always made me enchiladas, so I can't disagree with her.

"Every. Time."

"So, no enchiladas when I cook for you?" I ask.

"I thought we agreed that wasn't happening."

"I agreed to nothing," I counter.

With a sigh that speaks of long-suffering irritation, she changes the subject. "So, Charlie said October or November

IN THE BEAT OF THE MOMENT

when I asked her about dates. She said something about Jax's schedule being better then."

Running through Jax's calendar mentally, I whistle. "She's right but, fuck, if that doesn't give us any time."

"If you don't want to—"

"I already said I'd help." How many times is she going to try to let me off the hook? As much as the idea of wedding planning bothered me at first, once I commit, I commit. I stuff a tortilla a tad too violently and tear it.

"Okay, okay, jeez. Calm down, Karen."

I open my mouth to respond but shut it again. We're getting along—mostly—and I don't want to argue with her about this. "I thought the first thing to look at would be venues since those will be date dependent."

"That's...brilliant." Surprise colors my tone.

"I'm not a complete airhead," she says.

"I never said you were."

"You merely implied it." There's hurt under her anger. Does she realize I can hear it?

"I'm sorry." I sigh. "That wasn't what I meant to do. It's a good idea. What do you want me to do?"

Her breath blows through my phone. "I have a list of venues I think Charlie and Jax would like. Maybe we can go check those out together?"

I hum and slide the dish of enchiladas into the oven. "Okay. What day?"

"Hmm..." Blood rushes to my dick as that little sound reminds me of the other little sounds she made. *Down boy.* "Weekdays don't work well for you, right?"

I snag my laptop to check. My week is light, and I can easily shift some meetings. "I could probably make something work one day this week. What are you thinking?"

"Wednesday? Would that work?"

"Yeah. I'll pick you up at nine."

51

"AM?"

Barely avoiding the snort—there's the party girl I know—I try to keep the attitude from my voice. "Yes, Meredith. Nine in the morning."

"I'm gonna need coffee." Her warning has me struggling not to groan.

"That can be arranged."

Fuck me. What did I get myself into?

\*\*\*

Working at a record label—at least one like Reverb—is a lot like being a full-time actor. No one genuinely cares about their peers unless someone has fucked up, been fucked over, or is fucking someone else. Then it's all aboard the gossip train express. Needless to say, I'm not close to any of my co-workers, with the exception of my assistant.

"Good morning, Sybil."

"Morning, Nick." She hands me a stack of papers with a grimace. "Randa was looking for you already this morning."

Fuck. It's barely eight on a Monday morning. The coffee I've already had gurgles in my stomach with her warning. I leave my bag with her and take a deep breath. My muscles tense with every step down the hall to Randa's office.

Randa's assistant is the personification of a junkyard dog stereotype. After finally convincing her that Randa wants to see me, she picks up the phone.

"Nick Rhodes is here to see you. Okay." Hanging up the phone, her judgmental gaze lands on me. I'm dressed in gray slacks and a blue-gray dress shirt, but since I detest ties, I try to avoid them as much as possible. I also didn't shave this morning, so maybe that's why her lips purse like she ate a bag full of Lemonheads. "You can head back."

I keep another eye roll in check and open the door. Randa's

office is filled with bright sunlight that streams through two walls of windows. A portrait of her dad hangs above a leather couch, a subtle reminder that Randall Miller founded Reverb. Nepotism at its finest.

"You wanted to see me?"

Standing from behind her desk, she joins me halfway into the room. "I did. I want to talk to you more about our plans for Jax."

I keep my expression neutral and motion to the couches at the front of her office, and she nods. "What about Jax?"

"I was talking to some of the senior VPs," she starts, and my teeth grind together. Even though I've been here for twelve years and have worked my fingers to the bone, I've never made it higher than senior label rep. VPs are old cronies who have been here since her dad's reign. "Specifically surrounding the time frame with the tour I mentioned the other night."

Relief floods me. "Yeah, he asked about that too."

"I'm sure he did." I don't miss the way her lips thin. "We think the tour would do well to extend to eighteen months. We want a US leg as well as international with this one."

What. The. Fuck? No way can I sell Jax on an eighteen-month tour.

"Is there that much of a demand for him internationally?" Poker face engaged, I pretend I have no personal thoughts on how long Jax tours.

She shrugs. "It won't be a huge part of the tour. Maybe the last three months or so. I'll need you to research to find out the best places to get him seen."

Frustration flashes through me, invisible behind the mask. I nod. "Of course. Was that it?"

She stands with a nod, and I've been dismissed. Thank Christ. Leaving her office, I head back to my own and snag my bag from Sybil. She doesn't ask about my meeting and I'm grateful.

"Coffee?"

I nod. "Better make it a big one."

Closing the door behind me, I rub a hand across my stomach. This place is going to give me an ulcer by the time I'm forty. I toss my bag on my desk and sit in my chair, spinning to take in downtown LA in all its glory. Is this it? My sign from the universe that I've made the right decision to start something new?

"Shit." I'm glad I'm on this side of the recording studio. Would I have been in the same situation twelve years ago if I were Jax? My phone rings, a welcome distraction. I answer it without checking the caller ID, too caught up in plans to look.

"Rhodes."

"Nick?"

Not in the right frame of mind to talk to my sister, I scrub a hand down my face. I should have let it go to voicemail. But she usually doesn't call me during the week.

My eyes snap open, and my fingers grip the phone. What's wrong?

"Cara, what is it? Is everything okay?" Panic tilts my world sideways, my heart racing as I try to drag in several deep breaths.

"Oh. Oh my god, Nick, yes. Sorry, everything's okay." She rushes out. "You still have those?"

"Not very often." Right after Mom called to tell me about Emily, answering my phone—especially when someone was calling when they normally wouldn't—led to panic attacks. The attacks were worse with calls from a Nebraska area code. After years spent with a therapist, I finally have them under control. Mostly. Concentrated breathing helps my heart rate return to normal. Or as normal as it ever is when talking to my bossy older sister.

"I'm so sorry. I should have texted you first. I wanted you to answer your phone though."

She makes a strong point. If I expect the call, it's planned, and I'm able to react differently. But I also hate to talk on the phone. I tolerate it for work and check in with Mom every few weeks.

Sighing, I lean back in my chair. "What's up?"

"Mom and Dad's anniversary is soon."

"Okay?"

"It's their fortieth." She reminds me, like I need it. Always the big sister.

"I know. I'm going to send them to a restaurant in Grand Island. Or a weekend somewhere warm? Do you think Dad'd go for that?" Dad's favorite place is the farm I grew up on. The few times I've convinced them to visit me, he looks like a lost puppy surrounded by steel and concrete.

"They want a party." She pauses. "With all their friends and family. Here."

I haven't been back home since Randa showed up in Nebraska a month after I walked out of recording an EP to bury my fiancée. She had offered to let me try my hand as a label rep since I refused to sing anymore. Since then, I've flown my family here for the holidays or we've gone to other destinations, but never back home. My throat locks. Home. Is it really home anymore?

"They want you here." Cara's voice is quiet through the phone.

I shake my head. "Cara—"

"I know why you don't come home. I understand. But it's been years, Nick."

Twelve. It's been twelve years since I was in Nebraska.

"Cara—"

She plows on. "We've been planning the party for a few weeks. Mom and Dad have a tent coming. We found a caterer, a DJ. The whole town is coming. And all the aunts and uncles and cousins."

I lean my head back and rub the bridge of my nose as I wait to see if she has anything else to say. When she's quiet, I open my mouth. "The whole town?"

"They won't be there." She knows what I'm asking. Emily's

parents. "They moved out of Willow River a couple years after Emily…"

"After Emily died," I add in her awkward silence. My throat feels raw when I try to clear it. "You can say it."

"Nick."

"It's what happened." I attempt to shrug, but my shoulders lock as they tense.

"I know. It was a long time ago. And I know it's sad, but, Nicky, it's time. I don't want Emily's death to be the only thing you think about when you think about home. This will be a happy memory."

I have no more energy to fight this battle right now. "Let me think about it."

"Really?" She sounds surprised. "You'll actually think about it and you're not saying that so that you can say no later?"

"I will think about it." One side of my mouth quirks. "Besides, isn't that your MO?"

She laughs. "Guilty. Some days it's easier to tell the kids that I'll think about it than to debate why I'm telling them no."

I have two nieces and a nephew I've met a handful of times. I've probably been around McKenna more than I've been around those three. Caleb, Sam (call me Samantha, Uncle Nick), and Kristen. I wish we were closer, but the idea of going back to Nebraska has me breaking out in a cold sweat.

"When do I need to let you know by?"

"The party's not until the middle of October. You can tell me a little closer to that."

Eight weeks. I have eight weeks to build the courage to go home or disappoint Mom and Dad. Fuck me. Eight weeks to overcome twelve years.

"Okay."

"Okay?" The hope in her voice is a hot poker to the stomach.

"I'll let you know." I'm a suck-ass brother and son, disappointing my family by not coming home of my own free will.

Now they're at the point where they've asked. What will it look like if I say no? How can I say yes?

"Okay." A crash sounds on her line. "Dang it. I gotta go. Caleb, I told you not to try to stack that like—"

Her phone disconnects, but it sounded like everything was okay. Maybe my four-year-old nephew was playing with the Legos I bought him for his last birthday?

For twelve years, I've avoided weddings, anniversary parties, births, and any other celebration of love and commitment. Hell, I become a fucking hermit in early February to avoid all the bullshit associated with Valentine's Day. Now in the span of a week, I'm actively involved in planning a wedding and invited to a party celebrating nearly a lifetime of commitment. The universe has a fucking warped sense of humor.

# CHAPTER 7

*MEREDITH*

$\mathcal{T}$he alarm rings at the ungodly hour of eight. For a night owl like me, this is a prime hour for sleeping. Why do people willingly get up this early?

"Ugh." I smack at my phone and lie there, blinking up at the ceiling. "Time to get up, Meredith."

A knock at the door has me bolting upright. Shit. Shit. Shit. Jumping out of bed, I run to the door and throw it open.

"It's nine." Nick walks in without invitation.

"Give me fifteen minutes?" I'm not above begging at this point.

His eyebrow arches and creates tingles that shoot through my limbs at the perfect angle. Why does that one facial expression create such a riot in my body?

With a sigh, he sinks into my overstuffed couch. "Don't waste my time."

Even though my temper flares, I swallow it and acknowledge

my mistake. "I'm sorry. I flipped off my alarm and accidentally fell back asleep."

It's at that moment the reality of what I'm wearing—or not wearing—hits me. It's not something I usually worry about since I live alone. But the actuality of having him see me in only a tank top and panties isn't usual. Today, while he dwarfs my couch, I'm suddenly overly conscious of my lack of clothes, and I squirm with embarrassment. Hell, my bathing suits show way more skin, but there's something about being alone with him in what I'm wearing that has me grabbing a throw off the couch to wrap around myself.

I don't know why I bother since he is engrossed in his phone.

"Thirteen minutes." Shit. He's timing me? Rushing back to my room, I toss off the throw and pull on clothes that I think will work for today. Since a lot of the places on my list are higher end, I opt for a knee length floral print skirt and a royal blue sleeveless blouse. Slipping my feet into sandals, I hear his voice echo through the house.

"Nine minutes, Meredith."

With a squeal, I hurriedly make my bed and rush into the bathroom to toss some makeup in a bag, brush my teeth, and run my hairbrush through my curls.

"That's time." He glances up from his phone, surprise—and appreciation—flash across his face when he sees me standing in the hallway, ready to go.

I shrug. "I'm used to quick changes during shows."

He nods as if that makes sense and stands up. He's dressed in gray slacks and a dark blue dress shirt, the blue a similar shade to my top and the swirls in my skirt.

"Umm..." I pause.

"What?" When he turns around, sunglasses shield his eyes and hide his thoughts from me.

"Maybe I should change?" I motion between the two of us,

and the corners of his lips lift in a smile. "So we're not all matchy matchy?"

"I like it. Let's go." He ushers me out of the house, only pausing long enough for me to lock up, and guides us toward his car at the curb. The heat of his hand on the small of my back sears through my shirt and ignites my body.

"Are you sure you don't want to take my car?" I nod toward the Audi parked in the driveway.

"We'll take mine." A muscle ticks in his jaw, but his hand stays firmly on my back until we reach the passenger door so he can open it for me. "In you go."

The chivalrous gesture surprises me, but perhaps it shouldn't. I had a lot of misconceptions about him. Since the kiss, he's shown himself to be someone different from who I assumed he was. It's confusing, going from hating him to not. And the sparks he creates whenever I'm around him make it even more complicated.

He waits until I tuck my legs in to close the door, and my attention stays trained on him as he rounds the hood and slides into the driver's seat.

"I've never been in a Tesla before." The dash is like a spaceship.

He shrugs and puts his foot on the brake, making the car light up. "It's different."

"You don't sound like you like it very much."

Another shrug. "It's got a really good safety rating."

He got the car because of the safety rating? "Can I ask you a question?"

"You just did." The right side of his mouth kicks into a smirk.

"Smart-ass." I can't help the laugh that bubbles out. "How old are you?"

This time he barks out a laugh. "Why? How old do you think I am?"

"Are you avoiding my question?" I poke at his side, and he tenses.

"I'm thirty." The words are sharp enough to sting, and his knuckles whiten around the steering wheel.

What did I say? He went from laughing to douche in zero point two seconds. Whatever. I don't have to indulge his extreme mood swings.

I face the window and watch the neighborhood pass. The silence of the car is unnerving. There's nothing—no engine, no radio, nothing. I open my mouth to ask about music, but close it again, not ready for another dose of attitude.

Why is his age such a big deal? He's thirty—so what? With a sigh, I mentally count the number of hours I'm going to have to survive while stuck with him. Maybe volunteering him to help me with event planning wasn't such a great idea after all.

The car slows and I spy the sign of the drive-through coffee shop. It's a welcome beacon. I need caffeine to clear the confusion in my brain.

"Coffee?" I hesitate in confusion, despite the prospect of coffee. His hands have relaxed slightly around the steering wheel, but tension vibrates around him.

"You made me promise you coffee," he reminds me as we pull up to the window. He refuses my debit card when I hand it to him. "My treat."

Without thought, I lean across him to shout my order at the menu board. It's only as I'm pulling back that I notice the hard muscle under my hand. I want to dig my fingers into that thigh, just a little, but I restrain myself. Because I also notice how he's pushed back into his seat back like he can't stand to be near me.

"Sorry," I mutter and assign all my attention to putting my card back in my wallet and ignoring Nick.

We inch toward the order window, sitting in charged silence until he passes me my cup of frozen sugar and caffeine.

"Thank you." I lick the whipped cream that explodes out of the lid before I realize I'm the only one with a drink. "Uh-oh."

"What?"

"They forgot yours. Let's go back."

He shakes his head. "I didn't get one."

"Are you one of those guys who doesn't let people eat or drink in his car? Oh shit." I cringe and stare at my coffee in dismay.

He chuckles. "It's fine if you want to. I just...it's a distraction." There's a look of discomfort on his face. It tells me there's more to whatever he's *not* saying, but I'm too cautious to push him, well aware of how quickly his mood can shift.

"Oh."

First the safety rating and now road hazard distractions. What's next? Executing a three-point turn? Parallel parking? I keep my snarky comments to myself—he's not the only one who can switch moods faster that most cars shift gears—and busy my mouth with my drink. Distracted, my attention bounces around the activities of a fall morning in LA.

"I'm sorry." His voice breaks the silence, startling me. Clearing his throat, he continues. "I shouldn't have snapped at you like that. Earlier, I mean."

Age must be a sensitive subject for him. I shrug. "I've got a pretty tough skin. It's okay."

"It's—I take my responsibility as a driver seriously. It's my job to keep people safe."

There's more in his tone, but I doubt he'd appreciate my questions. So his attitude wasn't about his age, but about the car? What did I say? Rather than dwell on it, I move on. "Like I said, no harm, no foul. Ready to get our venue on?" Can we please just change the subject and stop being all tense and weird?

"As ready as I'll ever be?" He has a lot to learn about outings with me. "Where to first?"

"Head south. We're heading to Ranchos Palo Verdes. There's a golf course there that does weddings."

Hours later, even I'm ready to admit defeat.

"Could this place be any further away?" he complains, fingers once more wrapped around the steering wheel like he's choking the life out of his car.

"I organized them the best I could." I shrug and try not to let his frustration get to me. It's difficult to do when it's been a full day. We've either been in the car—which always seems to be stressful for him—or touring venues with events managers.

We'd started south near Long Beach and slowly worked our way north. After visiting four places, none of them had felt like Charlie and Jax. Despite Nick's thoughtful questions, nothing specifically stood out, other than my gut telling me they weren't quite right.

More than once today I'd heard what a lucky woman I was with a fiancé so involved in planning our wedding.

Every time I got that compliment, his smirk grew bigger. Can this car hold his fat head?

He sighs. "I know. It was a good way to check out the places. Seriously."

At a red light, he glances at me, and his look reinforces the compliment. Warmth fills me at his comment and I break eye contact first, staring back out the window.

"Think this place will have a charging station for your car?" I'm not exactly sure about how his car works, but I know after a full day of driving, it can't possibly go much longer.

"I hope so. If not, so long as we don't hit traffic, I can get you back to your house. I may need to hang out for a while, though, for the car to charge."

"Okay." Today actually hasn't been horrible. I haven't plotted his death once since this morning. Progress.

We cross the gated entrance of our final destination and stop at the valet station. He gets out and walks around the car, opening my door and holding out his hand.

Nope. Didn't feel a thing. No sparks. Promise.

"Ms. Pryce?" The woman who approaches us wears a fitted blush colored dress. "I'm Nikki. We spoke on the phone?"

I nod and shake her hand. "Hi, yes, thank you for letting us come take a look."

Late afternoon sun sprinkles through the trees, and the noise from LA's constant traffic is nothing but a distant memory.

"Absolutely. If you and—" She turns big brown eyes to Nick and bats her lashes.

"Nick. Nick Rhodes." At the touch of his hand, her eyelashes flutter like a butterfly on steroids. Jealousy shimmers and I shove the feeling away. He isn't anything to me. Who cares if Country Club Barbie wants to take him for a spin?

"Mr. Rhodes. Follow me and I'll walk you through what our wedding packages entail."

He glances at me, the smirk fading on his lips when he takes in my scowl. I motion for him to walk ahead and follow, arms crossed as I sulk—the third wheel again.

When we finally finish the tour, despite my feelings toward Country Club—Nikki—I know this is the place. The soft and hazy romance screams Charlie's name, and Jax will agree to almost anything to keep her happy.

"Do you mind if we explore a bit more?" I stare at the vista in front of me, imagining a sunset wedding. My heart clenches with jealousy as I picture it clearly. I want what they have.

"Everything okay?" Nick walks away from our tour guide and steps close enough to me that the heat from his body reaches between us. His cologne has faded through the day, but a tendril wraps around me, tempting me to lean in closer.

I shrug, not willing to get into the mess of my thoughts at this point in the day. "Of course. Why wouldn't it be?"

"We can look for different places," he suggests. Sunglasses perched on his head, he gives me his full attention instead of looking at the view in front of us. I can hear the gears turning as he tries to figure me out.

*Good luck, buddy. Feel free to pass any insights my way.*

I shake my head. "This place is perfect."

"I wouldn't know that by your reaction." He seems genuinely confused, and I sigh.

"It's just—it's been a long day."

"I don't think that's what you were going to say."

My sunglasses keep my eyes—and my thoughts—shielded from him.

"You do that a lot, you know."

"Do what?" I ask, even as I turn and walk in another direction. Any distance I put between us is gone as soon as he falls into step beside me.

"You start to say one thing, but then you change your mind. Jax tells me you don't usually have a filter."

"I've known Jax all my life." Deflecting, I stop and deliberately keep my back to him. The way he's acting right now? That's dangerous. It makes me think we're friends. It makes me want to spill all kinds of secrets.

"What were you actually going to say?" His voice is quiet, persuasive, and my resolve crumbles. Damn him.

"Jax and Charlie are getting married." I sigh, but don't say anything else. The wind plays with my hair, tugging on the big curls, and I try to tuck the wayward strands behind my ears.

"Yeah, I know." I hear his smile, but don't turn around to confirm its presence on his face. "You volunteered me for it."

The corners of my mouth lift.

"They have each other. And I guess...I'm jealous. They have this epic love story, and I'm just...me."

He doesn't respond, letting the silence stretch between us. Despite not talking, he hasn't walked away—there are no sounds of shoes scuffing on the gravel. But it's more than that. I can *feel* him standing next to me.

"You can't force those things," he finally says.

My laugh tastes bitter. "Oh, I know."

"What's that supposed to mean?" he asks.

"Dating on tour is hard, right? I saw how hard it was on Jax and Charlie to try the long-distance thing. Pass. But I've gone out on at least a dozen first dates in the last year, and there's never a second date."

The first few dates? Those were understandable. But as that number edged closer to double digits, I didn't get it. I tried funny, I tried quiet, I tried bold, I tried demure—whatever I tried, it never seemed to be what the guy was looking for.

"It'll happen."

"You don't know that," I counter.

"C'mon, great girl like you?" I stiffen at his word choice and remember the twist of his sneer when he had called me *little girl*. It must hit him about the same point since he curses. "Shit. That wasn't what I meant. I meant that I'm sure some guy is going to be lucky someday when you choose him."

The irrational sting of tears burns my nose, and I blink. His arm comes around my shoulders slowly, as if I'm a wild horse he's trying to tame. He squeezes me in a weird sort of hug, his warmth another piece of him trying to make me feel better.

"You're not the asshole I thought you were, are you?" I ask.

He barks out a laugh. "I guess not?"

"Cocky much?" I turn and catch him as he raises an eyebrow, the look on his face pure mischief. I groan. "Get your mind out of the gutter."

His laugh tells me that's exactly where his mind had gone. "Ready to go?"

"More than ready." I am exhausted.

He motions me ahead of him.

"Age before beauty," he jokes.

"You're such a dork," I tease him back.

*Keep telling yourself that, Mer.* Otherwise, I was going to find out I had bitten off more than I could chew.

***

Surprisingly, I'm earlier than Nick a few days after our trip to Sherwood Country Club. He'd agreed to meet me at a florist shop downtown on his lunch break to help pick flowers.

I'm wandering down an aisle of pink ranging from pale to hot when the bell dings. Nick steps out of the bright sunshine, the cuffs of his gray button-down folded up, revealing forearms I want to—

*No. Stop it.*

I don't want to do anything with his forearms. I don't even notice them.

"Hey. Been here long?" He steps closer, and the warm sunshine mingles with his cologne, overpowering the flowers and causing my breathing to go haywire.

I shake my head. "No, just got here."

"Sorry, I got caught by one of the VPs on my way out." A frown pulls at the corners of his mouth.

"I can do this if you need to get back," I offer. I didn't mean for this to interrupt his day. He's the one that volunteered for a lunch excursion.

He brushes past me, his long stride carrying him farther down the aisle. "Let's just do this."

*Oh boy. This is going to be fun if he's in this kind of mood.*

I roll my eyes but follow him down the aisle, biting my lip to avoid sparring with him in a public place.

"What colors?" he asks, motioning around the rainbow of hues. "Pink?"

I nod. "Charlie and I Pinterest boarded her wedding."

His brow furrows. "You did what?"

"We found colors she liked that worked together—rouge, blush, sand, and dark sage. And flowers she liked too." I pull up the board on my phone and show him.

"I didn't hear pink in there," he responds.

"Duh. Rouge and blush."

"What the hell color is that?"

"Pink," I toss over my shoulder and move down the aisle to containers with the colors I just mentioned.

"Pink is pink," he mutters, reluctantly trailing behind me.

Lifting one of the blooms to my nose, I breathe in the sweet smell of the peony. "Here, smell."

"I know what a peony smells like." He ducks away and pulls another from the bucket.

"How did you know?" My jaw is on the floor. Most guys recognize flowers by color—red flower, pink flower, white flower. But he called it by its name.

He shrugs and drops his stare to the soft petals being caressed by his fingers. I've never wanted to be a flower so bad in my life.

*Seriously, Meredith, get a grip.*

It's a flower. Not an act of foreplay.

"Seriously, how?"

"I tried to grow these on the farm I grew up on in Nebraska when I was in high school."

"Why?" I'm curious about his life prior to LA, but he's so close-lipped about so much in his past.

"Why?" He parrots and I nod. He lifts the flower to his nose and takes a deep breath before it comes out in a mournful sigh. Another breath and whatever emotion just overtook him is mostly gone, but still hovers at the edges. "Someone I knew used to love them."

"What do you think?" I ask, lifting the one I'm holding back up to my nose again.

"It's—" A massive sneeze interrupts whatever he was about to say.

"Bless you."

"Thank you—" Another sneeze causes him to shake his head.

"You okay over there?" I ask.

This time, he doesn't even get any words out when another sneeze racks him.

"Why didn't you say you were allergic?" I put the flower back and fish in my bag for the tissues Mom insists I carry with me.

"Not," he says, snagging the tissue I hold out for him.

I giggle at his next sneeze. "Doesn't seem that way to me."

"I grew up on a farm, I'm not allergic to a few flowers," he responds after blowing his nose.

"Oh dear. You're not the first fiancé sneezing his way through flower choices. Claritin works wonders," the clerk says as she joins us in the aisle.

"Oh, he's not—" Another sneeze interrupts my correction that Nick isn't my fiancé.

"Gesundheit." The clerk's attention shifts from me to him. "Several of our grooms-to-be end up waiting outside, and we take pictures."

"I'll st-st-stay," he stutters.

An hour later, we're back outside after I've picked several shades of pink roses and peonies, calla lilies, and some greenery to set everything off. Nick's eyes are red-rimmed.

"You remind me of Rudolph the red-nosed reindeer," I manage to say without laughing—barely—and point to his nose.

He bats my hand away. "Shut up."

"Awww, poor baby."

"I'm not allergic," he argues.

"The clerk said it's nothing to be embarrassed about."

"You both can kiss my ass."

"Grumpy," I drag the word out. "Does this mean you won't be joining me for cake testing the day after tomorrow?"

"I'm not allergic to cake," he responds.

"You said that about the flowers," I counter.

"I'll be there," he calls over his shoulder as he flips me the bird.

*Rude.*

# CHAPTER 8

*NICK*

*O*ur bakery appointment is at another shop downtown on Friday at five. I toss my laptop in my bag, grab my sunglasses, and wave a quick goodbye to Sybil. Randa's voice stops me at the elevator with my fingers an inch away from freedom.

"I'm losing my patience." Her voice has a bite of frost around the edges.

I turn to face her. "With?"

"Jax. I thought I made it clear I wanted the tour schedule earlier this week?"

She hadn't made it clear, the VP who stopped me on the way to pick out flowers with Meredith had. The snide comment about my lack of ability to deliver hadn't helped my mood, and I had shown up to the florist's ready to chew glass. Instead, I'd managed to succumb to a bout of hay fever and had only been able to nod or point to colors and flower choices from a safe distance.

"I have it," I hedge.

"Where is it?" Her red-tipped fingers tap against her hip.

"I'm just waiting on one of the venues to finalize. It's big," I assure her. "Otherwise, I'd have already dropped them."

She gives me a tight-lipped look—almost a sneer, but not quite—and nods. "Monday."

"Absolutely," I agree, blowing out a breath once she turns and heads back down the hallway without another word.

I'll have to check with my attorney on the paperwork for the label. There was a hang-up with one of the filings and that's slowed the process down. I drop my bag off at my car but choose to walk the five blocks to the bakery and get there right as Meredith pulls up in her car. The convertible top is down, and I cringe, picturing all sorts of catastrophic scenarios.

"Looking forward to sneezing at cake that much?" she jokes as she joins me on the sidewalk.

"Ha. So funny." I poke her side and she shies away with a giggle. "I already told you I'm not allergic to cake. Or flowers."

"We'll see." Her teeth nibble at the soft skin of her bottom lip, dragging my attention there. "Are we going inside, or should I ask to do the cake tasting out here?"

I pull the door open and motion her ahead of me with the conscious choice to not respond to her snark.

"Ah, you must be Meredith. Right on time. I'm Pete." The guy who steps around the counter is around my age, and his friendly look morphs into a grin as he steps toward us.

"Hi, yes. Nice to meet you." She shakes his hand and turns to me. "This is Nick Rhodes."

"Fiancé?" he questions and offers me his hand.

"Who, him?" She makes a gagging sound. "Ew. No."

The baker's grin widens at Meredith's words, and his posture straightens. My grip tightens around his fingers. *Back off, asshole.*

"So, I've never done this before," Meredith interrupts our staring contest, and I release his hand.

"I bet you're a natural," he says, and she responds with a throaty laugh that punches me in the solar plexus. "Let's get started."

*What the fuck was that, dude? What the fuck?* I trail behind them, trying to decipher the way Meredith's laugh hit me.

Pete the baker leads us to a large counter, and I suddenly picture him as the Pillsbury Dough Boy.

"What?" Meredith asks me quietly, her attention drawn from the plate of cakes in front of us to me.

"Nothing." I don't think I reacted to the silly nickname, but I must have done something for her to notice.

"Behave."

"Good as gold," I assure her.

Dough Boy explains that he has the different types of cake, and we can use what looks like an artist's palette of frostings and fillings to determine which combinations pair nicely.

Chocolate. Vanilla. Red Velvet. Lemon. Carrot. Meredith's nose wrinkles at the mention of the carrot cake, and Dough Boy excuses himself to check on a cake currently baking.

"You don't like carrot cake?" I ask once Dough Boy is out of earshot.

"What?" She glances up from the cake selection in front of us. "Why do you say that?"

"When he named it off, you made a face." Is it weird that I noticed that?

"Oh." Surprise has her lips parting as she looks at me. "I...no, raisins are disgusting."

"You can probably get the cake without the raisins."

"It's a vegetable. Cake shouldn't be made from vegetables," she counters with such vehemence that I laugh.

"Okay, then." I don't get to say anything else since Dough Boy returns.

"Sorry about that. No tasting yet?" He motions to our still full plates.

"Just trying to decide which to try first." Meredith beams at him.

"Try the carrot cake, it's delicious." He points out, leaning over Meredith and resting a hand on her shoulder. I want to knock his hand off, but refrain from anything other than glaring at said hand on said shoulder.

I sit back and wait for her response. This should be good.

Meredith looks over her shoulder at him. "Really? Okay."

Shocked, I watch her pick it up and smear it through the frosting recommended to go with it. The way her hand hesitates —that split second—is so obvious to me it's painful. How does no one else see it? She pops it into her mouth and chews slowly. It's apparent how much she hates the bite with how long it takes her to chew and swallow it.

"So, what do you think?" Dough Boy asks her. He's oblivious to her struggle, even though he's been solely focused on her since she told him that we're not engaged.

What if she had a boyfriend other than me? Dick.

"Oh, um." She clears her throat and reaches for the water bottle next to the plate of cakes. "You're right. Delish."

Did I take a turn into the Twilight zone? What in the ever-loving fuck? Pissed and getting more mad by the second, I've had enough. What was this bozo's name? Paul? Preston? No, Pete.

"Pete." I manage to tear his attention from her. "There's still a lot of cake here to try, so if you have something else you need to do, we'll taste and let you know when we're ready."

He swallows and nods. "Yeah, sure, of course. I'll be right over there."

He motions to a workstation, and I stare at him until he gets the hint and leaves us alone.

"What the fuck was that?" I whisper to her.

Meredith takes another drink of water. "What was what?"

"You said you hated carrot cake," I remind her.

She shrugs. "It doesn't hurt to try it."

I open my mouth to argue, but snap it shut again. Why am I arguing with her? If she wants to make an idiot out of herself and tell a guy she likes something when she doesn't, that's on her. "Let's just get this done."

I turn my attention back to the plate beneath me, hovering over the choices. The chocolate snags my focus and I slide the bite through the smear of raspberry filling and chocolate ganache. Lifting it to my mouth, my gaze locks on the berry color of Meredith's lips. She must have used a lip gloss. They're shinier and darker than normal.

I watch her mouth open around a bite of lemon cake. Watch her tongue lick along the fork, her lips wrap around it to suck it clean.

"Oh my god, this is heaven" she moans, her tongue darting out to savor the dark red stain left over from the berry filling that coats her lips.

Pete's whole face beams, his attention solely on Meredith. "I'm glad you like it."

Is he really flirting with her? In front of me?

*Why shouldn't he?* There's nothing between us. Nothing except a smoking hot kiss and fantasies I absolutely should not be having.

I picture leaning forward and devouring her mouth, my tongue sliding through the sweet cake and frosting until I find her unique flavor. Christ, every new bite brings those sexy sounds to her lips, and my dick kicks against my zipper.

"Nick? What do you think?" Her question catches me off guard.

"What do I think about what?" A glance at my plate shows that I've eaten everything, but it might as well have been cardboard since I don't remember any of it.

"Pete was saying that it's customary to do a traditional wedding cake with some lighter flavors, and then the groom's cake could be something else. Richer," she explains with a side-eye cast in my direction.

"Oh." I can't remember a single cake flavor. All I taste right now is our kiss from three weeks ago. "Okay, what are you thinking?"

"I like the raspberry cream stuff." She drags a finger through what's left on her plate and licks it clean.

"White cake and chocolate, both with raspberry," I manage. Fuck. Who cares about the cake when Meredith keeps flashing me her tongue?

Her face lights up and she turns to Pete. "That's brilliant. Can we do that?"

"Easily," he agrees with a wink.

I need some air. Some distance from the flirting between Meredith and the baker. Distance from Meredith.

Making an excuse that I need to make a call, I step back out onto the sidewalk and lean against the building. She's not mine. That's never going to happen. I don't do relationships, and somehow I don't think a one-night stand with a woman so connected to my friends is a good idea. I need to get my body fully on board with my brain here.

Nodding to myself, I straighten off the wall and turn to walk back into the shop to find Meredith coming outside.

"All good?" she asks.

"What?"

"The phone call," she reminds me.

"Oh. Oh, yeah. Just a quick confirmation call," I lie. "All finished in there?"

"Yep. Cake is ordered, and I have a date tomorrow night."

"A date?" My teeth grind together. I'm outside struggling with not kissing the shit out of her, and she's inside making plans for a date? What the fuck?

"Yeah."

"With Pillsbury Dough Boy in there?" I sneer and wave toward the building.

"Oh my god, listen to you. Grow up. His name is Pete and he seems like a nice guy."

"Pffft. Sure. Nice guy. Captain Oblivious," I grumble.

"What's that supposed to mean?" Her hands perch on her hips as she stares me down, full of fire.

"He made you eat carrot cake."

"Ugh," she yells as her head tilts up to the sky. "We're back to this again? Leave it alone. I ate it. It wasn't bad. I didn't die. And so what if I didn't like it? I'm going on a date with him because he asked me. It's not like I'm getting a lot of invitations. It's not like you're asking me, so why are you so wrapped around him asking me?"

"I didn't like him."

"Tough shit. He didn't ask you for a date, he asked me."

I step forward, but halt. What am I doing? Why does our arguing turn me on so badly that I forget every reason I shouldn't kiss her?

Taking a deep breath, I stare at her. "Sorry."

"Whatever." She throws her hands up and turns for her car.

My arm reaches out, not touching her, but she stops. "Seriously, I'm sorry. I... it's been a long day."

She's right. It's none of my business who she dates. And my pep talk lasted all of thirty seconds in her presence. I need to do a better job of stuffing my attraction down.

"Well, now you can go home and relax." She waves in front of us.

Placing my hand in the small of her back, I steer us toward her car.

"What are you doing?" she asks.

"Walking you to your car." Touching you the only way I can.

"Well, duh, yeah, I got that. But why?"

"It's not always safe down here. And I'd feel better knowing you were heading home safely."

"Aww." She reaches down, wrapping her fingers around my wrist. My pulse jumps under her touch, and I try to ignore the reaction. "Careful there, or everyone is going to know what a nice guy you are."

I frown—what's that supposed to mean?—but ignore her comment, and change the subject. "So what's next?"

She taps on her lip as she thinks. "Hmm. There are only a few more things to do. Invitations. Photographer. DJ."

"Invitations?"

"Yeah, Charlie and Jax gave me the list last night. We have about two hundred invitations to address and stuff."

"So how about you do the invitations, and I'll take care of the other two?" I really, really don't want to stuff invitations.

"Ha, nice try, buddy. I'm not stuffing two hundred invitations by myself."

"I don't wanna." I try a pout.

"I'll make it worth your while." Her words shouldn't conjure the images they do.

"How?" I croak.

She turns to me with an impish grin.

"Pizza, beer, and football." She ticks off the items on her fingers and then waggles them at me.

"Football?" That's a safe activity, right? There's nothing sexy about linebackers.

"How about Sunday you come over to my place, and we'll watch the games and stuff some invitations?"

"You like football?" She continues to surprise me.

"Duh. How do you think I knew about the game the other night?" She bites her lip, and I can't help but wonder if she's thinking about what came after.

I nod. "Okay, deal. But I'll bring the beer, you just take care of the pizza."

"And the invitations," she reminds me.

My fingers hurt just thinking about it. "Okay." My dick aches from the other things I refuse to think about.

She unlocks the door and leans toward me. The hug is friendly, quick, and so fitting with what I'm learning about her, I'm smiling by the time she pulls away.

"So you want to head over for the afternoon game? Say one o'clock?"

I nod. "Sure."

"'kay. I'll see you then. Thanks for helping tonight."

"I'm not sure how much help I was, but you're welcome." I wait until she's tucked her legs in and grab her door. "Drive safe."

She nods and waves, and I watch the little red car merge expertly into traffic before I walk back to my car at the office. Alone.

∗∗∗

"Unh-unh-unh. Hands." Meredith's voice freezes my hands inches from the next envelope and invitation.

"What?" I lift my hands but can't see why she stopped me.

"You're such a guy." She rolls her eyes and tosses a napkin at me.

A smirk twists my lips. "Never had any complaints."

She groans. "Yeah, okay, Casanova. Wipe the pizza grease off your hands and get back to work."

"Yes, my princess. It was your idea to order pizza," I grumble.

"Just wipe the pizza grease from your hands and keep folding." She points from the napkin to the stack of unfolded invitations that tower on the table between us.

The game kicked off an hour ago, and we've alternated watching the game, debating teams, and then sharing the differences between growing up in Nebraska, LA, and New York. We have been—dare I say it—getting along, for once.

"Isn't it too early to do this?" I wipe my hands and toss the napkin on my plate, then pick up another invitation to fold.

She shrugs. "Not really. The wedding's in about six weeks."

How have we already been planning for two weeks? But I keep that thought to myself.

"My fingers hurt," I whine.

"You've folded all of six invitations. Don't be such a baby."

"How about you do this part, and I'll address the envelopes?" I offer.

"No way," she argues. "Your handwriting is worse than a doctor's."

She's not wrong. Our plan had initially been to split the envelopes fifty-fifty. Until she'd seen the mess I made of the first address. I could admit a tiny bit of envy for her neat script.

"But I have a paper cut. See?" I hold up a finger, and she squints to examine it. I don't actually have a paper cut, something she discovers with a scoff.

"Uh-huh. Sure." She nods back to the invitations. "Back to work."

Grumbling, I pick up the invitation and stuff it into an envelope. "You're mean."

"Whatever." She bumps her shoulder into mine. "Slob."

"What?" I look down at my sweats and t-shirt. "What's wrong with what I'm wearing?"

"Nothing," she says quickly, but I swear I hear her mumble something about gray sweatpants.

"Yeah, they're gray. So what?"

"Never mind. Back to work."

"Okay, bossy," I gripe.

She bats her lashes at me. "*I've* never had any complaints either."

This new, teasing rapport we have is fun, but I can't help the way my attention seems to have a mind of its own. I drag my tongue across my lower lip while my gaze strays to her mouth.

"You'll survive," she tells me. Her phone beeps on the table, and we both look down.

"Pete, huh?" I ask her. "That's right, you two had a date last night."

She shrugs but doesn't pick up the phone. "Yeah."

"That good?" The sadistic part of me can't help but ask.

"It was okay. There just—wait, what am I doing? You don't want to hear about this." She shakes her head but still ignores the phone.

"I wouldn't have asked if I didn't want to hear." Maybe then my body will get in line with the plan. Meredith is not just a one-night kind of girl.

"He's hot." Not what I wanted to hear. "But there's no spark."

I consciously release the muscles in my jaw. "No spark?"

She shakes her head. "None. Another one bites the dust."

"Another one?"

"Like I said the other day, since I've been back, I've tried dating a few times. I've never made it beyond the second date no matter what I do."

"Jesus, Meredith." I drop the invitation in my hand. It's one thing to hear rumors about her on the tour, but for her to just admit to it?

"Not like that." She smacks my arm. "I mean, I've tried talking about books, being funny, being quiet, being knowledgeable about food or wine, and nothing. No second dates. No phone calls. Nothing."

"If that's the case, why is Pete texting you?"

"Oh. He asked me out again."

"So what are you going to tell him?"

"I'm going to go," she tells me.

"What? But you just said there's no spark."

"Maybe I wasn't trying hard enough."

Her head dips as she concentrates on addressing the next envelope.

"Meredith. *Meredith*," I repeat more firmly and wait until I have her undivided attention. "You shouldn't have to try to like someone, just like you shouldn't have to try to get someone to like you. They should like you for you."

"No one ever has," she mumbles.

"I do," I almost say. The words crowd my tongue and I swallow them back. Saying them wouldn't help either one of us. Instead, I settle for the end of sage dating advice. "I'm serious."

Her gaze, wary and a little vulnerable, holds mine for a long moment. "Just...let's get back to work." She grabs another envelope and focuses on writing out the address in painstaking detail.

So I do the only thing I can do since she won't listen. I grab another invitation and start folding.

# CHAPTER 9

*MEREDITH*

ick is due any minute, so we can go through playlist options for the DJ. And he'd better not be wearing gray sweatpants again like he did last weekend. The universe is cruel. How else could I explain Nick showing up at my house in the guy equivalent of sexy lingerie?

And he isn't allowed to be all insightful and supportive today either. I kind of miss Nick the Dick. That version was...easier for me to handle. To avoid.

Even if I did tell Pete thanks, but no thanks to his request for a second date.

And why did I do that?

All because Nick Rhodes told me that I deserved more. Not in those exact words, but still, that was the message I got. Well, and maybe that wasn't the only reason. But I'm ignoring the sparks of attraction that zing up my spine whenever I'm around Nick. Not gonna happen.

IN THE BEAT OF THE MOMENT

"Ugh." I flop onto my couch and take a deep breath. "Get it together, Mer. He'll be here soon."

As if on cue, there's a firm knock on my door.

"Come in."

"Hey." He stares at me from the doorway. "Nap time?"

I sit up quickly. "No, just...meditating. Come on in. Did you come here straight from work?"

He's in slacks and a button-down, but the shirt is cuffed and shows off his muscular forearms.

"Yeah, my meeting ran long," he sighs.

"I thought you and Jax were starting your own label?"

He snorts. "Paperwork is a bitch."

"Sorry."

"Eh." He shrugs. "What about you? How'd your second date with Dough Boy go?"

I can't control the laugh that slips out at the nickname, even though I shouldn't laugh. "You're awful."

"What's his name? Paul? Parker?"

"Pete."

"That's it." He snaps his fingers and points at me.

"You did that on purpose," I accuse. "You knew his name. And it didn't."

"What?"

"I didn't go," I say and head into the kitchen. "Are you hungry? I have a surprise for you."

He follows me. "What do you mean you didn't go? Why not?"

I pull the dish Mom brought over earlier out of the oven. Thank goodness she can cook.

"I just...I didn't want to go," I hedge. Why is he smiling at that? Trying to ignore the flutters that smile gives me, I lift the dish. "Look."

He lets me change the subject. "Is that what I think it is?"

Setting the dish on the counter, I whip off the aluminum foil. "Yep. Enchiladas. Mom made them."

83

"I thought you needed an enchilada break?"

"It's fine. Plates are in there." I point over his shoulder.

He doesn't move to the cupboard, but stares at me instead. "You had your mom make enchiladas because I like them?"

I nod and my cheeks heat under his scrutiny. "Yeah. Grab the plates."

This time he starts to turn around to the cupboard but turns back, his gaze locking on mine. "Thank you."

"You're welcome."

"Meredith, this could be the start of a beautiful friendship." He winks and starts dishing up the enchiladas.

The food was good—even though I kept complaining about needing a break from the deliciousness of red sauce, cheese, and corn tortillas. Mom made them. Of course they were going to be amazing. The conversation was easy as we ate. It was like the last few weeks of working together with a common goal had finally led us to this solid friendship. Maybe he was right—maybe we could actually be friends.

Until we had to choose music. Then we were warring factions intent on complete victory all over again.

"What do you mean 'no?'" What's wrong with it?

"The chicken dance makes people look ridiculous," he argues.

"That's what makes it fun." Obviously. I don't understand how he can't comprehend this.

He shakes his head. "No."

"You don't just get to decide by yourself."

"Why not? You vetoed Journey. All Journey songs. Who does that?"

"They're overplayed," I explain.

"They're classic. Classic can't be overplayed. Here, listen." Journey's "Faithfully" starts playing from Nick's phone, and he sings along.

Huh. He's got a really good voice. I've never heard him sing, which now seems impossible considering how smooth he sounds.

"How can you not love that line about loving a music man?" he says, pulling my thoughts from his vocals back to stupid, old Journey. "How perfect is that for Jax and Charlie?"

I sigh. "Fine. You can have this. If." I pause and he groans. "I get the Chicken Dance, the Electric Slide, and the Macarena."

"What? That's insane."

"Either I get them or you get no Journey."

"Jesus Christ," he mumbles and runs a hand through his hair.

"Take it or leave it."

"You play hardball." His face is a mix of amusement and begrudging admiration. "Fine. Fine. Deal."

He reaches out a hand, and I let his fingers wrap around mine. I also attempt to ignore the electricity that arcs up my arm at his touch.

And fail.

Clearing my throat, I drop his hand and paste a smile on my face. "Okay, now that you've admitted I'm right—"

"I admitted no such thing," he responds.

"Oh, you did. Admit it. Anyway, first dance. What are your thoughts?"

"Well, what are you thinking? Modern? Classic?"

"I have a few ideas. Let me find them." I scroll through my phone and pull up the mini playlist I created. My lashes flutter closed, and I sway as we listen to "Conversations in the Dark" by John Legend and Adele's "Make You Feel My Love." I round it out with Shawn Mendes' "Fallin' All in You."

"Well?" I ask as the last notes fade.

"I think I may have another option." He scrolls through his phone and presses something before setting his phone on the table and standing. "Try this with me?"

He holds out a hand, and I hesitate. If electricity arcs just from the two of us touching hands, what will this do? To hell with it. I let him pull me up as the song starts. His cologne wraps around me as his arms do, and I find myself inhaling the warm scent. It's faded but still there. My head finds his chest as I listen to the lyrics blend with the solid thump that vibrates against me.

"What song is this?" I ask after several lines.

"James Arthur's 'Falling Like the Stars.'" His voice is barely a whisper.

"I like it," I murmur. The lyrics describe love being a guide home and compare falling in love to falling like stars.

The song ends, and he stops moving us around my living room. I pull back enough to look at him. "It's perfect."

The silence stretches between us as I drown in eyes that remind me of a storm rolling over the ocean.

"You like it?"

The light sheen on his lips as they shape the words mesmerizes me.

"Yeah," I whisper.

His attention locks on my lips, and my tongue slips out to moisten them. I lean forward, desperate to taste him again, even though I know this would be a complication we can't afford. The way he looks at me tells me he's on board...until he's not. He clears his throat and steps back, breaking the spell of the song and the heady sensation of being wrapped in his warmth. My eyes snap open with the return of reality. And sanity. Mortification and relief fight for command of my body. Thank god he didn't close those few inches. And why couldn't I?

"I should go," he says. He seems awkward, not like the confident Nick I've come to know, and stands quickly. "I have an early meeting."

"Oh. Okay." The flash of disappointment that hits me is a surprise.

"Do you want me to send the list to the DJ?" he asks.

I nod. "Sure. That'd be great. We're still on for the photographer on Wednesday?"

"Absolutely. I'll see you later." He waves awkwardly and walks to the door. "Bye, Meredith."

"Goodnight."

***

"Seriously, Meredith, stay focused. You're planning Jax and Charlie's wedding. This isn't a date," I coach myself in the car outside the Sherwood Country Club the following week. Nick and I are about to scope out the location with the photographer. My heart refuses to slow down, and my palms grow damp. "Not a date."

Since Nick left my house last week, I have been repeating those words to myself like a mantra. I'd write it on my bathroom mirror like some weird affirmation if I wasn't worried someone else might see it. Then I'd have a lot of explaining to do.

I can't believe I almost kissed him again. I'm going to blame it on his cologne. That addicting smell is a bad influence. I need to stay out of nose reach at all costs. I also need to keep my lips away from him, but I can do it if I don't have to smell him. Right? Flipping down the driver's side visor, I check my reflection, jumping when a knuckle raps on my window.

"Everything okay in there?" Speak of the devil. Nick's voice is muffled through the glass.

With a sigh, I close the visor and get out of the car.

"Peachy keen." *Just berating myself for wanting to kiss you again. No biggie.*

"Didn't mean to interrupt a phone call. I just didn't want us to be late."

"I wasn't on the phone," I tell him.

"You weren't?" He leans down to glance in the car.

"What are you doing?" I ask, shoving him away from my car playfully.

"Checking. If you weren't on the phone, who were you talking to?"

He saw that? Mortified, the urge to bang my head against the steering wheel builds. "No one."

"No one?"

"Myself," I mumble. I get louder to respond to him before he thinks I'm weirder than I actually am. "Sometimes it's the only chance for intelligent conversation while planning this wedding."

I grin and he catches on to the teasing.

"I'm sure. Do you ever respond?" His lips twitch, and it hits me—it's rare to see him so relaxed since he's often wound tight and stressed from work.

"No, that would be weird," I say in mock seriousness.

He barks out a laugh, setting his hand on my lower back to guide us onto the grounds. I want to lean against him, to test that strength and feel that heat more fully. But instead, I straighten my shoulders and take a deep breath as we head toward the gazebo that overlooks a gorgeous hilly vista. A man and a woman with cameras slung around their necks are also checking out the view.

"Hello," Nick calls out, and the two people wave then head our way.

"Gorgeous facility. The views…" the woman mutters as they join us, and the man with her grins. These views are part of the reason I liked this location best. It's just as breathtaking today as it was the first time we visited.

"Forgive my wife," the man says. "She's a bit *focused*. Get it, focused?" The woman rolls her eyes, and I giggle at the bad pun.

"You must be Meredith?" she asks, reaching out to shake my hand. "I'm Marni, and this is my husband, Adam."

"Nice to meet you," I say and shake both their hands. "This is Nick Rhodes, my co-planner."

He perfunctorily shakes their hands and immediately jumps into interrogation mode.

"Have either of you shot celebrity weddings before?" His voice is terse, all business. Old Nick is back. I'd like to say I missed him, but that would be a lie.

Marni's smile is professional and practiced. "Actually, yes. We've both shot them individually and together. Last year we did a massive three-day wedding party on Kauai."

"And no issues with signing a non-disclosure?"

If he keeps up like this, I wouldn't be surprised if Marni and Adam tell us thanks, but no thanks.

"Of course not," Adam answers for the two of them.

"The pictures on your website are gorgeous," I interrupt and shoot a glare Nick's way. Why is he being such an ass?

"Thank you." Marni's genuine pleasure shines through when she responds to me.

"The one on the beach was my favorite," I tell her. A sand-castle had been in the foreground with a bride at the water's edge behind it and the sun setting over the water. It was mesmerizing.

"The McCall wedding…" Marni's gaze goes soft, and she reaches out a hand to intertwine her fingers with her husband's. "That one was a favorite of mine too."

"When we spoke on the phone, you said the wedding was the second weekend in November?" Adam asks.

"Yes. Does that work with your schedule?" Nick asks.

"Absolutely," Marni responds distractedly as her head swivels around us. "I'm sorry, the light is so perfect right now. Do you mind if we get some test shots?"

Nick's eyebrows raise at her request, but he nods, and the two move in separate directions.

"Are you sure about them?" His voice is so low it barely carries between the two of us despite how close we are.

"What is wrong with you?" I whisper shout, casting a furtive glance at Marni and Adam to make sure they're not listening to us.

"What? I'm not doing anything wrong."

"You're being a dick," I counter.

"I'm protecting Jax and Charlie."

"By being a jerk," I repeat. "You can ask questions and still be semi-decent about it. Or better yet, you could have asked me, and I'd have told you I researched them and they've done a bunch of celebrity weddings."

"Sorry. People with cameras. Jax doesn't always have the best luck." He has the grace to look sheepish. "You have to admit, though, they're a bit... strange."

I take in the two photographers currently engrossed on opposite sides of the lawn. "I can. But every website I went to said they're *it* when it comes to wedding photography."

He snorts. "Okay. Because you saw it on a website."

His attitude sucks right now, and I don't hesitate to tell him that. "If you don't think I'm planning this wedding correctly, be my guest. Let me know how it works out."

Hasn't he learned anything about me by now? I'm working hard on this wedding. How could today start off so promising, then turn into this? Whatever. I'm over it. I take a step back toward the parking lot, and warm fingers wrap around my arm.

"Meredith. Wait. Shit." His chest moves with the deep breath he takes. Is his heart racing right now? Mine is. Just from the loose way his fingers rest against my wrist. "I'm sorry. Really. You have worked hard on the wedding. I know you want what's best for Jax and Charlie too. If they're *it*, then okay."

"Seriously. Trust me."

This close, I can see emotion flit across his face. Regret and sadness are easy to recognize, but there's more, and my core throbs at the desire that shows itself momentarily.

"I trust you," he rasps while his fingers tighten against my wrist.

"Nick—" I start.

"Meredith, would you mind being my stand-in? I want to get

light reactions for bridal pictures," Adam calls to me from the gazebo.

"Duty calls," I tell Nick. I'm relieved to get some distance from him since I obviously can't heed my own advice to stay out of range of kissing him. "Sure!"

Walking over to the gazebo, I pose as directed by first Adam and then Marni as she joins us. Nick walks closer, his attention not straying from me as I try to concentrate on anything *but* him. But the heat of his gaze stokes a fire that isn't easy to ignore.

"Nick, can you join Meredith please? This'll give us some good ideas for the end of the ceremony," Adam calls.

*No. No, no, no, no, no.* I need the distance from him. But even as that thought crosses my mind, I discard it. I want to be close to him. I don't say anything out loud and watch Nick get closer, like he's walking to a guillotine until he stands awkwardly next to me.

"Oh, c'mon, you two, loosen up. No way would the happy couple be so stiff," Marni teases.

Nick wraps an arm around me and tugs me closer. While my heart rate has tripled, he's completely unaffected when he calls out to the two photographers. "How's this?"

"Perfect."

The right side of his mouth crooks up as he stares down at me.

"Having fun?" I ask, feeling my own lips curve in response.

"It's okay." He shrugs.

"Only okay?" I want to hear him admit that he's having fun. That I'm helping him have fun. I curl my fingers into his sides and he flinches away. "Is someone ticklish?"

"Nope." But the fact that his denial ends on a sharp intake of breath when I graze my fingers along his side again?

"Liar."

"Careful. Turnabout is fair play," he warns.

"I'm not ticklish," I tell him.

"Not necessarily my path to revenge." He quirks an eyebrow at me.

"Oh yeah?" I mimic his facial expression, enjoying this moment with him. We're not arguing. I'm not restraining myself from kissing him. This? This is easy.

"Yeah." He moves suddenly and dips me backward until my curls brush the ground and I'm digging my fingers into the back of his biceps.

"Yeah!" Adam calls out and whistles.

Maybe I should be embarrassed, but I'm not.

"Oh my god, you're a nut." I'm laughing so hard I can hardly get the words out, and Nick's smile lights up his eyes. Something twists inside me at the unfiltered happiness of this moment. For a split second, I wish all of this was real. That this was our wedding we were planning.

What the hell is that?

"Just remember that next time you think you've one-upped me," he tells me with a grin.

"Okay, okay, pull me back up." Surely Adam and Marni have captured enough already?

"Hmm, I don't think so," he responds. "What's it worth to you?"

"Haha, funny man. Joke's over."

"I could require you to pay a toll." He considers that thought.

"What kind of toll?" My voice is breathy, and I'd like to blame it on the laughter and the lightheadedness of being practically upside down. But that wouldn't explain why my panties are damp, now would it?

His attention flicks to my lips and back up. "I'm not sure yet."

"I'm sure you can think of something." This close, I can see the moisture left behind when his tongue drags across his bottom lip.

His head dips closer, and our breath mingles between us.

"I've always been a quick thinker," he whispers and closes the distance further. There's a ring of green around his iris that flares as we continue to stare at each other.

"Meredith—" My name is a whispered groan on his lips. A cross between pain and desire.

"That's great you two, thanks." Adam's voice breaks the spell between us, and Nick straightens us back up.

"Glad we could help," he says and clears his throat.

We may have helped the photographers, but what the hell just happened?

✦✦✦

I am in trouble. No ifs, ands, or buts about it. Nick is funny, fun to be around, and a closet romantic.

Shit. Shit. Shit.

Nearly everything else with the wedding is done. The country club is booked, the DJ has the playlist, and Charlie found a dress she wants to wear. Tonight, Mom agreed to watch McKenna while Charlie, Jax, Nick, Derek, and I enjoy a night out.

"It's fine. Everything is fine," I murmur under my breath.

If only that were true. Anxiety wars in a swirl with nerves in my stomach. Somewhere along the last few weeks, thoughts of killing Nick had faded. He'd become my friend, even if I didn't fantasize about kissing any of my other friends the way I did with him.

"What'd you say?" Charlie steps out of the bathroom in a forest green dress. Moving toward the mirror in my bedroom, she turns to check all the angles.

"I said you look great. That dress is amazing on you." She ducks her head at my compliment. "That green is really your color. Isn't that the same color you wore to the awards thing a few weeks ago?"

She nods and a blush brightens her cheeks. "Jackson likes this color on me."

I know what she's not saying and waggle my eyebrows. "On you or taking it off you?"

"Mer!" Her blush darkens, and I have to hold my stomach, laughter nearly making me fall over. Even without my shoes.

I've broken out my Louboutin ombre peep toes again and paired them with a black dress that shimmers when the light hits it. The shoes sit by my front door until we leave, and my feet are grateful for the stay of execution I've granted them. Since my makeup and hair are already done, I motion for Charlie to come closer. She hesitates.

"What?" I ask.

"I worry about you every time you get that look in your eye," she says.

I grin at the face she pulls. "Me?"

Her laugh is nervous. "You look like a cross between a drill sergeant and fashionista. The combination is scary."

I snort at her choice of words. "C'mon, goof. Let's finish getting ready so we can meet the guys at Eclipse."

When Charlie and Jax had asked where we should go, Nick and I said Eclipse simultaneously. I liked the atmosphere, and he liked the low-key nature toward celebrities. Even though we'd had different reasons, saying it together meant Charlie had practically swooned as she cast heart eyes at the both of us.

We'd spent a lot of time together the last several weeks, we both liked Eclipse. Who cares that we said it together like some super cute couple? The sooner Charlie got *that* look out of her eye when she looked at us, the better off we'd be.

***

My phone buzzes as we walk into the club. I hang back and pull it from my bag.

**D-MAN: I feel like shit.**

**MEREDITH: What? Why?**
**D-MAN: I have a migraine starting.**
**D-MAN: I don't think it's a good idea to come tonight.**
**MEREDITH: Derek.**

I whine his name in my head even as my stomach takes a nosedive. I haven't seen him since the last time we were here, but I *need* him here tonight. I need the distraction of a good dance buddy. Derek has always been my partner in crime. Why does he get a migraine tonight of all nights? I sigh and try to be a grown-up.

**MEREDITH: Feel better. Get some sleep. Call me in the morning.**
**D-MAN: *Thumbs-up emoji***

"There you are."

Nick's voice comes from next to my ear, the deep tone creating a shiver despite the heat that wraps around my body at his proximity. With his hand at the small of my back, he steers me to where Jax and Charlie sit at a table in the VIP section.

"Derek texted," I semi-shout to everyone over the music. It's quieter in this section than elsewhere in the club, but noisy enough that I can't use my normal volume. "He's not feeling well."

"Aww." Charlie's voice is full of compassion. "Is he going to be okay?"

I nod. "Migraine."

I slide onto the round bench of the booth and scooch around until I'm next to Charlie. Nick's leg brushes mine and I tense, trying to ignore the way he studies me with a lifted brow and how it heightens my awareness of our proximity.

A server comes by for our drink orders. Nick asks for a scotch, which makes me wrinkle my nose. I used to think scotch was sophisticated. So I tried it. Once. Yuck. Jax goes for a beer and Charlie orders a water, then all eyes shift to me. If the few minutes I already spent with Nick are any indication, I need to keep all my inhibitions firmly intact.

"I'll have what she's having." I point to Charlie, and the waitress nods and leaves.

Jax and Nick both stare at me like I've grown a third eye. "What?"

"You feeling all right, Mer?" Jax's face reflects his disbelief. Why is it so hard to believe that I want a water?

*Don't forget, party girl. You have a reputation.*

The first tour I went on, I felt so alone at first. I was doing something without my best friend, who I'd lived with for nearly a decade. We'd always done things together. In an effort to fit in, I went out and partied with some of the more experienced dancers. I was more comfortable by the second tour, but kept tagging along anyway. Until I was on Jax's tour, and then it was easy to bring him along and enjoy his celebrity status together.

"Why can't I have a water?" Defensiveness creeps into my voice, and I don't try to hide it.

Jax lifts his hands in surrender. "You just usually have shots. Shot time, right?"

His joke falls flat and his smile fades. A muscle ticks in Nick's jaw as he studies me, I'm sure remembering the last time we were both here.

"It's okay if you want to," he says quietly. "I'll keep an eye out."

His quiet words are a further reminder of the role he played last time as my rescuer. He says them because he thinks he needs to. Because, in his eyes, I probably *am* a party girl. Maybe I should order an actual drink, so they stop looking at me like I'm a stranger. I should be able to order what I want, but maybe a shot or a glass of wine or—

"Excuse me." I push at Nick, and his face morphs from confusion to concern. Whatever. I just...I need a minute. I keep pushing until he finally gets up.

"Mer? Where are you going?" Charlie starts to follow, but I wave her away.

"Just heading to the bathroom. I'll be back in a minute." Blinking rapidly, I try to lose the burn of tears that stings.

I know they don't mean anything by it. The fact is, I did this to myself by creating a version of myself to fit in, to be liked. I created a reputation that even my friends believe about me. It's a bitter pill to swallow.

The bathroom is empty and relatively quiet, the music muffled once the door closes behind me. The sting of tears is gone, but I'm frustrated by the reactions my order got. The only one who didn't react was Charlie.

"Maybe I'm being a little sensitive," I tell my reflection. Those memories from the last time I was here still pack a little bit of a punch, but my order isn't a big deal. Even Jax's reaction. He's used to joking around with me when we go out. He and Charlie have no idea about Nick's rescue before.

The fact that he had to rescue me still embarrasses me, though. I know better.

Cool water runs over my wrists as I stand at the sink, but the mirrors reflect what I don't want anyone to see. This is supposed to be a fun night, not one filled with my drama. Smiling, I wait until it looks more genuine than I feel. With a nod, I turn for the door, determined to enjoy the night. Nick kicked back against the wall across from the bathrooms causes me to jolt.

"Stalker much?" I snap. I'm not a fan of this hallway and stride past him back toward the club, but his hand wraps around my elbow. It's the heat of his fingers, not the pressure, that stops me.

"Hey." He pulls me closer and tries to capture my attention while I look everywhere but at him. Something I've learned by hanging out with him is that he has the power to see through my bullshit. "What's wrong?"

"Nothing." I shrug. "I'm fine."

He continues to stare at me. "Fine? Freaked out, insecure, neurotic, emotional? Or fine fine?"

*Don't react, Meredith, it's not funny.*

My lips twitch as I try to rein in my amusement. It was funny though. The fact that he could quote that from *The Italian Job* with a straight face makes it hilarious.

"Who do you think you are, Donald Sutherland?" I give up hiding my smile, and his grows in response.

"You know *The Italian Job*?"

"Duh." I attempt to step back, but his hand tightens slightly.

"So now that I have you talking again, what's wrong? Why'd you take off for the bathroom like the paparazzi were after you?"

"I didn't." Denial comes to my lips quick enough.

He stares at me, and hilarity fades until all that's left is a seriousness cataloged in the wrinkles of his forehead. "You did though."

"I—" Another lie sits on the tip of my tongue. I wasn't feeling well. I had to use the bathroom. I—

"You?" he prompts.

"I don't want to talk about it." It's enough of the truth. Tonight is Jax and Charlie's night. Why can't he be on the same page?

"Meredith."

I close my eyes to avoid the look on his face that accompanies the way his lips wrap around my name. Steeling myself, I open my mouth, ready to brush him off. But I can't. I can't keep fighting the pull he has on me.

"Why is it such a surprise that I ordered a water?" The words are out before I can bite them back, the hurt seeping back in around the edges.

His face softens, and his hands rub up and down my arms in a gesture meant to soothe. "Is that what this is about?"

The burn of tears is back, and I blink again, nodding. "Why is it a big deal?"

My voice is quiet, but he hears me. He picks up the way the

hurt builds in the waver of my words. He tugs slightly, and his arms come up to wrap around me. Besides the hug he gave me while we were checking out the venue, we've kept touching to a minimum. It's sanity saving. Friendly touches. Smacks on the arm, a bump of a shoulder or a hip. The dance and the photography posing were anomalies. And told me exactly why we *had* to keep touching to a minimum. As the warm smell of his cologne engulfs me, insanity returns. My body wants things it shouldn't.

"It's not. I'm sorry if we made you feel like it was." His lips graze my ear as he tries to be heard over the music. Goosebumps shiver down my body, and his arms tighten around me.

Good kisser? Check.

Better hugger? Fuck. Check.

I step back for self-preservation, but he doesn't release me right away. His electric blue gaze flicks to my tongue as I lick my lips. It's so quick, I nearly miss it in the dim light. But it's hard to ignore the electricity that sparks under his attention.

Two women giggle as they walk down the hall, their attention completely on each other and their conversation. It's enough of a distraction that it breaks whatever spell we were both just under. I step back out of his arms with a shake of my head. Taking a deep breath of non-cologne infused air—seriously, what black magic is in his cologne?—I try to reset my brain. Or is it my libido? Ugh, regardless, I need to plant Nick firmly in the friend zone. And friends definitely don't almost kiss their friends.

I'm determined to have a better night than how it started. And there's only one way to fix that.

"C'mon, let's go dance." Grabbing his hand, I pull him back into the safety of witnesses. At least out here I can avoid temptation, even if I can't avoid my imagination. "Try to keep up, old man."

***

Meredith from three hours ago is full of shit. The presence of other people does nothing to curb the way I want to attack him with my lips. And that's *before* I learn he can dance. And not only the swaying side to side seventh grade slow dance kind of dancing. The man has rhythm, and that rhythm has set fire to my nerve endings wherever he touches me. All. Night. Long. My only reprieve is when Charlie and I request songs we used to dance to in New York, and Jax and Nick bow out to go have a drink. But once those songs are over, she snuggles back up to Jax in the booth and leaves me to the mercy of my libido as it fights against the way Nick's hips keep time against mine. Chugging ice water as we sit around the booth for a break, I attempt to quench the fire that roars through me.

A bouncer stoops down to talk to Jax, and his chest deflates in a big sigh as the guy stands up and leaves our table. Jax bends toward Charlie while his hand rubs her thigh. The longer he talks, the more the happiness slips from her face.

"What? What is it?" Nick is next to me, the heat of his leg brushing mine. I shift my leg away and ignore the look he shoots me.

Jax and Charlie are looking around the club. The carefree atmosphere from a few minutes ago is gone.

"Fucking paps." Jax growls. "Someone must have posted that I was here."

I shrug. It's not the first time this has happened. Usually, it's a lot earlier in the evening.

Nick stands, towering over all of us. "Let's go."

We'd had a few hours of fun and, without any earlier interruptions, I'd started to think we were in the clear.

"This sucks," I complain as we head toward a rear exit.

Jax glances over his shoulder at me. "Sorry."

"Not your fault." He can't help that he's famous. Sometimes it's a few requests for autographs and other times, like tonight, it cuts short a night out.

"Did you guys have fun at least?"

"So much fun, Mer. Thank you," Charlie says. Jax interrupts, whispering something in her ear that has her nibbling her bottom lip.

*Okay then.* Some things truly are TMI, and whatever he said to her to create that reaction definitely falls into that category.

Nick leads us down the hallway to the alley side exit door. "Wait here."

He peeks his head out and motions for us to follow.

"Sorry, guys. It was fun until the sharks showed up." Jax's opinion of the paparazzi is almost as bad as his opinion was of Nick and Reverb. At least Nick redeemed himself.

Nick waves off the apology. "Don't worry about it. I ordered a car. They'll meet us back here."

It's hard to hear what he says after the loud music in the club. My hearing is muffled and sounds are muted. No one says anything else as we wait for the ride to show up. Jax is wrapped around Charlie, whispering in her ear.

"Did you have fun?" Nick's voice startles me from my other side.

"I did. You?"

His eyes glow in the little bit of light around us. "Yeah."

The look on his face has a giggle bubbling up. "You seem surprised by that."

He shrugs. "I don't usually dance."

"What made you tonight? You're pretty good BT-dubs."

He opens his mouth to say something, but closes it again as headlights wash through the alley.

"Ride's here," he says finally, and I brace myself to be the third wheel in the car with a canoodling couple.

"Jax, Charlie, you take this one. I've got a second one coming for Meredith and me." With that authoritative tone, no one questions him.

Jax and Charlie wave their goodbyes and slide into the car.

Taillights cast the alley in red for a moment, then the dark descends again.

"Shall we?" he asks.

His hand on the small of my back guides me toward the sidewalk and creates all sorts of delicious havoc through my body. Guess I'll be spending some time with my BOB tonight.

"Is there anything else we need to plan this week? Anything still left to do?" His voice is so low I have to strain to hear him.

Shaking my head, I hide the disappointment I feel. "Nope. You're off the hook. Everything is done and planned."

"Good." His response is clipped. Wow, tell me how you really feel. Is he that happy to be done hanging out with me? Good riddance—

He yanks me against him. The heat and push of his body pressing to mine ignites nerves and butterflies at the same time.

"Then I can do this."

# CHAPTER 10

*MEREDITH*

His lips crash into mine, surprising me for the second time with how soft they are. His tongue drags along my lower lip, and my gasp allows him to deepen the kiss as his tongue tangles with mine. The taste of him after craving him so long fizzes through my blood to pulse in my core. I want more.

Screw this. I'm not some meek and mild female to be a passive participant in the kiss, caught off guard or not. Spinning us, I shove him against the wall, licking into his mouth as my hands move from fisting his shirt to scrape the muscles in his chest. The friction tingles along my palms until my arms wrap around his neck. I press my body against his, lining us up from chest to hips and moaning into his mouth when my breasts press against him.

His erection digs into my stomach, and his hands wrap around the ends of my hair. They tug enough to move me into a different position for him to take the kiss deeper, the light tug enough to tighten my stomach with the need to touch him, to be touched by him. Little noises escape the back of my throat as his mouth leaves mine to trail along my jawline to my ear, and his lips discover the sensitive spot behind my earlobe. His hands skim the smooth black fabric at my waist in a way meant to tantalize, to tempt.

"Fuck. This. Dress." His growl vibrates against the column of my throat, and I tilt my head to give him better access.

"M-my dress?" It's one of my favorites, especially right now. The thin material is silky where his hands flex into my hips. His fingers shift to drag heat along the exposed skin along the open back. I arch into him, grinding my pelvis against his when his fingers dip below the fabric and rest along the top of my ass.

"Do you know how many guys were staring at you tonight?" His teeth and lips nip down my throat before he moves them back up, plunging his tongue back into my mouth. Is his taste from the scotch or is it just him? The spicy, fruity flavor creates a craving I have to feed.

"Get some!" The sound of a voice yelling down the alley breaks us apart. My chest pushes forward as I inhale sharply, refilling my lungs, and Nick's attention centers there. My nipples pebble further against my dress, poking against the silky material. I prepare myself for another one of those fire starting kisses. But instead, he takes a deep breath and steps back, adjusting himself in his slacks. The fact that he's as turned on as I am? My body lights back up, my core clenching with a need to keep going.

"I'm not even asking if I should apologize for that." His voice is hoarse.

I shake my head and comb my fingers through my hair as I try to ignore the ache between my thighs. "No one's asking you to."

His eyes flare with surprise, and he starts to reach forward, but the chime on his phone stops him. He pulls the phone from his pocket, breathing deeply once, twice. "Car's here."

My lips tingle as his hand burns against the small of my back, steering me until we're back on the sidewalk. I slide into the car first and he follows, the heat of his leg singeing mine.

If anything, tonight's kiss tells me that I didn't imagine how good the first kiss was. In fact, my memory downplayed it. What Pandora's Box did we just open up?

***

Soft lips drop kisses along my collarbone while bright sunshine filters in through the curtains.

"Mmm." Sighing, I attempt to lift my arms, but warm hands tighten their grip, preventing me from touching and reawakening the inferno that raged all night.

"Morning, baby." Nick's breath brushes across my skin, goosebumps shivering in its wake. His lips scatter my thoughts as they trace a pattern down my chest to lavish attention on the swell of my breast before his expert mouth surrounds my aching nipple.

I whimper with the need to touch him, and he releases his grip. My hands find the silk of his hair as I scramble for purchase with the nip of his teeth. My core pulses with the craving that only he inspires.

Warm hands tickle my sides to settle on my hips, and my stomach tightens as his mouth moves from one nipple to the other, tracing more patterns with nips that he gently laves with his tongue.

"Oh god." My hips lift against his, seeking friction, and my thighs drop open to urge him on, but he maintains the languid touches.

Faster. I need fire, not smolder. This slow pace is going to kill me.

His laugh vibrates against my breast.

"That's not my name." Teasing bites move down my stomach where his tongue swirls in my navel.

His scruff scrapes against my skin and fires nerve endings that beg for more.

"*More.*" My fingers slip off his shoulders as he moves lower, stopping to press hot kisses against my lower abdomen.

*No.* The whine builds as a whimper in my throat. He's so close to where I need him to be.

"Say it," he demands. The tone of his voice, coupled with how he's looking at me creates an acute ache, a burn only he can cure. I know what he wants. I hesitate, second-guessing what this is between us, and his fingers flex against my hips, driving out those doubts.

"*Nick.*" His nose rubs the line where my thigh meets my body. He skims it down one side and up the other as he hums, the vibrations rocking my core as it clenches.

"That's right, baby." His fingers flex against my hips to hold my legs closed, prolonging the sweet torture as my hands fist in the sheets.

"Nick. Please."

"I like hearing you say my name, baby. Especially when it's followed by please." His voice is full of gravel, deep and rough. But it's hard to focus on since my attention is now on his lips that move along the same maddening crease.

Down one side, up the other. Slowly. It's sweet torture, but torture all the same.

Growling, I'm desperate to have him fix the ache centered so close to where his lips are. The bastard laughs—laughs—as his tongue repeats the same pattern. I squirm, but I don't know if it's to get closer or to get away from the delicious torment.

"Mmm." He takes in a deep breath. "Does your pussy taste like apples?"

*My lotion.* I'll never think of anything else but the tone of his question when I breathe in that scent.

"Why don't you find out?" I challenge.

A smirk lifts his lips but, damn him, he still doesn't let my thighs part. "Is that what you want?"

I'm drowning in the ocean of his eyes as his gaze connects with mine. What secrets will he share with me? I want so desperately to know him.

I nod. "Yes."

His attention shifts, hiding his secrets again, but he finally releases my hips, and my legs part to accommodate his shoulders. His tongue runs from bottom to top, and I fall back, a cry rippling from my throat when he does it again. My breasts tingle, and I lift my hands, tweaking the nipples and lifting my hips against his mouth.

"Mmm. It does." It's the last thing he says as his tongue works magic on my body, swirling around my clit. He licks and sucks until I'm on the verge of coming. The orgasm is barely out of reach.

My hands grip his hair as I beg him to continue without words. I need to come so bad it hurts.

He stops, tongue disappearing and his warm weight vanishing.

I open my eyes, alone in my room, pajamas and sheets tangled around me.

"No," I whimper as I clench my thighs together. He's not here.

We'd shared the car ride like we hadn't just tongue fucked each other in a dark alley. He'd walked me to the door like he didn't feel the fire that flashed between us. My core pulses, my orgasm hovering at the edges.

"Fuck this."

I shimmy out of my panties and open my thighs. I graze my fingers down my stomach while my other hand pulls my tank top up to pinch and twist a nipple. A gasp leaves my lips involuntarily.

I'm so wet, so turned on by the dream that my fingers circle my clit easily. They drag around it to dip inside before I move them back to the hard bundle of nerves that begs for release. My toes curl into the sheet as I continue circling, pressing harder until the pressure carries me back to the dream, right on the edge.

"Please." I have no idea who I'm talking to. The universe, maybe? But it's Nick's voice that responds.

*I like hearing you say my name, baby. Especially when it's followed by please.*

The orgasm barrels into me at the phantom sound of his rough voice, leaving me whimpering and gasping. Every muscle clenches in pleasure until I'm a limp, damp mess with one hand buried in my pussy and the other on my breast.

My phone pings with a text as I'm catching my breath. I reach for it with a hiss as my palm drags across my sensitive nipple and relights every lust-filled thought in my body.

**NICK: Good morning**

Embarrassment crawls through me as the sweat cools on my skin from my fantasy about him.

**MEREDITH: Hi**

I almost make a crack about his ears burning, but isn't that only if I'm talking about him? What part of someone's body burns when you fantasize about them?

**NICK: I've been thinking.**
**MEREDITH: About?**
**NICK: You.**

How does that one word have my thighs tightening all over again? It's like I didn't just douse the inferno he's created.

**MEREDITH: Me?**
**NICK: I'm attracted to you.**
**MEREDITH: Thanks? I think?**
**NICK: You're attracted to me too.**
**MEREDITH: Don't flatter yourself.**

As if he won't remember the way I pushed him against the wall outside the club. And let's not forget who starred in my X-rated dream that inspired the orgasm I just gave myself. But that doesn't mean I have to acknowledge anything to him.

**NICK: Keep lying to yourself.**
**NICK: You have to admit, we seem to get each other going.**
**MEREDITH: And?**
**NICK: I think if we sleep together, we can get it out of our systems.**

A flash of temper spikes at his words, even if what he says is true. We are clearly attracted to each other. But friends don't have sex together, right? And isn't that what we are? Friends? I thought we were.

**MEREDITH: So the whole friendship thing? False?**
**MEREDITH: All I'm good for is a quick fuck?**
**NICK: What?**
**NICK: Shit.**
**NICK: No.**
**MEREDITH: You're pretty much saying you'll forget me as soon as you fuck me.**
**NICK: Dammit. That's not what I meant.**

Hurt mingles with my anger. Am I that forgettable? Is that all I'm good for? Is that why I've had craptastic luck with guys? Is that why Daniel...nope, not going there this morning.

NICK: I am attracted to you, even though I shouldn't be.
NICK: Fuck, that sounds even worse.
NICK: I'm attracted to you. But we're...
NICK: Complicated.
NICK: Meredith?
NICK: I'm sorry. I didn't mean it the way it sounded.
MEREDITH: So what did you mean?
NICK: I still want us to be friends. My attraction is making that hard though.
MEREDITH: So if we fuck, that's it? It goes away?
NICK: Harsh. But, yes, theoretically.

Will that work? Will sleeping with each other mean I can start fantasizing about Chris Evans again while I get myself off in the future? Sounds good to me. There's only one problem.

MEREDITH: One condition.
MEREDITH: I don't want Jax and Charlie to know.
MEREDITH: This is between us.
NICK: Agreed.
NICK: Second condition.
MEREDITH: Okay?
NICK: We stay friends. Even after.

I scoff and key in my response.

MEREDITH: Think pretty highly of your skills there, Casanova.
NICK: Do I need to repeat that I've never gotten any complaints?
MEREDITH: Whatever *eye roll emoji*
MEREDITH: So when are we doing this?
NICK: How about Friday at 7?
NICK: My place?

IN THE BEAT OF THE MOMENT

His place is definitely a better idea. Otherwise, how do I explain to Mom and Dad why his car is here all night? Maybe it wouldn't be anyway. We're having sex, not planning a sleepover. Anticipation curls through me, equal parts anxiety and excitement. If kisses like last night inspire my dream, what will it be like to actually sleep with him?

**MEREDITH: Okay.**
**NICK: And Meredith?**

It's like he's in the room with me, the sound of his voice the same as it was last night as it wrapped around my name. Goosebumps dance along my chest.

**MEREDITH: Yeah?**
**NICK: Don't plan on getting much sleep.**

# CHAPTER 11

*NICK*

The last few weeks would challenge the celibacy of a monk, and I'm not Catholic. It would be one thing if I didn't know how Meredith tasted or know about those sweet little sounds she made with my dick pressed against her center. Instead, I've created my own seventh circle of hell.

Meredith is funny, thoughtful, and beautiful. She's also a reminder of what it feels like to live instead of survive. The joy she takes in everything from flower selection to people watching is enviable. Add in her love of a good football game, and she has quickly become one of my favorite people to hang out with.

There is only one problem with that. Every time I'm around her, I want to find the nearest horizontal surface and spend several hours buried inside her until we both collapse from exhaustion. I hadn't started planning Jax and Charlie's wedding with the ulterior motive of sleeping with her, but that was no longer relevant to my dick. The struggle between the guilt of our first kiss—strike that, two kisses—and the fact that Meredith wasn't a stranger with no expectations, like the women I normally slept with, warred with the part of me that no longer fucking cared.

I'd nearly swallowed my tongue last weekend when she and Charlie first showed up. The black dress exposed smooth skin that I wanted to worship with my hands, my lips, my tongue. Her escape to the bathroom had caught all of us off guard, but I'd waved Jax and Charlie off and followed her vapor trail and waited for her outside the bathrooms. It was another glimpse of the girl—woman—she didn't show many people.

Over and over again, she has proven herself to be more than what I initially assumed. She's far from the vapid party girl I thought I met on Jax's tour last year, and it's a side many people don't get to see. The vulnerable side. Those big doe eyes filled with hurt and sadness had pulled me further under her spell. It was only a matter of time before I kissed her again.

*You fucking shouldn't have.*

A twinge of guilt pinches my stomach. I told her that this was a one-time thing. What if she wants more? She isn't like my normal hookups—picked up for a night of fun from whatever bar I happen to hit. But our texts last weekend were clear.

I'm overthinking this and frustrating the shit out of myself. Thankfully the doorbell rings as I shove a bunch of laundry into my closet. Music plays from the Bluetooth speaker on the counter. Dinner will be ready shortly. Tonight will be just fine.

"Hi," I say as I open the door. *Do not devour her in the doorway, asshole.*

"Hey." She's fidgeting, her fingers twisting in the strap of the small duffel that hangs from her shoulder. Arching an eyebrow, I widen the door to let her pass and take a deep breath of apples and sunshine. Her bag weighs next to nothing as I take it from her and toss it onto the closest couch to pull her into my arms. She stiffens before relaxing into me. What the hell?

"Everything okay?" My attempt to search her eyes yields

nothing. Her walls are up, and the only thing those dark depths tell me is that her mind is somewhere else.

"Of course. Why wouldn't it be?" She stretches to her toes and fastens her mouth to mine, her tongue brushing my lower lip until I let her in. Once her hands fist in the collar of my shirt, she lowers her feet and pulls me down with her. The movement pulls me off balance, and my hands grip her hips, fingers flexing into the soft material of her shorts.

This isn't right. She tastes the same, she feels the same, but my gut is screaming at me that something's wrong. She's not acting like Meredith. Not the one I've come to know anyway.

*Shut the fuck up*, my dick screams.

But it's too late. The lust is tempered, and I pull back to figure out what's going on. Her normally curly hair is straight and pulled back into a ponytail. I tug it once, and her eyes open with the pressure.

"You want something to drink?" I ask. She shakes her head, and I try another route. "No? What about dinner? Are you hungry?"

"Now you're talking." Her arms wind around my neck, and her breasts crush against my chest as she tries to pull my lips back down to hers. This is not the same Meredith I've spent the last few weeks with. Confusion mixes with guilt. Something's wrong and I can't pinpoint it.

Tangling my fingers with hers, I pull her arms down and step back. Maybe this will help lower the temperature in my apartment by a few thousand degrees because, fuck, it's hot in here all of a sudden.

"For food, Meredith," I say.

She shrugs and sends the shoulder of her shirt down to expose the tawny skin underneath. The contrived innocent look on her face tells me she knows exactly what she's doing. My body desires her, but my brain wants to know what's happening.

"I ate already."

Since the majority of my blood is pooled in my groin, it takes a minute for me to process what she said.

"What? What do you mean you ate already? I was going to make dinner."

"If you want to eat, I won't stop you," she says it like it doesn't matter to her. Eat or don't eat.

"What the fuck is going on?" My voice is sharp, but what the fuck?

"What do you mean?" Now it's her turn to look confused. "Isn't this what we planned?"

"You thought I was going to jump you as soon as you walked into the door?"

Is that really what she thinks of me? Even after all the time we've spent together in the last few weeks?

"It's just sex. Live from Nick's apartment for one night only." Her shrug has me seeing red.

"Well, that's blunt," I bite out.

"Since when have you known me to sugarcoat anything?"

This person looks like the Meredith I know, but she's certainly not acting like her.

*Get out of your head.* She's right. We agreed. Just sex. One night to get the attraction out of our systems and get back to being friends. Just friends. Maybe sex is like her reset button. Maybe something is wrong with me that I'm making a bigger deal of this than it should be.

"You're right." Smirking, I drop my voice and step closer to tug her back into my arms. She melts into me, and her stiff fingers move to the top button of my shirt. "Obviously, we both have experience with it."

Her fingers stop, her attention shifting from the button to my face while a line carves itself between her brows. "What do you mean?"

"What? Casual sex? I mean, I haven't in a while, but I don't deny picking up women for a night between the sheets." I take

115

advantage of her stillness and lean down to press a kiss behind her earlobe. My lips move to the shell of her ear. "I'm always safe and I never have any complaints."

That statement was supposed to pull her back into our flirty banter—either in text or in person—but instead, her whole body freezes.

"No." She breaks the connection between my mouth and her ear with a shake of her head. "That's not what I meant. What did you mean by 'we?'"

Is she concerned about the stigma of sleeping around? I'm an equal opportunist, and it's not like this is the 1950s. Sex is sex. "On the tour."

She steps back, and I'm not sure which is colder—the cool air that swirls between us or the cold edge to her words. "What about the tour?"

I shrug. "Look, no judgment. I don't care how many guys you hooked up with on the tour. Any of the tours, for that matter."

Her entire face shutters, the confusion replaced with a calm nothing that terrifies me with its intensity. Goosebumps erupt down my spine as the fine hair on the back of my neck stands up.

"How many guys did I supposedly 'hookup with' on the tour?" Her normally energetic voice is emotionless. Did she not want me to know?

"It's not like I ever got a number." I hadn't even seen it for myself. But there were definitely people willing to share her exploits with me. I couldn't understand it after spending all this time with her, but after I'd heard it from several people, I just assumed that was another side of her I hadn't seen. "People said —" That probably wasn't the right tack.

"People said what?" Her eyes flash, then harden to a brown so dark they're almost black. Of course she won't let me get away with cutting myself off.

"Umm…" I rub at the back of my neck. Whatever I tell her isn't going to win me any favors.

"They said what, Nick?" All the armor she has stripped off over the last several weeks is back, and I'm facing the same woman as the night of the awards show at Jax and Charlie's. The fire-breathing dragon ready to skewer me rather than kiss me. "What did *they* say?"

Fuck. "They said you liked to party. That you flirted a lot with a lot of different guys." She arches an eyebrow and I know she realizes I'm not saying everything. "Fine. Fuck, they said you were open for a good time."

The red in her cheeks fades and her body flinches like the words I say physically hit her. The way she swallows is slow and painful. Rolling her lips in, she bites down and nods. A few small steps move her to the couch, and she grabs the bag I tossed there.

"You're leaving?" A ridiculous question in light of what she's obviously doing.

"This was a bad idea." As she passes me, I reach out and snag her arm, forcing her to look at me.

"Meredith, wait." I'm not begging. Not quite. Her words are a bucket of ice water and a fire all at once. "What do you mean a bad idea? This isn't a bad idea." It *is* a bad idea if I listen to the brain attached to my shoulders. But I don't like her being the only one to admit this is a mistake. "I'm not a mistake."

Her lip quivers for a moment until she bites down on it. Hard. "No? If you had asked me, I would have told you. Instead, you chose to believe someone else's lies over my truths. Despite getting to know me. That tells me exactly how highly you think of me. God, I'm an idiot to have fallen for it, for your 'friendship.' So yeah, this is a mistake. *You* are a mistake."

I ignore most of her words and try to concentrate on the underlying message. I'm more confused than ever. "Told me what? I don't understand."

Her smile is bitter, a stark contrast to her mournful gaze. "I've had sex with one man. The same guy I lost my virginity to after we dated for two years. So what if I flirted or danced with guys while I was on the tour? Last time I checked, that wasn't a crime and it sure as fuck wasn't sex."

She tugs her arm from my numb grasp and leaves without another word. Sinking down on the couch, I spear my fingers through my hair. It never occurred to me to ask if what I heard was true. Even if what I saw didn't quite add up. *Dumbass.* I grab my phone and send her a text.

**NICK: I'm a moron.**
**NICK: I'm sorry.**

That phrase "when you assume, you make an ass out of you and me" flashes on and off in my head while I wait for her to text me back. Only I didn't make an ass out of her. That was *all* me and the assumptions I'd made from what I'd been told on tour. Turns out, they couldn't have been more wrong. And they are. With nothing but time to think about it, there's no way what I'd been told is even remotely true.

No wonder she wasn't herself tonight. With her limited experience, the original idea of casual sex is worse than it already had been.

A glance at my watch tells me it's been over an hour since she —justifiably—stormed out.

Anxiety tightens in a noose around my neck. Is she okay? Did something happen? She was really upset when she left here. What if she wasn't able to focus on the road? What if she wasn't paying attention? Fuck, I need her to text me back.

**NICK: Can you just tell me you got home safely?**

I pace from the living room to the kitchen and hold the phone like the connection between my hand and the device is going to make her respond. But thirty agonizing minutes later, without a word from her, I grab my car keys. Visions of an accident make me want to puke as I white-knuckle the drive to her parents' house. The red Audi comes into view, shining under the porch light in the driveway, and relief and guilt lash at me.

Swallowing around the lump that has crept into my throat, I park my car in the street and make my way around the back to her place—a converted pool house—thankful I don't have to face her parents after all that went down tonight. The quiet of the neighborhood is different than I'm used to. At the condo, the sound of the ocean drowns out my thoughts. And right now, the quiet means that the memory of my idiocy is in surround sound.

The main house is dark, and only a blue light shines from Meredith's window. My arm weighs a thousand pounds as I lift it to knock on her door. The muffled sounds that come through her door stop like she's muted her TV, but light still filters around the window.

The door opens six inches, her face hardening when she sees me. The slam of the door in my face stops me before I can even open my mouth. Well, fuck. *That went well.*

"Meredith?" Pitching my voice to be heard through the door, I knock again.

The blue light behind her curtains disappears, but nothing else happens. The light above my head turns off, and I realize I have a bigger fucking hole to dig myself out of than I initially thought.

"I only want to talk." I knock harder on the door. Maybe if I annoy her enough, she'll open it again and this time I'll be prepared. When she doesn't answer, I try another tactic. "I'm prepared to stand here all night and yell through the door, but something tells me you don't want your parents to hear what I have to say."

That does it. The door flies open, and the glare she gives me conveys her belief that a quick death is too good for me. I bite back the smirk that threatens. I figured she was right on the other side of the door, but saying "I told you so" will likely end up with her slamming the door in my face again or decking me. Either is a viable option at this point.

"Hi," I start.

"What do you want?" Her voice is raspy, eyes wary. "Here to humiliate me some more?"

Shaking my head in denial, I answer a question I shouldn't have to. A question she asked because of me and my dumbassery. "No, I...Can I talk to you?"

Her hesitation has me wanting to kick my own ass.

"I don't really want to talk to you." Her voice is quiet. Too quiet. Not like my Meredith. *My* Meredith? I don't get the chance to examine that thought when the door starts to close again, taking my timeline with it.

"Please?" I'm not above begging.

She looks down with a sigh. I don't say anything else, hoping she'll let me in—literally and figuratively.

"I don't have anything to say to you."

"I-I want to apologize. Please?" I try again. After several seconds of silence—I'm ninety percent sure she's going to say no —she finally nods, and I release the breath I've been holding.

"I'll be out in a minute."

This time she does close the door in my face. At least it wasn't a slam. It's not much progress, but it is a step in the right direction. Now I at least get the chance to apologize in person.

The pool glimmers blue in the darkness, and the surrounding shadows are cast in sapphire hues. My stomach knots the longer I wait for her. Is she actually coming out? Just when doubt has me ready to stand up and check, the sound of a door opening and closing rustles in the night. Turning from the water, I focus on her.

A massive sweatshirt reaches beyond her fingers while flannel pajama pants hide the rest of her figure from me. Hair that had been pulled up in a sleek ponytail is now bundled in a messy bun on top of her head, and her face is scrubbed clean of the makeup she had on earlier. She stops halfway between the pool and her house like she's planning her escape. Her arms wrap around her body, a form of protection, and she draws herself up as tall as her five-foot and change frame will allow her.

"Do you want to sit?" I motion to the two pool loungers, and her gaze pings between the two of them. I fucking hate that she seems so uncertain. "For a few minutes?"

Her nod is rough, but she makes her way to one of the chairs to perch on the edge. Her attention stays centered on the pool as I sit next to her in the other chair. Facing her, I clasp my hands between my knees.

"I'm sorry." I sigh and continue. "I was an idiot for believing something I'd heard but hadn't confirmed."

One shoulder lifts in a shrug.

"I should have asked you rather than assuming." *Thank you, Captain Obvious.*

A shiver works its way down her body, and her arms wrap tighter around her midsection. But she hasn't said anything, still even refuses to look at me, even though I know she hears me. "Mer?"

The irony isn't lost on me. It's the first time I've shortened her name, and I use it to feel closer to her after me and my big mouth pushed her away. Dark eyes flick in my direction.

"Maybe." Her voice is so quiet I have to strain to hear her. "Maybe I should thank you. No one else was willing to say anything to me about my reputation."

"Mered—"

"I love dancing. All my life. Any type." She clears her throat, and the sound is painful enough to have my own ache in sympathy. "I like people. They energize me. I like talking to them. Mom says I've never met a stranger." Her smile is self-deprecating. "I didn't think those were bad things."

"They're not," I begin, but I don't know what else to say.

"So tell me why." Her voice cracks and she pauses. "Why

would people take that and turn it into something ugly? Into something I'm not?"

Fuck. Running a hand through my hair, I want to scream. "Meredith—"

"Is that why you wanted to be my friend? Because you thought I'd be DTF?"

"DTF?" It takes me a minute. Down to fuck. Shit. "What? No. Of course not."

"That's right, Jax wanted us to 'clear the air.'" Her breath hisses between her teeth. "So you were my friend because Jax asked you to be. God, that's so pathetic, I can't tell which is worse. That I needed Jax to force someone to be my friend or that I'm apparently a tour skank."

The words provoke me to kneel in front of her. I hate that she stiffens when my hands drop to the chair on either side of her hips.

"Meredith. Look at me." She keeps staring at the pool, and I try the word I hope will work. "Please." Her eyes dart down to mine, unfathomable in the shadows created from the pool lights. "Did Jax want us to clear the air? Yes. But we more than did that. You're smart and funny. You like football. You *are* my friend. That has nothing to do with Jax and what he asked. I'm so sorry I hurt you. I didn't mean to."

Several moments of silence pass while I let her work through whatever is going on in her head. Her nod feels like a victory. "I know it wasn't intentional."

My hand closes over hers, and her whole body tightens until she forcefully breaks the connection.

"This was a mistake." She motions between the two of us. "It makes things too complicated. It's not a good idea."

"You don't want to be my friend anymore?" Panic claws up my throat until she shakes her head.

"No. I do. I think. I just—I think it would be better if we were only friends."

I'm relieved to even have the chance to be her friend. "Okay."

She's right. Having sex *would* complicate things.

*So?* My body is very much on board with our previous idea, but if she needs me to ignore the overwhelming attraction I have for her, I can do that.

I'd much rather have her in my life as a friend than not have her there at all.

# CHAPTER 12

*MEREDITH*

*N*ick's eyes reflect the glow of the pool lights as he kneels in front of me. Hurt continues to radiate through me and creates a chill through my body. How many people talked about me on the tour? How many people think the same thing about me he believed? I'm second guessing every interaction I had with guys—with everyone—on Jax's last tour. Does he know?

No. If Jax knew, he'd have told me. Or stopped the gossip altogether. Right?

"Can I ask you something?" My voice comes out softer than I want, and I clear my throat.

"Absolutely." Nick shifts back to the chair next to mine. "Anything."

"Who—who told you that I was easy?" The question is harder to push out than I thought. Twisting my fingers together, I wait for him to respond. He expels a breathy "fuck" and clears his throat.

"Do you really want to know? What good would that do?"

"I—I want to know if you heard it from one person or a hundred. What stories did you hear?"

He pinches the bridge of his nose. "Meredith."

"Please?"

Conflict wars on his face. "I don't think this is a good idea."

"And I think I have the right to know," I counter. "The rumors are about me, right?"

"You're right. But I just want to say, this is against my better judgment." He sighs. "When I came onto the last tour with Jax, two of the dancers approached me. One of them—Caleb? Clint?"

"Clint." My stomach twists. Clint had been a recent addition to the tour and gave me a hard time about everything I asked. If I said to start warm-ups at five, he wanted five thirty. If I wanted a spin there, he wanted it here. He was a total pain in my ass, plus he gave me the heebie jeebies whenever I caught him staring at me. I was glad when I didn't have to deal with him anymore after I quit.

"He told me there were concerns among the dancers. That you were hooking up with different guys every night and that you weren't showing up to practices or you were late. That most recently you'd hooked up with a few of the band members—at the same time."

He looks as green as I feel. Bile coats my throat, and I wince as I try to swallow the burning sensation back down.

"You b-believed him?" I can't breathe. My lungs won't work right. *Two guys at the same time?*

He nods. "At first. At least parts of it. But then I saw how close you and Jax were, and I started to doubt a lot of what those two dumb fucks told me. But I've learned that there's always a kernel of truth to the gossip. I didn't get the chance to ask Jax anything when Chicago happened. By the time I'd dealt with the fallout from that, you'd quit. Problem solved."

I nearly topple the lounger as I stand and bolt for the sanctuary of my house. Nick grabs my wrist and intertwines our fingers.

"Hey. Hey. Hey. Don't run away." The pressure behind my eyes warns me that tears are imminent. I don't want him to see. But he doesn't let go, and the tears gathering along my lashes slip through. "Meredith."

Warm arms surround me as he draws me into a hug I didn't know I desperately needed. Even though I didn't do anything to earn the reputation I got, I feel exposed. Raw. As his addictive cologne engulfs me, a sob erupts, and the rest of my tears run unchecked down my cheeks and soak into his dress shirt. Bunching the fabric across his back in my fists, I attempt to muffle my tears. I try to stop, to hide the hurt, to protect myself, but it's no use. My defenses have all crumbled down.

"Shh. It's okay." Warm hands run up and down as he whispers other nonsense words into my hair.

He moves until we're sitting back down in my chair, his arms wrapped securely around me. I want to get up, to go back into the house and handle this on my own. But it's nice to be able to lean on someone. As the tears slow and then stop, I sniffle and wipe my nose with my sweatshirt. I'm classy like that. With a shuddered breath, I pull back enough to put distance between the two of us.

"If I could go back in time, I wouldn't believe him. Or his friend," he shares.

"They wanted my job." My voice is hoarse, filled with teary remnants.

"I should have figured that out. I know that. Now." He blows out a breath and rubs his hands along his slacks. "Fuck. I'm sorry."

I don't say anything. What can I say? How could he have possibly known? I'm sure there are people out there who *do* exactly what Clint said I did. Hadn't I seen plenty of groupies throw themselves at Jax? At the band? Hell, any guy on our tour, from roadies to dancers, was fair game.

"So are we friends again?" He draws my attention back to him.

"Okay?" I shrug.

"You don't sound very convincing." He blows out a breath and wraps long fingers around the edge of the chair. "I really am sorry."

"I know," I assure him.

I *do* know. He wouldn't apologize unless he meant it. His bullshit tolerance doesn't strike me as being super high. I hate that he thought those rumors about me were true. Somehow it feels like I'm not good enough to be his friend. That I'm damaged. Unworthy.

"Get out of your head." His voice startles me from my thoughts before they can spiral further. "Whatever is going on in there isn't true."

"How—"

"I can see the wheels turning from here. I'd recommend you never take up poker."

"I'm pretty good at poker," I tell him confidently.

"Maybe with other people. Not with me."

Despite the heavy conversation, my lips lift with his comment.

"There it is," he breathes out.

"What?"

"Your smile. Or part of it anyway." He is such a dork. I bite my lip to try to hide the pleasure that threatens at the goofy expression on his face. "There. Right there. Don't move."

One arm wraps around my shoulders while he pulls out his phone with the other hand to angle the camera and capture the two of us.

"Wait, no, no pictures," I groan.

My eyes are swollen and gritty, my makeup long gone. Now is

not the time for any pictures. I try to duck under his arm, but he tightens it to pin me to him in an awkward hold. "Just one. I need one for your contact in my phone anyway. Smile, Meredith."

"Nick—"

"Cheese." I hear the shutter sound on the camera app and blink.

"Was my mouth open?" I punch him in the leg. "Lemme see."

Wincing, he rubs his leg and hands me his phone. It's not a bad photo. My mouth isn't open, instead curved in a half smile as I lean against him. My eyes are red and a little swollen, but there are worse pictures of me that currently grace photo albums on Mom's bookshelves.

"Fine. I guess you can keep it." I hand him back his phone and stand up out of the circle of his warmth.

"How about dinner?" he asks with a rapid change of subject.

"What? Like now?" I'm confused.

He chuckles. "No. I mean I want to cook dinner for you. As friends."

The clarification is painfully obvious after the last few weeks of not having to clarify.

"It's fine," I say. "Not necessary."

"Mer?"

"What?"

"I'm making you dinner. Tomorrow night. Six." He's not asking. The demanding tone of his voice sends a shiver of awareness down my spine. Friends shouldn't shiver from the growly demands of another friend. "Let me make tonight up to you."

Looking at him reminds me of the Caribbean Ocean we took a family vacation to when I was younger—the blue of his gaze is so clear, so deep, I could spend all day lost in it. Lost in him.

"Okay, fine." I nod. "Six o'clock."

★★★

My phone ringing drags me from my dreamless sleep.

"'Lo?" My eyelids feel cemented shut.

"Meredith?" The light chuckle has me instantly awake, and I sit up so fast I fall off the edge of my bed. "Still not a morning person, huh?"

What. The. Fuck? What did I do to piss off the universe so epically that karma is biting me in the ass this bad?

"Daniel?" Two years. Well, almost. Two years ago, I stopped answering his calls after I broke up with him and, eventually, he stopped calling. Why now?

"You okay there, Mer-Bear?" My molars grind at the use of his nickname for me. I used to think it was cute. I was sixteen, we had just started dating, and I was an idiot. Back then, everything he did was amazing, cute, perfect. Dark brown eyes I could get lost in and muscles I could read with my fingertips. On the first day of school my third year in New York, I had walked up and boldly introduced myself as his future girlfriend. The rest is a bumpy trip down a memory lane I'd rather avoid.

"How did you get this number?" I bite the words out, extricating myself from the twist of covers around my body.

"It's still in my phone," he says it like it's no big deal.

Shit. He's right. I haven't changed my number, so of course he has it.

"What do you want, Daniel?"

"Grumpy. Sounds like you need some coffee."

*Hang up.* My brain is screaming at me, but my fingers are paralyzed.

"What. Do. You. Want?"

He laughs like we're sharing some funny joke. "The company I'm dancing with was invited by the Los Angeles Ballet Company to come in and perform. Since I'm here in LA, I thought maybe we could get together, hang out, like old times? Maybe catch up?"

Old times, like all the times he belittled me? I was too loud, too immature, too much of a tomboy. I was too much of a prude before we had sex and too clingy after. No matter what I did—how I changed—I could never meet his expectations.

I must have been a serial killer in a previous life. That's the only reason I can figure that karma decided that first I needed to be told that apparently, I was known as the tour whore to at least two of my dancers, and now this?

Time the fuck out. Uncle. Hail Mary, whatever I need to do to rebalance the karmic scales, I'll do it.

"Mer-Bear?"

*Why me?*

"Are you serious?" Am I having a stroke? I need to google symptoms because the eye twitch I'm currently experiencing has to be one.

"Yeah, I was thinking you could come pick me up, and we could head to the beach—"

"I haven't talked to you in almost two years," I interrupt.

"Well, yeah, so we'll have a lot to catch up on."

"What makes you think I want to 'catch up' with you, Daniel? Did the two years of radio silence not register?"

"I got a new phone number, so you didn't have this one—"

"Even had I had your number, and you were the last person on earth, Daniel, I can assure you I *wouldn't* have called." No matter how much I try not to, the box of memories I have taped shut in the vault I locked it in opens like a floodgate. "Need I remind you that I walked into your dorm room while you were fucking someone else?"

"Why do you have to be so crass?" The hint of disgust I got so used to hearing in his voice is back.

"Oh my god, Daniel, I walked in on you with your dick shoved down someone else's throat." The words are practically a scream.

We hadn't planned to hang out that day, but I'd had a rough class and wanted to commiserate since Charlie was in practice. I had a key to his dorm room since he was constantly losing his.

His groan should have tipped me off as I opened the door. But like a moron, I'd kept going and found my boyfriend of four years with some girl I didn't recognize on her knees in front of him. I'm not surprised that he ignores that to complain about the way I've phrased his cheating. "You're concerned about how I describe it?"

He sniffs. "Still the same immature bitch you were in New York."

Before I can let the retort fly from my lips, there's a click. I don't hesitate for a second, blocking the number he called me from with shaky fingers.

I'd always felt like something was missing. Like I wasn't enough for him. His favorite phrase had been to tell me to grow up. *Immature.* Was I?

I need a shower, so I stomp into the bathroom, but even the spray of the showerhead doesn't wash away the memories. Images of fourteen-year-old toothpick me—a good enough dancer to get into the magnet school, but not good enough to get any major dance roles. Daniel had come along at the right time two years later and quickly learned to use my insecurities against me.

Anytime I did something he didn't like, he was there to cast judgment. To explain what I should say or how I should act. I'd tried to do everything the way he would want me to. I'd shoved my true self down deep anytime he was around. I wanted to be someone worthy enough for him to love the way I loved him. It had never been enough. *I* had never been enough.

I turn off the water and grab my towel. The embarrassment and anger I thought I had gotten past are as fresh today as they were then. And that frustrates me. I don't want Daniel to have this much impact on my life.

My phone chimes with a new text, and I'm grateful for the distraction.

**NICK: You okay with steak and baked potatoes?**

Chewing on my lip, I read his message a few times. Should I even go? I'm not in the greatest mindset to be around people. I'd rather curl up on my couch in my sweats with some popcorn, a big ass bottle of wine, and a stack of rom-coms at the ready. I'm ready to ask for a rain check when I get another message.

**NICK: You're not backing out, are you?**
**MEREDITH: I'm not feeling that great.**
**NICK: Bullshit.**
**NICK: This is my way of making up for yesterday.**
**NICK: If you don't come on your own, I'll just relocate dinner to your place.**

I'd rather not have Mom witness anything she can ask questions about. And if Nick's over, she'll definitely ask questions.

**MEREDITH: Fine. *eyeroll emoji***
**NICK: See you at 6! Don't be late!!**

*Don't be late, Meredith. That's so immature. Don't text with emojis, Meredith. How old are you, twelve?*
I click on a random playlist and attempt to drown out the four years' worth of negative comments. Too bad I can't delete *that* playlist from my mind.

***

At five fifty-nine, I knock on Nick's door, and a sense of déjà vu washes over me. Twenty-four hours ago, I'd stood here and given myself a pep talk that I could totally handle sleeping with someone who made my entire body light up like the Fourth of July. With only a kiss.

Tonight, the encouragement is less carnal. I'm only trying to convince myself to not run for my couch and stack of rom-coms.

"Hey, you made it." Nick's eyes light up as he takes in my jeans and slouchy sweater.

"Yep. I'm here."

Opening the door, he motions for me to enter. More aware of my surroundings tonight than I was last night, I take in his condo. Stacks of papers are haphazardly tossed on the table next to the couch, and three coffee mugs are stacked on top of them. I nearly trip over a pair of shoes by the door, and he grimaces before he picks them up and tosses them down the hall.

He's so put together in every other aspect I've seen that this is a funny surprise.

"Sorry about that." His grin is sheepish and charming.

It's how Daniel used to look at me when we first started dating. Thinking of him is a quick way for my contentment to fade, and I tuck my hands into my back pockets.

"You hungry?"

I shrug, and his gaze narrows. Scrutinizing. *Judging.*

"A little?" I say.

"Did you already eat?" I hear more attitude than is probably actually there, but sparks of my temper come to life to raise my defenses.

"No, *Dad.* I didn't," I snark.

He holds his hands up in the universal sign of surrender. "Truce."

I roll my eyes and turn to take in the monster TV that almost rivals Jax's and a big leather sectional. Why hadn't we hung out here while planning the wedding? *Because you're temporary*, says the voice in my head that sounds an awful lot like Daniel's. I swallow the bile that builds in my throat.

"Really? You have this, and you bitched about wanting to watch the game at Jax's?" My words spit out like weapons.

"Jesus, Mer, what the fuck? That was weeks ago." His brow is drawn in confusion while his eyes search my face.

I don't blame him. I'm acting insane. I don't want to. I can feel my attitude bubbling up, but my words all escape without my permission. I'm not angry with him, but he's the target, regardless.

"Sorry," I manage to choke out.

"Did you have a rough day?" He motions for me to follow him to the kitchen where two steaks sit, ready for a grill, next to giant baked potatoes wrapped in foil. My stomach growls, and he laughs. I nod since I don't trust myself to speak. He stops what he's doing to meet my gaze. "Is this about last night?"

"Ugh, no. Not everything is about you." I give up and turn on my heel, intent on leaving for the second time in twenty-four hours. "See? Bad idea."

"Whoa, whoa, whoa." He inserts himself between me and the door and leans against it. "Don't leave. Talk to me."

Wrapping my arms around my middle, I let out a deep breath as another sense of déjà vu swamps me.

"I'm sorry." I try to step around him to get to the door. "I'm not the greatest company tonight. I shouldn't have come."

"Wait." His long fingers wrap around my biceps, their heat singeing me through my sweater. "Take a deep breath. Talk to me."

"I can't," I finally manage to choke out.

"I have an idea." I don't get any other warning before he bends and locks an arm under my knees and another around my back. He carries me through the door that leads to his deck, setting me down in a chair and taking the one opposite. The smells and sounds of the ocean convince me to drag in one deep breath followed by another. "Now, talk to me."

"I'm sorry. I'm being a drama queen." *Drama queen.* I hate that phrase.

He shakes his head. "I don't think so. Everyone's allowed to have a bad day. What happened?"

Burying my head in my hands, I mumble out. "Nothing."

His chuckle is full of doubt. "Yeah, okay."

"I don't want to talk about it." I look at him but can't bring myself to meet his curious gaze.

"Name your demons and they can't hurt you." He sounds like he believes that.

"What?"

"I read that somewhere once. It made sense."

I blow out a breath. *Name my demons.* How's this? "My ex called me this morning."

"Your ex?" His attention is steady, the focus urging me to continue.

"He's in LA, wanted to hang out." Leaning my head back, I catch the purples and pinks that swirl in the pale blue sky. "Fuck. Two years. I haven't talked to him in two years. Then he calls me and pretends like nothing happened."

"What did happen?" His voice is quiet, his face turned toward the ocean. It's like he knows I can't be the center of his attention.

"He-he cheated on me." No one else knows about any of my past with Daniel. He's the first one I've admitted Daniel's adultery to in the two years we've been broken up. No matter how many times Charlie has tried to bring it up, I keep that shit locked down. Usually. But right now, it feels too raw and Nick feels like a safe space to unload.

"Motherfucker."

The vehemence in his voice fills me with warmth.

"He... has the ability to get under my skin. To get in my head." Sighing, I stand up. "I'm sorry I ruined dinner for you—again."

He shakes his head. "It's not ruined. Come on, let's eat. My mom always said food makes everything better."

"Sounds like a woman after my own heart."

"How do you take your steak?" He steers me back into the condo.

"However you cook it is fine." My response is nearly automatic.

He huffs out a laugh and turns me until I'm facing him. "No, seriously, how do you take your steak?"

"I'm good with whatever."

"Meredith. I eat mine medium rare."

Rare? I gulp. Yuck. "O-okay."

"I'll cook it however you want it. Just tell me." His voice fades, and he stares at me expectantly.

"I don't want to add any more work for you," I start. His eyebrows raise, and I sigh. "Medium well."

"There. Was that so hard?" He points me in the direction of a bottle of wine sitting on the counter. "Pour some if you want. Potatoes are ready, and I can have the steaks ready pretty quick."

Walking over to the bottle, I pour a glass for each of us and turn to hand him one, watching as he tosses the meat on a cast-iron skillet with a ton of herbs and spices I don't recognize. Tension ebbs from my shoulders the longer I stand there. I nearly don't hear him say that everything is done, but after a few minutes, we sit down across from each other at the small kitchen table.

Why is it that a man that checks most of my boxes for what I want in a guy also happens to be a guy I can't have?

Good kisser. Good hugger. Good listener. And now this. Damn it.

His food is the best I've ever tasted, to the point where I practically lick my plate clean.

"Finished?" He raises his eyebrows and indicates the finger currently tracking through what's left.

"Mmm." Dragging my finger through the last bit of marinade, I pop it into my mouth and suck the flavor off. His nostrils flare, but otherwise, nothing else about his smile changes. "I guess so."

He chuckles. "Glad you enjoyed it."

I laugh. "Not at all. Hated every bite. I should probably ask to speak to your manager."

"Haha, funny girl." He stands and grabs his plate. I follow behind with mine, and he takes both plates and stacks them in a sink that already overflows with dirty dishes.

"Aren't you going to get those?" My fingers itch to clean the mess.

"Eh, later." He walks away, and I trail behind him, the urge to turn around and take care of the dishes pricking at me. He hands me my glass of wine and grabs his beer. Sitting on the couch, he pats the cushion next to me. "Come hang out for a bit."

I sit down and turn my attention to my wine as it swirls up the edges of the glass like a small whirlpool. "So, I think turnabout is fair play."

"What do you mean?" He takes a pull on his beer, his upper lip shining with a layer of hops and barley.

"I showed you mine, so show me yours." Even though several inches separate us, I still feel his body tense next to mine. "What turned you into the man-whore who discusses casual sex so...calmly?"

Judging from the way his face shutters, I'm not sure I want to hear this story, even though I'm the one who asked the question.

# CHAPTER 13

*NICK*

Flashes of cold and heat alternatively pulse through my body. "Jax didn't tell you?"

She shakes her head. "He just told me you were engaged once."

A year ago, I'd sat on the deck less than twenty feet from us and told him about Emily in hopes that my story would light a fire under his ass for Charlie. Fortunately, he'd listened. I'm not sure what good sharing my story with Meredith will do. But she's opened up to me, and there's a sense of obligation that I need to share with her too. That need to balance doesn't make it any easier though.

"There's not much to tell." Draining my beer, I put the empty next to me. I get up and grab another from the fridge. She hasn't moved from her spot on the couch and stares at the wine in her glass like it has all the answers. If only.

"If we're going to be friends, I have to feel like we're equals."

Her voice is quiet, too reminiscent of how it was while we talked next to her pool. Fuck.

I don't want to open this lid again, but I understand what she's saying. I'm not sure what kind of douche fucker her ex was. Since he cheated on her, I'll take that as a sign of complete lack of intelligence on his part. She's an amazing girl—woman—and I've been privy to more of her vulnerable side and been the cause of more of her hurt than I care to be over these last few weeks. Sighing, I sit back down on the couch, pulling on memories I'd rather leave alone.

"I was engaged once. My high school sweetheart." I shrug. "Not much else to tell."

"That's all I get?" she asks.

"It's not much of a story."

"Fine. Okay." She stands. "Nick, I opened up to you about my ex. If that's all you think you need to share, I guess we're done and I'm going to go home."

She turns and heads for the door, and I'm off the couch and wrapping my hand around her arm without fully thinking that thought through.

"No, don't go."

"You summed it up best. 'Not much else to tell.'" Her words are bitter, and I know I've screwed up.

"I'm sorry. You're right." I steer her back to the couch. "I just... it's hard to tell this story."

The anger in her expression softens at my honest admission. "I can understand that. But I'd appreciate it if you would share it with me."

Inhale. Exhale. Another before I nod. "Okay."

"Emily and I grew up together, kind of like you and Jax, but in the same town. If there was a fishing or camping trip, we were there. Equally involved in making mischief." Images surface of white-blonde hair tamed into pigtails and big blue eyes that sparkled in the sun. A smile tugs at my lips. "She was my best friend."

"Until she wasn't?" Meredith guesses, and I nod.

"I was fifteen when I first started seeing her as more than a friend. We'd mostly gone through the awkward phase, and I was crushing hard. Figured that I didn't stand any sort of chance since we knew each other so well. Then one day I was talking to Melissa Green in the hallway. I didn't even know Emily saw us, but she lit into me on the bus home. Called me an asshole and then wouldn't speak to me for the rest of the ride." She'd been shaking with fury, and once she said her piece, she'd turned to the window and ignored every attempt I made to figure out why she was so angry.

"When I got home, my older sister Cara was over from her farm. She asked me where Emily was, and I let the whole story spill out. After she got done smacking me in the back of the head —literally—she told me that Emily was jealous. That she must like me if she was that jealous over a conversation with another girl. I told Cara she was full of shit and headed to my room, but I kept thinking about what she said."

"The more I thought about it, the more I started to see that maybe my big sister wasn't so full of shit. After everyone was asleep, I snuck out. Headed for the farm next to ours since that belonged to Emily's family."

"It took forever to wake her up, but eventually, she opened the window, whisper yelling at me to go home. Instead, I convinced her to come outside with me." My heart had pounded in my chest while I waited for her to come downstairs. "When she finally did come outside, we walked to her barn and climbed into the hayloft to talk." I can smell the sweet scent of the hay mixed with the horses below us. "I started off by explaining that Melissa had only been asking about an assignment we'd gotten in English. I told her what Cara had said, and her whole body froze, blue eyes growing wide as her cheeks turned a pretty shade of pink. That's when I figured out that my big sister might be smarter than me."

Meredith huffs a laugh.

"So I took a chance and admitted that I liked her as more than a friend, but I figured she wasn't interested in me like that. Since it couldn't hurt to put it all out there, I kissed her as soon as the words left my mouth."

"She liked you back." Her voice is a whisper. I nod.

"From that night forward, she was more than my best friend. She was my soul mate." I clear my throat, sorting through memories of high school until I land on the one I want. "The night of our senior prom, I asked her to marry me." I chuckle when Meredith's mouth drops open in obvious shock. "I used to be quite the romantic."

She mumbles something I don't quite catch.

"What was that?" It sounded like she said I still was.

"Nothing." Her response is quick and confirms my suspicions.

I bite back the smile at her quick denial, but let her win the point and don't push her.

"So she said yes, right?" she asks.

I nod, and my pleasure in her mumbled phrase fades. "She did. Fuck, we were young. But she was smart. She only said yes after I promised I wouldn't let our engagement stop me from going to LA. See, I'd been playing guitar and singing since I was a kid. Classic rock songs from my dad and hers, different songs from growing up that I liked. Until I started writing my own songs." I wince, recalling how bad those early songs were. "By the time we were graduating high school, I thought I'd gotten pretty good. So did she."

"What happened?"

"It took for fucking ever to finally break through and get signed by a label—Reverb, actually. Or at least it felt like forever to an eighteen-year-old kid. I was recording my EP when I got a phone call from my mom. Emily had been driving home from a store in Grand Island, and a truck driver had fallen asleep at the wheel. His truck crossed the center line, and Emily was killed on impact." The words are shards of glass that scrape my throat raw.

"Nick." Meredith's gasp is followed by her slender arms as they wrap around me. "I'm so sorry."

The soft weight of her body next to mine is real. Not some phantom dream. I must have heard "I'm sorry" a million times by now when it came to Emily. Why is it that those same words from Meredith give me back a little piece of my soul?

My arms tighten around her, and I take several deep breaths of her fresh scent as it brings me out of the dark and back to my living room.

I'm not sure how long we sit like that until she pulls away. I immediately miss the warmth of her body pressed against me.

"Thank you." She clears her throat. "For telling me about Emily."

I nod and focus back on her, locking her in my gaze. The compassion she exudes is like the warmth of a crackling fire on a snow day at the farm. She reaches out, squeezing my thigh with her hand in comfort. The heat of her palm transfers through my jeans and sends an electric current straight to my dick.

But I'm not sure which attracts me more. The fact that she's a good person or her extremely tempting appearance.

The sounds she'd made as she ate dinner had me ready to scatter dishes to the floor so I could feast on her, but I can't.

*Friends.*

Nothing more.

"Nick?" The way she says my name tells me she must have said it several times.

"Sorry, what?" Shaking my head, I try to clear the more-than-friendly thoughts from my imagination.

"If you hand me those cups, I'll take them to the kitchen for you." She motions to the coffee cups next to me.

It's so unexpected after what I've told her. But she stands and reaches out for me to hand them to her. I stare after her dazedly as she walks away. The sound of the water as it turns on wakes me back up fully. Standing, I lean against the door jamb and take in the sight of her. Water cascades momentarily from the kitchen faucet as she rinses one dish at a time and loads the sink full of dishes into the open dishwasher.

"What are you doing?" I ask.

She jumps, and I'm suddenly reminded of our kiss at Jax and Charlie's. The image of her loading my spoon into the dishwasher lays over this one.

"God. Don't do that." She clutches a hand over her heart and takes a breath. "You scared the shit out of me."

Why is she in here? It was like after she heard about Emily, she couldn't sit next to me anymore. "Sorry. Are you okay?"

"Yeah, sure, why?" She sounds confused but distracted by the dishes she focuses on.

"Well, you're in here." I motion to the living room. "After I dropped a ton of shit on you in there. Did I say something to upset you?"

She glances up. "No, of course not."

"Is—is this about what I just told you?"

She spins, water droplets scattering. "What? No."

"Then why are you in here, doing this, now?" I ask.

She shrugs. "You seemed like you wanted to be alone with your thoughts. You cooked, so I figured I'd give you time and clean up too."

The heat of embarrassment crawls through my body. There are more dishes in that sink than from tonight. "It's fine. I said I'd get it later."

"I'm already doing them, so there." She sticks her tongue at me and turns back to the sink. I laugh but join her and take over, loading the rinsed dishes.

Steam from the hot water in the sink billows around her face, creating a pink flush to her cheeks while her attention centers on what she's doing. In no time at all, my entire sink is empty, the dishwasher hums, and she finishes wiping the counters.

"You're a closet neat freak, aren't you?" I tease.

Her grin is self-deprecating, but she nods. "I can't cook, but I make a great housekeeper. It keeps balance. Mom or Dad cook, I clean up. And now that it's done, I can get out of your hair." She moves around me and grabs her purse.

"What?" She bounces so fast from one thought to the next that it's hard for me to keep track sometimes.

"Thanks for dinner. It was delicious." She won't quite meet my gaze, and her voice pitches higher than normal.

"You're leaving?" I ask.

*Welcome to the conversation, dummy.*

She nods. "I'm sure you have other things to do with your night."

I step close to her and hold up a hand to stop the ramble of words. "Meredith. You don't have to go."

"I do."

"Why?" What answer will she give me this time?

This close, the fruity scent of her lotion invades my senses, and my soul feels lighter somehow with each breath I take.

"Because." It's one word and doesn't answer my question, while at the same time it does.

A small grin curves my lips and draws her gaze to my mouth. Her quick inhalation tells me all I need to know. I get it. The temptation is torture for her too.

"Because why?" I step even closer to her, and she backs up until she bumps into the door behind her.

"Just because," she repeats. I move more into her personal space and run my nose along her jawline. She shivers in response.

"Because if you stay, you'll want this?"

I don't give her the chance to respond and slowly slide my mouth over hers. Dragging my tongue along the seam of her lips, I act like I have all the time in the world to savor her. She tastes like the red wine from dinner, but underneath that first taste is all Meredith. Sunshine and apples. I sink my teeth into her lower lip, and her gasp lets my tongue move forward to taste her more fully. She moans, and her fingers grip my shoulders. To push me away or pull me closer?

My answer comes with the way her fingers shift to my hair, her nails scraping lightly as her grip tightens. My hands trail along her sides to rest gently at her hips. Every other kiss we've shared has been a flash of fire, but this one is different. It's languid, a slow burn, and hits me harder than any of the others. My zipper digs painfully into my erection, and I flex my fingers against her hips before I drag them back up. Skimming along the sides of her breasts, I move them to tangle in her hair and shift her head so my lips can trace her jaw and follow with quick nips down her neck.

"Don't go." My growl vibrates against her neck, and my teeth sink into the tendon until she cries out.

Fuck, she tastes incredible. One hand finds her hip and the other moves to the hem of her sweater, dipping underneath to trace the soft skin with my fingers. Palming her breast through her bra, I relish the way she arches into me, pressing herself more fully into my hand. The feel of her pebbled nipple in the middle of my palm makes me want to fuck her against this door right here, right now.

"Wait." Her whispered word freezes my body, and my lips hover over hers. Eyes the color of molasses blink open. "What are we doing?"

"If I have to tell you that, I'm doing something wrong," I joke.

"No." The shake of her head has dark curls tickling my arms. "What are we doing?"

Her words, along with oxygen now making it to the head attached to my shoulders, clears the fog of lust slightly, but the satin of her bra against my palm makes my dick pulse in my jeans.

"Kissing?" I suggest with a smile.

Her lips curve too, but she shakes her head, her hand motioning between us. "What is this to you?"

Groaning, I shift my hands until they're both back at her hips in an effort to redirect blood back to my brain. "You have to know I'm attracted to you." She nods. "But I don't have anything else to offer you other than some epically great sex." I don't miss the way she flinches at my words. "My heart died twelve years ago. This." I sink my fingers into her hips. "It's all I have left to give."

"I'm attracted to you too." Her quiet words have me leaning down, ready to draw her lips back into a kiss. Her arms press against my shoulders to stop me. "But I want more."

"More?"

"I want it all." Sadness pushes out every other emotion. "I want an epic love story to go along with epic sex."

I imagine I'm not going to like the answer to my question. "So, where does that leave us?"

"At an impasse?" She shrugs. "Friends?"

Fuck. I step back. Releasing her body is a herculean feat, but I do it. *Friends.*

With a sigh, she retrieves her purse from the floor where she dropped it. She reaches up on tiptoes to graze my cheek with a kiss.

"Good night, Nick." Before I can respond, she opens the door. "I'll text you when I get home."

And with that statement, she becomes my favorite person. The fact that she realizes I need that reassurance after everything I told her tonight makes me want to pull her back into my arms and kiss her senseless. But I can't do that to her.

Nodding, I clear my throat. "Night, Meredith."

## CHAPTER 14

*MEREDITH*

*I* wake up early the next morning—I think the only time I've ever been awake at 7 AM on a Sunday morning is when I've stayed up until that time. But, after another X-rated dream that stars Nick and his masterful lips, sleep isn't an option anymore.

"Damn it." Groaning, I toss the covers off and pad to my kitchen in search of coffee until I remember I added it to my grocery list last week, but forgot to grab some. Armed with yoga pants and a strong desire for caffeine, I trudge through my backyard and walk into the kitchen at Mom and Dad's. The smell of coffee teases my nose as soon as I open the back door.

"Meredith?" Mom's coffee cup freezes halfway to her mouth.

"Coffee." I shuffle to the pot and pour a cup, adding some sugar and taking my first life-giving sip.

"Honey, why are you awake so early?" Mom comes closer to feel my face with her hand. "Are you feeling all right?"

"Haha, so funny, Mom." I push her hands away. "I'm fine, just awake."

"Before noon?"

I try to ignore the teasing. I won't be sharing that sleep was impossible after the earth-shattering dream orgasm I received at the hands—or lips—of the guy I've convinced to just be friends. And she'll see through any lie I try to feed her.

"Val, is there—Meredith, you're awake?" Dad stops as he enters the kitchen, eyes trained on me like I'm a ghost.

"Ugh." I sit at the table and lay my head down on my arms. "Am I really that bad?"

Both of them kindly choose not to answer that question.

"So, honey, since you're up, do you want to go to the farmer's market with us?"

Trailing behind my parents while they argue about the best stall to buy apples from or which mangoes are the ripest? Hard pass.

"No, thanks. I think I'll just laze around. Maybe catch the game?"

"Now, that's an idea. Val, do I have to go?" Dad turns a puppy dog expression on Mom, who punches him in the arm. Their relationship fills me with warm fuzzies. I want that. Someone to persuade to go run errands, someone to joke around with.

"You go get dressed." Mom smiles while he pouts and rubs his arm. He does what she says, though, and leaves the room. "You."

She points at me next.

"Me? What did I do?"

She gives me an indulgent look. "Nothing. Enjoy your coffee. Do you need anything?"

I shake my head since they don't sell coffee at the farmer's market. Standing, I refill my cup to the top and blow a kiss to Mom as I head back to my house. Sinking into the couch, my mind shifts back to the steamy dream that had woken me up.

Why does Nick have to be five-alarm-fire hot? Why does he

have to be such a good kisser? It's like a full body contact sport with him. The only problem is he's not interested in anything more than a hookup. But, if my recent dream orgasm is anything to go by, it might be worth it.

Can I ignore my attraction to him and continue the search for my person? That's what I want, right? My phone buzzes next to me and saves me from questions I can't answer.

**NICK: Hey, sleepyhead. Wanna catch the game today?**
**MEREDITH: Which one?**
**NICK: You're awake????**
**MEREDITH: So funny. \*angry emoji\***
**MEREDITH: Why does everyone think they're comedians all of a sudden?**
**MEREDITH: But yes.**
**NICK: Kansas City's in Denver. Wanna come watch with me?**

*No.*

*Yes.*

The answers to my earlier questions hit me like a bolt of lightning.

I *can't* ignore my attraction to him.

It's no longer a conscience thing since he's invaded my dreams not once, but twice. Not that I mind. Holy shit.

Is having sex with him so bad? I'm not with anyone. Neither is he. We're friends. And our chemistry is off the charts. I'm not seeing a downside here.

Do I want a relationship? Yes, but the right one. *The* one.

Right now, that's not happening. So why not Nick?

Would he still be interested in getting each other out of our systems?

There's only one way to find out.

**NICK: Meredith?**

**MEREDITH: Sure. Sounds good. I'll head over at 1.**

\*\*\*

As I stand on the other side of Nick's front door, nerves swirl in my belly. Now that I've made up my mind, I'm done. No more yo-yo emotions.

He answers wearing gray joggers and an old Kansas City t-shirt. His nostrils flare as his gaze travels from my head to my feet. After I made up my mind, today's outfit was planned carefully—a pair of denim shorts and a massive football jersey I'd convinced my parents I needed for Christmas one year. It's about four sizes too big, but it's comfortable. The shoulder keeps slipping down—it always does—to expose the lacy strap of my bra underneath. I shrug it back up with a grin.

"That's not a dress."

I giggle at his statement. "I'm wearing shorts."

I pull up the jersey and show off my shorts while I duck under his arm to get into the condo. Kicking off my shoes, I head for the couch. "Hey, by the way."

"H—" His voice cracks and he clears his throat. "Hey."

"You all right?" I bite at the curve of my lips I can't hide completely while he stands there with his hand still on the door.

"Yeah." Shaking his head, he closes the front door and watches me shrewdly. "What are you up to?"

"Me?" I ask. He nods while his eyes narrow further. "Nothing."

The silence is loud between us. "Do you want a soda? Beer?" he finally asks.

"Soda." Although liquid courage sounds amazing right now, I don't want him to think any of my decisions today are driven by alcohol.

Coming back to the living room with a drink for each of us, he sits down in the opposite corner of the couch, wariness emanating from him like some strange pheromone that seems to have my number.

"So, you're a Kansas City fan?" I pull up my legs to sit cross-legged on the couch and sip my beverage.

"Born and raised. Why? You a Denver fan?" He smirks before he takes a drink too.

"Not usually."

"But you are today?" He asks and groans when I nod. "Ouch. Can't even be on my team for football cheering?"

"That's boring. It's more fun if we both have skin in the game." He shifts at the word "skin," and an almost inaudible groan rumbles out of him

"You sure you're okay?" I repeat my question from earlier.

"Peachy," he grumbles out on a breath.

I bite the inside of my cheek, determined not to show my hand too fast.

"How do you feel about making this game more interesting?" I ask.

"What do you mean? Like a bet?"

I nod. "Something like that."

"What did you have in mind?" Is it me or did his voice get deeper?

"Hmm." I tap a finger to my lips while I pretend to think about the stakes. I know how I want today to start. "How about $5 for every touchdown and $1 for any field goals?"

He whistles. "That's pretty steep."

Shrugging a shoulder, I let the jersey slide down. "If you have a different idea?"

His head shake is barely perceptible with the way his attention rivets to the exposed skin of my shoulder. "Nope. I'm up for it if you are."

My eyes flick to his lap with his innuendo, and I move them quickly back to his face. I hold out a hand, his larger hand wraps around mine, and an electric charge sizzles up my arm.

"Deal." My voice is husky and I clear my throat.

I'm so distracted by my plan that it's hard to pay attention to the first quarter. Both teams seem to be evenly matched, so while they've only played fifteen actual minutes and spent about forty-five minutes on commercials, the score is zero-zero despite several attempts by both teams.

Blowing out a breath, I sit back against the couch. "Not much of a game."

He shrugs. "When they were talking about the match-up during the pre-game, the announcers said it would be close."

"What do you say we change our bet then?" I ask with as much nonchalance as I can manage, even while my heart is pounding.

"Why? Worried you won't make any money since no one's scoring? What, want to bet on yardage or something?"

*Or something.*

"Not exactly." I lick my lips, forging ahead with what I had planned all along. "How about for any score by our teams, the other has to lose a piece of clothing?"

His gaze sparks indigo fire as it clashes with mine, and his nostrils flare. "So, if I understand you correctly, strip poker, but for football? Strip football?"

Swallowing, I keep my focus on him. "Y-yes."

He purses his lips like he's considering the idea. With another glance at his lap, I see the outline of his erection visible through the cotton, and my thighs clench as I wait for his answer. I'm about to call the whole thing off when he speaks.

"You're on." His eyes glitter in challenge, and I squirm under his attention.

"Any questions?" My voice is breathier than I intended.

He smirks. "Oh, only about a billion."

"Ask away," I volunteer.

"Nope, I'm good. For now."

The game comes back on and interrupts a response I hadn't

formulated yet. Denver has the ball, and I wipe my clammy palms on my jersey as we both become more interested in the game than we were a few minutes ago. The announcer's voice pitches higher, and the ball sails through the air on the screen until it drops into the hands of the Denver receiver as he crosses the end zone.

"If I didn't know any better, I'd think you'd planned that." He glares at me accusingly.

I shake my head, but don't bother to hide my glee. "How could I control that?"

"I'm not hearing any denials from you," he argues.

"A bet is a bet." I remind him. It's still early in our bet, but I'm still curious what he'll choose to remove first. Will he play it safe? Or be a risk-taker?

Grumbling, he leans forward and grabs the hem of his t-shirt to tug it up and off. Deep v-lines that disappear into his pants morph to ridges of abs and a toned chest sprinkled with a light dusting of hair. There's a tattoo on his left pec, and I lean forward to see more clearly. I can't read the words, but it's a dandelion blown into wishes that morph into birds. He tosses his t-shirt at my head and distracts me from my ogling.

"Take the spoils of war, you brat." He leans back against the couch, his gaze jumping between the game and me.

"You're a sore loser," I counter, stealthily breathing in the cologne that clings to the soft cotton in my hand.

"I'll remember you said that." His voice is thick, full of promise, and I shiver. "When my team scores."

Kansas City scores less than five minutes later, and he smirks at me. "Well, well, well."

I don't bother to argue. I stand and lift the jersey enough to catch the snap on my shorts and shimmy them down my legs. The jersey still covers everything. With a page from his book, I toss the shorts at him. It's my turn to smirk as his gaze drags up and down my legs in a heated caress.

"I hope you didn't decide to go commando today," I tease while I settle back down on the couch. When the game comes back on, I feign more interest than I feel.

"Maybe I did." He stands, invading my space. "And maybe I didn't."

"That's not an answer," I counter. My voice breaks as he braces a knee on the couch and leans forward.

I lean back, looking up as his lips come within inches of mine. This is it. He's going to kiss me, and we'll forget the bet and just enjoy each other. But instead of his lips connecting with mine, he keeps going until his lips brush against my neck. The kiss is quick, but the following of his nose as he drags it along my throat and my jaw is devastatingly slow.

"It's the only answer you're going to get for now," he responds.

His fingers flutter against my knee before they glide up, up, up, coming close to where I crave them most. I close my legs, trapping his hand next to my damp panties.

"You're not playing fair." My voice is husky as need floods me.

"You're the one who created the game, baby. I'm just playing it." His fingers brush against the satin of my panties, and my legs open in an invitation for more.

He slides his hand away, turning to walk into the other room. The muscles in his back flex as he walks away, and I gulp in several lungfuls of air, absentmindedly turning my attention back to the TV when Denver completes another big yardage play on the field.

"Prepare to pony up," I call out to him.

Walking back into the living room, he carries a glass of water and watches the replay. With a groan, he sits back down but much closer to the middle of the sectional than where he had been. My pulse spikes as my attention shifts to him, and I completely miss the play that has him shouting in triumph.

"What? What happened?" I turn back to the TV in time to see

the QB throw an interception into the waiting arms of a Kansas City player. The interception results in a touchdown.

"What were you saying?" His electric gaze is filled with a mix of challenge and triumph.

"Now I'm starting to think you planned this," I complain, but reach under my jersey and undo my bra. I pull it through the neck of the jersey, and his gaze tracks the scrap of pink lace as it arcs through the air to land at his feet. Bending over to snag it, he rubs the lace through his fingers while a muscle ticks in his jaw.

His fingers stroking the light pink fabric have my breath catching, and I feel wetness between my thighs.

"It was your idea, remember?" His voice is full of gravel, raspy, and makes my panties damp enough that I shift against the couch.

Neither team scores for the remainder of the second quarter, and halftime comes and goes with both of us making innuendos about each other and our teams. Right after kickoff in the second half, I learn that—unfortunately—he is not commando under his joggers once they join the pile on the floor. His erection strains against black boxer briefs, but he doesn't acknowledge it. Sitting back down, he crosses an ankle over his knee while my attention stays glued to the bulge in his lap.

"Meredith?" The amusement in his voice has a different kind of heat climbing through my body. I blink and bring his face back into focus.

"Hmm?"

"Game." He points back to the screen, and I reluctantly pull my eyes away from him.

Yet again, Kansas City responds with another score, and his eyebrows lift as he looks at me expectantly. Smirking, I stand again and bend enough so I can reach my panties under the jersey. With another shimmy, I move them down slowly until they tangle around my ankles. His Adam's apple visibly bobs, and his attention doesn't stray from the pink fabric at my feet.

"I figured." His voice is a rough rasp of its former self.

"Figured what?" Mine is equally husky. I'm so turned on that the panties at my feet are soaked, and my arousal is obvious in the air around me.

"You like to match." His comment surprises a laugh from me. Smiling, I sit back down, careful to keep the jersey in place.

"Well, you know what they say about a woman's bra and panties matching," I tease.

"I don't think I'm familiar with what they say."

"They only match if she wanted someone to see them." I shrug and bite my lip as his whole body tenses.

"Fuck this." Tossing the remote on the couch, he stands and advances toward me. Even as he lowers to the couch, he pulls me to him. His lips capture mine as his tongue plunges into my mouth.

Finally. I don't think I could last any longer, but I was determined to tease him to the brink of sanity.

One large hand grips the end of my ponytail and moves my head so my lips meet his onslaught. His other hand lands like a brand on my hip, kneading me through the thick material of my shirt. But I want to feel him skin on skin. Enough foreplay. I whimper and my hands move to dig my nails into his biceps. I need him on the brink of control, just like I am.

He nips at my bottom lip before he drags me back under for another oxygen stealing kiss. His hand moves to my bare thigh under the jersey, and I moan as the friction sends arcs of pleasure to my core and I spear my hands through his hair. I shift to move the heat and pressure of his hand where I ache for it the most.

He breaks the kiss, and his lips move to lazily trace my jaw, his tongue and teeth nipping down my neck while his hand climbs higher to skate along my side. The caress is light, a tease, made more so by the way he drags a finger back and forth on the underside of my breast. My nipples tingle with each pass of his finger and tighten painfully against the rough material of the jersey.

"Nick." My hips lift against his.

"Hmm?" His hum vibrates against my throat.

"Touch me." Grabbing his hand through my jersey, I move it, arching into him when his hand closes around my breast. My nipple pebbles in the center of his palm, but he still doesn't move. I scrape my fingers down his chest and abs to rub him through the cotton of his boxers. Immediately, his hand clenches and his fingers shift to pluck at the tip. A ragged cry leaves my lips as he pinches and twists and connects our mouths to duel his tongue with mine. There's a direct line of pleasure from my nipple to my core, and arousal coats my thighs.

"Is this what you wanted, baby?" His fingers continue to work my breast while his other hand slides under the jersey to grip my hip. "My fingers at your nipples? Or did you want them some-where else?" His other hand moves until he's millimeters from my pussy, and I squirm to get closer. "Here, maybe?"

Opening my hips, I urge him forward. His fingers stay where they are, and I groan in frustration. "Nick. Please."

"Begging me so sweetly." His fingers move a fraction, but still don't connect, and my body lifts until his grip tightens around my thigh, holding me still. My breathing shallows with how strongly pleasure pushes against the wall he's constructed. "Ah-ah-ah. Not yet, baby."

His hand leaves my breast and I immediately ache for the pressure. Nerves shoot pulses of fire with the slide of his hand as it moves down to my other hip. Flexing slightly, he lifts me to straddle his lap, and his erection adds a delicious friction I *need*. Once I'm in place, he grabs the hem of the jersey to whip it off, and his mouth latches onto my breast as soon as it's free of the fabric.

"God." My hips move against him while my head tips back to push me further into his mouth.

Fingers move to my other breast and tug at the hardened tip, the electric pleasure/pain drawing a gasp as he switches sides. I need more. My core throbs, and I move my hand down my stomach, ready to add what I need to bring on the orgasm that strains to be set free. I brush against him, and my fingers barely circle my clit before his other hand cuffs my wrist to pull my hand away.

"Nooo," I whimper

"That's cheating, baby." His gaze clashes with mine. "You want me to touch you?"

"Please," I beg, and rub against him. His breath hisses out with the friction, but he keeps his eyes on me.

"This is all I have to offer you." His voice is serious, a reminder that nothing has changed for him since last night.

But it doesn't have to. I'm okay with this. It doesn't have to be anything more than crazy good chemistry.

I nod. "I know."

"What changed your mind?" His question causes a blush to fill my cheeks, and he arches an eyebrow while he waits. "What?"

"A dream," I finally admit.

"What kind of dream? Was I in it?" I nod, and his responding smirk is hot enough to melt candle wax. "What was I doing?"

"Making me come." My bluntness surprises him, and his eyes widen to reflect a ring of silver around the blue of his iris.

"With my hands?" One hand skates down my leg, dragging back up until his fingertips brush against the apex of my thighs. I squirm and am rewarded with a light pressure against my folds, but it's not enough. Not by a longshot. "What about with my tongue?" He runs his tongue around the shell of my ear, and my breathing shallows. "Or with my cock?"

"Fuck." I moan and yank at my hands trapped in one of his. "All of it. Everything."

"That's a tall order. I think I can handle it." His words make my thighs clench on either side of his. "What about our complications?"

I'm not willing to compromise on that. "Original rules stand. This is our little secret."

With a nod, he stands, and my legs automatically wrap around his waist, even while his hands grip my ass to hold me to him. The friction from our walk through the hall to the doorway has me ready to scream as my core aches with the delayed orgasm. His cologne is stronger in his room, enough that with a deep breath, my body trembles with pent-up desire. It's been driving me crazy for months. Now it surrounds me while I'm naked against him. He releases my legs to let me slide down his body. I rub against his dick with my descent and hiss at the throb the feel of him creates.

"You're overdressed." Running a finger around the elastic in his boxers, it's my turn to smirk.

"How rude of me." Within seconds, his boxer briefs are off, and he licks into my mouth while he lowers me to the bed that's unmade.

"You're kind of a slob, aren't you?" He acts like such a badass, like he has all his shit together. Now I know differently, and that knowledge makes me happy. Like I now get to see the real him.

"Are you going to judge my cleaning habits or participate in the orgasms I'm about to give you?" He doesn't give me a chance to answer. His tongue drives back through my lips, and his fingers once more find my breast to tug against the sensitive tip until I'm writhing beneath him, begging incoherently to let me come. Orgasms? As in plural? My questions scatter as his hand finally trails lower to trace the crease of my thigh in a silent request for entry.

My legs part and his fingers move to find my clit with an accuracy that tells me exactly how much he was teasing me before. I'm not sure whether to be mad or turned on, but desire wins as his fingers circle my clit before they pinch lightly. My toes curl as the orgasm continues to build at the expert way he handles my body. He slides two fingers inside and pumps while his thumb presses on the bundle of nerves. Flicking my clit, his movements create stars that spark in technicolor flashes. I moan into his mouth, and my hands grip his shoulders. The orgasm tingles in my toes and builds as his fingers continue to pump while his thumb alternates between circling and tapping against my clit.

"Fuck." Air saws in and out of my lungs while the pleasure builds to an overwhelming ache centered where his hand is currently tangled. His lips drop to my jaw and trail to my collarbone until they move farther down to find my breast.

His finger crooks inside me as his lips open to draw me in, his teeth nipping at the peak. My orgasm crashes over me all at once and locks my muscles even as my fingers grip his wrist, to push him away or keep him there, I don't know.

"One down." He doesn't let me fully recover before his lips drop lower to trace down my stomach. His fingers keep their motion as his lips and tongue join in.

With the first pass of his tongue, I moan as an orgasm aftershock pulses through me.

"Oh god."

"The name is Nick, baby." I sense his smirk even if my eyes are closed too tight to see it. Another drag of his tongue brings him to my clit. He circles and sucks while his fingers keep their rhythm. They don't stop. I grip the ends of his hair as the next orgasm barrels toward me.

"Nick, I can't. God, it's too much. Nick." He doesn't relent and sucks my clit into his mouth. I explode around him in a vortex of white light full of pleasure, my legs tightening where they rest on either of his shoulders. When did that happen? I start to come down and he pulls his fingers out, drawing them into his mouth as he sucks them clean.

His dick is hard and glistens at the tip as it reaches for me, jutting straight out from his body. "Mmm."

Why does the fact that he makes that sound as he licks the taste of me off his fingers make me think I haven't orgasmed yet when I've had two mind-blowing ones already?

Standing, he grabs a condom from the nightstand and turns back.

"You ready for me, Meredith?" The way he growls my name clenches my thighs again. I nod. "On your knees, baby."

I scramble into position, feeling awkward with my ass in the air as my head rests on my forearm. I can hear him move, but can't see him from my vantage point. Warm lips surprise me and drop to my ass. The nip of his teeth makes me jump, and his dark chuckle fills the room.

"I couldn't resist." The sound of the foil rips loudly in the quiet bedroom. I tense as his weight shifts on the bed. A warm hand glides down my spine. "Shh."

Hot, open-mouthed kisses follow his hand, trailing my spine to the dimple near my ass, and stoke the fire that had been waning as thoughts started to crowd in on the feelings he was invoking. He shifts forward, his hands moving to pinch and pluck at my sensitive nipples, and the fire reaches nearly intolerable levels again. I whimper and shift backward, ready for more. His hands move, gripping my hips as he lines up. With one full thrust, he pushes inside, and I gasp for air.

"Fuck me, baby. You feel amazing." He groans as he bottoms out and pauses. It's been two years since Daniel and, even then, he had a less than average sized dick. "You okay?"

I nod and release the breath I've been holding, relaxing around him. He pulls back until only the tip remains, and I whimper until he thrusts back inside. When he bottoms out again, his hands reach back around to cup my breasts as his hips begin to move. "Let me hear you, baby."

He tugs at my nipple with one hand while his other holds my hips steady as he pistons into me. "Ahh."

"My name." A slap on my ass accompanies the demand, the heat traveling to pulse through my core and spiking the pleasure that races through my body...

"Nick."

"That's right, baby. It's me."

Another slap, and I moan into the mattress.

I have never experienced this before. This pleasure and at the hands—literally—of someone who knows what I need before I do. Should I be embarrassed that I like the warm tingle of his hand as it connects to my ass? I don't have the chance to answer that question before he grabs my hair and tugs lightly until I'm kneeling in front of him. One muscular forearm bands my waist and keeps me upright. My groan morphs to a whimper as his other hand reaches down to slide through my folds and finds my clit to drag a finger around it. "Louder."

"*Nick.*"

He bites my shoulder as his arm releases me. I fall forward, and he moves faster. Another orgasm is building in my toes. Another slap, harder this time, and it shoots up my spine and begins to center in my core. "Oh god. I'm coming."

"Not yet." His fingers shift away from my clit, and the orgasm backs off.

At my whimper, his attention focuses back on my breast, and he begins to rebuild the fire. His pace increases again and, even without his fingers at my clit, my orgasm is ready to explode.

"Nick. I'm close. I'm so close." Everything in my body coils, centered on the pleasure that radiates from my core.

"Not yet." His words are bitten off while tension tightens his body. When his thumb moves back to my clit, I can't stop.

Screaming, I collapse forward under the force of the orgasm that buries me under tsunamis of pleasure. His body tenses behind me as, with his own growl, he pulses inside me.

# CHAPTER 15

*NICK*

Stretching across the bed, I reach for Meredith. Cool sheets instead of a warm body wake me up, and I crack an eye open. Rumpled sheets and the indentation where her head rested on the pillow greet me, but there's no sign of her.

"Meredith?" I sit up and call out her name. Maybe she's in the kitchen or the bathroom?

Hairs stand up on the back of my neck. That, along with the temperature of the sheets, tells me I'm wrong. But I still get up and look through my condo to confirm there's no sign of her. What the fuck? After recovering from the first round of epic sex, we'd ordered a pizza—pepperoni and cheese for her, meat lovers with pineapple for me. Her claim that my pizza choice sounded disgusting ended with her stretched out on my kitchen counter while I feasted on her until our food showed up.

We'd finished the game we'd missed part of earlier and then settled on an episode of *Lucifer*. I'd never seen it, and she had insisted. She told me we could binge-watch it once football was over. After gorging ourselves on pizza, she had persuaded me to clean up, which had led to round two—or was it three—for us in the shower. Something about her has me craving her more after my first hit instead of killing the attraction like I'd thought. Finished with nearly drowning in the shower, we'd crashed into my bed.

*"I don't cuddle." She freezes me with a look.*

*"Neither do I." I smirk. Flipping off the light, my fingers itch until I reach out and rest my hand on her hip. "This doesn't count."*

*"Whatever, snuggle slut."*

I'd gone to sleep with a smile on my face and—holy shit. Another realization hits. No nightmares of Emily last night. They'd been coming every night since the first one a few weeks ago, but last night I'd slept straight through.

That fact doesn't answer where Meredith is or what time she'd left though. The coffee pot is on and a note is scrawled on a tablet in front of it.

*Nick, yesterday was fun. Thanks for the Os. See you when I see you. - Meredith*

What in the actual fuck? I reread the note again, but it's the same frustratingly flippant one it was the first time I read it. *Thanks for the Os?* Is she fucking serious? Ripping off the page, I crumple it up and toss it toward the trash can.

It bounces back out, and I don't bother to pick it up—it can fucking stay there forever for all I care. Grabbing a cup of coffee, I head to the bathroom to shower and get ready for work, my good morning disappearing with the water down the drain.

My phone chimes as I head out the door.

**CARA: Any answer yet for the party?**
**NICK: Sorry. Haven't had time to check my schedule.**
**CARA: Liar.**
**CARA: Mom and Dad want to see you.**
**CARA: In and out? Same day? Any time really.**

CARA: Please come.
NICK: I'll think about it.
CARA: NICK!
NICK: I promise. I'll let you know by next Monday at the latest.
CARA: If you don't, I'm going to come out there and throat punch you.

I have no doubt she'll make good on her promise.

NICK: Next Monday.
CARA: Read this out loud.
CARA: Siri, set a reminder to text my beautiful sister next Monday about Mom and Dad's 40th anniversary party.
NICK: *eye roll emoji*
NICK: I don't use an iPhone.
CARA: Whatever. Too bad I know that's false since I'm getting iMessages from you.
CARA: Did you do it yet?
NICK: Fine, yes, I did it. Happy?
CARA: Ecstatic. Bye, Baby Brother.
NICK: Bye, Care-Bear.
CARA: *cursing emoji*
NICK: *laughing emoji*

My phone chimes several more times on my way to work, and I check it once I've parked in the garage at Reverb, hoping at least one of those chimes is Meredith apologizing for leaving without saying goodbye.

I don't know why what she did pisses me off.

But I'm fucking furious.

*Dude, get over yourself. You got laid. Don't be a pussy.*

I frown at the voice in my head that seems to be coming from my dick. Yes, we'd said only one night, but I'm still her friend.

Didn't that warrant her saying goodbye before she left? Was it better that she hadn't? My questions go unanswered since none of the notifications included a text from her.

**JAX: We gotta talk.**
**JAX: Randa can kiss my ass.**

Oh shit. What the fuck has already happened this morning? Why is everything going to shit? I ignore the texts and call him instead.

"Hello?"

"What the fuck happened?" I ask.

"Why is someone other than you calling from Reverb about tour dates that *go out eighteen goddamned months?*"

"Fuck." Randa usually doesn't go behind my back with my clients.

"Exactly," he clips out.

"She talked to me about that late last week." Pinching the bridge of my nose, I close my eyes and lean my head back against my car seat.

"I'm not touring that long, dude. I'm not uprooting my family that long, and I'm not being away from them that long, either. Ken would be almost two."

"I get it."

"Were you serious about the label you want to start up?" We'd talked about it when we were at his house, but nothing more concrete than I might file papers.

"One hundred percent. I've already found an attorney and he's helping me file papers." For the first time in a long time, I feel excited with the turn my career is taking.

"I'm in."

"I should have confirmation from the attorney later this week."

"What can I do to help?" He asks.

"Nothing. Wait. On second thought, don't commit to anything if anyone else from Reverb calls you. Play dumb if you have to. Just stall them." I take a deep breath. "And whatever you do, don't fucking sign anything."

"Will do. Want to come over sometime this week and we can talk details?"

"That'll work. Let me know what time." I nearly hang up, but Jax calls my name. "Yeah?"

"Thanks for having my back, man."

"You're my friend. Of course I have your back."

He chuckles. "We've come a long way since you were the biggest pain in my ass ever."

"Likewise, bro. All right, let me get inside and see what the fuck I can find out." I hang up and re-engage my mask. The one Jax and Meredith haven't seen in a while, but the only one I can safely show at Reverb.

✳✳✳

"Fuck." Spotting Meredith's red Audi in Jax and Charlie's driveway Thursday evening has heat crawling up my spine. But I'm not sure if it's heat from the memories of our night together or anger that I haven't heard from her at all. Not once. All. Fucking. Week.

She fucking ghosted me after Sunday, and I refuse to text her since she's the one who left without saying anything. I expected her to text at some point on Monday, but as Wednesday ticked over into Thursday, what she was doing was obvious. I don't play bullshit games, and I refuse to call her out on her shit since it's on her to reach out. She left me.

So why the hell do I feel guilty, like I've done something wrong, as I wait for Jax to answer the door? It's bigger than the guilt I already felt for fucking the woman Jax and Charlie consider a sister.

167

Shit.

Jax opens the door with a smile on his face. "Hey, man, come on in."

"You sure now's a good time?" I motion to Meredith's car and hesitate. I don't want to interrupt if something else is going on.

"Who? Meredith?" The look he gives me is funny. Like he can't figure out my hang-up. "She's talking to Charlie about a job opportunity."

We walk through the house, and I hear Meredith's laughter. My cock perks up for the first time in a week. Fuck. Reaching down, I covertly adjust myself, thankful Jax is leading the way.

"Nick." Charlie's greeting is just as warm as the one I got from Jax, but Meredith stiffens. "Jackson said you were going to stop by."

I return Charlie's hug and nod at Meredith, whose attention is captured by anything *but* me. "Mer."

"Nick."

"Don't tell me you guys are fighting again." Jax's attention pivots between the two of us.

"No." We answer at the same time.

Charlie pauses as she sits and sends Meredith a questioning look.

"Okay?" He shakes his head. "Whatever. Let's talk label, Nick."

"Do we want to go somewhere else?"

"Why?" Jax asks. "Whatever you have to tell me involves Charlotte too."

That's salt in a wound from before, and I quickly correct the misunderstanding. "No, nothing like that. It just looked like you were in the middle of something when I got here."

"We're done." Charlie smiles. "And I want to hear what you've come up with."

I sit down in one of their patio chairs while Jax picks Charlie up and settles her back in his lap. They're adorable. My heart stings as memories of how I was with Emily lash at me. Seeing Meredith shifts the sting to guilt, and I clear my throat.

"All the paperwork is filed, and I can now tell you all that Arrhythmic Records is a licensed business registered in the state of California."

"Arrhythmic Records?" Charlie's nose wrinkles as she pronounces the name. "Doesn't arrhythmic mean lack of rhythm?"

"You trying to tell us you have a heart condition, old man?" My temper flares at Meredith's snarky question. If we were alone, I'd show her heart condition.

*No. One night, remember?*

Clenching my fists, I take several deep breaths and count backward from ten.

"No, smart-ass. It's like when you see the love of your life and your heart stutters. Just like the love of the right music makes your heart skip a beat." My gaze burns into hers until our staring contest forces her to look away. "I nearly named it after someone close to me, but... it... it didn't work out."

Those beautiful eyes, full of understanding and empathy, lock on me. Her scrutiny makes me uncomfortable. I don't tell them that the name I first came up with—EmJay after Emily Jane—created a pain so acute in my chest I thought I was having a heart attack. "I played with a few names until it hit me. Music has always been a driving force for me—for you too, Jax. Any future artist we sign to the label should have that same philosophy. Good music needs to touch people. The right song can inspire laughter or tears. Make you soar with love or agonize when it gets ripped away. That's how I landed on Arrhythmic."

Jax nods. He understands what I'm talking about. Something tells me that all three of the people here with me understand the power of music I described.

"Nick, that's...that's beautiful." Charlie swipes at a tear that runs down her cheek, and Jax presses a kiss against her temple.

We talk for a little longer about the rest of the details I've locked down and my plan for giving my notice at Reverb first thing Monday. We're working through details of how Jax will notify Reverb of his intent to change labels and how to leave with the rights to his current catalog when a cry breaks through the monitor.

Charlie stands. "Duty calls."

She comes back out of the house a few minutes later, a crying McKenna squirms in her arms. Jax jumps up to grab the baby and bounces her gently.

"What's wrong, Kenny? Daddy's princess not feeling good?"

"I think she's teething," Charlie says, and I notice that she and Jax both have shadows under their eyes, though hers are darker.

"I should get out of your hair. You guys should be relaxing instead of trying to entertain us," I say.

Meredith stands and says her goodbyes with a hug for the three of them before she turns to me with an awkward wave. "Bye."

*Excuse me?*

I don't even get to open my mouth to say anything in the short time it takes her to walk away. Fuck that noise. I say goodbye too and trail after Meredith as quickly—and as inconspicuously—as I can. I'm quick, but she's still nearly to her car by the time I catch up to her.

"Meredith." Her shoulders tense, and the keys jangle in her fingers as she turns around.

"Yeah?"

Without the buffer of Jax and Charlie, I feel less certain. Like that makes sense. "You left."

"Well, yeah, Mac wasn't feeling well and—"

"Not tonight. Last weekend. You left and you didn't say goodbye. Why?" I hadn't planned on getting into all this here, but it's as good a place as any.

"What do you mean why?" A spark of temper flashes, but

instead of unleashing it, she swallows whatever retort she nearly made. "Nick, we agreed to one night. That's it. We hooked up. It's done."

"I'm not an idiot." My voice is louder than I want, and I lower it. "I know we said one night. But it doesn't excuse you leaving the way you did. Or your fucking note."

"What was wrong with it?" The fact that she pretends to not know what I'm talking about has my own temper on the rise.

"Thanks for the Os?" Why do I have to explain this?

She shrugs, and my jaw clicks together. "It is what it is."

"I thought we were friends?"

"We are." Her confusion furrows her brow.

"Friends don't ghost each other, Meredith." I shouldn't have to tell her this.

"Not like you were blowing up my phone." The hurt is under her breath, under the snark. She smirks and sticks out a hand. "Hello, Pot. I'm Kettle."

Stepping closer, I invade her personal space until she either needs to drop her hand or risk grazing my chest. The fire goes out of her, and her hand falls. Disappointment flashes, and I move until the heat of her body presses against mine. My dick twitches in my shorts.

"Why?" I ask. I need to know the reason she left without a goodbye. It's been driving me insane all week, and I'm not letting her go without an answer.

From this close, the flash of hurt, of anxiety, is clear before she can mask it behind the tough girl facade she's so fond of.

"You said you only wanted one night." If I hadn't seen the other emotions flit across her face, the quiver in her voice would be a dead giveaway to everything I need to know.

Inching closer, my lips graze hers as I shake my head.

"What if I said I wanted more?" I ask quietly.

She blows against my lips on a breathy exhale.

"More? What do you mean more?"

The interest is there in her espresso-colored gaze. Coupled with hope and wariness, their spark draws me further under her spell. "One night wasn't enough."

"That's it?" The spark dims, and while she tries to mask that hurt, the happiness on her face is now shaky around the edges.

"I should have called or texted you after last weekend," I admit.

Her shrug pisses me off. Does she think so little of herself that she doesn't deserve someone to check in on her? Especially the guy she slept with? Fuck.

"Meredith, you deserve someone who is going to look out for you. Who's going to check on you to make sure you're okay. From here on out, I commit that I will be that type of friend. What if." I lick my lips, and her gaze traces the path my tongue takes. "What if we agree to hook up for the time being? Still friends, but more?" She hesitates, and I continue. "Then, if you find Mr. Right, I'll back off. We'll just be friends again."

She tilts her head as she thinks about my offer. "Friends with benefits?" Grimacing—I hate that label—I nod. "Until I find someone I'm interested in dating?"

I tamp down the jealousy that flares at her question. At the thought of another guy worshipping her body. I nod again.

"Shake on it?" When her hand pops up in front of my face, I flinch.

"I think we can do better than that." Crowding her further against her car, I slant my lips against hers and take the invitation as her mouth opens under mine. I slide my tongue in to taste her for the first time in nearly a week. Fuck, she tastes amazing. My hands tangle in her curls, and I tug slightly, my dick hardening to diamonds with her whimper. With a flex of my hips, my erection presses against her stomach, remembering the way she felt pulsing around me as she came. The smooth skin is a temptation, and I nip at her jaw and trail a layer of kisses to the pulse point at her throat. I don't even try to resist a bit of those vibrations under my lips. When she gasps, the smile on my lips breaks my contact with her. Her lips are swollen from my kisses when her eyes flutter open. Her body presses against mine. Close, but not enough.

Mine. At least for right now.

# CHAPTER 16

*MEREDITH*

**NICK: How long until Lucifer and the detective finally get together?**

*W*hat the hell? Does he not know Binge-Watching with Others 101? Ignoring his text, I click on his number instead.

"Rhodes."

*"You can't watch those without me."* I hadn't seen them yet, either, even though I could use my own Netflix account and binge them all. Where was his self-control?

"What?"

*"Lucifer.* You can't watch without me. Don't you know the rules?"

"Rules? What rules?"

"The binge-watching rule. If we're bingeing together, no bingeing ahead."

"Christ." He barks out a laugh. "Any other rules I should be aware of."

"How many episodes did you watch?"

"I don't know. One or two?"

"Second rule of binge-watching, no spoilers." His laughter makes happiness bubble up inside me, but I don't want him watching any more without me. Tom Ellis is HAWT-hot. "Nick."

"What? Sorry. I didn't know there were rules. You could come over, and we can re-watch the ones I've seen."

Heat licks through my body. "That, old man, is called Netflix and chilling. And something tells me we wouldn't get one episode watched if I come over there right now."

His voice drops an octave. "Oh really?"

"I'm on to your game."

"Come over." The sound of his voice alone right now makes me squirm.

"Sounds like you only want a booty call." Something has me hesitating, but I don't know what or why. The sex with Nick last week was amazing, so what's stopping me? His voice drops further and prevents me from adding to my argument.

"I'll show you a booty call."

✳✳✳

Days later, I'm still thinking about how good Nick is at phone sex. Is there anything he's not good at?

"Girl, why do you look like the cat that got the cream?" Derek's scrutinizing look takes me in from head to foot, and I hide my blush in our hug.

"What? What are you talking about?" He sits back in his seat, and I follow suit on the other side of the table, grabbing the menu to look at it. The movie finally wrapped last week, and he texted for a lunch date—gasp—on a Thursday.

His finger lowers my menu, a perfectly contoured eyebrow raised as he studies me intently. How does he get his eyebrows that perfect? Also, how does he always seem to have the ability to see into my soul? Jeez. I try to lift the menu back up as a shield. When it slaps down to the table instead, I sigh.

"You are glowing."

I fidget at that, glad that I don't blush as easily as Charlie. "D, I don't know what you're talking about." *Deny, deny, deny.* Yanking at the menu, I pull it back up. "Lemme look at the food, I'm starving."

Mmm. Cheeseburger and fries. Yum. I keep the menu up even though I know what I want to order, but its protection is short-lived.

"You had sex." His voice booms through the dining room, the din of conversation stopping at his announcement.

"Shh." I smack him with my menu and hunch down in my seat. "Go ahead and say it louder for the cooks who didn't hear you."

"Oops. Sorry." He has the grace to appear chagrined. "So who's the boy toy who popped your one-man cherry?"

"Oh my god, you're awful." Covering my face with my hands, I groan. "I'm not having sex."

Or at least we hadn't had sex again since the first night I was with Nick. Yeah, sure, he'd dry humped me to near orgasm outside of Jax and Charlie's, but we'd finally come up for air and, since the invitation to his place wasn't forthcoming, I headed back to my house. I texted him when I got home, per his request, and once that was done, BOB was my best friend for the rest of the night.

Is it sex if it's with your vibrator? Asking for a friend.

Since Jax and Charlie's, I hadn't seen him. Other than our "booty" call, we'd only talked once for a few minutes after he submitted his resignation. Turned out Reverb didn't need any notice, and he was asked to leave right away. But otherwise, he had his life, and I had mine. Not much had changed with this new arrangement, besides the fantasies I no longer had to feel guilty about.

"Bullshit. I know sex glow when I see it. And, honey, you have sex glow all over you so strong I can smell it."

The server's nose crinkles as she approaches our table to take our order. "D. Shut up."

He bounces in his chair while he orders and gives me a few moments to confirm that yes, I want the cheeseburger and fries. He unloads on me again as soon as the server walks away.

"Sooo. Anything you want to tell me?"

I laugh. "No."

"Mer!" he whines. "Since no one is currently giving me sex glow, I need deets."

Rolling my eyes, I grab my drink from the server as she returns and take a sip of the ice water.

"Meredith Rose Pryce. Details, now."

"The triple name doesn't work since you're not my mom," I tell him.

"Mer." He gets up and rushes my side of the table with a hug that nearly suffocates me.

With a smirk, I give in. Only a little. "I don't kiss and tell."

He laughs. "Bitch."

When he pokes my side, I squirm away with a glare. "No."

"Please? Pretty please? Pretty please with sugar on top?" He bats his eyelashes at me, and I throw my straw wrapper at him. Taking another sip of my drink, I hope it can cool me off as memories with Nick flood me as it is to give myself time to respond.

"Fine." I finally relent on a breath. "What do you want to know?"

"Well, obviously, the man can satisfy based on the glow you're sporting."

I duck my head and nod. "That's an affirmative. I've, um...I've never had multiples before."

His eyes widen comically. "The fuck you say?"

I groan. "Or oral until recently."

He reaches out and pats my hand. "You poor deprived soul. Sounds like karma brought you a present. Your ex was a lazy fucker."

Rolling my lips into my mouth, I don't respond. Derek knows nothing about Daniel other than I dated a guy I lost my virginity to. But I don't want to think about Daniel right now. Instead, I center my thoughts on Nick, on the memories of his mouth and —lunch arriving breaks me out of those thoughts, and I grab a fry.

"Who?" Derek asks.

"What?"

"Who is this magical bringer of the Os? The master of your sex glow? Woman, I need a name to write him a thank you card on your behalf."

I grab my burger with as much nonchalance as I can fake. "Nope."

"What do you mean nope?" He takes a bite of his sandwich and watches me while he chews.

"You don't need to know his name," I tell him. If I tell him it's Nick, he'll go from encouraging me to shutting it down faster than I can blink. He's definitely not a Nick fan.

"Do you know his name?"

The question causes the fry I'd popped in my mouth to slide painfully down my throat, and I cough as I glare at him.

"What the fuck, Derek?"

"What what? What's with that look?" he asks innocently.

"Do you think I'd sleep with a guy and not know his name?"

Maybe Derek had known about the gossip from the last tour and hadn't told me.

"Baby girl, that was a joke. Obviously a poor one if it has you more pissed than a mosquito in a mannequin factory."

His absurd comparison defuses the anger and has me laughing instead. Damn him and his southern sayings.

"Fuck. I just thought of something." He puts his sandwich back down. "Is he a spy? CIA?"

"Oh god, Derek, you've been watching too many soap operas."

He shrugs. "I already told you, baby girl. With no action here." He motions to himself. "I gotta find entertainment elsewhere."

"Well, now that the movie's done, maybe you'll have more free time to meet someone."

"You volunteering to be my wing woman—Ohhh—does that mean I get to meet Mr. Sex Glow Giver?"

"Nice, Derek. But no. No chance." *Not when you have already.* "And if you need a wing woman, I'm your girl."

What Nick and I have isn't exclusive. He's already agreed to the arrangement we have becoming null and void when I meet someone. So why do the words stick to my tongue like I don't want to say them? Why does the thought of going to the club as Derek's wing woman make me feel guilty?

"Fine." Derek pouts for a minute until his face brightens. "This means I get more details since you're keeping him anonymous."

What did I get myself into?

After finally satisfying Derek's curiosity at lunch—to the point that he now knows I liked getting slapped on the ass—I head back home. Since both Mom and Dad are at work, I have the pool to myself. Perfect. I need to think about everything that has happened in peace.

Talking about having sex with Nick brings it all back to the surface after I successfully kept it shoved down since it happened. It might be my inexperience talking, but I had *never* experienced sex like that. I hadn't expected much from Daniel since we'd both been virgins, but Nick took everything I thought about sex and amplified it to rock star status. I thought orgasms only existed by the work of my vibrator or my fingers. Yes, I'd heard about oral—I'd even given Daniel several blow jobs—but he'd never reciprocated.

I'd second guessed my decision to sleep with Nick after I didn't hear from him. The longer it went on, the more my doubts solidified to anger. Was his friendliness toward me only so he could get in my pants?

Seeing him at Jax and Charlie's, the urge to scream at him warred with the desire to kiss him. Back to square one. I'd been relieved that McKenna had been fussy, and I'd used that as my opportunity to get out while the getting was good. I hadn't planned on Nick following me or practically fucking him against my car in plain sight. Had Jax and Charlie glanced out their window, they would have seen us. Since I haven't heard from either of them all week, I think we were undiscovered.

My phone buzzes with a text from Nick, and my body throbs just seeing his name on my screen.

**NICK: Wanna hang out tomorrow?**
**MEREDITH: Don't you mean Netflix and Chill, old man?**
***wink emoji***
**NICK: You want to watch more Lucifer?**

Before I can respond, my phone rings with an unknown number.

"Hello?"

"May I speak with Meredith Pryce please?"

I don't recognize the voice, and hesitancy makes my voice tremble. "This is she."

"Meredith, we haven't met, but we have a mutual friend— Charlie Bryant? This is Garrett Harrison."

Immediately, my body relaxes. "Hi there."

"I got a text from Charlie earlier this week telling me she had the perfect candidate for the Assistant Choreographer job we have an opening for." *Thank you, Charlie.* "Apparently, that's you?"

I take a deep breath and launch into my list of training and move on to the tours I'd both danced and choreographed for.

"I caught Jax's show when you guys were in LA. You did the choreography for that?"

"Most of it. Some of it was recommendations from the other dancers." Maybe I shouldn't have told him that, but it's the truth.

"Hmm. Would you be interested in coming in one day next week? I'm sure Meric would want to meet you as well. You can run through everything with him too."

"Oh my god—I mean, yes, absolutely."

"Great, let me check Meric's schedule, and I'll get back to you. Have a good day, Meredith."

"Thanks, you too."

I wait until I'm off the phone to squeal. My phone pings to remind me that it buzzed several times while I was talking to Garrett.

**NICK: Kidding.**
**NICK: When I make you come, there's nothing 'chill' about it.**
**NICK: Meredith?**

Now that my panties are thoroughly soaked, I get up and head for my house as I type my response.

**MEREDITH: Sorry. Phone call. I may have a job.**
**NICK: A job? You've been looking?**
**MEREDITH: Duh. I'm not a total sponge.**
**MEREDITH: And correction, I've had several jobs over the last year.**
**NICK: Oh, yeah. Like what?**
**NICK: Sorry. That sounded rude when I read it back in my head.**
**MEREDITH: It was, jerk. A couple of small dance gigs. Day stuff, mostly.**

NICK: **What's the job now?**
MEREDITH: **The casting company that hired Charlie for Dylan's video is looking for an assistant choreographer.**

I'm pissed I missed a chance to meet Dylan Freaking Graves. Charlie has all the luck.

NICK: **That's awesome.**
MEREDITH: **How are things with you?**
NICK: **Startups are a bitch. I'm glad we're not still planning Jax and Charlie's wedding right now.**

His text causes a pang of sadness to prick. I'd liked spending all that time around him. Had I not been as fun to be around?
*Chill, Meredith, don't be such a girl.*

MEREDITH: **I bet.**
NICK: **So, how about it?**
MEREDITH: **How about what?**
NICK: **My house? Tomorrow night?**
MEREDITH: **Are you sure you have time to spend with me?**
NICK: **Huh?**
MEREDITH: **Since you're glad we're not still planning the wedding.**

Asshole. I roll my eyes and wait for his response.

NICK: **Shit.**
NICK: **That wasn't what I meant.**
NICK: **I just meant that there was more free time to spend it planning with you. I liked planning the wedding.**
NICK: **If you come over tomorrow night, I can apologize in person.**

I snort a laugh.

**MEREDITH: Is that what it's called now?**
**NICK: Haha. An actual apology.**
**NICK: Please?**

Something makes me hesitate. I don't just want to be a booty call. FWB, sure. I can handle that.

It's the please that does it. He's not usually one to use that word.

Maybe it's time he and I set a few more rules about our situation.

**MEREDITH: Okay.**
**MEREDITH: Let's start with some Lucifer and see how things go.**

★★★

Will I ever not be nervous standing outside of Nick's condo? Rolling my eyes at my own stupidity, I knock. It's not until he answers the doors in basketball shorts and a faded t-shirt that hugs his chest and shoulders like a lover that my nerves take over, filling my stomach with roller-coaster riding butterflies. When he sees me, his whole face lights up. Add the five o'clock shadow that covers his jaw, and I am officially toast.

The smell of his cologne tickles my nose.

Scratch that. I'm more than toast. What's more than toast?

"Hey." Drawing me inside the condo and into his arms, he wraps himself around me and breathes deeply. "You smell nice."

The vibration of his chest under my ear combined with the hints of cologne and laundry soap from his shirt have me so turned on I'm shaking.

Hello, world, I'm Meredith, and apparently, the smell of laundry soap is an aphrodisiac for me.

"Hey," I respond back.

With a brush of his lips over my hair, he releases me and heads for the kitchen.

"You hungry? I made grilled cheese sandwiches." Popping his head back out of the kitchen, he sends me a glare. "You didn't already eat, did you?"

I giggle at the look on his face. "No, I didn't already eat. I am hungry. Grilled cheese sounds perfect." I take the plate he hands me and get comfortable on the couch. "I haven't had one of these in years."

"Years?" His voice echoes from the kitchen. "Shit. You like them, right?"

Staring at the crisp, golden perfection on my plate, I can't wait to dive in. "I don't remember not liking them. This smells so good."

He walks in with his own plate and stops next to me, offering a bottle of water he had in one pocket. He sits, the heat from his thigh creating slivers of fire that lick through me. Pulling out another water for himself, he puts it on the table and nods at my sandwich.

"Eat up."

I eye him warily—not one-hundred percent sure he won't prank me somehow—and lift the sandwich. The first bite explodes in my mouth, and the moan I make has his gaze growing hooded as it fastens on my mouth. "Oh my god, what is this heaven?"

He smirks. "Right? A few years ago, I went to this resort—Indigo Royal. One of the owners there, who is their head chef, made the most amazing grilled cheese sandwiches. I badgered him until he gave me the recipe. It's all about the cheese."

I nearly choke on my laughter. "Really?"

He nods, eyes serious even though a half smile kisses his lips.

"Brie and Gruyere are required with a third cheese being the chef's choice. From there, you can add anything you want so long as you balance it. I happen to love bacon on mine, so that's what you got too."

He polishes his sandwich off in four bites and grabs his water. His throat muscles working as he drinks should not be sexy. Or mesmerizing. But they are.

"Meredith?"

Blinking, I bring his face back into focus.

"You gonna finish that?" He motions to my half-eaten grilled cheese.

Holding it to my chest, I push him away with my other hand. "Mine."

The look he gives me has a response echoing in my body, in the way it softens against his on the couch. But he doesn't make a move. He plays with the ends of my hair, wrapping my curls around his fingers as I finish my sandwich. Once I'm done, he leans closer, and I lick my lips to prepare for his oncoming assault. I barely catch his smirk as his fingers wrap around my plate and tug slightly. Biting my lip, my attention fastens to the way his ass fills out the gym shorts he's wearing as he carries both plates into the kitchen. The sound of a microwave and smell of popcorn call me like the pied piper. I follow and lean against the doorway to take him in.

Clearing my throat, I wait until he turns around to bring up my next topic. "Can I talk to you about something?"

"Yeah. Sure. What's up?"

"Well, I wanted to check with you... I guess to make sure we're on the same page." I say.

"Same page for what?" His brow furrows with his question.

I motion between us. "For our FWB."

"FWB? Oh, friends with benefits." He nods. "What about it? We already agreed not to tell Jax and Charlie."

"I still like that rule."

No way do I want my two best friends to know about this. And since Derek can't keep a secret to save his life, he's out too.

"Agreed."

"But, well, I mean, I guess I should tell you that I don't sleep around." A flash of guilt hits me thinking about my promise to be Derek's wing woman. This isn't the same thing though.

Nick nods. "I remember. Vividly."

I barely repress a shudder at the memory of our argument about my reputation. "I just... I'm wondering... You said before that you didn't mind picking up girls at bars and—"

He holds up a hand to cut off my awkward ramble. "If I'm sleeping with you, I'm only sleeping with you."

"Until I find someone I want to date?" I remind him.

A muscle ticks in Nick's jaw, but he nods.

"Of course."

Turning around, he grabs a bag of popcorn from the microwave and dumps the buttery goodness into a big bowl dwarfed in his hands. When I glimpse his face, a smile is back and the muscle tick is gone. Maybe I imagined it?

"Ready to Netflix?" I don't stop the laughter at his grin. The way he waggles his eyebrows tells me that he's dying to add the words "and chill" at the end of that question.

"You're awful." I snag a massive handful of popcorn and retreat back into the living room. "Bring on the devil."

# CHAPTER 17

*NICK*

"I should go." Meredith is kicked back on the couch while she watches something on my Netflix account. I'm sitting next to her, scouring the paperwork I need to finish for Arrhythmic. My brain feels like I've pureed it through a blender, but I need to get through the documents in my hand before I can reward myself with the brown-eyed beauty currently supine on my couch.

Frowning, I put the papers down. "Why?"

A huge sigh gusts out of her, and her whole body deflates. "I haven't been home except to shower and grab clothes in the last few days."

"So?" I ask.

So what if it's been nearly two weeks since our Netflix and chill turned into a sleepover that didn't involve much sleep?

For two weeks, we've watched football games, binge-watched *Lucifer*, talked about all sorts of things, and hung out at the beach. For almost every night for two weeks, she has been next to me in bed, usually after a mind-blowing round of orgasms. Panic burns a bitter trail up my throat and threatens to strangle me.

It's been nearly two weeks of no nightmares.

"Don't you think we need some space?" she asks.

"Do you?"

"Nice deflection." She wrinkles her nose and stands up from the couch, but I grab her hand and reel her into my lap. "I need to go home."

"Why?" My nose buries itself in her curls, and I breathe in. My heart rate slows with her in my arms.

"I shouldn't stay."

"What does that mean?" I turn her to face me but don't say anything else. It wasn't *can't stay*, it was *shouldn't stay*.

Her eyes search mine, the emotions flashing too quickly for me to identify any one in particular. "It makes things too sticky."

"Too sticky?" What the fuck does she mean by that? Granted, our situation feels more than friends with benefits, but who the fuck cares?

"Too blurry," she clarifies.

Fuck this. I grip her hips in my hands and lean forward for my lips to graze her neck.

"Stay."

With a shake of her head, she starts to squirm in my lap, but not to get away.

Shifting my hands, I palm her ass and squeeze, leaning down to nip the spot where her neck and shoulder connect.

"Stay," I repeat.

*Keep away my nightmares.* I keep that thought to myself, refusing to admit she's the reason they're gone. They've been more frequent since Cara called about Mom and Dad's party. Except when Meredith is next to me at night. It's like they never happened at all.

"Nick." Meredith's tone is a mix of no-nonsense and breathiness as my lips and hands continue to map out my strategy. My fingertips brush the underside of her breasts, and my name on her lips ends on a whimper.

"Stay." My blood is a persistent thrum of lust that moves and pools in my groin.

"I shouldn't." It's a whisper, a half-hearted attempted as she moves against my hands. Her head is thrown back as she pushes herself closer to me. The fact that I've won this war has exhilaration coursing through my blood. I need her. Now. Shifting my hands to her thighs, I stand, and my dick jumps at her husky cry of surprise and the way her arms and legs tighten around me.

"I've got you."

✱✱✱

Her smooth shoulder is a magnet for my lips before I even fully wake up the next morning. She groans and snuggles deeper into her pillow while her ass wiggles against my dick, my morning wood all about some action as it reaches toward her.

She stayed. No nightmares.

*I can't let her go.*

My phone buzzes on the nightstand and pulls me from that dark thought.

**CARA: If you continue to ignore me, I'm going to tell Mom it was you who broke her special occasion serving platter.**
**NICK: Fuck. That was like 20 years ago.**
**CARA: Think she's going to be over it?**

The serving platter had been passed down to Mom by her grandma. Shit.

**NICK: I'm not ignoring you.**
**CARA: You are. I've asked you every day for weeks for an answer about the party.**

Dread coils my stomach with the need to make a decision I don't want to have to make. I don't want to disappoint Mom and Dad, but the thought of going home—of facing those demons—scares the shit out of me. My gaze drifts to where Meredith shifts next to me.

Meredith.

She can go with me. She's banished the nightmares. She can be a distraction from the memories too.

**CARA: Am I ever going to get a response? Or should I call Mom now?**
**NICK: If you call Mom, it's only to tell her I'm coming.**
**CARA: Wait, what?**
**CARA: Seriously??**
**NICK: Plus 1**
**CARA: *GIF of fainting woman***
**CARA: I'm dead. You've succeeded.**
**CARA: Enjoy being an only child.**
**NICK: *eye roll emoji* Don't be so dramatic.**
**CARA: Did I have a stroke?**
**CARA: You did say you AND you're bringing someone?**
**NICK: We'll be there.**
**CARA: Holy Shakespeare.**
**NICK: What the fuck?**
**CARA: Clean up your language when you see your nieces and nephew. EEK. I'm so excited!!**

Rolling my eyes, I'm glad Cara isn't here to see me, otherwise her palm would connect with the back of my head.

**NICK: Maybe be less of a crazy person when I see you next?**
**NICK: I'll text you flight info, but we'll rent a car from Grand Island.**
**CARA: Mom and Dad are going to flip. Text me. Love you!**

**NICK: *smile emoji* Love you too.**

"You look happy." Deep brown pools blink up at me from my pillow, and her mass of curls creates a halo of chaos around her. Her fingers reach up and trace my lips. "What brought this on?"

I drop my phone and concentrate on her, brushing a kiss against her soft lips. "My sister."

Her lower lip pouts and I steal another kiss. "I always wanted a sibling. Jax was close, but he didn't count."

"Aw, poor Meredith." I tease her. "How would you like to have mine when we go to Nebraska next weekend?"

She sits up so fast she nearly knocks into me. "What?"

Laughing, I push her back down. "That was an invitation. Would you go home with me next week?"

"Why?" Her skepticism is clear.

"It's my parents' fortieth wedding anniversary."

"No, well, yes, I wanted to know that too. But why are you inviting me to Nebraska with you?"

I shrug. "I thought it would be fun. Show you around a farm."

She wrinkles her nose. "I'm not really a country girl."

I chuckle and clutch her closer to me. "I haven't been a country boy in twelve years. You're good. It'll be a short trip, a weekend."

Her eyes clash with mine. "You're serious?"

"I wouldn't have asked you if I wasn't."

"But..." She trails off.

"But what?" I prompt.

"Meet the parents? Where does that fit in with all this?" She motions between us.

"I want you with me. Isn't that what matters?" I pout. "Don't you want to go with me?"

Biting her lip, she blinks several times before she responds. "Can I think about it?"

"Yeah, of course." Shit. I was so sure she was going to say yes, it never occurred to me that she might say no. "Let me give you something else to think about."

Capturing her lips with mine, I give her at least three somethings to think about.

*★★★*

"Earth to Nick." Jax's hand waves inches from my face and I jump.

"What?" I blink and his in-home studio comes back into focus. He'd texted me earlier to ask if I wanted to spend some time working on his next album. Since he was currently my only artist, I headed to his place.

"Dude, where were you just now?"

My lips twist in a grimace, and I shrug off his question. "Sorry."

His face turns from easy-going to serious the longer he studies me. "You okay?"

"Yeah, man, sorry. Label shit."

He shakes his head. "I call bullshit."

I hold the lie for about ten seconds until my face falls. Running a hand through my hair, I confess what's really diverting my attention. "My sister called. Guilted me into going home next weekend for my parents' anniversary."

Since he knows about Emily, he's quick to understand why the thought of that fills my veins with ice.

His eyes widen. "Oh shit."

I nod. "Yep. I haven't been home in years. Twelve to be exact."

"You never went home after—"

"No." Not once after I buried Emily and came back to LA as a rep for the same label that was going to make me a star.

"Fuck. So you're going?" he asks.

"Yeah. It just...it has my head wrapped up right now."

"I get it. You sure you want to do this? Would you rather

listen to demos instead?" Not only is he the only artist, he's also a co-owner and has gotten the lead on some demos for us to listen to.

"That'd be great. I'm not in the right mind for this shit." Tossing the pad of paper and pencil on the couch next to me, I lean back and scrub a hand down my face. The sound of his chair spinning around drowns out the deep breath I let out.

My fingers itch with the need to text Meredith to ask if she's decided she'll go with me. I need her to go with me. Fuck. Panic claws through me and suffocates me at the thought of going to Willow River without her.

"...I like them, especially that refrain in the middle. What'd you think? Nick? Nick?"

"Sorry, what?" *Get your shit together, Rhodes.*

Shaking my head, I try to push thoughts of home into the box they've decided to explode from.

"Dude, still Nebraska?" he asks.

"Fuck, I'm sorry."

He smirks. "I know it's bad if you're apologizing."

Barking out a laugh, I toss a notebook, and he dodges it. "Smart-ass."

He shrugs. "Got you out of your head for a second. What's up?"

"It's nothing." I wave him off. "Just Nebraska shit."

"I think there's more to it than that."

Fuck. Is he psychic? I look down and find a geometric pattern formed by the flecks of color in the carpet at my feet. Guilt churns in my stomach. "So, I've been hanging out with a girl for a few weeks."

His jaw drops. "Like exclusively?"

I shake my head in quick denial. We're friends. With amazing benefits. And yes, she's not sleeping with anyone else and neither am I, but still. "No. It's not like that. It's...casual."

His lips thin and his jaw hardens, the big brother in him

coming to the forefront. Not that he knows I'm sleeping with his surrogate sister. "Define casual."

Shit. This is worse than the time I had to confess to Dad that I didn't want to be a farmer. "It's—It's just sex. For both of us."

That's all it can be. It's not like Meredith isn't getting anything from it—I've more than made up for that selfish jackass she dated in her past. That douche nozzle had no fucking clue.

"So what about it?" The confusion is clear in his voice. I don't blame him for being confused. I'm confused.

"I asked her to go to Nebraska with me."

He shakes his head. "Wait, back up. You did what? How is that quote unquote 'casual?'"

I try to ignore the guilt that sits like a rock in the pit of my stomach. But not because I regret my invitation. "Yep. When I'm with her—the nights she's with me—I don't have nightmares of Emily's accident." I don't add that she's been with me every night for nearly two weeks. "I'm hoping she can do the same thing when we go back for the weekend."

His gaze turns shrewd. "And why does she think you invited her to go with you?"

"She knows the score." We've been over this. Meredith and I.

"Score?"

"Anything with me—it's temporary. It's physical. Nothing more." My voice cracks with the last sentence.

He arches an eyebrow. "She knows that, or she's okay with that?"

"Jesus Christ. Both. It's not like it's some big secret."

The only secret I have isn't with Meredith. It's hiding who this woman is from Jax. But if I admit to him that it's Meredith? I might be able to dodge the well-deserved punch that accompanies *that news,* but I can't dodge what's coming after. The fallout with him. Potentially losing my partner with this label.

He is quiet as he watches me, wheels turning in his head as he processes what I've said.

"It's not like I'm screwing Jessie," I tell him.

He grimaces. "A—never talk about screwing and my sister in the same sentence. Two, same applies to Meredith."

"Meredith isn't your sister," I remind him.

"Just—no. That would be like me talking about your sister."

"My sister married her high school sweetheart." I shrug even though the guilt sucker punches my kidney.

Part of me wants to come clean, to tell him about Meredith and me. But what would I tell him? That I'm fucking the girl he considers the next thing closest to a sister? Fuck.

"Not the point." He levels me with a stare, and my heart rate spikes as he studies me. Finally, he shrugs. "So what's the deal? You worried she's gonna think it's more than it is?"

"No." Yes.

Maybe?

No. I've never kept the truth from Meredith. She knows we're not in a relationship. She knows why I invited her.

"So...?" he prompts.

"She didn't agree. She said she wants to think about it." The panic I keep pushing down climbs back into my throat.

"Sounds reasonable."

"What if—" I have to work a swallow around the lump of dread that sits on my vocal cords. "What if she says no?"

His confusion is apparent on his face. "But you said it was casual? Who cares?"

"Fuck." I run my hands through my hair as I stand and pace the small room. "I can't go there by myself."

If Meredith says no, then I'll need to call Cara and come up with some excuse. I can't be there. Not by myself.

Jax's hand on my shoulder stops my pacing. "Then I guess you better hope she says yes."

# CHAPTER 18

*MEREDITH*

$\mathcal{I}$t's Sunday, and I haven't been home except to get more clothes. I've told Mom I'm staying with a friend and, being as relaxed as she is—hell, I lived in New York for eight years by myself—the only thing she told me was to let her know if I needed anything.

I haven't brought up going home again after Nick's persuasive attempts to keep me here the other night. He also hasn't brought up going to Nebraska again. But there's a tension between us that wasn't there until I asked for time to think about it. The sex continues to be phenomenal, but it's like there's a disconnect between us. I'm not sure if it's real or in my head. I know why he wants me to go with him. He's been so open with what happened with Emily that I understand his hesitation to go home.

Guilt gnaws at me. He deserves an answer. But what's the right answer? My initial inclination is to say yes, but is that really what I want? That debate is almost paralyzing in its intensity, and the need to explain it to him pushes at me.

"Wait." I yank my lips away from his.

The announcer's voice blares through the TV, but we've been so caught up in each other, I don't remember who's playing, let alone what the score is. I sit up and bite my swollen lip, tasting his flavor with my tongue. It would be so easy to dip my head back to his and ignore the voice that tells me to talk to him.

The fire visible when his eyes open is enough to make my core throb. He takes several deep breaths, his chest moving up and down, and his heartbeat races under my fingers. Studying me, his face turns serious.

"What? What's wrong?" He cups my cheek.

"I—I need to tell you something."

His hands move to lightly rub my back.

"You look so worried. Whatever it is, you can tell me." Concern has crept into the corner of his eyes, but I doubt he's even aware it's there, doubt he knows that his mask isn't quite as intact as it used to be with me.

"It's about the other day. Remember how I told you about my ex?"

His teeth click audibly, and a muscle ticks in his jaw with his nod. "Yeah, that fucker cheated on you."

Humiliation washes through me even after two years.

Glancing down at my hands against the gray of his t-shirt, I nod. "I just—you've been honest with me. About everything. About Emily." I don't miss the way his muscles tighten when I say her name. My heart breaks for him even as the words I need to say wrap around my tongue, clinging to the opportunity to stay hidden. "I—I need to tell you something."

"Okay…" His brow furrows, and the way he holds himself is another sign of his confusion. "So he didn't cheat on you?"

"Oh no. He did. He cheated." I take a deep breath and keep my gaze on my fingers. "But this is about me."

"You?" he asks. "What did you do? Did you cheat too?"

I lift my face quickly. "What? No. That's not it at all."

197

"So what is it?"

"I just—I was never enough for Daniel, you know? I was always a screw-up. Even though I tried to change who I was to make him happy. He—he made me feel bad."

"He hurt you?" His fingers tighten against my arms and I shake my head.

"No. Not like that. He told me things. I was immature. I was too loud. I was bad at sex," I mumble that last part.

"What?" he asks.

I don't want to repeat it again, so I nod.

"So if I act weird. That's why. I-I don't want to be that person again. But it seems to be a habit in any relationship I'm in. I try to change who I am. But it doesn't matter what I change. I'm never enough." His flinch at my use of the r-word reminds me that this —while fun—is physical only.

"You don't need to change, Mer. Not for anyone."

"That's easier said than done."

"Meredith." He exhales my name on a breath.

"Why? Why am I not good enough? What's wrong with me?"

"Come here." He tugs me back to him, and his warm hands splay across my back. "Daniel's decision to do what he did? That had absolutely nothing to do with you. Maybe he hadn't been honest with himself. Or with you. There's never a reason to cheat. He was a mouth-breathing moron who didn't deserve you then and doesn't deserve space in your head now."

"Mouth-breathing moron?" I can't help but smile a little at that.

"Fuck yes. Forget that douche dick. Anyone would be lucky to have you love them and should love you back as much, if not more. And as for the sex?" He leans up to nip at my jaw. "If it were any better, I'd be dead."

Heat filters through my blood, and I turn my head to slide my lips over his, intent to pick up where we left off.

"Your phone," he mumbles against my lips while his fingers flex into my hips.

"Ignore it." My fingers spear through his hair to pull his mouth back to mine. Too bad the buzzing of my phone against the table distracts me enough that I sit up with a sigh. He looks pointedly at my phone and leans forward to bite a kiss against my neck before he lifts me off of him to stand up. His erection is obvious through the thin cotton of his pants, and I clench my thighs together while I grab my phone.

I've missed a call from Derek that he followed up with a text.

**D-Man: Girl, climb out of your sex cave and answer my damn call.**
**D-Man: Where are you?**
**D-Man: I'm at your house.**
Shit. My fingers fly over my keyboard as I respond.
**Meredith: I'm not home.**
**D-Man: No shit.**
**Meredith: What's up?**
**D-Man: I want to hang out.**
**D-Man: Come home if I can't meet MSG.**
**Meredith: MSG?**
**Meredith: Wait.**
**Meredith: Mr. Sex Glow?**
**Meredith: Derek!**
**D-Man: He's not losing that nickname anytime soon in my book.**

Grumbling, I stand and have slid my feet into my shoes by the door by the time Nick comes back out of the kitchen.

"Where are you going?"

"Derek's at my house," I explain.

He walks closer and pulls me into a hug. "I don't want you to go."

I sigh and tighten my arms around his waist. "I don't want to go either. But I'll come back after he leaves, okay?"

He nods against my hair. "You better."

His kiss lights every single nerve ending in my body.

"We'll pick this back up when I get back," I say and smile at his laugh.

Blowing him a kiss, I wave and close the door behind me.

Thank god Nick lives so close and I make it home a few minutes later. Derek must have conned the key from Mom, since he's busy making himself at home in my kitchen.

"You have no food," he whines into the refrigerator.

I shrug. I haven't been home much, so I haven't been to the grocery store lately. "Sorry. There's wine. Mom and Dad probably have food."

"Wine is good." He grabs an open bottle from the door and pours a full glass for each of us. "Now tell me everything. Where have you been? Why do I feel like I haven't talked to you in years?"

I follow him into the living room where he flops on my couch.

My shrug is a half-hearted effort to play off his questions. "I've been around."

"I think the correct word you're searching for is under." He smirks and sips his wine.

"Derek. Jesus." Embarrassment wars with amusement at his witty comeback, and I take a drink from my glass to hide my reaction.

"Hashtag truth."

"You're such a perv." I push at his arm, and he swears as he bobbles his drink.

"No, honey, a perv would be asking for more details after last time. I had a mini orgasm just listening to you. Speaking of." He winks at me. "My dirty mind requires more details to digest."

"Tell your dirty mind tough shit. That vault is closed." I way overshared last time. I mime zipping my lips and ignore his pout. "It's not happening. But I want to talk to you about something else."

I need some advice on what to tell Nick about his invitation to Nebraska.

"Talk to me about the something else, and I promise to listen, but reward me with some details?" The waggle in his brows has me clutching my stomach as giggles erupt, followed by hiccups.

"Oh my god." I wipe at my streaming eyes and take several deep breaths. Finally, the hiccups are gone, and I can speak again. "You seriously aren't going to let me off the hook, are you?"

"Nope. But I will be a good friend and listen to whatever you want to talk to me about right now. I'm all ears." He rests his head on his fists, attention focused on me.

"Sooo...I got asked to go to Nebraska next weekend," I start.

He sits up. "What, like for a job?"

My fingers twist in my sleeves. "No. Ni—" Jesus. I clamp my lips closed as Nick's name almost escapes. "The guy I'm seeing. His parents are having a party. Their fortieth anniversary."

His eyes nearly bug out of his head. "He wants you to meet the family? Isn't it a little soon for that?"

"It's not like that. He—he wants me to go back there for moral support. He—he's had some bad memories tied to home. I can help him with those. It's not a boyfriend/girlfriend thing. We're only friends."

"Friends don't tap the ass of their friends." He says it so matter-of-factly, I choke on the wine I just swallowed. "Shit, sorry."

I wipe my mouth with my sleeve and wave him away as I cough. "Drinking around you is hazardous to my health."

Once I'm finally able to breathe without my lungs burning with aspirated wine, I shrug. "We are friends. We agreed to add the benefits part. But he is, first and foremost, my friend. It's not just about the sex." He opens his mouth to speak, but I cut him off. "And yes, the sex is still fan-fucking-tastic, pun intended."

"Bitch. I really do hate you." He may be glaring at me, but his words lack any heat.

"You love me," I argue. "But, Derek, it's not only the sex. He's thoughtful and he cooks these amazing dinners. I swear I've gained ten pounds just from his food. But more than that. He sees me. He asks me questions and he *listens* even when I don't say something out loud."

"But you're just friends?" He rolls his eyes in response to my nod. "Denial ain't only a river in Egypt, girl."

"What do you mean?"

"You like him." He says it like it should be obvious.

"Duh, we're friends, genius."

"No, not like that. Not like you like me. You *like him* like him."

I snort and drain the rest of my glass. "What are we? In junior high?"

"I'm not hearing you say no." I refill my glass, and he holds out his. "You're catching feelings, baby girl."

"What? No, I'm not. I mean, he's my friend. So of course I care about him."

He shakes his head. "The lady doth protest too much."

"Friends," I repeat.

Nothing more.

"Mmm-hmm. What if he's catching feelings too?" he muses, and my heart stutters in my chest.

"What?"

Why aren't my lungs working right anymore? I blame the wine I breathed in.

He shrugs. "It's not out of the question. And he *did* invite you to meet his family. For an anniversary thing. Isn't that close to a wedding thing?"

Derek has a theory about dates at weddings. You only take someone you have feelings for, anything else is a complication.

"I dunno. Maybe?" I down my wine again and grab the bottle for another refill.

Nick is thoughtful, he talks to me, he listens to me. He cares about me. A question lodges itself in my brain, refusing to go away, and I gulp.

What if Derek is right?

\*\*\*

**NICK: Where are you? I thought you were coming back over tonight?**

From my spot splayed on my couch, I squint at the screen in the darkness, blinking until his words make sense.

**MEREDITH: My house.**
**NICK: Why?**
**MEREDITH: Derek just left a little while ago.**

Luckily, he'd Ubered over earlier so he could Uber home. We'd polished off three bottles of wine talking about the Nebraska invitation. That reminds me. I concentrate on my phone and key out a text.

**MEREDITH: Is the Nebraska invitation still open?**
**NICK: If you mean if I meant what I said earlier, yes. Come with me.**
**MEREDITH: OK.**
**NICK: OK?**
**MEREDITH: I'll go with you.**
**NICK: Thank you.**
**NICK: Come over.**
**MEREDITH: You only want a booty call.**
**NICK: I wouldn't turn it down. \*wink emoji\***

**NICK: We have unfinished business, remember?**
**NICK: I miss you.**

Those three words wrap around my confused heart.

**MEREDITH: Can you order me an uber?**
**NICK: Why?**
**MEREDITH: Derek and I had some wine earlier.**
**NICK: How much wine?**

How much wine had I had? Three bottles between the two of us. But the third bottle was more me than Derek.

**NICK: Meredith.**
**NICK: How much wine?**
**MEREDITH: *shrugging emoji***
**MEREDITH: I'm fine. Just order me an uber and I'll come rock your world. *devil emoji***

I don't get an immediate response from him, but that's okay. He'll text me when the car is supposed to be here. Thoughts of Nick remind me of his cologne—the warm, spicy scent wraps around me and makes me feel cared for. Treasured.

"Up we go." Warm arms lift me against a solid chest.

"Nick?" My eyelids refuse to open to answer my own question.

"Shh." His lips brush my hair as he maneuvers us down the hall.

"What are you doing here?" My voice is muffled by the thick cotton of his shirt as I bury my nose in the soft fabric.

His chest vibrates against me with his laughter. "Taking care of you."

Derek's words surface. *Does* Nick have feelings for me? The merry-go-round of questions in my head makes me feel sick.

"Arms up." His command is a murmur that I comply with as he pulls the shirt over my head.

There's a slight chill in the air until he finishes undressing me and pulls back the covers to tuck them around me. I want to call him back, but my lips and tongue feel heavy. And then I don't need to when he lifts the covers, and his warm weight settles behind me. His arm curls around my stomach and tugs me back against him.

"I'm glad you're here," I mumble.

"Sleep, Mer." His lips are feather-light against my shoulder, the last thing I feel as my mind drifts off again.

Waking up the next morning reminds me of a benefit of turning over a new leaf—no hangovers. It's been a while since I'd woken up with one, and definitely not after drinking so little.

"Ugh." Bright sunlight slants through my blinds. The white light adds to the throb in my skull.

"There's water and ibuprofen next to you." I whip around at the sound of Nick's voice behind me and immediately regret the action since my stomach doesn't stop rolling.

"What are you doing here?"

Leaning against my headboard in a t-shirt and basketball shorts, he's absorbed in his phone but manages to point to the nightstand on my side of the bed. "Ibuprofen. Water."

"Okay, okay, Mr. Crankypants. Jeez." I turn more slowly until I can crack one eye open to spy the glass and two small pills next to it. The water is cold and burns an icy chill to my stomach. I groan again as I lay back down. "Kill me now."

"Don't tempt me." There's a bite to his voice that I'm awake enough to notice. Come to think of it, it was there a few minutes ago too.

"What's wrong?" He ignores me, and I push at his arm. "Nick, what's the matter?"

His eyes remind me of a storm roiling over the ocean. Dropping his phone next to him, a muscle ticks in his jaw. Why the hell is he so pissed?

"I was planning on waiting until you were less hungover, but if you want to do this now, we can. What the fuck were you thinking?"

The tone in his voice sparks my own temper.

"What are you talking about?"

"Anyone could have fucking walked in here last night. You were passed out cold on the couch with your fucking front door unlocked." The fire in his glare tells me to swallow the response that I leave my door unlocked more often than even I want to admit. It's behind the gate to Mom and Dad's yard, so I don't always remember to lock it.

"If you're so pissed at me, why didn't you say so last night? Why are you here?" I counter, trying to sit up. Flashes of skin remind me that I'm naked under my sheets, and I tuck the sheet more securely around me. His nostrils flare, and his glower sparks with sapphire flames, but he ignores the peep show he just got.

"You were too drunk to hear me last night. And I'm here because someone has to make sure you can take care of yourself."

"I'm a grown-ass adult. I can 'take care' of myself." He rolls his eyes, and my fingers itch with the desire to slap him.

"Since you obviously do an amazing job yourself," he scoffs.

"What's that supposed to mean?" Pretty sure I know what he means, but I want to hear him say it.

"You know exactly what it means. I'm talking about at the club when I had to rescue you from that asshole."

Done with being judged and with that being thrown in my face—again—I roll over and face the window. I don't even spare a glance over my shoulder with my next words. "Feel free to leave at any time. I would say don't let the door hit you on your way out, but I wish it would."

He grabs my shoulder and turns me to face him again. "You don't get to ignore me right now. I'm fucking worried about you."

"You have nothing to worry about," I snap back.

"Who's going to look after you if I'm not there?" The fire in his gaze dims with his concern. "I wanted to strangle you once I saw the door was unlocked when I got over here last night." He releases a breath and leans against the pillows. "Meredith, you have to promise me that you're going to make better choices. You can't always rely on someone to remind you."

"Nick, it's fine. I'm fine." I tell him.

Blue eyes blaze open, and a swallow strains the muscles of his throat. "Meredith, promise me. I don't want anything to happen to you."

As quick as it came, my anger deflates. Emily. That's why he's always so wrapped up in my safety. He couldn't save her—he was thousands of miles away. But he won't let himself off that guilt train. I make a decision and shift until my head rests against his chest and feel his heart racing under my cheek. Strong arms come around me, and he holds me so tightly it steals my breath.

"I promise," I say quietly.

Note to self. The pressure on Nick—the new label, the trip back to Nebraska, his guilt over Emily—it's intense. He doesn't need my shit right now. I can make that promise.

He's taken care of me, listened to me. He's become my friend. I can be his rock right now.

# CHAPTER 19

*MEREDITH*

$\mathcal{F}$or the last several years on tour, it was normal to stay up all night. It was easy to do. So being exhausted on Wednesday, barely past nine o'clock at night, makes me feel old. But the stress of these last few days has been mentally exhausting.

This week has felt both a thousand years long and not long enough. The closer Friday gets, the closer we get to leaving for Nebraska. The closer we get to that date, the more my stomach ties in knots.

Nick is a different person than the one I've spent the last few weeks with. He's distracted, cold. Standoffish. At first, I think it's because of the night at my house, but if that's it, it isn't the only reason. If he's not ignoring me, his emotions boil over, and I find myself in crazy arguments over nothing. Anything from as silly as immediately washing my coffee cup to the ringtone on my cell.

But he needs me right now. Not normal me. But the one who tries to be more understanding. And I'm not complaining about the amount of angry sex followed by make-up sex these arguments seem to lead to. I'm surprised the sheets haven't disintegrated from the heat we create. But the yo-yo of emotions, the eggshells I've spent the week on, all of it has me second-guessing my agreement to go with him. At least a half a dozen times I've opened my mouth to ask if he'd rather I didn't go, but the fear of rocking the boat we're in always closes it before I say anything.

My jaw cracks with a yawn as I lean against Nick, who is surrounded by papers on the couch. I swear after the last few days, his ass has become fused to the couch, complete with paperwork accessories. "Wanna watch something?"

"Hmm?" He doesn't glance up from his phone.

"You wanna watch something?" I wiggle the remote under his nose and laugh at the way he jerks back slightly.

"Jesus." He pushes the remote away and goes back to his phone.

"So that's a no to watching something?"

He grunts in response.

Okay then.

I miss the man I've spent time with. I trail my hand along his leg and brush against him through his joggers, deliberately moving back down. On my second pass, his dick kicks against my fingers. By the third pass, he's hard against my hand. Cupping him, my lips brush against his jaw. My fingers trail to his waistband and dip beneath to wrap around him. He stills, but he doesn't put his phone down.

"What are you doing?" His voice sounds strangled.

"Nothing." I don't try to hide the grin on my face.

"Doesn't seem like nothing." His voice returns to its distracted tone.

I'll show him distracted. I push his waistband down until he pops free and lower my head, ready to pull him into my mouth.

"Christ, Meredith. Really?"

I freeze, inches from his erection, my mouth open but my

attention locked on his face. The tone of his voice chills me worse than any New York snowstorm I lived through. He drops his phone to the stack of papers next to him and turns distant eyes on me. I sit up and wrap my fingers around each other instead of him.

"I have *actual* work to do before we leave Friday."

His words whip against me, and the lump that forms in my throat makes it hard to swallow.

"I-"

"I don't fucking care if you watch something or not." He stands and stalks to the kitchen. The slam of a cupboard echoes in the silence between us.

Usually when we argue, he sticks around, and the heat between us builds until it funnels into a different outlet. He's never walked away from my touch. Until tonight.

He's under a lot of pressure. Not only do he and Jax want the label to succeed, but he's going back to a place full of memories of his dead fiancée. But those aren't justifications for his behavior. I don't deserve to be on the receiving end of his piss-poor mood.

My car is out front. I don't have to stay here. I walk back to the bedroom and smile at his attempt to make the bed, even though I'm confused and frustrated. The wrinkles on his side are a stark contrast to the smooth fabric where I made my side. My side. I have my side of the bed at his condo. A bottle of my shampoo sits in his shower. Surely that has to mean something, right? What if he regrets asking me to go with him?

When I don't have a clear answer to that question, tears overflow to stream down my cheeks. I sit on the bed and wrap my arms around a pillow. The fluffy cotton muffles my tears. What if Derek is wrong and Nick doesn't return the feelings I've started to admit to myself I have? I need to get up, grab my phone, and go. But what does it mean for Nick and me if I do that?

His cologne wraps around me as strongly as his arms do. The

room is dark, and I'm under the covers. What time is it? The last thing I remember was telling myself to get up and go.

"I couldn't find you." His arms tighten and tuck me back against his chest. "I was afraid you left. I wouldn't have blamed you since I acted like a grade A asshole. I'm so sorry."

Warm lips brush against my hair, and tears clog my throat again. I bite my lip and stay silent to hold them off. "Mer?"

I shake my head and try to keep my voice even. "It's fine. Don't worry about it."

"Are you sure?" I nod, and his breath blows across my neck. Goosebumps pebble down my arms. "I really am sorry, baby."

I know he is. That's why I choose not to fight this battle.

He has a lot going on—in real life and in his head. He'll be fine as soon as we get to Nebraska and he sees it's not that big a deal. We'll be fine.

By Thursday night, I doubt if we'll even make it to Nebraska. Our flight is early in the morning, and I'm stuck as I stare at my half-packed suitcase. I am stressed the fuck out. I've brought over a bunch of different options and asked him to help me. He said he was nearly done with some paperwork—a few more minutes, according to him—and he'd come back to his bedroom. It's been an hour, and I still don't know what to pack.

I push my temper down and try to keep the peace. I watch him from the edge of the hallway, he seems to be a million miles away as he reads through a different stack of paperwork. Files are scattered over every inch of the couch, and the urge to tidy everything up intensifies my anxiety.

"Nick?" When there's no answer I try again. "Nick?"

I give it another minute without a response.

"Nick, are you listening to me?"

"What?" He blinks and looks up. "Sorry, this is that paperwork I told you about. I need to get it to the attorney no later than tomorrow."

I get it. It's important. He told me it's the partnership agreement with Jax. But that knowledge doesn't stop the frustration that simmers in my veins. I want to make a good impression on his family. "I've been asking you all week what I should pack. I'm not sure about your parents' party or the weather or what I need for a farm. Could you help me—"

"Fuck, Meredith. I don't care what you fucking pack. Pack something. Christ. Why is this so difficult?" he snaps like I'm a nuisance, his gaze immediately falling back to his papers.

The burn of tears stings my nose. Taking a deep breath, hurt zips through me. I can't. I can't deal with him like this. This is too similar to the situation I put up with for years from Daniel, and I refuse to be this person again.

Fuck this. Fuck his attitude. Fuck him. Walking to the hook I persuaded him into buying for coats and bags, I grab my purse and slip it over my shoulder. No movement from the couch.

Why do I expect differently? Shit, my suitcase. Maybe I'll leave it. Does Jax have a key? Wait, then Jax would need to know why I need it. Nope. I walk to the bedroom and zip up the suitcase. It thumps to the floor and rolls behind me on my way back to the front door.

He doesn't glance up. It's like I'm invisible. But even as upset as I am, I need him to hear me. I don't want him to worry.

"So…" Pent up tears clog my throat, and I clear it to try to get rid of them. "I'm gonna go."

His gaze focuses on me like he's seeing me for the first time. The distant blue of his eyes clouds over with confusion. "What? Why?"

I can't help the mirthless laugh that escapes. "This isn't a good idea."

And fuck if saying that doesn't feel like déjà vu. But it didn't hurt this bad the first time I echoed those words.

"I'm confused. What isn't a good idea?" He's not lying. The confusion on his face is visible from here. It doesn't make it any easier to get the words out.

"My going to Nebraska with you."

"What?" He puts the papers down next to him without breaking eye contact with me.

"I'll make it easy on you. I won't go. I'm sure the airline can give you credit for the ticket—" He stands, scattering files and papers to the floor. They almost remind me of big, fat snowflakes when it used to snow in New York—the big snows that would mute the chaos of the city for a bit. The last paper flutters to the ground, breaking the spell. I shift my attention back to him. "I'm gonna go."

I turn, one hand on the door, and the warmth of his hand wraps around my other wrist. It's a soft touch, but it burns me anyway. "Mer."

*Do* not *cry in front of him, Meredith.*

I blink rapidly while I face the door and try to will the combination of angry and sad tears to stay put. One deep breath and another. I refuse to turn around, but am paralyzed to leave. Physically, I could easily pull out of his grasp and walk out like I did that first night. But he'd have a little piece of me anyway.

"Don't leave. Please." The pleading note to his voice hurts. How is it that part of me wants to walk away, and the other part wants to turn around and fall into his arms? "I'm sorry. I want you to come. I haven't changed my mind."

Mom used to say something to me whenever I apologized. "Actions speak louder than words."

He draws in a breath, blowing it out. "I know. I've been a real asshole this week."

I'm not sure what to say to that. "If you're looking for a disagreement, you're barking up the wrong tree."

He doesn't move, but the press of his fingers soothes the bruises my heart has gotten this week.

I stay silent, and he continues. "The attorney has been calling me for this paperwork every day, and it's a fuck ton to get ready. I'm...I'm dealing with a lot of shit right now." I understand what he's saying, which is even more frustrating. But it doesn't excuse him using me as the trash can for all his emotions. "I'm sorry. Don't go."

He steps closer to my back. The genuine regret that radiates off his body, coupled with his words, weakens my resolve. My hand drops from the door, my body still.

"I'm sorry." The words are a whisper as soft lips graze my shoulder. Arms wrap around me and pull me closer. "I'm sorry."

I let myself be reeled against him and am treated to another kiss, a longer press of lips, followed by his warm tongue. The caress lights up my body even though my heart feels raw. I want to feel good. To make him feel good. I tilt my head and am rewarded by another drag of his lips once he gets better access.

"Do you forgive me?" The murmur vibrates against the column of my throat as he traces lazy kisses down my neck. His hands shift and reach up to cup my breasts.

With a moan, I nod. "Yes."

I'm not sure if I'm responding to his question or to the way his hands move on my body.

"We should head to bed. We have an early flight." His words are followed by a nip of teeth at my earlobe.

It's not until hours later, as he sleeps fitfully next to me, that the doubt returns in a slimy wave. It drowns me in second guesses. Should I plan to go with him tomorrow?

# CHAPTER 20

*NICK*

$\mathcal{M}$y heart hammers as I bolt upright in the darkness.

"Shit." I rub a hand over my chest and try to recall the dream that jerked me awake.

Definitely not the Emily one. That one always stays with me long after I wake up. But this one? This one is like a ghost—nothing left except the chills that travel my body. The fact that I can't remember adds an edge of panic—a new piece of the hell these dreams bring.

Meredith shifts next to me, a line furrowed between her brows even in sleep. Fuck, she's put up with a lot of my shit this week. Too much. The shit I spewed at her, the way I spoke to her. I couldn't stop. Even after I told myself that she didn't deserve it. She didn't deserve my anger or frustration. And she damn sure didn't deserve the rejection I dealt her the other night.

Normally, the sight of her mouth so close to my dick would be enough to have me focused only on her, on getting her naked and under me as fast as possible. The paperwork would have waited. Instead, I'd pushed her away.

Fuck. I'd been terrified that she left. That I'd fucked it all up. I'd come into the bedroom to grab my shoes to go track her down and found her asleep with a pillow clutched like a lifeline in her hands.

The relief at seeing her practically leveled me. Why she's here, why she's put up with my ass, is beyond me. Thank fuck she's going with me, even if I can't figure out why. I wouldn't go with my grumpy ass at this point. Lying back down, I wrap my arms around her and pull her to me to bury my nose in her soft curls. I inhale the comforting smell of her shampoo as her warm weight rests against me.

She's my friend. My talisman against the nightmares.

I need her.

My lips brush her shoulder, and my voice is barely a whisper as my arms tighten around her. "Don't leave me."

She mumbles something in her sleep, and I freeze. I don't want to wake her up. Instead, I match my breathing to hers, but it's no use, I can't drift back to sleep. Shadows recede and the light climbs through the room, barely gray when the alarm starts on my phone.

"Hey, sleepyhead. Time to get up." I jostle her in my arms as I wake her up.

She groans and buries her head against my chest.

"Too early."

My laugh is raspy. "I know. I'm sorry. This was our best flight option."

"I know." Her voice is muffled.

Cuddling her in my arms, I drop a loud kiss to her cheek. "If I promise you coffee, will that work? We have to get up."

"Mmm." She stretches and sits up.

"Good morning." Half of my mouth lifts in a lopsided curve. Staring into her eyes, I vow not to be a dickhead.

"Morning," she responds.

I open my mouth to thank her for putting up with me for the last week, but close it again. What the fuck can I say? Thank you seems so insignificant. Apologizing isn't enough. Her kiss is quick, chaste, and shows me how unaware she is of the struggle I'm having with words.

"I'm gonna grab a shower. You promised me coffee." Her soft smile lifts the weight of dread from my neck for the first time since I made my promise to Cara to come home.

Getting out of bed, my body automatically turns to the bathroom, ready to follow her.

"No. No time right now." I mumble to myself with a shake of my head. Tossing on a pair of shorts, I head to the kitchen and make us both a cup of coffee. When I come back to the bedroom with the two cups, I'm surprised to find Meredith already out of the shower. She's wrapped in a towel while she puzzles over her suitcase. Water runs trails down skin my lips are intimately familiar with. "Coffee, milady."

Distracted, she returns my kiss for a moment before turning back to her suitcase. I know it's serious since she nearly forgets the coffee cup in her hand. After she hasn't moved for several moments, I wrap my arms around her and rest my chin on her shoulder.

"Everything okay?"

"Um." Chewing on her lip, her face has a panicked expression I've never witnessed. "Just trying to figure out clothes."

"I wouldn't mind if you go without." I smirk at her and laugh when she sticks out her tongue.

"Haha. I'm not meeting your family in a towel." I've been so caught up in my own head, I've completely ignored what this experience is going to be like for her and the fact that she's nervous too.

"Whatever you wear, you'll be fine." Kissing her shoulder, I stay where I am.

"I will?" The uncertainty in her voice has me tightening around her.

"Absolutely." I promise.

The smile she gives me sparks a need to brush my lips with hers. I pull back sooner than I want while the need to get to the airport on time hangs over us like a building storm.

She's dressed and packed by the time I'm done with my shower, and we're on our way to LAX fifteen minutes after that. Her hand weaves with mine in the back of the car.

"Doing okay?" she asks. Her hand squeezes to give me comfort I don't deserve after my behavior this week. Too bad I'm a bastard and I'll take what I can get.

I shrug. "I'm not sure."

My stomach churns the closer we get to the airport, and anxiety locks my voice until she leans her head against my shoulder.

"It's going to be okay. I promise," she says.

I hope she's right.

Her reassurance helps ease some of the tension in my shoulders, but doesn't touch the pit of anxiety that grows with every mile closer we get to Nebraska.

The three-hour flight from LAX to Dallas is uneventful. I've upgraded us to first class, and we're barely airborne when Meredith is asleep, dark circles under her eyes. I order a scotch and soda and toss it back before I lean back and succumb to my thoughts of what to expect. It's a riot in my head that only allows me to doze. Waking up as we land, I nudge Meredith awake and kiss her temple where she rests it against my shoulder.

"Sleep well?" I ask.

She nods, yawning. "How long is our layover here?"

"We have about two and a half hours. Getting hungry?" We hadn't had anything to eat yet, and while the thought of food doesn't hold any appeal for me, I can't imagine why she wouldn't be ready to eat by now.

She nods. "Starving."

We grab our carry-ons and walk up the ramp to the closest directory.

"So what are you in the mood for?" Her innocent question as she looks at the different choices has a smirk twisting on my lips. "Nick? Ugh. Get your mind out of the gutter."

She laughs and pushes at me, but I grab her hand and reel her in for a quick kiss. "My mind was more in the bedroom, but you're right. Food first. Burgers?"

She shakes her head and points at the map. "Tacos?"

Nodding, I interlace our fingers and steer us in the direction of the restaurant she pointed to.

"Need to use the restroom?" When she declines, I reluctantly release her fingers. "I'll meet you at the restaurant?"

With a nod, she merges into the people around us until she reaches the restaurant and ducks inside. A few minutes later, I stand at the same entrance and scour the tables for her signature curls. I finally spy them at the bar, where she laughs at whatever the bartender says to her. Jealousy spikes, hot and hard, and completely irrational. She's not mine. Not like the jealousy says she is. But that voice doesn't care.

*Mine.*

I join her at the bar and my hand reaches out with a mind of its own to land on her hip. Call it what it is. I stake my claim to the bartender, whose interested gaze continues to devour my—Meredith. Does she even realize? Glaring at him, I wait until he walks away before I look at her.

"What was that?" Her attention bounces between me and the guy who wisely chooses to go to the other end of the bar.

"What was what?" I ask.

"You're acting all jealous," she teases.

"I'm not jealous. Because I get to do this." I yank her to me and drop my lips to hers. The rest of the world fades as I deepen the kiss and absorb the little whimper that escapes her throat. When

I finally pull back, her dazed expression comes back into focus. The warm brown of her eyes sparkles under the lights around the bar. Her cheeks are flushed, her lips swollen from our kisses, and I dip back in for another quick taste.

"Were you guys ready to order?" It's a different person than the guy flirting with her earlier.

She straightens and rattles off her drink and food order while I scan the menu and order the first thing that looks good. With the interruption gone, I turn back while words rush to my lips. I need to tell her what I think of her. How special she is.

"You're beautiful," I murmur.

"What?" She shakes her head like she doesn't understand what I said.

I can't explain the nerves that swirl in my stomach as I reach out to wrap my hand around hers. This is Meredith. Why am I nervous?

"I mean it. You are beautiful. And not only on the outside. You're a beautiful person. What did I do to deserve you?"

She ducks her head with a shy smile. "What brought that on?"

I blow out a breath, frustrated with myself. "I've acted like a total ass this entire week, and you're still here."

"We all have rough spots." Her shrug says it's no big deal to her. And she means it. It's not. This is who she is.

"I'm sorry." I clutch her fingers as hurt for her wars with anger at myself.

Her gaze softens as it locks on mine, and her fingers tighten in return. "It's okay."

"I—I walked in here earlier, and it hit me when I saw that guy flirting with you—"

"He wasn't flirting with me," she interrupts.

"He totally was," I correct her. "I'm lucky to have you in my life. I don't know what I would have done if you weren't here."

"You'd have figured it out," she reassures me.

I doubt it, but I don't get to voice that before the server is back, and our conversation moves to safer subjects that don't make my stomach turn in on itself.

Walking to our next gate, I vow not to let my shit spill out onto her. To make this weekend as easy as possible for her since she's doing everything in her power to be there for me.

# CHAPTER 21

*NICK*

*T*he Grand Island airport is so much smaller than I remember, but Meredith's attention bounces everywhere. Her head is in constant motion as she checks out our new surroundings. I tow her along toward the exit and focus for both of us since her attention is distracted by everything else.

While the majority of me pays attention and navigates us to the car rental counter, there's a sensation between my shoulder blades I can't shake. A tension that wasn't there until we stepped off the plane. My stomach wants to rebel against the tacos I ate at lunch, but I swallow the bile that coats my throat.

"You okay?" Her eyes stay on me as we stop, and people flow on either side of us. They grumble as they shift, and some of them throw us dirty looks as we stand and stare at each other.

"F—" My voice cracks and I clear my throat. "Fine."

Her face tells me she doesn't believe me, but she doesn't ask any more questions. Her fingers find mine, and she reaches up to kiss my cheek.

"It's going to be okay. You'll see." This time she pulls me toward the exit. "Do you want to go grab the car and I'll pick up our bags?"

I nod but immediately want to grab for her hand once she lets go to walk in the direction of the carousel that flashes our flight information. Taking a deep breath, I turn and walk to the car rental counter. I'm not surprised there isn't a line.

"Can I help you, sir?"

Sir. Like I'm old. Considering the kid behind the counter barely looks old enough to drive, maybe to him, I *am* old.

"I should have a reservation. Nicholas Rhodes."

He nods and focuses on his computer screen while his fingers fly over the keyboard.

"Right, Mr. Rhodes. You requested a mid-size, and we have you in a Ford…" My hearing blips out with the make of the car. I don't even hear what type of Ford.

*No. No way.*

Grinding my teeth, I barely manage to spit out the words. "I specifically requested the car be anything *but* a Ford."

Emily had driven a little purple Ford Focus. It had been the first car her parents bought her at sixteen, one I'd teased her about relentlessly. I'd named it Barney, and I never let her drive if it was just the two of us. It was the same car she was driving when the truck hit her. But according to the whispers I'd overheard from her dad to mine, the car had been unrecognizable. My stomach threatens to revolt, and I lock my jaw, refusing to move as I glare at the kid in front of me.

"I'm sorry, sir. Yes, I see that right here." More frantic typing as the kid seems ready to piss himself. "I—I don't have any more mid-size vehicles right now that aren't reserved. I—I—let me just check with my manager."

He scurries off as Meredith walks up and wraps her arms around me.

"Whoa. What's wrong?" she asks softly.

*Do not lose your shit.*

Do not lose your shit *with Meredith.*

She has zero to do with this. Rather than the risk I run in opening my mouth, I shake my head. Her arms tighten around my midsection, and her head rests right where the tension is balled between my shoulders.

"Want me to handle this?"

Inhale. Exhale. Nod.

"Okay." She steps toward the counter as the kid comes back. His eyes ping between the two of us, shoulders visibly relaxing once she waves to get his attention.

I nod toward her, and the kid clears his throat. "Yes, ma'am. I'm so sorry. I don't know what happened—"

"Don't worry about it." She says warmly and tries to diffuse the tension that surrounds us.

"I talked to my manager. He's authorized us to go to a different category of rental car. An upgrade to a Rav4."

"Would you be okay with a Toyota?" She glances back at me and I nod. It's not my preference, but my options are limited if I have to rent a vehicle.

She turns back to the counter. "Yes, that would be fine. Thank you so much."

A few minutes later, keys in hand, she walks back to me. Her arms wrap around me, and her head rests against my heart. "Breathe."

I follow her direction, breathing in, holding the air in my lungs for a beat, and blowing it out.

"Do you want me to drive?" she offers.

Shaking my head, I unlock my jaw. "I'm okay."

Or at least I hope I will be.

An hour later, the regrading as I turn from the paved road onto my parents' driveway is a punch in the gut. Gone are the ruts my truck bumped up and down on like a trampoline the last time I drove the familiar path.

"Are you all right?" Meredith's voice unclenches my jaw, the waver betraying her own nerves.

I nod and glance at her quickly while the house gets closer. The white tent set up next to the barn is a reminder of why we're here. "You? You've been pretty quiet since we left the airport."

It's not like her. This quiet, reserved version is a woman I rarely see.

"I'm okay." She shrugs, but the flutter of her hands in her lap is a dead giveaway to her nerves.

Stopping the car near the house, I thread my fingers through hers and bring one hand up to my lips. "Thank you for coming with me."

Her fingers are clammy in mine, and I bend toward her, intent on brushing a kiss against the lip she's nibbling.

"Nicholas Landon Rhodes!" Mom's voice carries from the front porch, and I immediately straighten, feeling like a high schooler caught necking with his girlfriend. In fact, it's exactly what she said on numerous occasions when Emily and I got distracted in my truck. There were many, many discussions about being safe. The number of times Dad was forced to mumble his way through "the talk" scarred us both for life. "You get out of that car and give me a hug."

I wrap my hand around Meredith's, bringing it to my lips, and unbuckle my seat belt. "Time to face the music."

Her smile is shaky, but she unbuckles as well. The sound of her car door echoes mine.

The happy sound Mom makes is the only one I get before she darts down the stairs and throws herself at me in a cinnamon-infused hug. Her arms grip me with a strength and familiarity I've known all my life, while her sniffles have my shoulders tensing.

"Mom." Wrapping my arms around her in comfort, I wait until she pulls away. Tear tracks shine in the late fall sunshine.

"Nicky." Her hands grip my cheeks, and joy stretches across her face. "My baby is home."

Meredith's expression might as well form cartoon hearts as she watches the exchange from the safety next to the car.

I roll my eyes but hold still in Mom's grasp. "Mom."

She chuckles at my whine, and her gaze flicks to Meredith. "Nothing to be embarrassed about, Nicky."

*Nicky?* Meredith mouths at me. Her grin is her usual impish one, her nerves hopefully forgotten. I shrug, not sure what to say. The only time Mom doesn't refer to me as Nicky is if she triple names me. And those times never result in anything good.

"Mom, I want you to meet Meredith. Meredith, this is my mom, Beth."

Meredith walks slowly over to us while her hands wipe at the imaginary wrinkles in the skirt she insisted she change into at the airport.

"Mrs. Rhodes, it's nice to meet you."

The fact that Meredith extends a hand and doesn't crush Mom to her in a hug is another tell of nerves. Meredith is a physical person, and she doesn't usually shy away from hugs.

Mom smiles and takes Meredith's outstretched hand. "You too, Meredith. But please call me Beth. How do you two know each other?"

The panic on Meredith's face has amusement curving my lips. Her eyes dart between Mom and me, and I swoop in to loop an arm around her tight shoulders and kiss her temple.

"We met through Jax," I explain.

Mom's eyebrows skyrocket to her hairline, and her attention locks on my hand around Meredith's shoulders. But she doesn't say anything else and nods like nothing is amiss.

The crunch of tires on gravel has the three of us looking back to the driveway. My sister beeps her horn frantically as she pulls the minivan up behind my rental. It barely shuts off before Cara is out of the car and throwing herself at me in a death grip.

"Jeez, y'all act like I'm the prodigal son or something," I joke, hugging my sister back.

Cara's eyes are misty as she pulls away from me, but she laughs as she motions to the kids who climb out of the car. Caleb is first, his four-year-old legs moving even as they hover in the air.

"Mama, mama, is this Uncle Nicky?" I turn a glare to my sister. I had hoped the nickname would die with the current generation all older than me.

Apparently not. It would seem, to my entire family, that everyone delights in the nickname that makes me sound like I'm Caleb's age.

She nods. "It is."

Little arms wrap around my knees. "Hi, Uncle Nicky. Wanna play with me?"

"Umm…" I look at Cara for help.

"How about in a little while, buddy? Uncle Nicky just got here. Why don't you go ask if Grandpa will take you to see the horses instead?"

He beelines for the house and the front door slams behind him.

"You must be Meredith. I've heard so much about you." I choke on the lie, but can't call bullshit on Cara's remark when a nine-year-old with platinum blonde hair in braids joins us and hides behind her mom. "Kristen, this is your Uncle Nicky and his friend Meredith. You met him a few years ago."

The last time I had seen Kristen, she had been Caleb's age and just as talkative. Peering around her mom, she waves at me with a wary expression, sending a similar gesture to Meredith.

"Mom." Kristen pulls Cara down to whisper into her ear.

"That's fine, Kris. You can head in. Keep an eye on Caleb for me, okay?"

She nods and follows her brother's trail at a less exuberant pace.

"Not very talkative?" I ask.

Cara shakes her head. "No, she turned eight and suddenly turned into my shy child."

"No Sam?"

"Sam-*antha*," comes the snarky reply from the open passenger door of the van.

Cara's gaze turns heavenward, and her lips move silently. Surely, a fourteen-year-old girl can't create that kind of response, right?

Hot pink patent leather Doc Martens stomp down from the passenger seat. Streaks of hot pink are visible in hair that is darker than her sister's and closer to Cara's color.

"Samantha, right, okay. Remember me?"

The eye roll she gives me would be enough of a response, but she goes above and beyond.

"Sure, the absentee uncle I've met, like, three times in my whole life." She gives me a peace sign. "Hey there, Unc."

"Samantha Anne." My sister's voice causes me to do a double-take between her and Mom. When did Cara start to sound so much like Mom did as we were growing up? "Manners or your cell phone stays in my possession longer than it already is."

The sullen teenager pastes a syrupy sweet smile on her face. "Better, Mom?"

"Lord, don't let me kill this child." Cara's voice is barely audible, the words mumbled under her breath.

"Hey, I'm Meredith. I love your shoes. Where did you get them?" Meredith approaches the teenager much the same way I would equate how Chris Pratt faced off with the hungry velociraptors he trained in one of the Jurassic movies. But her genuine smile and curiosity have Samantha dropping the hostile act, and the sarcasm written all over her face softens as she glances down at her shoes.

"From Zappos. They have all kinds of colors. I had a gift card for my birthday," she explains.

"Those are awesome, can you show me?" Meredith pulls out her phone and clicks on something, rotating it to hand it to Samantha.

Cara blinks—stunned—as she gestures to Meredith and Samantha and tosses a grin my direction. Even Mom seems surprised by Samantha's about-face. Shrugging, I open the rear hatch on the rental and grab our two bags.

"Mom, where am I putting Meredith's stuff? And mine?"

She shifts her attention from the miracle unfolding in front of her as Samantha giggles at something Meredith says.

"Oh, um, your room. Both of you." When my mouth hits the dirt at my feet, she laughs. "I am aware, Nicholas, that you are an adult. Don't make me regret my decision."

★★★

The sounds of a farm in the morning are as familiar to me as breathing, so it's no surprise that I'm up early. Lying in my childhood bedroom with Meredith snuggled up against me creates a weird sensation in my stomach. It's one I can't name, but feels an awful lot like happiness. Having Meredith next to me is different—Emily and I never had the chance to do this. It's a new memory, one that has the tension easing from my body.

I glide my fingers across her hip to brush against the warm skin of her stomach.

"Mmm." She wiggles her ass against my already hard length.

"Morning, baby." My fingers move north to settle on her breast as my lips graze the skin behind her earlobe.

"Well, good morning to you too." Her voice is a low murmur while her back arches her breast further into my palm.

"Sleep well?" My thigh parts hers as my fingers tweak her beaded nipple.

"Yes." Her response is breathy, both an answer to my question as well as an exclamation over the sensations I'm creating in her body. "Y-you?"

"Mmm-hmm." I murmur. Bending over her, my lips drag hers into a kiss before I tangle our tongues and twist her body beneath mine. "I had the best dream. You were there."

"I was?" Her legs part to wrap around my waist, my dick inches from her slick pussy.

"Mmm." I hum my response as my nose moves along her jaw.

"What was I doing?" The laughter in her voice is my Meredith. The nerves from yesterday, the stress from the last few weeks, are gone. It's only me and her, skin to skin.

"I could tell you." I nip at the column of her throat. "But I'd rather show you."

My lips are a breath away from hers when a knock at the door interrupts me.

"Nicky? I'm making breakfast. Your favorite. It's nearly ready."

I groan into the pillow next to Meredith's head and my dick instantly deflates. "Thanks, Mom, we'll be down in a few minutes."

Cock-blocked by my mother. Does she have a radar? The squeak on the second stair from the top signals her descent back to the kitchen. Those squeaks are the same ones I'd learned to avoid as a teenager when I snuck home well past curfew.

Meredith pushes at me until I roll off of her. Lying on my back, I contemplate my ceiling. At one point, Emily had put those glow-in-the-dark star decals up there, but they either fell down or Mom pulled them down since they're long gone.

"Your favorite?" she asks.

I chuckle. "Biscuits and gravy. Bacon. Hash browns. Heaven."

She giggles. "We should probably get dressed then."

I groan. "Probably."

"I don't want your family to get the wrong impression of me."

Rolling back toward her, I pin her back to the bed. "My family adores you."

It was true. Meredith had connected with Surly Samantha, joked around with Cara, and helped Mom clean up after dinner, all while charming Dad with her knowledge of old-school rock-and-roll music and football.

My family loved her. She fit in with each of them. And the best part about it is she was here next to me last night—my talisman against memories that continue to push against the fortress her warmth provides me.

Her shallow breathing and the way that heat sparks in her eyes have my dick perking back up.

"Later." She pushes against me and I fall back in the bed. She tosses the covers back and adds an extra sway to her hips on her way to her suitcase. "Like what you see?"

With a groan, I move my hand to grip my cock.

"Get dressed." My voice is rough, full of unfulfilled lust.

"Aww. Poor grumpy Nicky. Now who's not a morning person?" Her voice is all sweetness and sass.

Tossing off the covers, I close the distance to her and pull her against me, bruising her mouth with a kiss.

"Still you." I swat her ass and chuckle at her hushed yelp. "Get dressed."

One hand rubs her ass while the other grabs her clothes. "I was doing that until someone distracted me."

We're dressed and heading downstairs when I respond. "By the way, a promise is a promise."

"What?" Her hand grips the rail as she stops to glance at me.

"You said 'later' earlier. I'm holding you to that promise." I drop to the stair next to her and crowd her against the wall full of family pictures. "There are lots of places I want to show you while we're here."

"Y—you do?" Her breath comes in pants and her pupils dilate as her chest rises and falls to brush her breasts against me.

Nodding, I move close enough that my breath mingles with hers. "Want a tour later?"

"No." Her response surprises me. "I want that tour right now."

I smirk and brush my lips against hers. "Later."

# CHAPTER 22

*MEREDITH*

*N*ick Rhodes is a damn tease. To sit through breakfast and not react to the way his fingers coast closer to my throbbing core drives me crazy. My thighs clench to try to achieve some relief from the heat of his fingers as they walk along my thigh. My attempt to ignore him is short-lived, and I catch his smirk out of the corner of my eye as he brushes the center seam of my jeans. My sharp intake of breath draws attention from his mom.

"Everything okay, Meredith?"

Coughing to cover the way I shift in my chair, I nod. "Sorry."

"Nick, feel up to helping your old man move a few bales this morning?" According to Beth, Nick's dad, John, had already put in several hours of work and had brought the crisp air of fall into the kitchen as we were all getting ready to eat.

Disappointment rushes in when Nick removes his hand from my thigh completely. "Sure, Dad, now?"

He nods. "Your mother and sister have told me I'm only allowed to work until two."

Beth swats him on the arm. "We have close to one hundred people coming over for the party this evening. You'll be working here. Same as me."

Nick's muscles tense at his mom's words. I wouldn't take him for someone averse to crowds. He's always done fine at the after-parties on the tour, but tonight, it's people who know him. People he hasn't seen since he was with Emily. Or at her funeral.

He's been like this since we left LA yesterday morning. It's a roller coaster between the Nick I've come to know and lo—*like a lot*—and a person I haven't seen in months. I thought he was going to drag the rental car person over the counter. He'd surprised me before that with what he said at the restaurant in Dallas. I hadn't flirted with the bartender, but secretly, his jealousy had warmth blossoming in my chest. It told me more than he did that his feelings toward me were stronger too.

"Mer?" Nick's voice breaks through my thoughts, and I blink. Three sets of eyes watch me curiously.

"Sorry, what?"

"I'm gonna help Dad for a bit and then come back here and take you on that tour I was telling you about earlier." Is it me or does he emphasize the word *tour*? Did someone crank up the heat in this house? I nod and exhale a deep breath.

"Okay."

A smirk covers his whole face. The urge to kiss it off him burns brightly, but I refrain, both conscious of our audience and not sure how he would feel about a PDA like that in front of his parents. If they think anything is amiss, neither of them says anything.

After helping Beth with the dishes from breakfast and exploring baby photo albums of Nick, it's nearly lunchtime and neither John nor Nick have made a reappearance at the house.

"If I know John, he had several things on the list he needed help with." Beth hands me a cooler of sandwiches, chips, and a few sodas. "You'll probably find Nick closer to the barn. It's John's least favorite set of chores. Oh, here's John now."

Through the window, we see Nick's dad pull up in his old truck. Beth motions to the door, and I start my walk down the gravel path to the barn. Cool wind bites through the jacket Nick bought me for the trip. Shivering, I tighten my grip on the cooler, hoping to find him sooner rather than later. Preferably somewhere indoors and out of the wind. My Southern California blood is not thick enough for Nebraska in late fall.

As I get closer to the barn, I start to call for my wayward boyfriend. *Boyfriend?* "Don't let Nick hear you, Meredith," I mumble to myself. Taking a deep breath, I raise my voice. "Nick?"

Animals answer me, and I can't help but jump a little at the unfamiliar sounds. Blowing out a breath, I try again. "Nick?"

Turning the corner, my mouth goes bone dry. Nick has a hay bale hefted to one shoulder. His flannel from earlier is gone, and the white t-shirt he had on under it pulls across his chest, revealing muscles shadowed by white cotton. He is sex on a stick. Every farmer fantasy come to life. Wowsers. He drops the hay on a pile and smiles at me.

"Hey, sorry. Dad had a few things for me to do, but that's the last of it." He grabs the hem of his t-shirt to swipe at the sweat on his forehead. The muscles in his chest and stomach ripple and flex with the movement.

"A—aren't you cold?" Another shiver racks me as I ask the question. I can't tell if it's because of the cold or because of the way he looks. Maybe both?

Definitely both.

Barking out a laugh, he shakes his head. "No. But you are. Come on."

He grabs the cooler in one hand and laces our fingers together with the other to pull me into the dimly lit barn. There's a sweet smell of hay mixed with the scent of horses. We stop next to a ladder that goes through a hole in the floor above us.

"Up you go." He boosts me up several rungs and follows. The heat of his gaze on my ass makes the climb harder than it should be. Once at the top, there's a large door on the outside of the wall that's propped open on one side, but a small half circle of hay bales blocks most of the crisp air. A blanket covers the floor.

"What's this?" I ask as he climbs the last few rungs.

He walks to the blanket, brushes his hands against his jeans, and sits, patting the floor next to him. "Come sit. Let's picnic in style."

"Picnics usually involve summer." I shiver again, giving him a dubious look but dropping next to him as close as I can to absorb his body heat. "Or at least warm weather."

He chuckles and unwraps the sandwiches and chips. It's silent as we eat, and once we're done, he leans back against the hay, pulling me with him.

"Are you okay?" I hesitate to ask the question, to disrupt this moment of peace we seem to have found. It's the first time in over a week that he seems relaxed.

He shrugs. "It hasn't been too hard being back. Having you here helps."

His words create a warmth in the pit of my stomach. Eyes that match the color of the October sky outside catch mine and hold my gaze. They heat as his attention flicks to my lips.

"It does?" The heat spreads to my fingertips at his nod and the happiness that plays on his lips.

"It does." He confirms. Lowering his head, he brings his mouth millimeters from mine. "I promised you a tour earlier."

"You did." My lips brush his with my answer.

"The hayloft was the first stop on that excursion." His mouth curves in a half smile. "It's why I set up the hay bales like this."

I wrinkle my nose, not sure why. "It's only hay."

"This." He snakes an arm around my waist and aligns our

bodies so his erection presses against me through his jeans. "Is one of my favorite places on the farm."

"Why?"

"Privacy." With that word, his lips connect with mine, and he deepens the kiss instantly.

My fingers curl into his hair, and my nails scrape lightly against his scalp. The denied pleasure from earlier returns, fueling the ache in my belly. He rolls us until I straddle him, and his hands move to my ass to rub me against him. His erection presses against the center seam of my jeans, ratcheting that ache to a five-alarm blaze that burns through my blood.

My hips keep the rhythm for us and allow his hands to move and tangle with mine even while his tongue continues its assault on my mouth. I need more. More of him. More of this moment. I break the kiss and sit up, rolling my shoulders to shrug off my jacket until it tangles around my wrists.

Releasing his hands, I yank it the rest of the way off. When his hands reach up to cup my breasts through the thin fabric of my sweater, I arch into him. His thumbs graze the nipples that poke through my bra, and fireworks sizzle through my blood. My hips falter as my brain short-circuits, focused only on the fireworks that stem from his fingers on my breast.

My head falls back, pushing me further into his hands. "Oh god."

Sitting up, he drags kisses along my jawline. His hands fall to the hem of my sweater to tug the soft material up, tantalizing me as it drags along my skin. He only breaks the connection between his lips and my neck long enough to pull the sweater over my head before he dives back in. My fingers yank at his t-shirt with a desperation I can't explain. His chest hair springs against my palms as I smooth my hands up, relishing the feel of his erratic heartbeat. With a flick of his wrist, my bra disappears, and my breasts brush against the warmth of his chest. My nipples tighten further at the contact, and I pull him closer. Skin on skin, the heat ratchets higher between us.

Ordinarily, he would have sped up by now, but he keeps his movements slow, unhurried. Why? The urge to know what he's thinking intrudes on the pleasurable fog enveloping me. I open my mouth to ask, but the only sound that comes out is a moan as he lowers us down and settles into the cradle of my thighs. The friction of him through our jeans scatters any thought that isn't centered on the way he drags hot, open-mouthed kisses to my collarbone. Moving south, his sure fingers unsnap my jeans. The zipper is loud in the decadent silence between us. His fingers move to dip below the waistband of my panties and slide along my folds until he circles my clit. I cry out, my legs wrapping around him as the building climax tightens my muscles, and his fingers still.

"Shh." He warns. My teeth clamp down on my lower lip to bite back another cry for him to keep going. "I'm gonna need your help, baby."

I kick off my flats, and my hands fly clumsily to the waistband of my jeans and panties. I drag them both down far enough to kick them the rest of the way off while his fingers continue their delicious torture. His lips trail down the slope of my breasts until his tongue wraps around my nipple to suck it into his mouth, and the ache centers between my thighs only to be stoked higher by his touch.

My fingers weave through his hair and pull him closer. As if that's possible. *"Nick."* I lift my hips restlessly. "Fuck me."

His mouth leaves my nipple with a pop, goosebumps dotting along my body with the absence of his mouth once he stands and toes out of his boots. My attention locks on his fingers as they undo the fly on his jeans and drag them down until he can kick them away.

"You're so beautiful." His eyes trail an azure fire from the top of my head down to the tips of my toes while his words wrap around a heart that is already his. He pulls a foil packet from his jeans and laughs at my raised eyebrow. He definitely planned for this with that in his pocket. "Need all sorts of tools on a farm."

I giggle. "I bet."

With a rip of the foil, he rolls the condom onto his length and kneels back down. His hands trail along my legs to position them where he wants them, and desire thrums inches from where his dick stretches toward me. I lift my hips against him as he settles between my legs once more. Impatience has me digging my nails into his ass.

"Now," I order.

He pauses and his gaze searches mine. "Slow."

It's a groan, even as he shifts to line up the head of his dick and sinks slowly into me. The pressure, the pleasure, the emotion —it's all building to a point of white heat that threatens to consume me. His powerful gaze lights that fuse.

"*Nick.*" Closing my eyes only succeeds in blocking that one sense, but it heightens all the others, the feel of him stretching me is overwhelming, and I can feel the emotion building behind my eyes.

Sliding out until only his tip remains, he pauses a beat. My fingers tighten against his sides and urge him forward with a snap of his hips. The heat of his mouth claims mine, and his tongue mimics the retreat and thrust of his dick. He's driving me to the brink of insanity while he keeps my orgasm barely out of reach.

A calloused finger drags down my side, pulling goosebumps along my ribs. I writhe until he pauses in the spot that makes me squirm for a different reason. This time with his retreat, his finger dips to circle my clit again and again as his rhythm continues. Pleasure arcs from my core to my breasts. My toes curl, and my fingers tingle where they scramble for purchase on his arms. Finally, he speeds up, and the orgasm shimmers at the edges.

"*Please,*" I whimper.

His control snaps with my plea, and his hips piston against mine while his finger continues its maddening pattern.

"Come with me." His words are a groan in my ear as his finger teases the bundle of nerves and presses down.

White-hot pleasure bursts behind my eyes as my muscles tighten. My orgasm pulses around me, wave after wave swamping me. His mouth captures my cry moments before it can escape and draw any attention to what we're doing up here.

His pace picks up again until his own muscles tighten with the beginning of his orgasm. His lips break from mine and his head falls forward, his mouth close to my ear. "Oh fuck, Emmmmm."

The pleasure disappears like a flipped switch as what he says registers. I freeze even while he pulses inside me.

Emily.

He fucking called me Emily.

The best sex of my life and he calls out another woman's name. Holy shit. *Holy shit*. What do I do?

I don't know what to do. I can't think. Can't focus.

He pushes up, his breathing ragged, and brushes a kiss against my frozen lips. I'm paralyzed by his words. Worry creases his brow.

"Are you okay?" he asks.

He must have noticed the stiffness in my body.

Willing my tears to stay back, I attempt to ignore the look he's giving me that tells me way more than I want to know. Based on his face, the genuine concern in his eyes, he doesn't even know what he did.

Sadness drags icy fingers where warmth resided a few minutes earlier. A fissure opens in my heart. It's my own fault. I shake my head. "No."

"What? What happened? Did I hurt you? Did a piece of hay stick through the blanket? That's happened before—"

Just like that, his words add another layer of ice, and my heart cracks further. This feeling is my own issue. He hasn't changed his mind. This is only physical release with a friend. "You've done this before?"

He flushes and sits up, breaking our connection. "Well, yeah."

The cold air that rushes between us has nothing to do with how my insides cake in ice.

I don't need to ask with who. But I'm a masochist. "With Emily?"

He flinches when I say her name, and that one movement confirms my suspicions without saying a word. Standing, I make my way to my clothes and dress as quickly as I can. Two can play the silent game.

"You knew I wasn't a virgin when we met." His voice holds traces of anger and confusion once he finally succumbs to the awkward silence. "For Christ's sake, I was fucking engaged. I'm not sure why you're upset."

The laugh that bubbles up holds zero mirth. "I'm not upset by that. Of course I know you were engaged. And no, I'd say based on the amount of man-whoring you did, you were definitely not a virgin."

"Well, tell me how you really feel." He steps toward his clothes and starts to toss them on with sharp movements.

"I don't want to be put in a position of comparison. That's not fair."

"What does that even mean?" he asks.

"You're going to make me say it? Really?" Saying the words that are running through my head makes them real. More real than they are right now. I turn and step toward the ladder until his fingers wrap around my wrist to stop me.

"What the fuck? If this is some game, I'm fucking over it by now. Just tell me. What are you talking about?"

Facing him, I blow out a breath and count to ten as I try to rein in the emotions that swamp my body. "What am I talking about? God, Nick, are you serious? You brought me to the same place you used to hook up with your fiancée. That was the best sex of my life. Until…" The words lodge in my throat.

I don't want to say them out loud.

"Until what?" His face is a mix of confusion, concern, and anger. Who knew that was possible?

"You called her name." I swallow around the lump in my throat, and a burn sears through my stomach as I breathe through tears that I refuse to shed right now.

He rears back as my words slap him. "What?"

"You heard me."

"I did not. I didn't call out Em—" He breaks off on a swallow.

"So you can't say her name now, but you have no problem calling it out in the middle of sex?" I push.

"I didn't call out her name," he denies.

I can't help but stare at him. "Why would I lie about something like that?"

He opens his mouth to respond, only to close it when one doesn't come.

I take another step to the ladder, desperate to get some separation from him.

"Meredith." He moves closer to me, panic clear on his face.

Ever the masochist, I smile softly at him even while I take a step back. "I'm not leaving. Well, not leaving Nebraska."

"Where are you going?" he asks.

Shrugging, I tell him the truth. "I'm not sure. I just…I need some space."

"Fuck." He drags his hands through his hair while misery lines his face. "I'm sorry."

"I know." I won't say it's okay, but I know he didn't mean to. Sadly, it doesn't change anything, and the universe has now bitch slapped me back into reality. "I'll see you later."

When I step out of the barn, the cold wind hits me full force. I spin with no idea where I would even go—my choices in this new place are limited to the barn I walked out of and the house I'm not sure I want to walk into anymore.

But I promised Nick I wouldn't leave. I promised him I would go with him to his parents' party. I check the time on my phone and realize it's almost time to get ready.

Sighing, I walk back to the house and brush at the tears that won't stop. I don't hear anyone after I slowly open the door, and relief floods me. I get all the way to Nick's room without seeing either of his parents. It's a good thing since I don't know how to explain my tears, but I'm not strong enough to stop them right now.

Shower stuff in hand, I head for the bathroom in the hall and lock the door. My clothes smell like hay, and I strip them off and kick them as far away from me as I can. Steam fills the room, and I step into the warm spray, desperate to wash away the pain of the last few minutes. Under the hot spray, I lean my head against the tile while the water runs over my back and shoulders. Trying for some yoga breathing, my attempt to clear my head is pitiful and just leaves me exhausted in the shower. I can't stay here all night.

*Just a few more minutes.*

I'll start to move again in a minute. Leaning my head against the shower wall, I drift, only to startle when the curtain drags back and Nick steps in behind me.

"What are you doing in here?" I ask.

"I needed you." He wraps his arms around me and tugs me back against him until his head drops to my shoulder.

"I locked the door." I'm not sure what else to say.

"I picked the lock," he teases, sounding proud of himself.

"So I see." I turn back to the spray and try to step out of his arms, but they tighten, and his lips brush against my shoulder.

"I'm sorry." He kisses my other shoulder. "This place has me all mixed up."

It's no excuse, but I understand. Or, at least, I want to.

Deep down, I knew this weekend was going to be hard, especially given his behavior that led up to us leaving. I spin and wrap my arms around him as his heartbeat vibrates under my ear.

"I know."

"Are we okay?" The sound of anguish in his voice has me blinking away tears. I nod.

He needs me. I can be his friend.

*Friends don't shower together.*

The snarky voice has me sucking in a breath, but I push it down and will it away to concentrate on the steady rhythm of his heartbeat.

"We'll be okay," I assure him.

I'll make sure of it.

# CHAPTER 23

*MEREDITH*

*a*fter the emotionally charged shower, the silence in Nick's room is just as awkward. I don't know what to say, and he must not either. We're like two ghosts that get ready in tandem. It's a different experience from how we got ready to leave his condo yesterday, or even our playful banter from this morning.

The dress Derek helped me find for tonight is dreamy—the teal fabric floats around my knees, and the tan faux suede boots match the dress in a way that he convinced me looks amazing. I'm just glad the boots have a bit of a heel, otherwise I would look like a kid playing dress-up. Makeup bag in hand, I leave the room without saying anything to Nick. The gray blue dress shirt and charcoal dress pants he picked for tonight make the blue of his eyes pop.

I keep my makeup simple, neutral—a soft brown eyeshadow and pale gloss. At the last minute, I dab some of the gloss on my cheeks to add some color back into my face. I don't have time to straighten my hair like I'd planned, so instead, I scrunch some curl back into it and pull it back into a loose ponytail. Nodding, I give myself a little pep talk to hopefully remove the drawn look visible on my face.

"You're here with a sexy guy—a broken, sexy guy—but he's sweet. Clueless, but sweet. You can do this. You can be here for him."

Finished, I shut the light off and step back into the bedroom. Nick curses and whips the tie back off his shirt. He struggles, but finally it's on and straight, and he stands in front of his bedroom mirror. His tug at the tie and the expression on his face tell me how much he hates it, and I can't help but laugh at the picture he creates. Caleb's pout has nothing on Nick's.

"It's not going to kill you, you know," I say with a laugh.

He glances up in the mirror, and his eyes flare as they travel my body. "You look...Meredith, you look incredible."

My pulse jackhammers at the combination of his words and the expression on his face. Smiling, I step closer and yank on his tie. "Thank you. You're not so bad yourself."

He leans down, brushing a soft kiss against my lips while my traitorous heart picks up more steam. Ever since the hayloft, he's treated me like I'm made of glass.

"You ready?" His gaze searches mine, but I know what he's looking for. I shove my hurt from earlier down deep and paste a smile on my face.

"If you are." The next breath I take is filled with his cologne. The scent splits me in two—part of me is strengthened by the familiar smell while the other part of me wishes I was anywhere but here.

Taking my hand, he entwines our fingers, and we walk slowly downstairs to rush through the cold dusk. The glowing white tent beckons, and heaters have been set up around the perimeter. It's cozy in here as people mingle with Nick's parents and his sister and her family.

I see Caleb's platinum blond head chasing after another little boy close to his age. Samantha is with a group of teenage girls, and Kristen is reading a book by herself at a table while Cara and the guy who must be her husband dance nearby. It's idyllic. It makes me want to someday celebrate my fortieth wedding anniversary like this. Pain pricks with a question that surfaces— will I ever get to that point?

An hour into the party and Nick and I deserve Academy Awards, considering how well we act like everything is fine. It's not the time for me to dwell on it. He needs me. I've repeated that to myself over and over again, and the advice seems to be helping. But every time someone new walks into the tent, he tenses. It's the only reminder I have that he's not comfortable here. Despite the tell, he plays the perfect boyfriend—introducing me to friends he grew up with and his parents' neighbors. He jokes with his brother-in-law about raising a teenage daughter. I've lost count of the names of the people I've met, but everybody welcomes me with open arms.

I catch Cara steal her husband, Troy, and tug him in the direction of the dance floor. She gives Nick a pointed glare.

"You want to dance?" He squeezes my fingers with his invitation.

Other couples besides Cara and Troy are on the dance floor, taking advantage of the slow, romantic music. Nodding, I accept the hand he holds out to me. Once we reach the edge of the dance floor, he twirls me into his body and shifts us until my ear rests against his chest. The sound of his heartbeat relaxes me further while his cologne wraps around the two of us.

"How are you?" His question startles me enough that I lose my rhythm, but he covers my stumble.

Breathing deeply, I let it out while I consider his question. "I'm okay."

His lips brush my curls, and his arms tighten. "Are we?"

"Are we what? Okay?"

He nods.

"We're fine." I remember the last time we joked about the word fine and a pinprick of pain shoots through my heart. Are we okay? I'm not sure. It's not his fault I've started to fall for him. He's been honest all along about what our relationship is. "How are you?"

Based on how he's acted tonight, anyone else would assume he's nothing more than a successful local boy who made good. That he's dealt with being back home as if it's a regular occurrence rather than twelve years between instances. A few months ago, I wouldn't have known the mask for what it was. But with me, he dropped that facade so long ago, it's like it never existed.

"I–" His heart speeds under my cheek. "This is weird. Surreal."

"I can only imagine." My words are quiet, but he hears them.

"I *can't* imagine being here without you. Thank you, Mer." His words and the way he says my name create small pinpricks in my battered heart. But he doesn't realize that. My feelings are mine and I own them.

"You're welcome."

That dance isn't our last of the night. When we're not on the dance floor, his hand rests in the small of my back or our fingers are linked. I listen to him tell stories of his time in LA to anyone who asks. And *everyone* asks.

No one brings up the fact that he hasn't been home in twelve years. No one brings up Emily.

"Having a good time?" His lips press the spot below my ear.

I nod. I've also heard all sorts of stories about him as a kid and shared some style tips with Samantha and her friends, who all complimented my outfit. "I am."

"Good. Let's go dance some more."

Smiling, I let him lead me to the dance floor, but I'm not paying attention and run into his back as he freezes between two tables full of people.

"Everything okay?" I grip his hand and try to look around him to see where his attention seems riveted.

Two new people have come into the tent and appear to be the same age as Nick's parents. The woman's blonde hair is pulled up into a bun while the man's is obscured by a faded green hat that touts Willow River High School. "Nick?"

As if my hand suddenly burns, he drops it and shoves his hands into his pockets. But there are no words. He hasn't said anything. All the hurt, the anger, and the sadness I've pushed down come back to the surface. The rejection stings more than I would have thought from dropping my hand.

"Nick? Who is that?" My voice is quiet.

"Tha—" His voice cracks and he clears his throat. It's a painful sound. I reach out, but hesitate with inches between my hand and his arm. I don't know if he would welcome this touch from me or not. "That's Karen. And that's Graham. Michaels."

He says it like I know who they are. "Are they friends of your parents?"

"You could say that." His voice has lost all its life. "Considering I was engaged to their daughter."

My mouth drops open until I snap it shut. I hadn't asked him if Emily's family lived nearby.

"Did you know?" When he doesn't answer, I finally let my fingers land on his arm. He jumps. "Nick?"

He shakes his head, and his eyes don't leave the couple hugging his parents. "I'm sorry, what?"

"Did you know they were coming?" A heads-up would have been nice.

Memories are one thing. I can't even compete with those. How can I compete with flesh and blood people?

# CHAPTER 24

*NICK*

Fuck. Fuck. *FUCK.*

Cara had told me they weren't coming. Even after she said that, I thought they would show up any minute. Every time someone came into the tent, I braced myself to see them. Until I didn't think I had to. After several hours, I'd begun to think Cara was right, and I was safe.

Joke is on me, though.

"Nick?" Meredith's voice wavers behind me. It's muted like she's behind thick glass.

The guilt that has gnawed at me since she told me I called out Emily's name in the hayloft is replaced with shame. I forget about everything else as I stare at the two people who, despite twelve years passing since I've last seen them, are as familiar to me as my own parents.

A mixed wave of guilt and shame swamps me, made worse at the look on Meredith's face when I shrug away from her fingers that rest so cautiously on my arm.

I can't do this. My only plan is to retreat from the chaos of emotions that heads in my direction.

Spinning, I grip Meredith's wrist to yank her behind me while my body searches for any exit not close to the two people who look so much like Emily. It hurts to see them, but I can't look away. She'd had her dad's eyes and smile and her mom's hair. I slam my eyes shut and push through several groups of people, only vaguely aware of Meredith's apologies behind us.

It's only when the warm air of the tent gives way to the chilly, dark October night that I can breathe again. I continue across the yard while she scrambles to keep up with me in her heeled boots until I reach the safety of the barn. I can't go inside. Claustrophobia tightens around me like a noose and directs my feet to the back of the barn, away from everyone.

"Jesus. Stop." She jerks out of my grasp.

Regret settles in my stomach at the red print around her wrist barely visible in the muted glow from the light on the side of the barn. Her shiver doesn't help my state of mind. It's freezing, but I didn't stop to think about that or anything else. I needed to get away as fast as possible.

"What the fuck was that about?"

"I—I couldn't be there right now," I tell her. Locking my hands behind my neck, I stare up at a sky devoid of stars. It's too cloudy tonight to see anything. Of course, one of the few nights away from the big city and the universe still decides I don't deserve to see them.

"Why? Don't you want to say hi to Emily's parents?" she asks.

I flinch at her use of Emily's name, like it's commonplace, and my anger rises to the surface.

"You don't understand anything." Her face shows her confusion, but hurt quickly crowds it out. "Fuck. How could you? You're only a little girl."

Her face morphs again as anger burns away every other emotion that washed across her face. "So I'm too young to understand hurt and loss? I'm too young to understand that you could be upset?"

"How could you? How could you possibly understand any of this? Christ, what are you, twenty-two?" I motion in the direction of the tent.

"Old enough, obviously, to be your fuck buddy," she spits back at me.

"How else was I going to get through this weekend?" I needed her here. I need her to understand why she's here.

It's not about the sex.

Well, not completely.

Meredith steps back and stares at me in the silence.

"So I was only here as a distraction?" Brown eyes that blend with the shadows around us search mine. She's searching for something that just isn't there.

Her voice cracks on the last word and she spins away, her arms wrap around her body to try to block the wind as it whips behind the barn. But she can't ignore what I have to say. I *need* her to hear me.

"Why else would I have invited you?" She shrugs like that's an answer. Stalking over to her, I spin her back around and grab her gaze with mine. "Why did you think I invited you here, Meredith?"

"I—" She shakes her head and stops.

"You?" I prompt.

"What does it matter what I thought?" Her voice has gone quiet, and her attention bounces everywhere except me. "I'm here, aren't I?"

"Did you really think there was something more there? That what? I was bringing you home to meet the parents? For what? Some schmaltzy happy ending? This isn't a Hallmark movie, Meredith. You knew the score before we ever started fucking."

She wrenches herself away from me and holds out her hands to stop any advance I might make toward her. Not that I'm going to. My feet are firmly planted, paralyzed by every emotion that beats at my body.

"You're right. I knew what I was signing on for. If I didn't, you calling out Emily's name while we were fucking in the hayloft earlier was a message I received loud and fucking clear."

A swallow works its way down her throat. The fact that I can see it in the dark shows me how painful it must feel. My own throbs in sympathy.

I push that feeling and every other emotion back into the box they belong in, locking it and tossing the box into the dark corner of my mind. I should have never opened it. I know better.

"I just thought I was your friend too. And friends don't treat each other the way you're treating me. I'm not your dirty little secret, Nick." Her voice is thick with emotion.

"How naïve can you be? How fucking immature that you don't get how painful it is for me to see Emily's parents again." Pain is an all-consuming fire intent to destroy my body from the inside out, burning away every memory—good and bad—with the woman in front of me. Dredging up one that flickers in the flames, I use words I know she'll understand. "This was a mistake. Bringing you here was a mistake."

She nods and draws one shaky breath, followed by another. "You're right. This was a mistake."

She walks away from me quickly, back toward the house with her arms wrapped around her body.

Fine. Forget her.

Instead of following, I head in the opposite direction of both the house and the party. I've done my required socializing. Having roamed the fields for as many years as I did, the next field I find myself in is familiar, as is the one after that. Reality blurs with memories of distant laughter. Two kids chase each other in these fields, and the sounds of their happiness echo around me.

Finally, I approach a wooded area that borders a neighboring farm. The boundaries between the two are somewhere in the darker forest, but what I'm looking for is right near the clearing.

EM+NR.

I trace my finger around the rough heart carved crudely around our initials as my lips curve into a smile. I'd loved to tease Emily about her initials also being her nickname. *For now*, was always her response.

"FUCK!" My fist crashes into the tree below the carved heart. Pain radiates through my hand into my arm, and the cold seeps through my dress pants as I sink to the ground at the base of the tree.

Staring out into the darkness, I startle as an owl calls nearby, and I'm pulled from the blurs of thoughts that consume me. With the return of consciousness come the waves of remorse. They crash over me—not enough to drown me—but enough to make me despise myself more than I ever have. I drop my head to my hands, my accompanying groan loud and out of place in the quiet sounds of the night that surround me.

"Fuck."

What the hell did I do? Flashes burst through my brain, helpful reminders of all the poison I'd thrown at Meredith. I close my eyes as the pain that accompanies those memories makes me want to throw up.

I'd promised not to let her take the brunt of my emotions.

When I finally stand, my joints creak from the cold ground, and I dust the moisture and dirt from my pants. I keep walking in a different direction as I pass several other fields to approach the house from a different angle. My dress shoes are ruined by the time I step back onto the gravel driveway, and my stomach churns as I think about what I can say to apologize to Meredith. She didn't deserve the shit I spewed at her earlier.

Instead of being her friend, I'd used her as my personal verbal punching bag. The red mark on her wrist comes back to mind, and I realize it had been more than verbal. I'm debating on if I can kick my own ass or not when the crunch of gravel behind me joins a pair of headlights that light up the barn in the distance.

I stop and turn, unsure why someone would be coming out to the farm this late since the party would have broken up about an hour ago, if my watch is any indication.

Seeing my sister's van, I figure one of the kids forgot something and wave her down. She pulls alongside me and the window rolls down to show Cara glaring at me like the time I let it slip that she had a crush on Danny Perry in junior high.

"Um, hey?"

"Get in." It's the no-nonsense mom voice that moves my ass to the passenger seat of her car.

Not the fear that even at thirty-five, she could still probably kick my ass.

I barely get the door closed when the car starts to roll forward again. She doesn't say anything else, and I sit in silence since I value my life and my curiosity to find out what has her panties twisted will likely get me killed. I use the quiet to keep thinking about my apology. This awful day had started out with so much promise.

Bounding out of the car as it pulls up to the house, I call a "thanks for ride" to Cara and step inside. I take the stairs two at a time up to my room, expecting to find Meredith. Cold silence greets me.

"Meredith?" I turn and knock on the bathroom door in the hall. Empty.

Back downstairs, I check the living room and the kitchen, finally retracing my steps to the entryway. I toss on a coat—fuck, it's cold out here—and run to the barn. I'm breathless by the time I yank open the door.

"Meredith?"

Animals startle but shuffle back to their disturbed sleep. I jog back over to the tent and poke my head in, finding Mom talking to a woman I don't recognize.

"Mom." She glances over and excuses herself while the woman keeps clearing tables. "You seen Meredith?"

"She's not with you?" I shake my head, and she shrugs. "The last time I saw her was when you two lit out of here like your behind was on fire."

She gives me a pointed look and I feel the heat of a blush in my cheeks.

"We weren't doing anything like *that*," I defend.

If only that had been why we disappeared.

"Is she back at the house?" Mom's concern wrinkles her forehead, and I squeeze her arm in comfort.

"She must be. I may have just missed her. I'll go back and check again."

"Okay. I'll be up soon. I'm almost done here."

Waving, I head back to the house and find Cara on the porch steps.

"Were you waiting for me?"

She nods. "You took off before I could tell you."

"Tell me what?" I move my legs in place, anxious to keep searching for Meredith.

"That you're a fucking moron." I stop fidgeting, and my eyebrows climb at her use of an f-bomb.

"What?" That distracts me from my need to find Meredith.

"You. Are. A. Moron." She says it slowly like she's lecturing a child.

"I heard you the first time," I growl through gritted teeth. "I don't know why you think that, but I don't have time for this shit. I need to go find Meredith."

"She's not here." Her voice is resigned, final. Disappointed.

"What do you mean she's not here?" Ignoring Cara, who opens her mouth to respond, I bound back upstairs. Meredith's suitcase is missing. What the fuck?

Cara is waiting for me when I show up in the kitchen, more confused than ever.

"Well, where the fuck is she?" I'm tired of this game.

"Shh." Her glare shoots blue fire at me, and I only barely remember Dad would have been in bed for a while now. Morning comes earlier for him than anyone else.

"Where did she go? Is she at your house?" I'm already headed for the door, not bothering to wait for her answer.

"She's at the airport."

Spinning, my vision goes sideways enough that I reach out for the counter. "Airport? Why is she at the airport?"

The glare she gives me asks if I'm as stupid as I sound. "She's there because I took her."

"Why did you take her to the airport?"

"Are you serious right now?" Her hands go to her hips as she stares me down.

I squirm under her scrutiny and attempt to defend myself. "I was coming back to apologize."

"Apologize for what exactly?" But it's the look on her face that gets me.

It's the same one Mom used to get when she already knew the answer to the question she was asking and was giving me the chance to confess.

"I—" Dragging a hand through my hair, I sit in one of the kitchen chairs and stare at my destroyed shoes. "I said some pretty awful shit to her."

"Oh yeah, I know," she scoffs.

"She told you?" I glance up sharply. I'm not sure how I feel that Meredith tattled on me to my sister.

"No. I fucking heard you, moron. I saw you bolt from the tent right before I noticed Graham and Karen. I came after you to make sure you were okay." Her voice is brittle and cold. "Imagine my surprise when I barely made it to the barn in time to hear you call her a mistake."

Shit. Wincing, I open my mouth, but nothing comes out. I'd forgotten I'd said that.

It hits me then. It's for the best that Meredith left. Whatever is —was—between us was temporary and selfish on my part. Hell, even our friendship was tenuous at best. It's better she finds that out now before I fuck it up worse.

"Thanks for giving her a ride." Christ, I'm exhausted. Tired and sore. I shuffle to the stairs to start my climb back up. "Tell Mom for me that Meredith left?"

"That's all you have to say?" Her shock barely registers.

"She was worried about her when I was looking for her."

"Nick."

I ignore her calling my name until she stops. My bedroom still smells like an orchard in summer once I close the door.

Cara's right. I'm a fucking moron. Too bad I learned that lesson too late.

# CHAPTER 25

*MEREDITH*

**W**alking away from Nick, my ears strain, and I wait for him to call me back. It hits me halfway to the house. He isn't going to. It's that realization that crumbles the pretend walls around my heart.

Once they crumble, tears run unchecked down my face. Tears of anger and frustration. Tears of hurt. Yet again, I'm not good enough for the person I chose. I'm immature. I'm impulsive. I'm a baby. I don't measure up to what they want or what they had. Am I ever going to learn?

"Meredith." A voice calls out to me, but not the one I want to hear. "Meredith, wait up."

Cara runs up behind me, stopping me on the porch. I swipe at my cheeks and try to hide my hurt, but I know I don't manage to do that when she pulls me in for a hug.

"Oh, sweetie." The pity in her voice is almost my undoing.

"It's okay." I don't sound okay, but instead attempt to fake it 'til I make it. "I'm fine. It's fine. I—I need to get out of here. Do you know if Uber can get me to the airport?"

I step out of her embrace, and she follows me up to Nick's room, where I left my phone. My bag is next, and I toss the few items I had around the room into it.

"My brother is an idiot." Her pity-filled gaze follows me from her perch against the doorframe. I shrug in an attempt to appear more nonchalant than I feel.

"We were always temporary. Scratching an itch. FWB. Friends with benefits." I clarify to answer the question on her face.

"If that was the understanding, why are you moving like your feet are on fire?" She's quick to call me on my lies. Just like her brother.

"I just—" I cough and try to clear the tears that threaten to choke me. "We were friends, I thought."

Based on what Nick said, apparently, I was wrong about that too. She nods in sympathy but doesn't say anything else while she watches me gather my few belongings. If only I could erase Nick from my heart as quickly as I erased my presence from his room.

"For what it's worth, I haven't seen him as happy as he was with you in a long time," she sighs. "I really do think he cares about you."

I don't believe her, but I don't contradict her either. I also don't stop the tears that make their way down my face as I tap my phone to order a car.

"Uber or Lyft?" I ask, my voice thick.

"Neither." I'm about to protest—I can't stay here anymore—but stop as she continues. "Come on, I'll give you a ride."

I shake my phone. "No, that's okay. I don't want to take you away from the party."

She waves away my protest. "It's fine. Troy can use Mom's car to get the kids home. I'll text him."

Once her text is sent, she ushers me to her van. There's not much to say on the hour-long car ride to the airport, and I'm grateful for the ability to not have to pretend right now. Instead, she tells me to put the radio on a station I like. Finding one with pop music, I settle back in my seat and stare out the window as the mile markers tick by.

It isn't until she stops in the passenger drop-off zone that she clears her throat to speak. "Do you want me to say anything to him?"

I shake my head, the curve of my lips a sad shadow of the way I normally feel. "There's not much left to say."

Her forehead wrinkles with her frown. "I'm sorry. Want me to smack him around for you when I get back?"

My lips twist into a bigger smile at the image her words conjure. "No. Don't do that." I reach over and give her a quick hug. She was my rescuer tonight. "It was nice to meet you, Cara. Please thank your mom and dad for me and tell them I'm sorry I had to leave so soon."

"I will. Take care of yourself, Meredith."

I wave, and her taillights disappear while exhaustion settles over me like a weighted blanket.

"Come on, Meredith, let's go see about getting a ticket." Steeling my shoulders, I head to the counter of the airline we flew out here with, hopeful they have a flight that leaves soon.

As luck would have it, there's a flight from Grand Island, Nebraska to Denver with a flight from Denver to LA in the morning. I don't bother to tell the airline employees about the other ticket in my name—the one Nick bought for me. I just plunk down my credit card for a new ticket. Once through security, I settle into a seat near the gate and wait for the flight to board.

Curious, I check for hotels near the airport in Denver for the night. Holy shit! $400 for one night at the hotel connected to the airport? That's insane. Scrolling, I finally give up and resign myself to an airport sleepover at the terminal to make sure I won't miss my flight.

A couple sits down in the row in front of me, kissing and cuddling until an announcement asks for Mr. and Mrs. Springer to come to the podium. I don't mean to eavesdrop but, sitting so close, I overhear the airline upgrading the two of them to first-class for their honeymoon. How is it that they look like they're twelve and married? They're babies.

*You're just a little girl.*

The memory of Nick's words slices sharply against my heart, and my stomach cramps at the expression on his face as he'd flung those at me. Breathing through the cramp, I flex my fingers against my thigh until it recedes.

The tear that tracks down my face makes me angry. Yet again, I was good enough to sleep with, but not good enough for anything else. This is Daniel all over again. But worse. So much worse. I had thought I was in love with Daniel. But those feelings pale in comparison to the ones I have for Nick.

What's wrong with me? Why do I constantly have to fall for guys who don't return my feelings? Why do I pick the wrong guys to give my heart to? Am I ever going to find a love like Jax and Charlie's? Maybe it's pointless to search for something that doesn't seem to exist for me. Maybe I met my soulmate in New York and passed by him and didn't know it.

The announcement to board comes over the loudspeaker, and I stand as the questions circle. It's only once I'm seated in the plane as it taxis down the runway that I let my heart shatter completely.

He didn't come for me.

✱✱✱

By the time the Uber pulls up to Jax and Charlie's the next morning, I've managed about twelve minutes of sleep and sipped on black coffee that could substitute as roofing tar until my stomach rebelled. The LA sunshine is too bright, too *happy*, too everything. Even my dark sunglasses aren't enough to block out the bright light that finds all the scars for my thoughts to poke at.

"Mer? What are you doing here?" Charlie's shock is evident when she sees me and urges me into the house. She grabs my suitcase from my numb fingers and sets it by the stairs.

I'd come here from the airport since I told Mom I'd be gone through the weekend. I don't want to show up early and have her question the truth out of me. I need time to not think for a while. If I could have afforded a hotel on my credit card, I would have done that. Too bad another charge would have inspired a stroke. I would have gone to Derek's, but he went home to Louisiana to visit his family. So here it is.

"Can I stay here for a few days?" My voice breaks, and she wraps me in a hug.

"Of course. What happened? What's wrong?"

"I'm an idiot." With those words, I burst into tears and let her lead me to the couch.

"Mer? What's wrong?" Jax comes down the stairs and stops in the doorway. McKenna is wrapped in a sling-like contraption slung around his shoulders and her feet kick happily.

Realistically, I know that nothing physically happens to the heart once it gets broken. But when it throbs painfully in my chest, I rub at the ache like I can somehow get rid of it.

"I'm an idiot." Sniffling, I wipe at my streaming eyes.

"Did something happen with Nick?" Charlie asks quietly.

My focus swings from Jax to her.

"We figured it out shortly after you two left," he explains as he sits next to Charlie.

"You did?" I *am* an idiot. Of course they did.

"Why didn't either of you say something to us?" Her voice is soft and only makes me cry harder.

"We—we—we—" I can't get anything else out for several minutes. Charlie comes and sits next to me to wrap an arm around my shoulders. "We agreed. We were temporary. We didn't want to disrupt your friendship with either of us."

"Either of us?" Jax stands, and the image of him pacing while he cracks his knuckles with a baby strapped to his chest is almost comical. "There's no choice to make. Mer, we choose you. Since you're here crying, I can only imagine that Nick said or did something to hurt you. He can go to hell."

"No." I shake my head. "He needs your friendship too. Promise me." Jax opens his mouth, but I stand up and repeat my demand. "I'll leave right now unless you promise me, Jax."

"Fu—" Jax shoots a glance to Charlie while he grips the back of his neck. "Fudge."

"Promise me."

"Okay, all right. Fine. I promise."

Charlie rolls her eyes at him and pulls me to sit back down beside her. "So you were together—even if it was temporary. What happened?"

"I can't compete with a ghost." It's the only explanation I have.

"Emily?" Jax asks. The surprise must show on my face because he continues. "Nick told me."

I nod. "Partially."

"There's more?"

Huffing out a laugh, I nod again. "I have the worst taste in guys on the planet. Probably in the universe. I'm never enough. For Daniel. Or for Nick."

"What do you mean by that?" Charlie asks.

"I need to start at the beginning. Let's start with Daniel."

# CHAPTER 26

*NICK*

When I step onto the porch, the sun is on the rise and the air is cool and still around me. I finally gave up the charade of sleep after several hours. Lying in a bed that had smelled like Meredith meant that every word I said to her, every selfish decision I had made in dragging her to Nebraska to help distract *me*, had played over and over in my head. It was like an earworm of a song stuck on repeat, and the refrain forced me up far earlier than normal.

Frost has settled over everything as far as the eye can see, encasing life in a layer of ice that sparkles in the early light while my breath puffs out in front of me. Zipping up my jacket, I start to walk a path that twelve years ago was familiar enough I could walk it in my sleep. I think I did at least once or twice. It was the only explanation I had from coming to and not knowing how I got where I was.

After getting the phone call from Mom about Emily and driving home like a bat out of hell, I hadn't been able to sit behind the wheel of a vehicle for weeks. The only way I could get to the cemetery was to walk, since I didn't want to ask anyone for a ride and have to explain my reluctance to drive.

Those first few weeks, I had walked from the farm to the cemetery several times a day. In that month I was home, I must have walked the three miles over a hundred times. But today feels different. If anyone spotted me along the main road, they'd assume I was a stranded motorist. But this early in the morning, the only company I have are my own thoughts.

The gates don't seem as big as they do in my memory. The cemetery is peaceful while the frost evaporates in ribbons of mist as the temperature warms up.

Emily's headstone is near the rest of her family—mostly grandparents and great-grandparents. A relative who had died in childhood based on the dates on the headstone. Hers is the next shortest timeframe. All the headstones are overgrown, and flowers left the last time someone was here disintegrate as I clear the brush away. Dropping to my knees, I don't feel the cold that seeps through my jeans.

"Hey there, Em." A ball of guilt lodges in my throat. "I'm sorry I haven't been here in a while. If you could, I'm sure you'd kick my ass for staying away as long as I have."

My lips lift my frozen cheeks as I imagine Emily nodding her head emphatically, arms crossed over her chest. She never let me get away with anything, before or after we started dating, often playing my conscience and keeping my ass out of more trouble than I could have imagined.

My smile fades as I continue. "I—I couldn't. Once I left, I was afraid to come back, to have to relive the pain I left behind. Not that you didn't come with me to LA. Just not in the way we planned."

I'd imagined beach walks at sunset, showing her all the places I had discovered while I fought to get myself signed. She had told me she wanted to go to Disneyland when she first got there. I'd laughed but agreed only to make her promise I didn't have to wear mouse ears. We both knew I was going to wear them anyway.

"Mom and Dad just celebrated forty years together. Forty. Can you believe it? That's a lifetime. Would that have been us? If you were still here? We'd probably have at least one kid by now. Maybe more."

She had wanted a big family since she was an only child.

"There was a big party last night. Your folks showed up. I, uh, I brought someone here with me. A friend... I think. Or at least she was." After last night, I wouldn't be surprised if she hates me. "I didn't want to come alone. And she—Meredith—keeps away those dreams. The ones I told you about. I don't have them much anymore, but they scare the shit out of me. But with her, they're gone."

"I think you'd like her. She's sassy as fuck and calls me on my shit like you used to. She makes me laugh. She's... she's a reminder of what it's like to live my life versus surviving it." Running my hands through my hair, I look up and blow out a breath as I stare at the bare branches of a tree overhead. "Fuck. I fucked up, babe. I hurt her. You'd definitely kick my ass for the shit I said."

"I thought I'd find you out here."

Startled, I drop my face down, and my eyes land on Graham as he makes his way down the cemetery path.

Standing, I reach out to shake his hand. "Graham."

He clasps my hand but also pulls me in for a hug, slapping me on the back hard enough that I wince. "How ya doin', Nicky?"

I shrug. It's as noncommittal an answer as I can think of since I probably can't say "I feel like shit for being an asshole."

"I'm all right, Graham. You and Karen doing okay?"

He waves off my question and tugs on the bill of the faded cap he's had since he coached the football team at the high school before Emily and I graduated. I've only seen him without it one time since—Emily's funeral.

"You're out here early." He studies me—warning me against any more bullshit—with his comment.

"What do you mean?"

"Trying to get here early enough to avoid running into us later?"

"What? Of course not." That hadn't originally been my intent, but I definitely would have appreciated avoiding the awkwardness of this conversation.

He gives me a look of disbelief but doesn't call me on my bullshit. "You took off so fast last night, we didn't get the chance to catch up."

"Sorry about that. I—" I start to give him an excuse, but he keeps talking.

"Who was that pretty young woman with you last night?" The weight of his gaze makes me want to look anywhere but at him. I settle for staring at the etched words in Emily's headstone.

*Gone too soon.*

"She's...she's only a friend." The words stick in my throat, and the lie tastes bitter on my tongue.

"Boy, I've known you since you and Em were running barefoot through the cornfields and driving your mamas both nuts. That's the second time you've lied to me this morning. How about you take a turn with the truth?"

Well, shit.

Shame heats my face when he calls me out. "She's...it's complicated. She's not Emily."

He scoffs. "No one is saying she has to be, right?" As I shake my head, he continues. "Your new young lady—"

"Meredith," I supply.

"Meredith doesn't have to be Emily. She shouldn't try to be. She just needs to be herself."

I'd said something similar to her. To be herself. That someone would be lucky enough to be with her exactly as she was. But then I'd told her she was too immature, too young to understand. Bile burns up my throat as I recall her face as I tossed those words at her.

"Based on the look on your face, I'm guessing you did something stupid that you need to make right." I open my mouth to explain, but he waves me off again. "I don't need to know the particulars. But I will say that Emily would want you to be happy. She was always such a happy, positive light in this world. She'd want us all to be happy. It's why Karen and I moved away. We needed a fresh start to help us heal."

"I-I heard you'd moved." Cara had said so, had used that as her reason for why they weren't coming last night.

"Five years ago or so, now," he sighs.

"Did it help?"

He shrugs. "We think so. We're happy in Grand Island. Karen volunteers with the church and I have a poker game every Thursday night where a bunch of us sit around and smoke cigars and lose money at Texas Hold 'Em." The picture he paints of his new life provides a sense of relief, of happiness. "Not a day goes by that we don't think about Emily. About the hand the universe dealt that took our only child from us way too soon. But she would hate for us to honor her memory with tears."

The burn in my nose tells me those tears are closer than I want to admit. Even Graham's eyes are rimmed in red.

"I'm sorry—" I start, and he interrupts me again.

"Nicky, the accident wasn't your fault. Shit, you were thousands of miles away when it happened. Accidents are called accidents for a reason. They can't be planned for. But don't put your life on hold because you're afraid to open back up."

"I'm not afraid of—" When he shoots me with another glare, I swallow the lie. "I don't want to forget her."

I motion to the headstone at our feet.

He claps a hand on my shoulder. "You won't. We'll always

have her in here." His other hand motions to our hearts. "And don't avoid us next time you see us. We'd love to hear all about your life in LA."

I shrug. "It's not been much of a life."

He laughs. "Well, I guess it's time to fix that, isn't it?"

He makes it sound simple. Easy. But I'm not so sure.

✱✱✱

Two days after Meredith left Nebraska, I'm back in California. I knock on her door and hope like hell she'll actually answer since it's impossible to get her to respond to a text or phone call. Not that I blame her.

"Meredith?" Knocking again, I try to see through the front window. Everything appears dark. "Meredith, you there?"

"Nick?" The voice behind me—Meredith's mom, Val—stops me mid-knock. I spin as guilt pushes at my tongue to confess everything. Shame keeps me quiet. "What are you doing here? Do you and Meredith have more planning to do?"

"Planning?" It hits me. Wedding planning. That would have been the only reason Val would think why I was looking for Meredith. "Oh, the wedding. No, um, I had a question and I tried calling and texting her, but she hasn't answered."

"Strange. I know she has service. She texted me yesterday to let me know she was having a great time and might extend her trip." Thoughts stop like a record scratch in my brain.

What? Where the fuck did she go? Great time? What the fuck?

"Do you know where she happened to go?" My conscience is lodged in a thick ball in my throat and makes swallowing a herculean feat.

"She mentioned something about a spa trip with Derek." She shrugs. "But I'm not sure where exactly."

Fuck. Dead end. "Okay, thanks."

"Do you want me to tell her you're looking for her if I hear from her again?" Her offer makes my guilt feel one hundred times worse.

"No." My voice comes out harsher than intended, and I soften my tone. "That's okay. It's not urgent. I'll catch her when she's back."

She looks at me curiously but smiles and waves goodbye before she walks back into the main house.

Shoulders slumping, I head back to my car. I don't drive away right away as my thoughts whirl with different options of where she might be. No way would she have left Nebraska and immediately headed on another trip. But maybe she's staying with Derek?

Damn it. I don't have Derek's contact info. But Jax does.

With that light bulb, I drive the few minutes to his place without bothering to call. I practically bolt from my car once I hit his driveway and only slow down enough to ring the doorbell after the code Jax had given me doesn't work. I must have keyed it in wrong, but I don't have the patience to try it again.

In my haste, I don't bother to think through any other reason why my code won't work and definitely don't expect the right hook that comes at me as soon as the door opens.

"FUCK." Grabbing my eye, I double over as pain radiates through my skull. I want to laugh when I hear Jax's voice echo my same exclamation as he holds his hand, but pain sings through my body. Dumbass better not have broken anything—on me or him. "What the fuck was that for?"

One hand clamped over my throbbing eye, I use my other to focus on him. Anger radiates from him in red hot waves. His jaw is locked and, if looks could kill, I'd be a pile of ash on his driveway by now.

"You're going to fucking ask me that, asshole?" Well, I'm fairly confident he's either talked to Meredith, or he knows where she is.

"Is Meredith here?" Straightforward is best right now. Something tells me anything else will likely get me punched in the face again.

His nostrils flare. "Like I would fucking tell you that."

"Jax—"

"Meredith made me promise that I'd still be your friend, but she didn't make me promise I wouldn't deck you, asshole. I'm so fucking pissed at you. You lied to me," he grits out.

"What? When?"

"The studio, remember? If I had known it was Meredith you were talking about—that you were screwing around with her— I'd have told you then not to be a dick. Any other girl in LA, and you fucked with her. You made her fucking cry."

"Jax, I'm sorry. I—"

"Save it. I don't want to hear it. I'm still your friend—something you should be on your knees grateful for to Meredith for making me promise that shit. But I'm not helping you with her. And we're not talking about this." He waves a hand in between us.

She made him promise to stay my friend? If it's possible, I feel even worse than I did before, and I don't mean the burn in my eye as it currently swells shut.

"Please. I just want to talk to her." Fuck. The whine in my voice is obvious, even to me.

He stands firm at the door. "She doesn't want to talk to you."

"She'll talk to me if I'm here." Hopefully. Maybe.

"Has she answered any of your calls or texts so far?" His eyebrow lifts with his question. He already knows the answer.

"Well, no. But—"

"If she wanted to talk to you, she'd have answered. Even if it was to tell you to go fuck yourself." How much did he toss in the swear jar with all the f-bombs he's dropping? The errant thought comes and goes as he steps forward and pulls the door mostly shut. "Listen, against my better judgment, I'm going to give you some advice because you look like shit."

"That would be the black eye you just gave me," I snark. When he glares at me, I motion for him to continue. "Okay."

"Don't try to talk to her before she's ready. I did with Charlotte. And it backfired into a bigger mess."

Nodding, I remember the damage control of said mess. "I only want to apologize."

He shakes his head. "She won't hear it now."

"I fucked up."

He snorts. "Yeah, you did."

"Thanks. Dick." He grins at my attempt to joke. "How much did she tell you?"

The question sobers him. "Enough. She told us about Daniel too. If I ever see that asshole, he's next on my list to punch." He grimaces as his hand clenches into a fist.

Surprise has me reeling. She really did tell them a lot if she told them about Daniel. I motion to his hand. "Anything broken?"

He shakes it out. "I don't think so."

"You kind of need it for the next album. Even if you do go back to Reverb."

"Fuck that. I'm not going back to Reverb. But." He nods toward the house. "It might be a good idea for us to find somewhere else to work for now."

I nod. I've already hurt Meredith enough. The last thing I want to do is rub salt in those wounds.

## CHAPTER 27

*MEREDITH*

"It's Halloween." Derek doesn't even say hello as he barges into my house almost two weeks after my failed trip to Nebraska.

"Is it?" I double-check the date on my phone. Holy shit, he's right.

Time has blurred in a weird warp.

One second, I'm hiding behind Jax's front door as I eavesdrop on Nick as he tells Jax he's sorry—I both relish and regret that Jax punched him—and the next, I'm back home and pretending I was away on some fantastic spa weekend with Derek and didn't just get my heart broken.

It helped once Garrett called and offered me the assistant choreographer job. I even met Claire, the new director who works at Arabesque. She told me she could read the heartbreak all over me. When I asked her how, she said we were kindred spirits. I haven't gotten the chance to ask her about that since she's been on location for a video, but work gives me something I need—an excuse to disappear for hours and not have to keep up a facade of being my "normal" self. Jax and Charlie know the truth. So does Derek. At some point I'll come clean to Mom and Dad, but I'm not there yet.

"You're going out." Derek flops on the couch next to me, snagging the remote to stop my binge-watching marathon of *Say Yes to the Dress*. "Correction. We're going out."

"Derek," I whine. "Look at me. I'm nowhere near ready to go anywhere. I don't want to. I don't feel like it."

I like my plan of obsessively watching brides pick overpriced dresses while I stuff my face with popcorn. I bet Mom has Halloween candy I can steal too. Maybe one of my excuses will stick. But I underestimate the powers of persistence from one of my best friends.

"A, that's what I'm here for. B, you may not want to, but it'll be good for you, and C, see the response to part B."

Standing, he tugs me off the couch and steers me toward my bedroom and bathroom. Shoving me into the bathroom, he demands I shower while he goes in search of something for me to wear. I'm embarrassed to admit I don't remember the last time I showered, but the hot water feels fantastic, and I lean my head back as I let the spray massage the exhaustion from my scalp and neck.

"Wash your hair!" His voice booms through the door.

"Okay, okay." Sheesh, it's like he knows he has to tell me what to do all of a sudden. So much for hiding out in my shower until he leaves. I quickly finish, and with a cinch of my robe, shuffle into my bedroom. It appears as though Hurricane Derek has made an appearance—clothes are scattered everywhere.

"What did you do? Pull out every dress I own?" I spy the red dress and the black dress I've worn around Nick, and my heart twists painfully in my chest.

Definitely not those. Anything but those.

"Your closet is insane," he responds. "Everything is way too organized, freak. I couldn't work my magic like that."

"This is going to take me forever to fix." I motion to the clothes everywhere.

He waves me off. "I'll help you fix it later. Look what I found!"

He's like a kid in a toy store as he holds up the dress I wore last Halloween. It's a black dress with purple octopus tentacles stenciled around the skirt. I'd found it last year when Derek and I decided to do costumes from *The Little Mermaid.* He was Ariel and I was Ursula.

"It won't make sense this year." I point at him. "And you're not dressed up either."

He shrugs and motions to his all-black outfit. "I have a mask in the car. I'm going for a version of *Phantom of the Opera.*"

"I don't even have the makeup for this anymore."

He arches a sculpted eyebrow at me. "Who are you saying this to exactly?"

In less than five minutes, I'm in the dress, my Steve Madden heels laced up my legs, as I sit on a stool in my kitchen. True to his word, he creates an Ursula look with the makeup I have on hand—purple and blue shadows, dark eyeliner, and a dark purple lip. As soon as the makeup is set, he runs to grab my hair dryer and straightening brush. When he puts them down, all my thick curls lie straight to the middle of my back.

"Come on, Mer, get excited for me. It'll be fun." He reaches over to wrap me in a bear hug while we wait for the Lyft.

"I'm trying." I am. Really.

From our vantage point in front of the house, Halloween decorations dot the lawns and houses while the last few trick or treaters hit up the houses at the end of their route. I can hear the spooky music from the house next door where my parents went for a Halloween party. Halloween used to be my favorite holiday of the year. Dressing up in fun costumes, candy as a kid, parties as an adult. What was not to like? Today just feels…hollow.

My phone buzzes and I tense, only relaxing when I remember that I blocked Nick's number shortly after I came home.

Like a masochist, I'd left it on to read through all his texts and listen to his voicemails those first few days at Jax and Charlie's. But I had to move on, and I couldn't do that with his words still seeping through the cracks.

I'd deal with seeing him again once I saw him at the wedding.

The text is a picture of Jax, Charlie, and McKenna.

"Oh my god, that's adorable." I show Derek the picture of Charlie as Princess Jasmine, Jax dressed as Aladdin and McKenna as Abu.

"I can't believe she got him to dress up," he complains.

Jax had never dressed up when we asked him to, and it frustrated Derek, who had lots of ideas for costume trios.

"Charlie asked him." I shrug. "If she asked him to shave his head, he probably would."

He nods as the car pulls up. "Very true."

I shouldn't be surprised that we arrive at Eclipse, but I didn't ask. Their Halloween parties are the best and I should have known. So what if this place is now tied up in memories of Nick?

Squaring my shoulders after I get out of the car, I turn back to Derek. "We're not in Kansas anymore, Toto."

He settles his mask on his face, and we comment on all the costumes that wait by the door.

"Let's go have some fun." He tugs me forward and nods at the bouncer. I love that he knows people like this since we're inside a few minutes later.

"Drink?" he yells over the music.

"Water?"

He glances at me with a raised eyebrow, but we head to the bar to get him a drink. I take a sip of my cold water, and my attention shifts to the people who crowd the dance floor. Once he tosses back his shot, I get yanked into the chaos.

"Let's dance, baby girl." He winks and hauls me behind him.

It's not long before I get lost in the music, moving with him as songs merge from one to another. I'm about ready for a break when Derek gets asked to dance by a hot AF Prince Charming he's had his eye on for most of the night.

I motion that I'm headed to the bar, and nab the first open stool I see while he gets his groove on. The bartenders seem overwhelmed by tonight's crowd.

"Happy Halloween." The voice belongs to a face with a mustache, but the rest of the man is covered in his costume.

"Happy Halloween," I say hesitantly.

He smiles. "Think the Sea Witch Ursula would let the Dread Pirate Roberts buy her a drink?"

Of course. That's why his costume seemed familiar.

"I love *The Princess Bride*. Sure. Water?" I ask.

"As you wish." The fact that he stays in character has delight tilting my lips.

He snags the bartender's attention and orders a water for me and a beer for himself.

"Should I call you Ursula tonight?" One side of his mouth kicks up as he hands me my drink.

I laugh. "No. I'm Meredith."

He takes my hand in his to bring it to his lips. "Pleasure, beautiful Meredith. I'm James."

He is a nice guy. Not like the guys who normally pick up girls in clubs and definitely not the type of guy who I've encountered here in the past.

"Is Halloween in LA always so...extra?" He motions to the crowd around us, and I smile.

"It is," I confirm.

"Are you from here?" He takes a sip from his beer.

I nod. "Born and raised. Obviously you're not?"

"No. I recently moved here from San Antonio."

"What's that like?" I ask.

"Different from here. More...tame," he finishes with a laugh.

"What brings you to LA?"

"A job. I graduated college last year, and an engineering firm here offered me a job." He's a chemical engineer, and he starts to explain what he does, but it's hard to follow. He must see the dazed look on my face because he stops with a shrug. "Sorry. I didn't mean to geek out."

I smile. "Don't worry about it. I wish I understood more about that."

"What about you?" he asks. "What do you do?"

"I'm an assistant choreographer for a production company that specializes in music videos."

"That's a thing?" His eyes widen behind his mask.

"Yep."

"How did you land a job like that?"

"I was a dancer on a few tours before I choreographed the last one I was on."

"Anyone I'd know?" This guy seems too good to be true. He's easy to talk to and seems genuinely interested in what I have to say.

"Jax Bryant?"

"Seriously?"

I nod. "He's from Texas too. Austin."

I don't share that I've known Jax since I was in diapers or that I've been to Austin half a dozen times through the years.

"What's your favorite place to visit?"

His question makes me stop and think. "Depends. If I want nightlife, New York and Nashville are both great. For quieter spaces, I like some of the smaller venues we hit up in Montana."

He nods. "Any favorite restaurants? I'm still learning my way around LA, so include those too."

I give him a few suggestions and end up laughing at the faces he makes when I share some of the restaurants to avoid too. We have a lot in common as far as music and TV. It's like the universe finally gives me a break by sending me James. When he asks me to dance, I nod and let him lead me to the dance floor. The music shifts from upbeat to something slower, and he steps closer.

His hands respectfully stay at my hips as mine curl around his neck. But when I take a deep breath, I don't get the hint of bergamot. Vanilla and leather. He's not Nick. My heart needs to get on board with my brain here. James seems like a nice guy. He's exactly who I would have looked for two months ago, but the lack of spark between us frustrates me to the point of near-tears.

"I'm glad I met you tonight." His voice is low in my ear. "I almost didn't come out."

"I'm glad you did," I respond.

"I was wondering, maybe I could take you to dinner one night this week?"

I pull back and notice his eyes are almost the same shade as mine. "Like a date?"

He nods. "Yeah. What do you say?"

# CHAPTER 28

*NICK*

$\mathcal{H}$ow did I fucking forget it was Halloween? All I wanted was a quiet drink where some noise would drown out my thoughts. Instead, I have to fight for both a barstool and the bartender's attention.

"Johnnie Walker. Neat." One drink now that I have the bartender's attention. Then I'm going home. Away from this mess. Thoughts or no thoughts.

Drink finally in hand, I stare at the amber liquid and hope it has some answers. Jax still hasn't given me any advice on Meredith. He did tell me that she went back home after we were supposed to have gotten back from Nebraska and also let it slip that she got a job with the video production company that did Jax's *Dreamer* video. Other than that, he clams up whenever I try to bring up her name.

I've continued to text and call her with zero response. I even tried stopping by her house one day last week, but if she was home like her car in the driveway suggested, she pretended not to be. Maybe I'll finish my drink and try again tonight.

Nodding to no one in particular, I take a sip and lift my gaze to see what crazy costumes are on display. Lots of girls with animal ears dressed in normal club wear. A redhead in a corset top with a pirate hat tilted on her head gives me fuck-me eyes, but I keep my gaze moving across the bar and up to the raised dance floor as memories of other times swamp me.

Meredith dressed in the siren red dress the night she needed to be rescued. Meredith in the black dress designed to drive me crazy during our night out with Jax and Charlie. Meredith in a dress with octopus tentacles, her hair silky, the curls that are so much a part of her personality, gone.

Wait. What? Blinking, I measure how much liquid is in my glass and confirm I've only had a sip. That's no drunken mirage. She is on the dance floor dressed like... Ursula from *The Little Mermaid*? But a sexy version.

Red shrouds my vision as I take in the way she leans against some weirdo in a black costume. Dude has a black scarf wrapped over his head, and a mask obscures most of his face. His hands curl into her hips, and I'm up off my stool before I can draw my next breath. Who does that asshole think he is?

"She says no, asshole." I answer his request for a date as I step up between them.

Meredith's gaze whips from the guy in front of her to me. It flashes with anger until she turns that espresso-colored gaze back to Don Juan.

"Actually, I was about to ask what night works for you." She reaches for him again and I grab for her hand.

Fuck this.

"Hey." Don Juan tries to step between us again, and I freeze him with a glare. "Find your next mark, Don Juan. She's taken."

Her nails prick my skin where they dig into my fingers as she tries to pry my hand off of her wrist. I loosen my grip but don't let go completely. We're almost to the stairs when Derek steps forward. I wave him off—she's safe with me—and he steps toward the guy who continues to stare after us.

She doesn't say anything, but she also doesn't make our trek through the club any easier as she continues trying to unlatch my fingers from her wrist. The universe is, for once, on my side, and no one else attempts to stop us as I pull her into the corridor. An employee exits a storage room, and I use the closing door and distracted employee to my advantage and yank her inside. I plant myself in front of the door before I release her.

"What the fuck is your problem?" Her chest heaves with anger and she pivots away. Spinning back to me, she slams her fist into my stomach. I grunt, but otherwise don't move.

"He had his hands all over you." I bite the words out through clenched teeth.

"You're insane. He had his hands on my hips because we were dancing."

"He had his hands on your ass," I counter while red clouds my vision again. I know what I saw.

"You're insane," she repeats. "But I'm not going to argue with you. Excuse you."

She tries to shove past me, but I shift my weight. She changes angles but doesn't succeed in getting around me.

"I want to talk to you," I tell her.

"Tough shit," she snaps.

"Mer." I only need her to listen to me for a few minutes. To let me explain. To apologize.

"Why should I talk to you after you embarrassed me like that?"

"I embarrassed you?" I scoff and all thoughts of an apology scatter. "I fucking had to rescue you again."

"Listen to me." She steps into my face. "You may be older than me, but you *aren't* my dad. You're nothing to me. Based on your own choices." Her eyes widen with words that seem to surprise even her.

Ignoring her, I fasten my gaze on hers. "Why aren't you responding to my calls? To any of my texts?"

She twists away from me to pace in the small supply room.

"Meredith."

"I blocked you."

*Blocked me?*

"What? Why the fuck would you do that?"

"Oh my god, Nick, you really are stupid, aren't you? I don't want to talk to you. There's nothing left to say that you didn't say in Nebraska."

Her words land direct hits, and my stomach sinks with the confirmation that I seriously fucked up. "What about us?"

Her laugh is bitter but lures my attention to her plump lips. I want to sample the color to see if she tastes like the fruit they remind me of. "There is no us."

"Meredith." How can I get through her defenses?

"The wedding planning is done," she continues like I didn't say anything.

"That's not what I'm talking about and you know it," I finally snap at her.

She drops her head back to expose the long column of her throat, and my dick pulses in my slacks at the urge to lean down and trace that line with my tongue. "Ugh. Why are you doing this?" The intensity of the pain reflected when she looks at me sucks the breath from my lungs. "You made it loud and clear. I'm too immature for you. I'm not enough. I'm too young to understand—"

"I'm sorry." I step toward her. My arms lift helplessly as she finches away. "I shouldn't have said that. I didn't mean anything I said. There was a lot going through my mind while we were there—"

"That's an excuse." She still won't let me get away with the bullshit.

I nod. "It is. And the truth is, there's no excuse for the way I treated you in Nebraska. What I said to you—"

She shakes her head and lifts her hand while her skin pales. "Stop."

"I'm sorry." It's a desperate whisper.

"And what about calling Emily's name?" She acts like I need that reminder.

"I didn't mean to." I try to pull her into my arms. When she lets me, I let out a gusty sigh. "She was the last one I was there with like that and—"

"I don't want excuses." She ducks out of my grasp and takes several steps back to put space between us. "I was willing to take anything you would give me. Whatever small piece of your heart you would let me into. But I wasn't important to you. You showed me that, and I can't unlearn it. I can't do this anymore. I can't keep trying to push into your heart when you don't want me there. I can't keep pushing myself down for someone else. I want somebody to *want* to give me their whole heart. To find someone to love who will love me back. Me. Just as I am."

"Love?" Icy panic filters through my veins. "Emily—"

Tears line her lashes, but she blinks them away. "I understand. I do. But I can't compete with a ghost. I can't keep letting you yank me along while I hope you'll give me a little more. I can't just be a friend with benefits. I can't have sex without emotion anymore because somewhere along the line, I fell in love with you. I didn't mean to. I tried not to. But here I am."

"Meredith." My brain blinks off. All the words and emotions that have been swirling inside me these last few weeks, gone in an instant. *She loves me?*

"Please." Her anguished voice warbles over the word, and her rapid blinking tells me more tears are coming. "Let me go."

Stepping to the side, I release her and refrain from reaching out to stop her as she rushes to the door and slips through the smallest opening she can to get out. I'm frozen in the same spot a few minutes later when an employee walks in, startled at my unexpected appearance.

"Sorry." I head for the back exit. I'm not interested in seeing Meredith wrapped in another man's arms. Once outside, I order a car, grateful I don't have to fight the distractions that play through my head to drive back home.

My condo is dark as I open the door, but my gaze unerringly locks on Meredith's jersey on the couch where I left it earlier. I'd found it under the couch cushion yesterday, the piece of white material sticking out between the pillows. There are other clothes in my room, folded and sitting on top of the dresser. She'd never asked for space to put them away, and I'd never offered it.

I'm a selfish asshole, taking whatever she was willing to give me and giving almost nothing in return.

"Fuck." Stalking to the fridge, I reach inside for a beer. I pop the top and pace the condo until I'm back in the bedroom. I can still see her lying in the bed and feel the weight of her in my arms when I would tug her against me to drift off to sleep. She'd been my shield from nightmares I didn't want to face.

Nightmares that haven't returned even though she hasn't been next to me in weeks. I can't do this. Spinning, I make my way back to the living room to unlock the patio door and walk outside. I smash into one of the chairs that face the ocean.

"She loves me." The sound of crashing waves is my only response. "I'm an idiot."

I should have seen that. Fuck, I should have predicted it. She has too kind a heart. Whereas mine has been dead for a while, hers is very much alive. Capable of loving.

"I mean, yeah, I care about her." She's my friend. Like Jax. Like Charlie. Or at least she was. "But love?"

I need to let her go. I screwed us up because I pushed her for more. Not only have I lost the opportunity to taste her, to feel the silky skin against mine or the way her curls tickled my palms, but I've lost her friendship too.

Maybe someday I can earn it back.

So why does it make me clench the beer bottle in my hand to think about her with Don Juan as her plus one to the wedding? Or another guy at the next cookout?

She deserves someone who can make her laugh, can see through the facade she tries to use if she's hurt or upset. She deserves someone to place stupid bets on football games, to teach her to cook so she can feed herself rather than relying on someone else.

Someone who isn't selfish. Who appreciates the love she has to give. Not some selfish bastard with a dead heart.

✶✶✶

The setting sun creates a perfect vista in front of the decorated altar. Candles flicker in the light breeze, and soft music plays through the speakers.

It's perfect. But why is the officiant the only one at the alter? Where's Jax? He should be up there waiting for Charlie. I swivel to search the rows full of people I don't recognize to look for his familiar face. Pachelbel's *Canon in D* starts, and I know—I just know—that Charlie is getting ready to walk down the aisle to an empty alter. What the fuck is going on?

Standing, I try to move toward the back of the chairs. I have to find—

"Jax," I say as he tugs on my suit jacket.

"What are you doing? Chill the fuck out." He stands next to me as everyone around us rises.

"Wait, shouldn't you be up there?" My attention moves back to the alter. Don Juan—the moron in the black costume who was with Meredith at the club—now stands next to the officiant as he stares intently at someone walking up behind me on my right.

"Oh, she's gorgeous." Charlie's eyes fill with tears, and my head swivels to see Meredith walk down the aisle on her dad's arm.

Fuck.

She's a vision in white lace, the curls I love to spin around my fingers tamed to waves that hang down her back. A bouquet of pink peonies mix with other flowers and cascade from her arm. The joy written on her face has my heart pounding.

Beautiful is too simple a word. Stunning? Alluring?

"Exquisite." Emily's arm links through mine while her head leans on my shoulder. All the guests turn as we focus on Meredith while she moves the rest of the way to the altar. Her dad kisses her cheek and sits next to her mom. The sense that she's the most beautiful bride I've ever seen wars with the feeling that this isn't right. I want to open my mouth to say something, but I'm frozen.

"Please be seated." The officiant smiles at all of us standing before he shifts his attention to Meredith and Don Juan. "Dearly beloved, friends, family, we come here together today to witness Meredith and—"

Emily nudges me and distracts me from what the officiant says next.

"What?" I ask.

"What, what?" She looks at me innocently and points back to the ceremony going on in front of us. "Shh."

"A very wise man once described love perfectly. 'Love is a friendship caught on fire. In the beginning a flame, very pretty, often hot and fierce, but still only light and flickering. As love grows older, our hearts mature and our love becomes as coals, deep-burning and unquenchable.'" The officiant nods. "That's how Meredith and—"

Jax snorts and wrenches my attention to the three people that sit around me. "Dude, do you remember how much we hazed him when Meredith first introduced us?"

I want to scream, no. No, I don't fucking remember.

What the fuck is going on? I've only seen this guy once. What the hell is Jax talking about? I open my mouth to ask, but Charlie slaps him on the arm.

"Quiet," she scolds.

He bites back a laugh but focuses on the couple at the altar, and I do the same. But only for a second.

"He's describing you." Emily's blue eyes burn with an intensity I've never seen before.

"What?"

"That love is a friendship spiel. That's you and Meredith."

I shrug her off and move to grab her hand. My hand slides through hers as she starts to disappear in front of me. Startled, I reach for her again.

"But I'm with you," I tell her, even though the words crowd at my lips to stand up and claim Meredith as mine. *Mine.*

Emily's smile is bittersweet, and I swear the warmth of her palm cups my cheek as I breathe in sweet pea lotion. "Say something."

"If anyone has just cause why these two should not be lawfully wed, please speak now or forever hold your peace." My attention darts to the officiant as he scans the crowd.

"Say something." My gaze moves back to where Emily was, so real I still feel her warmth pressed against me. But she's not there.

"Em?"

"Say something," her voice repeats.

"Em? Where'd you go?"

"Say something." She's fading and I can hardly hear her.

"Emily?" Panic takes hold and I stand, spinning in place as I search for her. "Emily, quit playing around. Where'd you go?"

"Say something."

"Emily!"

The only response I get is my harsh breathing as I bolt upright in bed. My shout echoes against the dark walls of my bedroom.

"Fuck." I'm drenched in sweat, the sheets twisted around my legs.

Untangling myself, I stand and walk to the bathroom to flip on the shower. As the water warms up, I shed my boxers and finally get to step into the hot spray. The dream still clenches icy fingers around my heart, and I lean my head against the wall to let the hot water stream down my shoulders as the dream echoes in the bathroom with me.

*Love is friendship on fire.*

*Say something.*

Like a flash of lightning, it hits me. I straighten and slick my hair off my face. It came on so slowly, those embers glowing, growing until it's all that's left.

I want to be the one to make her laugh, to see through that mask she puts on for everyone else, and comfort her when she's upset. I want to snuggle on the couch with her and argue football games. Play strip football again. I want to teach her to cook so we can take turns in the kitchen. To be the man who earns her love.

My heart pounds painfully in my chest. A reminder that I *am* alive.

And that I love Meredith.

# CHAPTER 29

*MEREDITH*

I've barely walked in the door from work when my phone rings. Dropping my bags, I fish it out of my hoodie pocket and answer Charlie's call.

"Hey, Charlie, what's up?"

"Mer, what are you doing tonight?"

I don't even have to think about it. I'd had dinner with James last night—he had given his number to Derek after Nick dragged me away at Eclipse. While he is a nice guy, I'd told him I was just coming out of a relationship and didn't want to lead him on.

How could I contemplate another relationship since I was still in love with someone else? That was that. No dates for a while. "Nothing, why? Wanna have a girls' night?"

I'll invite Claire. At work, we seem to have become the three amigas.

"I wish." McKenna starts to wail in the background, and the sound gets louder as Charlie picks her up to soothe her. "I know, baby, I know."

"What is it? What's wrong?"

"McKenna isn't feeling so hot." Charlie sounds close to tears too, but I keep that thought to myself. "She's teething and running a fever and only wants Mommy right now."

"Aww. Poor baby." I have no idea what that's like, but Charlie being close to tears is something I'm not used to hearing. McKenna not feeling well is taking its toll on her too. "Do you need me to go grab something for you? Where's Jax?"

Her sigh is heavy through the phone. "Jackson has the label launch party tonight. I was supposed to go with him, but no way will McKenna be okay with a sitter."

"Okay?" Dread builds in my stomach. I'd already explained to Jax and Charlie that even though I want to support Jax, based on what had happened with Nick, I didn't think it was a good idea if I went.

They both claimed they understood, and I didn't even realize that tonight was the party.

"I don't want Jackson to not have anyone there he knows. Nick invited a bunch of people to network with, but Jax needs a friend there."

"Charlie."

"I know, I know. I wouldn't ask normally. But he was really nervous."

"Ugh." I already know I'm going to say yes, but I really, really don't want to see Nick. Well, mostly. A small part of me does. The masochist in me.

"I'll owe you big time for going. Double. You did plan the wedding happening next weekend too." McKenna's wails pick up in volume again, and I hold the phone away from my ear. "I'm gonna go see if I can help Ken feel better."

I don't even agree to go when the call ends.

"Okay then."

Wiping my palms on the yoga pants I'd worn to work today, I head for my bedroom and rifle through my closet until I find a black cocktail dress that should work. It's a little fancier than normal with a lace hem, but I can also wear my black and red ombre peep toes, and I need the confidence they provide if I'm going to face Nick tonight.

Thirty minutes later, I've finished my makeup for the night and pulled my hair back in a fancy ponytail since I don't have time to straighten it and make it to the party on time. I don't let myself think about Nick until after I'm in the car I ordered. I'd considered driving myself, but I'm too nervous to deal with LA's traffic snarl today.

My stomach flips and twists in a gymnastics routine that would make an Olympic hopeful proud. The party is at a downtown LA hotel where Jax and Nick managed to reserve the pool area for the night. Nick had shared the idea with me when we were still…something and I had loved it and pictured myself as his date. It was such a naïve thought that I could kick myself.

"Keep it together, Mer," I whisper as I exit the vehicle. My legs shake as I walk to the elevator, and I blame the slow-moving machine for the continued acrobatics that leave my stomach sitting like a lump in my throat.

"Mer, you came." The relief on Jax's face tells me exactly how nervous he is. If that isn't a clue I catch, the way he crushes me to him as he hugs me is another tip.

"Nervous?" I laugh at his nod.

"It's weird. I can get on a stage and sing, but the thought of trying to market the label to people Nick invited tonight makes me nauseous." I listen halfway, but the other part of my attention pings around the rooftop while I look for Nick. "He's talking to the events manager."

"Who?" I try to play dumb.

"Goof." He rolls his eyes. "Nick."

"Oh." My nonchalant voice sounds more like I inhaled a balloon full of helium.

He reaches out to clasp my shoulder. "It's gonna be okay. I'll be here all night and I'll be your buffer."

I shrug, the breath hissing between my teeth once Nick walks back into view. Charcoal slacks and a light gray shirt mold to his body in tailored perfection. Even shielded by mirrored aviators, the heat of his gaze burns me. Jax turns to see what I'm looking at.

Nick takes a step toward us and seems to reconsider and retreats in the direction he came from. With him no longer in my line of sight, I pull a deep breath into my lungs.

I'd like to say that's the only encounter, or even the closest encounter, we have.

The party is in full swing by the time I make my way to the bar for a club soda refill. I've had one glass of wine but prefer to keep my inhibitions firmly in place since there is a risk of running into Nick. Jax has run interference between us all night, but when I left him a few minutes ago, he was deep in conversation with another artist about signing with their label. I'd spotted Nick deep in conversation with Dylan Graves. If Nick weren't there, I'd be fangirling all over the hot British rocker. Instead, I'll be happy that he seems to be distracting—

"Scotch. Neat." His voice shouldn't still have the power to drag goosebumps down my arms, but the traitorous reaction doesn't take that into account. Taking the glass the bartender hands me, I turn to look for Jax. "Meredith."

My name on his lips freezes me, and the warm hand at my elbow nudges me back toward him. Back toward eyes that remind me of the Caribbean in the sun.

"Hey." Uncertainty pinches his brows while an awkward smile tilts his lips at the corners.

"Hi." I wrap both hands around my glass to avoid reaching out to him.

"You look beautiful."

"Don't." My voice is a whisper, but his compliment leaves me breathless. I shift again to leave, but his hand once more cups my elbow.

"I'm sorry. I've...can we talk?"

Shaking my head, I can't stop the wayward tear that slips through my defenses. "Nick."

His scent surrounds me as he steps closer, and his finger is soft when he wipes away the tear. But I flinch at his touch.

"Please?" It's the lack of confidence in his tone that sends a pang through me. "About the other night—"

I hold up a hand. "I can't."

This time, I don't let him keep me from walking back toward Jax. I take a sip of the club soda, the cool carbonation soothes the burn of tears in my throat.

"You okay?" Jax's attention shifts from me to Nick.

I nod. "Yeah."

Maybe. I can't go through an encounter like that again and say the same thing though. Jax sticks close to me for the rest of the night. I think he feels bad that my behavior is more forced than it was earlier in the evening. That's saying something since they haven't been natural all night anyway. I'm ready for this party to end so I can go home and call Derek and unload all the emotions that swirl in my stomach. I only need to make it through the speech and that's it.

The music that plays over the speakers stops, and Jax and Nick both step up to the microphone.

What is Nick holding?

Why is he holding his guitar? I don't have to wait long since Jax makes a few comments and passes off the microphone.

"Thanks for coming, everyone. Y'all have a good time?" Nick smiles as he's met with applause and a few catcalls. "Jax and I appreciate your support for Arrhythmic Records. When I first named the label, someone asked me the question about how I came up with it and if I had a heart condition." He smirks, and heat climbs into my cheeks. "I told this person that I named the label because music can make your heart skip a beat, like when you look at the love of your life, your heart stutters."

My own heart falters with the memory.

"I didn't know it then, but this person—this beautiful woman —she does to me what good music does. She makes my heart skip far too many beats." He pauses and steels his shoulders on a deep inhale. I hold my breath, desperate for him to keep talking. "But I messed up. Bad. Pushed this woman away when I realized the effect she was having on me. So here's hoping that good music can tell her how sorry I am and how much I love her."

What did he say?

I don't believe it. No. I can't have heard all of that correctly. How much he loves her? Me? I try not to get my hopes up. Maybe I misunderstood him.

The song he starts to play is new and, to everyone's surprise except for Jax's, he begins to sing. His voice is a mix of smooth whiskey and smokey honey. It reaches out to wrap around me as the lyrics of the song tell me about a dream where friendship ignites to love, about the realization and the need to speak up and claim that love before it's too late.

By the time the song ends, tears spill down my face. Thank god for waterproof makeup, otherwise I'd resemble a raccoon by now. With the fading of the guitar, Nick's gaze locks on mine.

I have to talk to him.

A DJ starts a song to fill the silence, and a few glances come my way as I make my way toward the stage, but otherwise people go back to their own conversations.

Nick drops to the ground as I reach the stage, and butterflies flutter in my stomach. He doesn't say anything, just reaches forward and weaves his fingers with mine. Then he starts to lead me away until a voice stops us.

"Nicky, surely we rate a hello."

Spinning, I spot Cara and her husband and Beth and John. My breath stalls once I see who is behind them—Emily's parents. My attention snaps to Nick as my heart gallops in my chest. I steel myself for the sting of rejection, for him to drop my hand, but it doesn't come.

"Jeez, y'all. You couldn't give me five minutes to talk to Meredith? I have some things to tell her," Nick groans. He tries to tug me away, but my feet stay planted.

"Is this what you were talking about earlier in your Facebook post?" It's Emily's mom who speaks up, and I picture myself as a cartoon character with my jaw on the floor.

I look at Nick. "Facebook post?"

He shrugs. "I'm friends with Karen and Graham on Facebook now."

"When did that happen?"

"A couple of—wait, not the important thing right now. Do you mind?" He asks the three couples who surround us.

Cara waves him away. "Go win back your girl, Nicky."

This time, he successfully leads me behind a row of potted shrubs that line the rooftop. He stops and his attention shifts to our intertwined hands. After several moments, his eyes refocus on mine.

"What did your post say?"

He groans. "This is why I don't share on social media. If I had known my family was going to surprise me today, I wouldn't have."

"Nick." I grip his hand. "What did it say?"

"I asked them to wish me luck. That I was going to do something big to see if I could win you back."

"So what you said back there?" I wave in the direction of the stage.

"It was true," he nods. "All of it. I fucked up so bad in Nebraska. In that week leading up to Nebraska. I don't deserve you, but I needed you to know how I feel."

I don't deny what he said. He *did* screw up. Epically.

"How do you feel about me?" I nibble on my lip, scared I'm

going to wake up and this will all have been a dream.

"Don't you know?" He doesn't try to hide his smile or the roll of his eyes as his hands lift to cup my cheeks. He steps closer, and the smell of his cologne wraps around the two of us in a cocoon of bergamot. "You brought me back from the dead. Before I met you, I was surviving, existing but not living. And then you hurricaned into my life. The more you hated me." Heat fills my cheeks. "The more I wanted to push your buttons."

I laugh because he had enjoyed exploring which ways fired my temper. Like a little boy pulling on my ponytail. One of his fingers tangles in a curl and wraps around it.

"And then I peeked below the surface. I saw someone who was kind, thoughtful, funny, sexy. You are everything. Just as you are. I wouldn't ask you to change to be with me. Just be with me." His voice cracks and he clears his throat. "I'm so afraid I'm too late. That I pushed you away. But I had to try. To tell you."

I lick my lips, and a shiver runs down my spine. His gaze heats as it tracks the movement of my tongue. "To tell me?"

His gaze moves back to mine. "I love you. Everything. Everything about you. The way you're so crazy about cleaning and organizing, the fact that you cook science experiments instead of dinner, the way your curls wrap around my fingers," he tugs on the one currently wrapped around him. "I love how you make me laugh, how you make me live. I love you."

I lift to my tiptoes, and my lips brush against his to stop his words. The second our lips connect, he takes over. Slanting his head, he deepens the kiss as his tongue licks into my mouth. One hand weaves through the ends of my hair and tugs my head where he wants it, while the other hand flexes against my hip to hold me closer. He breaks the kiss—far too soon for my taste—to lean his forehead against mine. "Stay with me. Be mine."

I nod. "Why is that even a question? Of course. I love you."

"Say it again," he whispers.

I brush his lips with mine as I repeat the words. "I love you."

"My three favorite words." His smirk makes me roll my eyes until he leans forward and connects our lips again.

"Get a room," Jax mutters as he walks by us on the other side of the bushes.

"Great idea." The way Nick looks at me creates an azure fire that licks along my skin. He weaves our fingers together and tugs me toward the elevator.

"Don't you have to stay? Shouldn't we say goodbye to your family?" I stop and glance over my shoulder, though I'd rather ignore the niggle of responsibility.

"Jax can handle the rest of the party. And as for my family?" He tugs out his phone with his free hand and sends a text. "They'll meet us for brunch."

"Brunch?" I ask as he tows me with him onto the elevator. I giggle and snuggle into his embrace as his arms wrap around me.

"I have plans for you until then." His hands find my hips and squeeze.

"I'm all yours." My words end on a moan as his hands shift to my ass.

"I love you." His voice is a growl against my ear when his lips graze the sensitive spot below my earlobe.

"I love you." I'll never get tired of telling him, of reminding him. Just like I'll never get tired of hearing those words from his lips. My arms wrap around his neck while my fingers toy with the ends of his hair. "Take me home, Nick."

# CHAPTER 30

*MEREDITH*

"I don't know about this." I hesitate at the doorway to the kitchen, reluctantly moving forward when Nick pulls me the rest of the way in. He's been quicker to smile over the last few days, quicker to laugh, and it rings out in the kitchen now.

"Baby, it's a kitchen, not shark-infested waters," he tries to console me.

"Not even sharks would eat my experiments."

Tugging me into his arms, he grazes a kiss on the top of my head. "It won't be that bad. Promise. Let's get started."

His hand comes down and smacks my ass, and my senses all sit up and take notice. I squeeze my thighs together. "What am I making again?"

His heated sapphire gaze appraises me and gives me the idea that maybe we can avoid this cooking business. I press closer to him and meet his gaze through my lashes.

"Stop that." He swats me again, more playfully and with less heat, and I resign myself to at least one lesson. "Homemade pizza. We're going to start with the dough."

It sounds so delicious that my stomach growls. "You're buying the pizza when I screw this up."

"Is that a wager?" His voice has dropped to a husky whisper.

"Yep."

"So what do I get when you successfully make pizza?" he asks.

"What do you want?"

Yanking me closer again, he lowers his lips close to my ear, his erection digging into my stomach. My breath comes in shallow pants with the heat building through my body.

"You," he growls.

"You're on." I wink.

As I slide the first pizza in the oven an hour later, I turn to Nick. Shockingly, it actually appears edible.

"I did it!" With a squeal, I launch myself into his arms.

"You did." His voice holds a raspy quality that makes me lean back to look at him. Flour streaks across his black t-shirt and there are even some specks of it in his hair.

"We're a mess." I run my fingers through his hair, and he reaches up and swipes a finger across my face to show me the smudge of flour he wiped away.

"We're about to get messier." Stepping forward, he pins me to the counter as his arms cage me on either side. "I'll take my winnings please."

His mouth latches on to mine, and his hands boost me to the flour covered counter while he steps between my legs.

✱✱✱

Candles flicker in the soft breeze as the sunset creates hues of pink and orange across the sky. Today has been amazing. Mom sits at a table and talks to Mama Danielle, Jax's mom, while she holds a sleeping McKenna. The baby is adorable in a pale pink romper that makes her look like the petals on a flower. She's long since lost the headband we'd found to match it, more interested in chewing it with her new bottom teeth.

Standing on the edge of the dance floor, my attention shifts to the center to find Jax and Charlie. Their eyes are locked on each other like the rest of the world doesn't exist. Jax wore a tuxedo for the occasion but tossed the bow tie as soon as the pictures were over, and Charlie looks like a princess in a strapless white dress with a skirt covered in layers of lace.

Warm arms wrap around me, and Nick's cologne tickles my nose as he rests his chin on my shoulder. "Beautiful."

His soft lips press against me as I lean into him. This last week has been incredible. If friends with benefits Nick had been boyfriend material, boyfriend Nick is something else entirely. He had even taken on the brave task of attempting to teach me to cook. Both my face and body heat with memory.

"You're far away." His voice is quiet in my ear and pulls my attention back to the swirling couples on the dance floor.

"Thinking about pizza." His arms tighten around me, his lips hot against my neck. I lean back into his kiss, thankful for the up-do Derek gave me today.

"Pizza, huh?" Warm breath vibrates across my skin as he lowers his voice to a growl. "We should do that again soon."

My breath catches when my core throbs in response. I nod.

"Yes, please." Turning around, I interlace our fingers. I love the way ours seem to fit together effortlessly. "Dance with me."

I don't have to tug very hard to get him to follow me, and moments later we sway to the soft music. My head finds his chest, and I listen to the combination of the music with his heartbeat. "Have I told you how handsome you are today?"

My voice is a murmur and so is his response. "I vaguely remember something about my being hot AF. Is that what you meant? I'm not sure an old man like me can keep up with all you kids and your new-fangled vocabulary."

I laugh. "You're such a dork."

"You love me anyway." His arms tighten and pull me closer.

"I do." Squeezing him back, I reach up to graze his jaw with my lips.

"You look so beautiful today. I think it's bad luck to upstage the bride," he says.

Charlie had chosen a pale pink chiffon bridesmaid dress with a lace overlay on the bodice to create the shoulders.

"I think Jax would tell you that Charlie is the most beautiful woman here today." I breathe against his tuxedo jacket. As Jax's best man, Nick was also in a tux and he's wearing the hell out of it.

"I'll agree to disagree with him." His lips graze my hair, and both of us fall silent for the rest of the song.

"Hey, you two."

Lifting my head, I see Jax and Charlie standing in front of us. I let go of Nick and turn with a smile toward the happy newlyweds. Are they still newlyweds since this is technically their second wedding?

"We're getting ready to leave." Jax reaches out and shakes Nick's hand before he pulls him in for a manly hug while Charlie wraps her arms around me.

"We wanted to say thank you for this beautiful day." Her eyes are luminous with unshed tears.

"Don't start that now." My own tears burn my nose. Jax pulls me into a hug and Nick does the same with Charlie.

"We'll be back next week," Jax says.

"Think a week in Hawaii will be long enough?" I tease.

"If it were up to Charlotte, we wouldn't even be gone that long." Jax grins at Charlie's blush and he turns to Nick. "Try not to sign any new acts until I get back. Did you tell Meredith?"

"Not yet." Nick smirks. What's that expression all about? Suddenly, I'm dying of curiosity.

"Tell me what?"

"Jax and I signed three new artists this week. One of them was Dylan Graves."

"Really? You signed Dylan—" Glass shattering interrupts my squeal. I turn and see my co-worker Claire staring slack-jawed at Nick instead of at the broken glass at her feet.

"D-Dylan? You signed Dylan Graves?"

Nick looks at me and I give him a shrug. He turns back to her. "Yeah. Why?"

"Nothing. No reason. Oh." She looks down as if only now seeing the broken pieces of the champagne flute she had been holding. "Oh. I should see if they have a broom."

She scurries off, and Nick turns back to us.

"Your friend is weird."

"She's not weird. She's sweet. I hope she's okay." Charlie steps forward. "Maybe I should—"

"Maybe you should just come with me, gorgeous. Honeymoon, remember?" Jax pulls her to his side.

We say our goodbyes, but Jax turns back around at the edge of the dance floor.

"Tell Meredith the other thing."

Nick groans and pulls me back into his arms, spinning me to the song.

"Tell me what?" I ask when he doesn't say anything right away.

"I love you." He leans down but I dodge his kiss.

"I love you too. Tell me what?"

He looks so uncomfortable, my curiosity is on pins and needles. Closing his eyes, he blows out a breath before opening them again. "Jax talked me into recording the song I sang last week. We're going to start production on it next week when he gets back."

"Nick." I step back, but he doesn't accept the distance and boosts me until my feet don't touch the ground anymore. "That's…that's incredible."

"You'll always come first. I didn't want to do it without you being on board. If you say the word, I'll cancel the production right now."

"Count me in." I lift my hand, and the scruff on his jaw that scrapes my palm creates a shiver. "We'll do it together."

"Together." It's the last word he says right before his lips claim mine.

# EPILOGUE

*NICK*

"$\mathcal{I}$ need more coffee," I growl into Meredith's ear as we snuggle on the couch on Christmas morning.

"Who are you telling?" She yawns and burrows into my arm while her eyes drift shut. "If your nieces and nephew were over here at six, what time do you think they woke up Cara and Troy?"

My sister and brother-in-law are both passed out on the couch while the kids play with the insane number of presents Meredith shipped out to Nebraska for the holiday. Cara and Meredith had conspired to get us back here for Christmas.

I get the impression that any time those two team up is going to mean trouble.

"With as fast as they tore through all the wrapping paper here?" I snort. "I'm guessing five thirty there."

She giggles and yawns again. "Isn't that what time we fell asleep?"

My body heats with the memory of our private Christmas celebration last night. "Something like that."

She leans her head against my chest. My lips find her curls, and I gently shake her. "No, no way. You gotta get up. We have someplace to be."

I stand and tug her up.

"I should pick up all the wrapping paper." She looks around at the remnants of paper and tape that cover the floor.

I manage to get Sam's attention away from the makeup bag Meredith got her. "Sam."

I imagine there's an eye roll for the nickname I refuse to give up, but I don't see it. "Yeah, Uncle Nick?"

"Would you mind cleaning up the wrapping paper for Meredith?" Tacking on Meredith's name guarantees Sam's undying love and devotion.

"Sure."

That taken care of, I drop a kiss on Meredith's nose and pull her with me. We grab our coats and step outside into the bite of the cold wind. "We're driving."

Jesus. I shiver. I definitely am a Southern Californian now. Weather like this didn't used to bother me so much. My hand threads with hers, and I drop her off at the passenger side of the car and round the hood. The roads are deserted this early on Christmas morning, but I go slower than normal, the route unfamiliar by car.

"Do you know where you're going?" she teases.

"Pretty sure." The gates to the cemetery come into view, and I pull through them and park at the crest of the hill. "I want you to meet someone."

She stares at me before she glances through the window.

"Are you sure?" Her attention shifts back to me.

I nod. "It's time."

Getting out of the car, I stop by her door, but I let her open it once she's ready. Her lips move, and I want to ask her what she

307

said once her door opens, but I let her have those moments to herself. We walk in the direction of the headstone with snow piled around it as I interlace our fingers. She stops, and I follow her lead and stand next to her.

"Meredith, this is Emily. Emily, Meredith." If she thinks this is crazy, she doesn't act like it.

"It's nice to meet you, Emily. I've heard so many stories about you from Nick and Cara. I feel like I got a chance to get to know you already." Her voice fades off.

"They're mostly good stories," I continue. "Usually more embarrassing for me than anything else." She leans her head on my shoulder with a small smile. "I'm not sure if you're able to look down on us from heaven—or if you do, I hope you pick your moments. But I'm not sure if you knew or not that Meredith moved in with me recently."

It had happened so gradually that by the time we figured out most of her stuff was already at the condo, it seemed like a foregone conclusion. But I still asked her, she still said yes, and she made a big production of getting a frilly pink key for the front door.

A gust of wind blows against us, the ice-tipped fingers digging through the layers of clothing. "Anyway, I just... I thought it was time to introduce the two of you." Nodding back to the car, I tighten my hand around hers. "Wanna head back?"

"One sec." Her hand tightens in mine and she turns to face Emily's headstone again. "Emily, I'm sure you know how special Nick is. I bet you experienced all those same amazing things I do. I want you to know how much I love him. He's my other half. I'll take care of him, I promise. And I'll remind him exactly how lovable he is and how loved he is. Always."

It's the wind that stings my eyes and has me blinking, nothing else. Two tears make their way down her face when she turns back to me, and I use my thumbs to wipe them away before I drop a kiss to her lips and release her. "I love you."

"I love you too."

"Let's head back," I say.

Our drive back to the farm is quiet, which worries me. She usually isn't quiet. What is she thinking? My own head is filled with what comes next for us. I stop the car next to the house and turn to her. "Take a walk with me?"

Snowflakes have started to swirl through the air. Big, fat snowflakes that hold the promise of a white Christmas after all. It was all she had talked about—a white Christmas in Nebraska. She stares at the falling snow and glances at me and nods. "Okay."

We set off on our walk, and I tuck both our joined hands into my pocket to keep them warm. I should have brought gloves. Too late now.

"Where are we going?" she asks.

We pass the barn, and her head swivels back and forth to take in her surroundings—the fields blanketed in fresh snow—while the crunch of our footsteps fills the otherwise quiet air.

"I figured a walk in the snow would be fun."

"I love it." She stops and lifts her face to the sky while snowflakes coat her hair and eyelashes. "Snow is magical."

"Says the Southern California girl," I tease.

She pushes at me and grins. "I lived in New York."

"So what's with the snow obsession?" I ask.

"Even if it snowed on Christmas, it was never like this. More sort of gray."

We walk along empty fields until we approach a copse of trees. I stop and tug her into my arms. The breath that comes out is a shaky mist in front of me.

"You okay? Need to take a break, old man?" She teases me back and I chuckle.

"Not a break. Just wanted to stop here." I look around. It's perfect.

"A year ago, I hardly knew you. Other than the fact that you were Jax's annoying friend who talked too much." She scowls at me, but a smile hovers on her lips. "And in one of those weird moments, I thought that the only way to get you to be quiet was to kiss you." My cock perks up at the memory of that kiss, but I ignore him. "I now think that was Emily making her move. Using the universe to help her out. She knew way back then that you were perfect for me. I was the dumbass who took months to recognize it." Her laughter has my heart beating faster. "Two months ago, I nearly lost you. And I walked through these fields and talked to Emily—and her dad—who set me straight. And I'm so fucking glad they did. I can't imagine my life without you in it. It overwhelms me sometimes how much I love you."

She opens her mouth to speak, but I silence her with a finger against her lips. "So, I have a question I need to ask you."

Reaching into my coat pocket, I pull out a pale blue box, and my heart gallops faster with her quick intake of breath. I drop to one knee.

"I've talked to your mom and dad, and they gave me their blessing to ask you. Meredith Rose Pryce, will you marry me? Be my wife, my friend, the mother of my children. Be mine. Always."

Time and my heart both stop as I wait for her answer. The world rushes back to life with her nod. Surging off the ground, I claim her lips with mine and kiss my fiancée in the falling snow on my family's farm in Nebraska. When I break the kiss, her palms cup my face.

"I love you. Yes. Always."

I pull the ring from the box and slide the cushion cut diamond on her shaking finger. As I bring her hand to my lips, the ring sparkles like crystals in the snow that falls around us. "You're stuck with me now."

"Pretty sure I can handle that." I tug her against me while one hand tangles in her wild mass of curls and the other anchors around her back. My lips brush hers once, twice, until they hold, and I deepen the kiss, our tongues tangling together. When I break the kiss, a smile stretches my lips. "Think this wedding will be any easier to plan now that we have experience?"

Her giggle echoes in the fields of snow around us before she pulls my lips back down to hers, sealing our laughter with a kiss.

THE END

∿

Thank you so much for reading!

**Before you go!** Want a glimpse at life with Nick and Meredith in the future? Turn the page and see what life with them is like three years in the future.

WAIT! BEFORE YOU TURN THE PAGE...

~

Just a quick note before you keep reading. You'll see Nick, Meredith, Jax, Charlie, and even McKenna in this bonus epilogue. You'll also see characters from future Heart Beats books.

I have it on good authority, it's not really a spoiler, but just wanted to give you fair warning. ;)

Happy reading!
XOXO,
Breanna

# BONUS EPILOGUE, CHAPTER 1

## 3 YEARS LATER

*MEREDITH*

"*J* don't want to tell everyone today," I say, looking at Nick from the passenger seat of the Tesla Model X he bought me as a wedding present.

"What do you mean?" He glances at me quickly before reaching over and interlacing our fingers. He draws our joined hands up to his lips to press a kiss against my hand. "Why not?"

I shrug, nerves filling my belly at the idea that my life—our life—is about to change drastically. "It's Ken's birthday today. It's her special day."

No one has called McKenna by her full name since she was a baby. But she doesn't seem to mind her nickname.

"Mer." His tone tells me he knows I'm not being completely honest.

"All the books say to wait to say anything too. At least until the twelfth week."

The hand not currently enveloped by his rests against my still flat stomach. I'm a mess right now.

Joy. Nerves. Love. Nausea.

I take a deep breath as queasiness takes over the nerves. I thought I'd gotten the stomach bug that Ken and Charlie had a few weeks ago. Turns out I had a bug alright. But more the nine-month variety.

Ugh.

I hope the morning sickness doesn't last that long. I crack my window. Maybe the rush of fresh air will distract me.

"We're almost at twelve weeks," he reassures me. "It's going to be fine."

"We're going to have to get a bigger house." Having a baby in a one-bedroom condo on the beach isn't going to work, at least, not for long.

"We'll figure it out," he says as we turn into the neighborhood. "We've talked about getting a bigger place."

"When we got pregnant." My breath hitches, the panic teasing its way through my chest. I try to breathe through it. We'd been married for a year and decided it was time to start trying. I'd gotten pregnant right away—that first month we started trying. But at seven weeks, I'd started spotting, and we lost the baby.

My doctor said it was safe to try again the following month, but I couldn't. I wasn't ready. I felt like I had failed. Until I'd talked to someone in one of those online support groups and accepted that it wasn't my fault.

Things like that happened sometimes. The relief in hearing those words from someone who had experienced it helped the grief fade.

When I was ready to try again, I didn't realize it would take as long as it did. Nearly a year and a half of ovulation monitoring and doctor's appointments and month after month of disappointment and doubts when it didn't happen.

Nick pulls into the driveway and puts the car in park before looking at me.

"Babe." He squeezes my hand. "We are."

His face is a mix of happiness and concern. Concern for me even when I know he grieved too.

"What if—" I swallow around the lump in my throat. "What if…"

He smiles sadly, immediately understanding the words I can't manage.

"You're already further along now than you were before," he says softly.

"Eleven weeks," I whisper.

"That's why you don't want to tell everyone." It's not a question, but I nod anyway. "Come here."

He pulls me into an awkward hug across the console, and I breathe in the comforting scent of his cologne. Shifting his head, he grazes my lips with his in a soft kiss.

"I love you." His words are exactly what I need to hear right now.

I take a deep breath again and hold it for a beat before letting it out.

"I love you." My fingers wrap around his neck and pull his lips back to mine. Instead of the chaste brush of our lips, I open my mouth under his, moaning when his tongue dips and tangles with mine.

I score my fingernails through the short hair at his neck, and he reaches down, gripping my hip, the heat of his palm branding me through my skirt.

A rap against the windows has us breaking apart like guilty teenagers. Dylan is laughing hysterically in the driveway.

Nick pops his door open, pushing him out of the way. "Dick."

"They have nice things called mattresses for that type of activity," he jokes.

Flustered, I step out of the car and smooth non-existent wrinkles from the flowy skirt of my blue sundress. The weather is hot for February, so I leave my sweater in the car, rounding the hood to stand next to Nick and glare at Dylan.

"When was the last time you made out in a car?" I challenge.

How I was ever starstruck by this goofball is a question I'll never be able to answer. He has now been relegated to another irritating big brother I never wanted but love anyway.

He shrugs. "I prefer the bedroom."

"I'll just bet you do," I counter, teasing. "Now that you're a boring married man and all."

He bows his head. "Touché. Truce?"

I study him for a minute before finally placing my hand in his. "For now. Let's just see what your wife has to say. Where is she?"

"I was running late so we rode separately," he says as we make our way to the door. He keys in his code for the door, and we enter a pink bedecked chaos. If it's princess, pink, or glitter, it exists in some form in this house.

"I can see Ken's been at it again." Dylan whistles as we take in the explosion of pink around us.

"Daddy can't say no," Charlie says with a smile as she hugs all of us. "Come on, everyone's out back."

Dylan starts to follow her, but Nick's warm hand wraps around my wrist, halting our progress.

"You're sure?" His cobalt-colored gaze studies me as he waits for my answer.

I nod. "Yeah. Is that okay?"

Reaching down, he presses a kiss against my cheek. "Of course. We can wait. Whatever you want."

His fingers drift, tangling with mine as we head out to the backyard.

"Mer!" The small cry echoes across the yard.

"Kenny!" I cry, lifting her up as she launches herself at me. She smells like cotton candy and sunshine. "Hi, love bug."

"Guess what!" She reaches out an arm to bring Nick closer to us.

"What?" he asks, amusement plain on his face as he studies the brown-haired chatterbox.

317

"It's my birfday." Her little face is so serious that he and I glance at each other with a smile.

"It is?" I ask.

She nods solemnly. "Yes."

"And how old are you?" Nick plays along. "Sixteen? Seventeen?"

"No, silly." She rolls her eyes. "I'm only three."

She lifts three chubby fingers and shows us both before squirming to get down.

"Hey, Ken," I call as she starts to run off.

"What?" Her pink dress flares around her with her spin.

"You have presents." I point to the pile where Charlie placed the wrapped package we brought.

Her gaze tracks my finger, and her eyes go wide when she spots the haphazardly stacked mountain.

"Ken, you want to go bounce more?" Thank goodness for Mom, who distracts her. Since Charlie's parents live in Colorado, Ken has become a surrogate granddaughter.

"Oh, yeah. Bye!" She scampers toward an inflatable bouncy castle.

"Jax is too much." I wrap my arms around Nick and roll my eyes.

He huffs a laugh in agreement.

"Jax is too much what?" a voice asks from behind us, and I turn and grin at the over-indulgent dad.

Jax walks up, a baby kicking happily from the sling on his chest. Eight-month-old Mason James Bryant has a gummy grin for both Nick and me as he squeals from his contraption. I make a mental note to look up YouTube videos on how to use those.

"Mason!" I smile at the baby and trace a finger down his nose to end with a boop on the tip. He responds with a giggle and more drool.

Mason was born when Nick and I were almost nine months into the whole "trying" routine. Sex loses its luster when it's scheduled by ovulation cycles, no matter how sexy I find my husband. Just saying.

Nick and Jax fist bump over Mason's head, and Nick gestures to the princess carnival around us. "What's next, dude? A pink elephant?"

Jax just grins. "Nah, couldn't get the elephant, but we do have a unicorn."

He points, and I turn to see a small pony with a white, glittery horn tied around its head.

"You are out of control," I tell him.

"I said the same thing," Charlie says, wrapping her arms around his waist and tickling Mason's moving feet.

"She's only three once," he defends.

"And when she was two, you had a princess parade," I remind him, remembering the actual parade of princesses that had occurred every hour through their backyard last year.

"It's fine," he argues. Charlie just laughs and starts unstrapping Mason from the carrier.

"I'll take him, and you fire up the grill." She reaches up, brushing a kiss against his jaw while his arm bands around her, holding her against him for several moments.

"Bro, while we're young. I'm starving," Nick jokes.

Jax releases Charlie to flip Nick the bird before dragging him to the grill.

"Where's Claire?" I ask Charlie.

"I told her she needed to go sit down over in the lounger with some lemonade." She shifts the baby in her arms as he grabs for her hair. "C'mon, buddy, time for a diaper change. Be right back."

Charlie heads for the house, and I move in Claire's direction. She's exactly where Charlie said—sitting in the lounger with a glass of lemonade. Her blond hair is piled on top of her head, and a pink wrap dress stretches across the bump that makes her look like she swallowed a massive beach ball.

"Hey. I'd get up and hug you, but... " With a smile, she trails off and gestures to her belly before resting her hand on it.

"I got you, girl." I reach down and squeeze her in a hug. "How are you feeling?"

"Ugh, like Shamu swallowed a polar bear. Or a hundred." She grimaces.

I can't help imagining myself that pregnant and try to temper the little thrill that zips through me.

"You look gorgeous," I tell her.

"No, you look gorgeous." Waving in my direction first, she gestures back to herself. "I look like I need my own zip code."

"I disagree, but I won't keep arguing," I relent. "So, tell me what's been going on? I never see you anymore."

With my recent promotion, my schedule has ramped up lately as hers has eased with her upcoming maternity leave and we haven't seen each other in several weeks. I'm dying to know how she's feeling and what I should expect now that I'm expecting.

# BONUS EPILOGUE, CHAPTER 2

*NICK*

*I* watch Meredith settle next to Claire and I can't help but smile at the happiness on her face.

Fuck, she's gorgeous. Inside and out. And I'm the lucky bastard that convinced her to marry me.

And now she's pregnant with our child. Anxiety and grief from the loss of the first baby knot up my stomach, and I rub at the ache.

"Dude, you alright? You're breathing funny," Jax says, looking at me as we stand next to the grill with Dylan.

"What?" I shake my head. "Sorry, I'm good."

Better than good.

And it sucks that I can't share it with my two best friends. But Meredith has asked to keep our secret, and I'll do anything to keep that smile on her face. The miscarriage and the trying have taken a toll on her, and more than once, I've caught her crying because she thought she had done something wrong. Fuck that noise.

I remind myself that it wasn't meant to be. That there was a reason for what happened. It's what I finally allowed myself to believe after Emily died and I fell in love with Meredith. It's the only thing that kept me sane in those early days when I would hold my sobbing wife, my own eyes wet, while we both grieved something we wanted so much.

Dylan's gaze follows mine, and he slaps me on the back.

"Hate to interrupt—again," he says with a wink. "But did you get the chance to listen to the latest track?"

"The one you recorded this morning and sent me like an hour ago?" I ask. He's crazy if he thinks I've done anything like that. I'm good, but I'm not that good.

"No, the other one. From last week."

I nod. "It's good."

"No other changes?"

The song hadn't been hitting right at first, and we'd made several changes to it over the last week.

"Jax listened to it too," I reassure him. "I think it's good as is."

Jax nods as he turns the food. "It is. Damn good. Show off."

"Couldn't have done it with you both." He lifts his beer, and Jax and I do the same.

"Jackson Matthew," Charlie's voice calls out from the doorway as she steps back outside with Mason in her arms. "Are you almost done?"

He grins and nods. "Yes, gorgeous. They're done now. Let's eat."

***

Meredith grabs a plate for Claire—who looks like she's about to burst any second—and one for herself. Barely sitting down, she pops back up again, and my heart rate increases irrationally. Am I going to be like this for the next twenty-nine weeks?

"Mer, everything okay?" I ask, setting my plate down and

looking for any signs that something is wrong. She's been struggling with morning sickness that hits more at every other time than it does in the morning. It makes zero fucking sense to me, but what do I know?

She nods. "I'm okay, just…"

She trails off and swivels her head like she's looking for something in particular.

"What do you need, baby?"

"I want a pickle."

"A pickle?" I ask, surprised. That's new. I don't think I've ever seen her eat one.

"Mer, you feelin' alright?" Jax asks. "You hate pickles."

"I do not," she counters quickly.

"You do. Ever since you at the whole jar full when you were seven," he reminds her. "You threw up so much your mom nearly took you to the emergency room."

I glance at Val, who just shrugs and nods.

"You haven't eaten a pickle since," she confirms.

"Nick." Her pleading gaze turns to me.

I smother the smile that threatens at the look on her face—confusion and hope—and nod.

"I got you, baby."

I finish fixing my plate and grab two pickles before sitting next to her. She immediately takes the first and chomps into it with a moan that has my jeans fitting a little tighter.

Resting my hand on her thigh, I don't bother with the second pickle on my plate. It's for her anyway, which she knows since she grabs that next. Jax looks confused as he studies her intently.

"What the heck, Mer? You pregnant or something?" he finally asks.

All the ladies freeze, and Meredith glances up with the pickle still between her fingers like a kid caught with her hand in the cookie jar. *Oh, baby, you do not have a poker face.*

Her eyes are wide as she turns them to me.

"Meredith?" Charlie asks, a small smile curving her lips as she stares at my wife.

Val hasn't moved either, her focus glued to Meredith.

"I—ugh—I," Meredith starts before glancing at me. I nod and let my own grin loose to stretch across my face. She blows out a breath before she finally nods. "We weren't going to say anything today, but yeah, yes. We're pregnant. Eleven weeks."

Everyone starts talking at once while Val sprints from her seat to wrap her arms around Meredith. Jax reaches out to shake my hand and hands Mason to me.

"Here, you're going to need practice," he says.

Holy shit. He's right. I stare down at Mason and realize that soon, it'll be my baby in my arms.

"I love you," I mouth to Meredith.

"Love you too." Her smile is everything I need in this moment, and I make a vow to make her as happy and as comfortable as possible as we wait for our little one to arrive.

I can't imagine how life could get any better.

"Um, guys," Claire's voice is tremulous as she raises it to be heard over everyone else. "My water just broke."

# PLAYLIST

Nick and Meredith's playlist is full of upbeat anthems like Dahl's "Can I Kiss You?" and Sia's "The Greatest" to heart-wrenching songs like Tate McRae's "you broke me first." It also has some swoony ballads like John Legend's "Conversations in the Dark" and James Arthur's "Falling Like The Stars."

Want to hear their full playlist? Check out the playlist on Spotify by searching for the "In the Beat of the Moment" playlist.

# A NOTE FROM BREANNA

Early on in Written in the Beat, I knew that Meredith was going to need her own story—she just had too much to say to only be a side character.

The surprise was when Nick decided to declare himself her hero. He was *never* supposed to be anything more than the jerky label rep that Jax had to fight with to keep his relationship with Charlie.

Nick kept his story—losing his high-school sweetheart tragically—a secret until probably the fourth or fifth re-write/edit of Jax and Charlie's story. But when I started the story, it just flowed out of me. It was there, begging to be discovered. And suddenly he became the unlikely hero for the quirky and fun-loving Meredith.

After wrapping Jax and Charlie's story, I started diving in to Nick and Meredith last fall. We'd recently moved and I was ready to keep writing through the pandemic that had turned the world on its head. I was still writing when my entire world flipped yet again.

On December 7, 2020, my husband of nearly seventeen years, passed away in his sleep. Our relationship wasn't perfect, but rather an imperfect one that each of us continued to choose every day for the nearly twenty years we were together. Not only had I lost one of my best friends, but my four children had lost their dad shortly before Christmas.

Those next few weeks are a blur. I focused on getting up, taking care of the kids, and trying to make sure that Christmas was as "normal" as it possibly could be. It wasn't until after the holidays that I opened my laptop again and read Nick's story with a renewed vision. Suddenly, I no longer had to imagine how it felt to lose someone you loved. I was dealing with his grief in real time.

My husband was a big cheerleader for me when it came to my writing and my dreams to publish. If you've read Written in the Beat, you've seen the dedication to him there. He believed in me before I fully comprehended the ability to believe in myself.

It's been over eight months since he has passed and we've experienced so many firsts as a family. Birthdays, anniversaries, first days, experiences…they all morph to focused grief that includes sadness for myself as well as the children we created together who still struggle to understand why their dad had to go.

Grief is a funny thing. There can be happiness in the sadness and anger. It's a huge melting pot of emotions that we continue to sift through on a daily basis. I've also heard grief described as a button and a ball. The buttons are emotions and the grief is a ball that never goes away…it can shrink in size, but it will always be there to make memories bittersweet.

For those of you experiencing grief, know you are not alone. My heart goes out to each and every one of you. Find love, find hope, and find the strength to move forward. To carry on the memories of your loved one in a way that honors them.

Sending you my love,<br>
Breanna

# ACKNOWLEDGMENTS

Holy cow! The fact that I'm at this point in the process of book two is mind-boggling. I can't believe it!

To you beautiful readers out there! Yes, you!! Some of you started this journey with me in Written in the Beat and some of you are just now joining this universe. For taking the chance and reading either Jax and Charlie's story or Nick and Meredith's, thank you! I hope you enjoyed their stories as much as I have enjoyed writing them.

For my family—thank you for supporting me in this dream. For asking for a signed paperback, for sharing my work with others, for your love. I couldn't have done this without you! I love you!

Claire and Alina—You two are the A&C to the ABCs, my author wives, and two of the best things to ever have happened to me. Thank you for your love, your support, and the shenanigans that make us *us*. Thank you for brunches and Friday night zoom calls and for being there to provide a safe space to cry when needed! Love you two to infinity! <3

Editor Jess—Thank you for your continued guidance and polishing of Nick and Meredith's story. For your help in making me a better writer and story-teller! I promise eventually to stop using dangling modifiers…someday!

Beth—I don't think anyone loves Nick and Meredith the way we do! Thank you for that! For your friendship and for crying when you read them over and over again. You just tell me what and I'll bring a bottle to Michigan and Mackinac in 2022!

Kate Farlow—You truly are a graphics goddess and have become an amazing friend over the last year! Thank you for turning my vision of Nick and Meredith into a gorgeous reality with your graphic prowess!

Ladies (& gents) of the RWR and HEA—Thank you for your excitement, your encouragement, and your help in navigating this crazy journey of author-dom(authorship?)!

To my ARC team—the fact that I can type those words is crazier than anything! So many of you found me early in this journey and your love of Jax and Charlie have kept me going. I hope you love Nick and Meredith just as much!

To everyone who helped me create, mold, and polish In The Beat of the Moment into what it is—thank you! I can't imagine this journey without you! XOXO

# ABOUT THE AUTHOR

Breanna Lynn lives in Colorado where she attempts to keep her two sets of twins (affectionately referred to as the Twinx) from plotting to take over the world with the help of their partners in crime—dogs, Ella & Kronos, and kittens, Nala and Deku.

A classy connoisseur of all things coffee, Breanna spends her time keeping the Twinx from taking over the world. When not coordinating chaos, Breanna can be found binge reading, listening to music, or watching rom-coms with a giant bowl of popcorn.

To stay up to date on the ramblings of her (often over-caffeinated) mind, Twinx Tasmania, or the latest news on her latest happily ever after, sign-up for her newsletter here: https://app.mailerlite.com/webforms/submit/i2t1c4. Subscribers receive exclusive news, content, specials, and giveaways!

You can follow Breanna on:
Website: https://breannalynnauthor.com/
Readers Group:
https://www.facebook.com/groups/breannasbookbaristas

# WRITTEN IN THE BEAT, CHAPTER 1

*CHARLIE*

*M*y scuffed black Converses make loud squeaks along the concrete floor in the otherwise quiet cinderblock corridor. I've been here before—it's one of the best places to catch a concert in Denver even if the drive from Boulder is a pain in the neck with all the traffic.

But I've never been behind the scenes and never anywhere in this building when it wasn't teeming with people and music. The directions Meredith gave me take me from one look-alike hallway to another, the industrial smells of cleaning product, paint, and air conditioning irritating my nose.

Finally through the maze, I approach two hulking figures with SECURITY emblazoned across their overly-muscled chests.

I force a smile and swallow around the lump of nerves in my throat. "Hi."

"Name, miss?" Neither guard looks anything but emotionless, I'm sure accustomed to all sorts of fans who try to do or say whatever it takes to get behind the scenes without the right access. My smile falters and I clear my throat.

"Charlie—um, I mean Charlotte Walker. Meredith Pryce said that she would tell security..." My hands flail as I gesture at them. "That I was coming?"

One guard narrows his eyes as he assesses me from the top of my head to the bottoms of my battered sneakers while the other guard runs through a clipboard dwarfed by his meaty hand. The urge to fidget under the one's scrutiny is so strong that I can't help but squirm, my excitement to see Meredith dimmed by the awkwardness in dealing with two strangers.

It feels like an eternity before the one with the clipboard looks up. "You're clear."

Scurrying between the two bulky behemoths, I put them out of my mind as the sound of pounding music at the end of the hall captures my attention. Like the Pied Piper, the notes draw me closer until I pause in the doorway. The source of the music is a complicated-looking stereo system in a room full of dancers that work through a routine.

Meredith is here, her petite frame and dark curls vibrate as she calls out steps louder than the music beats through the room. Mirrors line one wall and the scents of wood polish and sweat engulf me, the smell familiar, bringing a pang of nostalgia after over a year without it.

"Turn, down, pivot, and...stop." Meredith's elfin stature is belied by her drill sergeant voice calling out the steps. She spots me in the doorway and a broad smile stretches across her face and, with a clap of her hands, she releases everyone from the rehearsal. "All right, good job, everyone. Let's call it and we'll see you back here at five for warm-ups."

Sweaty dancers file past me, swamping me with memories of being one of them, leaving a class exhausted but excited after putting my body through that physical rigor.

"Girl, you best get your scrawny butt in here!"

I step into the now vacant room, and Meredith squeals in excitement before she launches herself at me. I'm wrapped in an apple lotion-scented hug that takes me back to being an awkward fourteen-year-old girl from Boulder meeting her much cooler roommate from California for the first time at the arts magnet school we both attended in New York. It's her signature scent and never changes, a source of comfort I've missed since we've been separated.

"Too long! Missed you like crazy!" she says.

Tears burn the back of my nose and I laugh to clear the sensation. "Missed you! You've become quite the jet-setter."

After two years spent at the magnet school, we spent another four years studying contemporary dance and ballet at a private academy in New York before finishing there. Some days I still feel like a stranger in my home state, in my life here.

After the academy, Meredith signed on as a dancer on a music tour before she became the lead choreographer for this one. Jax Bryant was a rising pop artist, and, knowing Meredith, I'm sure the dancers work hard during his shows. The year since I left New York hadn't worked out for me the way I'd imagined.

"Ha! Thanks to Jax." She says with an impish look.

"Please." Pushing at her shoulder, I ignore her modest statement. "You earned it."

She shrugs. "You're better now, right? I could get you on like that."

It's been a year since my surgery for multiple stress fractures in my right foot and ankle, and despite long hours of physical therapy, I'm still not sure I'm one hundred percent. Meredith left New York and embraced her future, but is dance even an option for me after a year away?

I moved back home and have spent months as a babysitter for Bella, my baby sister, while I've rehabbed and tried to figure out a plan. Bella is a full-time job and I love her to death, but the only dancing I've done involves teaching youth classes at the local studio on a part-time basis. Techniques that I spent years honing are rusty, practiced only in the shadows of the studio when I find free time.

My face twists in a grimace. "I—I don't know if I'm ready."

The look Meredith gives me is one I know well. "Shut up. I'm sure you're ready."

"What about all the traveling you do? A new city nearly every day must be exhausting and confusing and—"

"Fun and adventurous," she interrupts with a grin and a wink. "Plus, the eye candy's not bad to look at, either."

A laugh bubbles out of me at her cheeky statement. When we'd go out in New York, she was the center of attention, flirting and dancing with whoever caught her eye. I'd always felt so awkward and tongue tied with any of the guys who approached me. It had been easier to watch from the sidelines.

"We need to jet if I'm gonna be back here in time for warm-ups. Stay put, let me go change and we'll get out of here."

We'd made plans to grab a late lunch, then I'd stay for the concert. Since tomorrow was a down day for the tour, we planned to hang out before she had to head for their next stop tomorrow night.

She snags her water bottle off the floor before heading in the direction of the other dancers. The music changes to a new song, and a rock beat fills the air. I circle the empty room, my fingers trailing across the smoothly polished barre before skimming off as I step back. I draw a deep breath as my eyelids flutter closed. The notes of the song pulse their way inside me, rushing through my blood, my body moves, absorbing the vibrations as the song takes over. I take classically trained moves and alter them to fit the harder sounds.

The music pushes everything else out. My ankle twinges, a reminder of the screw still embedded there. Pushing that sensation away, I let the music take over, and everything else fades— the doubts that I won't ever completely recover from my injury, the concern that I'll only ever be Bella's nanny, the excitement at seeing Meredith again. It all disappears.

My feet groan and echo across the floor, accompanying the song and erasing the tension knotted under my skin. Nothing exists but the flow of my body as it bends to the notes surrounding me.

Want more? Check out the rest of Jax and Charlie's story in Amazon or Free in KU!

Made in the USA
Columbia, SC
28 September 2021